ISEKAI VETERAN:
MENDICANT

CJ HOLMES

Bongosian Press
www.bongosian.com

TABLE OF CONTENTS

ASSURANCES

"You look tired, my friend." The Duke of Nurr, Cuelar Frenzio, inspected his old acquaintance more with hearing than with sight. Cuelar's beast trait was large ears, many-folded and intensely sensitive. He was also blessed with a half-back of soft gray fur, but it was his ears he valued. From the sound of his friend's heartbeat, Prelate Edmond DeGray was ragged with stress and sleep deprivation.

The stress was mainly due to the pesterings of Disciple Lucia, the newly-powerful matrix of the Chapel of Compassionate Light located in the bricktown slum. She had been going quietly about her business for years, giving food to the hungry and overseeing religious services for the poorest of the city. Her tiny chapel was nothing compared to DeGray's magnificent Basilica of Majestic Light, yet lately she had eclipsed the ambitious prelate: she had the patronage of Prince Estevan and his mother Queen Diana; she was rectress of the new school built in the name of the Missing Disciple; she had a say in the management of the school's extensive glebe; she had taken to telling people that the wealth of the church was in the hearts and minds of its worshipers and not in extravagant buildings.

Worst of all, she kept bringing large groups of people to DeGray's basilica to show them the Fragment of Sun, that miraculous artifact that lit the whole of the basilica's dome and its awe-inspiring illustrations. Blue-white light the color of the sun rippled down gently from the dome's oculus to the sanctuary floor in a slow aurora. Those who stood in its effect often reported feeling exposed, as if the one god Olyon was inspecting them and choosing to love them in spite of their sins and shortcomings. That too was a gift from the Missing Disciple, and every time Lucia reminded them of that fact it was like she was taking credit for finishing DeGray's great work. Worst of all, these crowds were common workers and the poor. Low people. DeGray had not spent more than a decade of his life refurbishing the creaky old temple into a grand basilica for them, he had built it so the wealthy and well-born would have a suitable place to pray and attend holy days.

"She was here again," said Edmond, "this time with a hundred of them. Church doctrine says we're open to everyone, but I wish she wouldn't bring them *here*. And she claims to have found another candidate for her little Arts School. She'll demand another increase in her budget."

Cuelar steeped a pot of jota while they talked. They were prominent men but they enjoyed these evening sessions together without servants or attendants. Alone together in the prelate's office they could be honest.

"I'm surprised she needs the funding," Cuelar said, "since the Colares estate got added to the school's glebe."

"She shouldn't," grumbled Edmond, "but the Colares family was stripped because of their assaults against the estate DeLanion left to the prince. It got put into the same foundation with the same rules: educate the poor and turn them into civil servants."

"Ah," said Cuelar, understanding, "and he only funded the school's basic scholarship role, not its training new practitioners of the spiritual arts."

Edmond nodded, and accepted a cup of hot jota from Cuelar. "That famous musician, Bibi, funds the music program. DeLanion funded reading and math. Church leadership funds the future healers and disciples. The buildings are donated from other sources. I could admire her management skills, if she would just stay in bricktown."

They sipped their jota in silence for a few minutes.

"I have the king's payment prepared," Edmond said at last, pointing at a heavy wooden chest, "but how are you going to move it? A ton of gold isn't very large, but..."

"...it still weighs a ton," finished Cuelar. They had made the joke often when raising and managing the vast stores of wealth required to rebuild the basilica. "How are you going to account for it?"

"I won't," smiled the prelate. "This is my secret repair fund. Leadership will never know the gold is missing."

Cuelar went to the chest and opened it, to ensure the gold was there.

"Cuelar," asked the prelate, looking anxious, "can you really manage the public end of this mess? DeLanion was supposed to just disappear, quietly. Janocas Colares complicated things for us when he ransacked DeLanion's properties. People know the palace was involved because of him. If people keep talking like they have been, Leadership will send someone to investigate."

Involvement from Leadership would be bad, for both of them. They had conspired to pay the king of Lavradio to kill DeLanion, under the pretext that the Unity Church had ordered it. In truth the Council of Guardians, widely know as simply "Leadership", had done no such thing. The scheme only worked as long as DeLanion disappeared quietly, but Janocas has fouled that up.

"You don't have to worry about that," said Cuelar, as he checked the pot and refreshed their tea, adding more water and more berries to the pot before pouring. "Janocas was my choice, so it's my mess and I will take proper care of it. DeLanion threatened your basilica, and was a threat to the future of my kingdom. We did the world a favor when we convinced the king to remove him, and you will never be censured for it. I promise."

The prelate, reassured by his reliable friend and ally, thanked Cuelar and drank from his cup.

From his seat across the table, the duke could hear the prelate's heart accelerate. He reached across the table and gracefully relieved him of the delicate clay cup so he would not drop it. Edmond's teeth clenched, audibly grinding together. His lips turned blue. As his heart pounded faster and faster, the man's eyes bulged and veins in the whites burst. When the heart died, so too did the man. Cuelar counted nineteen seconds, from ingestion to heart death.

Cuelar poured all the poisoned jota into a canteen using a small funnel, rinsed everything, made a new pot without poison, and put one of the cups in the small cabinet where Edmond kept such things. He staged the scene to tell a story: the prelate was drinking jota alone and reading a stack of boards. A letter from an acquaintance in Unity City pulled at random from Edmond's in-box sat on his desk. He had died in the night, working, with nobody to witness it.

4

The prelate's private diary was kept in a drawer, stacks of thin wooden boards arranged by date. Cuelar scanned through them, substituted a couple day's worth of entries with forgeries of his own, then put everything neatly away.

The gold got packed into a special rucksack made of rare monster hide and bone, capable of carrying more than a ton of weight if your back was strong enough to bear it. Then he activated the ancient artifact he always wore around his waist, the one that gave him strength enough to carry the pack across town without significant effort. It was the kind of thing the church liked to confiscate, but to someone who was born without great stature or strength it was too useful to give up.

"I'm sorry old friend, but you've become a loose end. In a quest for dominion nothing can be spared." The prelate's empty eyes and clenched face looked up at the ceiling, unresponsive.

Nobody had seen Duke Frenzio enter through the prelate's private entrance, and nobody saw him leave.

RESURRECTION

Nowhere-Everywhere

It knew this place, the place between lives. It had been here before, though It could never remember the place when It was alive. A million distant souls winked in the darkness like stars, while a relative few plummeted in some direction or other leaving a thin trail behind them that faded in moments. Normally It would be one of them, hastily going to its next place as Fate or Design or Chance would have it. Never did It choose. Rather, It was Pulled.

Strange, that there was no Pull this time. But there was a string, a Tie to somewhere. It followed the string, Pulling Itself for a change, to the faraway end of the string. To a world orbiting a blue-white star, itself orbited by the three moons Silenz, Boraz, and Crevist. The string led down to a large continent, to a stone ledge clinging to the side of a lonely hill covered in a thin blanket of snow gleaming in the light of two of the moons. A cairn was there, covering a body.

Now here was a quandary. If this was Its body, and Its body was dead, from where was It thinking right now? The question was a good one, and It added the query to Its Sphere of Mysteries where all such unsolvables lived.

It could cut the tie that brought It here, that was an option: It could wait in the waiting place with the other souls and contemplate the flow of Time until the next Pull. If

Its past was a statistically reliable sample, Its chances of being Pulled to a place worse than Tenobre (the name of this place) was about eighty percent. Its chance of finding another Emristar was closer to zero.

Or It could Live Again, in Tenobre.

As lives go, it hadn't been the worst. It graded itself A for heart; C for effectiveness, on account of brevity; F for survival, again on account of brevity. It was forever earning Fs in survival. But if It Lived Again then the grade wasn't final. It might even live to middle age and earn itself a coveted C. Coveted by Itself only, as there was no one else to compare grades with.

Spinning the wheel of Fate again was illogical when there was a perfectly promising life to be lived right here. It just required a little work to get the body started again.

First, It had to unbury the body. Even as an entity of pure spirit It could, if It focused hard enough, pluck the rocks up and throw them aside. This took a little time, and loudly scattered the stones down the steep hillside.

The body was well-preserved but naked. The people who had ended the life had also taken its material goods. And yet, someone had thought to bury the body in a scenic location and in possession of a good long knife, the weapon of a strong foe killed in combat. Remorse. Care. Honor. At least one other person hadn't liked the way things turned out. Likely not the person who had poisoned the body.

The spirit waited for sunrise, meditating on the grand view below while It drew in vast amounts of mana to nourish Its existence. Forests ran for many kilometers. North lay the older untouched stands, and to the south were many miles of coppiced stumps managed for lumber and firewood. Far to

7

the south a grayness gathered in the sky as city people woke with the dawn and started their fires. It was time.

This body that was dead had no spirit or life of its own to aid in healing. It was also foul with poison and decay. It would have to be repaired and detoxified and inhabited with a single word. Any other body would have been too much to attempt, but the spirit had known this one intimately when It was alive so the feat was possible.

The spirit took all the mana it had gathered and formed Itself into a detailed mimicry of what the body had been in life, healthy and whole down to the last hair follicle. When It was as perfect as It could be made, the spirit struck itself into the corpse, and transformed dead flesh into a living person.

Lavradio, North of Girona

The first sensation was always pain. All the feelings of being alive, without order or understanding, was chaotic noise that the newly awakened consciousness groped at while trying to make sense of millions of unsorted nerve endings. The confusion was perceived as agony. Amid the static came signals that were recognized: this is hand touching rock. That is light touching eyes. This is chest, heaving for breath. The entity had done this before, several times, and knew how to explore and move all the parts of the body it could find, discover where everything was connected, and gradually bring order to all the sensory inputs.

The screaming was an entirely normal part of the process. It stopped once he figured out that he had ears, that some of their sensation was the noise of himself screaming, and where the vocal cords were and how to use them again. The blindness too, was resolved in time. The only unusual part of this awakening was the amount of filth. A black putrescence covered him from head to foot. The moment his sense of smell was discovered he dry-heaved uncontrollably while he frantically tried to crawl away from the puddle of ichor that reeked of poison and rot.

He found snow and rolled in it, then found some fresh snow and rolled in that. Then, he learned to stand by grasping the rocky wall and pulling himself gradually up on shaking legs. With his new-found voice he first thanked the god Olyon. He didn't believe in the One God of Light exactly, but he believed in the existence of the divine power and Olyon was as good a name for it as any other. And, if the divine being had a home nearby (in the astronomical sense) then there wasn't any reason he couldn't live inside the local star.

Finally upright, he uttered the Prayer of Cleansing thinking to wash away the remaining filth, but what he got was a cyclone of wind that knocked him off his feet with a yelp and nearly dragged him off the ledge. He dug his newly-discovered fingers desperately into any crack and crevice in the rock he could find to keep from being flung out and dropped into the forest below, narrowly averting another untimely death. When the storm finally passed, both he and the hilltop were sparkling clean and a little raw.

After some searching he was able to find the long bronze knife which had been thrown into a recess of the ledge. He couldn't remember how he knew to look for the knife but there it was: a long single-bladed knife with a sharp chisel-shaped point, freshly shined. Having a weapon was good. The tang looked long enough that he could remove the handle and remount the blade onto a spear, which would be ideal for him.

The morning was cold and the ground was snowy. Being naked here was not great. Nor was the lack of food or water. But he had a knife and he had, if he was careful not to destroy himself with it, magic. He was fairly sure he was north of Girona, which meant the safe house was south and east. The safe house would contain clothes and money and be a good place to rest for a few days. That was, assuming he could find it.

His name, he remembered, was Taylor DeLanion. And he would call this life World 12.1.

Girona, Bricktown

On cold winter nights all three priests of the Chapel of Compassionate Light slept in the same bed. The aged Matrix Lucia, with her pair of broken horns and cloudy vision, slept on the side that was easiest to get out of. Her husband Brother Mika slept on the opposite side, with the younger Sister Lorena between them to keep them both warm.

Lucia's eyes weren't much good for detecting visible light any more, but she could see spirit light quite well. What other practitioners felt as a vague feeling of another's spiritual arts, the Matrix could see as plainly as sunlight. So when a massive source of spirit gathered itself in the north like a sun rising from the wrong horizon, it woke her.

Lucia rose and dressed in pre-dawn darkness, adding layers of felted wool to combat the cold. She lit a small stove using the arts and made the largest pot of jota she could, then took a cup with her to the dormitory next door. Lorena caught up with her, and helped her up the stairs to the big second-story balcony that looked north. She sipped and watched the north horizon, while Lorena went to fetch the pot and some more cups.

The dorm was only half-complete, but the first floor was fully occupied. The Fragment of Sun Taylor had created and hung in the basilica had the power to awaken the Light in others. Especially, it seemed, children. Nearly every time she took groups of people into the basilica to witness his "gift to the city" another potential practitioner was revealed.

Lucia had tapped the most likely among them (by talent and disposition) as candidates for training as practitioners of the spiritual arts, taking as many as she could handle. A few candidates' families declined the free education, preferring to keep their children in the family occupations, but most of the families were eager to give their children to such a prestigious profession in the Unity Church. There were some candidates who had unstable homes, and those resided in the hastily-built dormitories.

In a few years they would be ready to make the journey to Unity City and the School of Spiritual Arts, thence to swell the school's pool of practitioner candidates to the breaking point. Lucia would need to find a way to spread out their entry enough not to overwhelm the Arts School, and she was already in regular correspondence with the deans about it. For decades the church had recruited practitioners almost exclusively from first families, descendants of the first disciples for whom the church was a family profession. Only occasionally did they bring in the odd outsider, usually some accidentally discovered talent too promising to be ignored. Here in Girona they had collected no fewer than twenty candidate practitioners, all of disciple-class talent: enough to double the yearly intake at the Arts School. Whereas most of the Arts School candidates were only healer-class talents, all of her arts students were of the higher disciple-class talents.

Facilities for the candidates were tacked on to the school Taylor had founded to teach writing and math to the public. With the addition of Bibi's endowment for music, and the church's funding for preparatory arts, the school had been awkwardly renamed "DeLanion's School for Math, Scripture, and Music" but everybody was calling it "DeLanion's". It was another of Taylor's gifts to Girona. The boy believed education was for everyone, so he built a place that gave the common person a chance to learn.

Lucia and Lorena were soon joined by Mika, and after a little time two of the city's healers joined as well. Healers, like disciples, were practitioners of the spiritual arts but they had less spirit. All of the people present had, either by long practice or decades of exposure, become highly sensitive to movements of spirit required for the spiritual arts. What was happening in the north right now was to their eyes either a calamity or a miracle. To someone with the right senses, it was if a new sun was igniting just over the horizon.

Lucia let her own spirit bloom wide, as big as the dorm, and sampled the distant light that mingled with her own. The nearest description for what she was doing was "tasting" and the far-away spirit tasted just like their Missing Disciple. "It's him," breathed the matrix at last, releasing weeks of tension and uncertainty. "He's completed Sandim's Return. If you've ever wondered what a being of pure spirit is like, there is your answer."

"Will he come back to Girona?" asked one of the healers.

"I hope not," said Mika. "The palace would be obliged to try to kill him again. Things could escalate."

"He'll stay away," Lucia told them all, "for now. He's young, and wants to get on with his adventures. For a while, we'll have to watch him through the *Luminous Histories* as Phillip the Younger."

Taylor's teachers had recorded his anointment twice: once as Taylor DeLanion in Girona, and again as Phillip the Younger from 'the wilderness'. The phrase was a seldom used term for a practitioner, usually from a wealthy non-church family, for whom life in the church meant rejecting their past. It was Dean Garsharp's idea, as a way to let Taylor travel without bringing his complicated past with him. That was what they had told Taylor when they asked him to choose a practicing name.

The secondary reason for the double anointment was to give Taylor a documented cover identity in case one of his powerful enemies made it impossible for him to stay in Girona, or in case Leadership decided to make him quietly disappear. The days of Leadership enforcing strict discipline on disciples was long past, but Taylor had been summoned from another world using an ancient summoning room. To a few people, like the disgraced Ambassador Serano who had tried to have him killed, Taylor's origin felt like a threat to the church.

Lucia was herself a disciple, trained during a time when Leadership had been adamant about enforcing oaths of loyalty on practitioners. Leadership's reform of the Art School had ended in disaster: their hand-picked loyalist disciples became scourges that had to be purged at enormous cost to both human life and the church's reputation. The reforms were repudiated and all disciple issues were returned to the Art School's deans. Lucia and others her age would never forget that the current balance of power with Leadership could not be taken for granted.

Together, the five of them prayed for the safety of Phillip the Younger.

Lavradio, North of Girona

It was snowing. He was naked, he didn't know exactly where he was, and it was snowing. It didn't take Taylor long to realize he would have to chance a few prayers just to make the run to his safe house, even though his magic was unstable. He had no money and he was pretty sure letting himself be seen would be a bad idea. He could attempt to steal clothing and food from an isolated house, maybe a woodsman's hut, but Taylor wasn't a fan of theft and everything he needed was at the safe house. He just had to get there.

Measuring out his spirit in the smallest amounts he could, he invoked blessings of endurance and warmth over a wide area including himself and everything within three meters. The snow around him immediately began to melt. He had maybe thirty kilometers to run, and he was going to leave a trail of melted snow behind him the whole way. The good news here was the falling snow would cover his trail.

If he had a choice, the forests of Lavradio wasn't where Taylor would be right now. He'd rather be back in Emristar, a wealthy nation in a technologically advanced world where he had actual family who loved him. His adoptive parents and two older siblings were probably giving up on him about now. After all, what choice did they have? He had disappeared into thin air, in front of witnesses, and there was no way to track him here. He had been summoned to a different world and Emristar lacked both the scientific and magical technology to follow him. After six months, plus however long he had been recently dead, they would have no choice but to get on with their lives.

If you counted all the reincarnations and soul transfers he could remember, this was Taylor's twelfth world so far. It was a bronze age civilization, with a single inhabited continent called Tenobre. Most nations were governed aristocratically, and they spoke a single language called Unity. Nearly everyone had some kind of animalistic features like claws or fur, and not having such a "blessing" made you a pitied "smooth skin" like himself. There was one religion, the Unity Church, that worshiped the sun god Olyon. Magic here was was controlled by the church, whose body of scripture included their canonical spell book the *Book of Prayers*. If you had a little talent and the church happened to find you, then they might train you and anoint you as a healer. If you were very talented and you passed ethical muster, then you could be anointed as a disciple.

Taylor had been fortunate to connect with a semi-retired disciple only a few weeks after being summoned here. The king of Lavradio might not have taken a real interest in his summoned guest, but Disciple Lucia certainly had. She had arranged a crash course for him at the hands of the three best teachers she could lay her hands on, and had seen to his anointment as fast as possible. The church didn't have enough disciples to go around so they were eager to put him to work.

There were a lot of atypical aspects to Taylor's anointment: he was only twelve years old; he never went to the School of Spiritual Arts in Unity City where priests and practitioners were normally trained; he had an unusual amount of spirit; he wasn't a member of any of the first families that usually supplied practitioners; and his anointment was recorded twice.

"They knew," he said out loud, halting his jog. His teachers had told him the alternate name would let him travel and work without carrying the "summoned from another world" baggage with him everywhere. But then why have two names at all? They had prepared a second identity for him in case his old name became unusable.

The last words Micas had said as she poisoned him to death was that the church had put a bounty on his head and Duke Frenzio was trying to collect. But Micas didn't work for the duke, she was Queen Diana's creature through and through. The queen was far more ruthless than Taylor had imagined, but that didn't change the fact she was competent. The only reason she would kill off someone who was an ally and who wasn't a threat to the realm was if her husband the king had ordered it. The king, on the other hand, didn't have a lot of ethical qualms when it came to picking up a loose windfall here and there. If someone, anyone, offered King Joaquim Odemira enough money then he would have no qualms disposing of Taylor.

It was possible that Leadership had paid the king. Or maybe it was just Duke Frenzio duping the mentally lazy king. Either way, it seemed his teachers had anticipated this predicament.

"Dean Garsharp," he muttered to the snow, "you're a dodgy old codger."

Well then, he couldn't go back to Girona and he couldn't use his own name. In fact he should leave Lavradio entirely, just as soon as he had himself in some kind of order. If he was going to be Phillip the Younger then he needed to do something about his appearance, and he would have to rethink his other identifiable traits. One thing was for sure, he couldn't keeping singing in public. He had become famous for his performances, and singing would out him as Taylor in a minute. That fact alone made him regret needing a new identity. He was going to miss performing.

"Food," said Taylor out loud. His eyes had found fruit high up in a tree, dried up and wrinkled and probably frozen inside. Winter fruit was an excellent find: it would keep him going for the rest of the day.

Taylor laid his knife on the ground and used his toughened fingers and toes to scramble up the tree. With his slight frame he had no problem climbing high enough to knock down twenty of the little brown treasures. He jumped down, then had to consider how to carry them all. There was another tree nearby, older than the rest, that had fallen under the twin pressures of too many years and too much snow. Taylor used his arts to strip the best fibers he could get from a still-living branch and form them into two items: a couple meters of rope and a felt sack. The sack had to be felt because delicate threading and weaving was way beyond his magical abilities right then. Felt was simple to shape, and sturdy enough to withstand his poor control. It wasn't a very good bag and it might not last more than a few days, but it would let him carry his forage. The winter fruit went into the bag. The rope went around his waist, and the knife and the bag were tucked into the rope.

With one fruit in hand Taylor resumed his travel at a brisk walk, peeling and snacking on the sweet chewy flesh as he went. He might have been naked but thanks to the spiritual arts he was warm. He was armed with an excellent bronze knife. He had food and he knew how to find more. He might not know precisely where he was, but he knew how to get where he was going. He would avoid the city of Girona entirely and instead aim for the highway that ran east out of the city by setting his course southeast. The highway would be literally impossible to miss. As soon as he found a marker on that road he would know exactly where he was, and how to get to his temporary home.

Two fruits later his attitude was fully restored, and he broke into an easy lope that would chew up the distance.

LEO'S DETOUR

Everything had been going fine, until suddenly it wasn't. Prince Leonardo had found himself with two extra weeks before he had to be home, and their gurantor train was fast enough to carry them all to Gallia for a short vacation. Their gurantor's name was Bonita, and she was a massive creature even compared to her own kind. Her six legs pulled a luxury car and a cargo wagon like they were children's toys. Her intact horns, magnificent and back-swept, were a warning to anyone who might get in their way. She was secretly a sweet animal, though: she would probe their pockets with her trunk, looking for fruit.

Gallia was warmer this time of year than Lavradio, where the nights were getting cold and the snows had already begun. They had enjoyed nine days of beaches and balmy sunshine away from the usual pressures of embassy life, then turned Bonita and their carriage homeward.

He traveled with his trusted entourage of guards: Rita, Nunio, and Jorgo, all from noble families and all with combat-enhancing beast traits. His fiancé Farava was with them, a beautiful young woman from a Unity first family that had produced many members of Leadership. She had her own two attendants with her: a healer-practitioner named Esther, and a guard named Malisa. The seven of them and their most essential luggage fit easily into the luxury carriage where they could rest comfortably between turns driving.

Their personal mounts, appalons, rode in the cargo wagon. The thin snowfall was no challenge for Bonita's bulk, especially on such a wide and well-kept road.

Leonardo, known as Leo among his entourage when nobody else was around, knew he was fooling himself. He liked to think he was traveling in a low-key manner like some mild mannered knight or baron, unremarked by anyone. His large frame and dark mane of hair running vertically from scalp to the middle of his back was a dead give-away to anyone who had met an Odemira. Binding his hair in silver clasps and riding around in a massive carriage dedicated just to him and his well-dressed retinue was fairly screaming for attention. But as long as he kept his manner relaxed, didn't affix anyone with the royal glare, or introduce himself as a prince then nearly everyone was willing to temporarily believe the fiction that he was some wealthy person of no great import and he was best left alone.

Half a day from their destination in Girona was where misfortune struck. The carriage's front end was wrenched several feet to the right, throwing all the riders to one side. The gurantor screamed, which is a sound they seldom make, and heaved itself free by breaking the harness and nearly overthrowing the carriage. Then she spun about and swiped the front with her horns. Everything loose in the passenger compartment went flying towards the opposite side: books, cushions, luggage, food, drinks, playing cards, musical instruments and people all careened together from one side to the other into one cacophonous heap. The exception was Leonardo, who sailed through one window of the car breaking the shutters to land free and clear of the whole mess. He cleared his head just in time to watch the ornate vehicle balance on two wheels for an eternal moment. From inside he could hear a chorus of "no no no no no" before the vehicle made up its mind to crash onto its side.

The appalons broke free of the cargo wagon and fled in all directions.

Bonita was thrashing and bellowing, and trampled the ground around herself as if fighting some unseen enemy. Twice it kicked the overturned vehicle and sent it sliding and crunching against the cargo car, eliciting new rounds of panicked shouts from the riders inside. Leo tried approaching the rear of the carriage to attempt a rescue but almost ended up flattened when the beast kicked it again.

The mayhem ended as inexplicably as it began. The gurantor fell down dead and the afternoon became quiet.

Half an hour later, Leonardo was faced with a choice. They could stay here, make camp by the carriage, and hope to be found. They could go forward to the next village. Or they could take the essentials and hike back five kilometers to an old hunting lodge belonging to his family.

There were assorted bruises and strains, but Esther sorted out most of them using the arts.

They had two immediate problems. Nunio had been driving, but he was nowhere to be found. And Malisa could barely breathe.

"I've used all the arts I can on her," Esther explained, worried for her friend, "but she's struggling. Her lips are blue because she isn't getting enough air, but I don't know what to do for her. It doesn't seem like poison, but prayers aren't helping."

Farava knelt next to the stricken woman, holding her hand.

"We stay here, with Malisa," Leo decided, "and we'll make camp in the carriage. Rita, look for Nunio again."

Rita started retracing their path, to find out where Nunio fell off. Jorgo gathered wood, while Leo moved the clutter around in the carriage to make room for everyone. The interior was a wreck, but everything they could want to survive the night was in there.

An hour later their situation remained the same. Rita returned with no news of any sign of Nunio. Malisa's breathing became more labored, and continued attempts by Ester to heal her still weren't helping. Their only progress was they had a fire going. They ate jerky and dried fruit, because nobody felt like cooking. Nobody felt like doing much of anything. All they could do was watch for trouble and hope to be found. Ideally, they should be found by someone with a carriage large enough for them and all their luggage. Farava put on a brave face, but eventually started to weep silently over her friend and guard.

Leonardo would need to split his party. Two would go forward to the next town to find help and the rest would stay behind to tend Malisa.

"Leo," Ester said before he could give the order, "someone is coming. An arts user. They probably sensed me."

"Maybe they can help," Farava said hopefully.

"They're very powerful," Ester added. "A disciple."

Jorgo stood, "let me talk to them, in case they're dangerous."

"No noble airs," Farava warned him. "Disciples hate that. Say please and thank you."

"What for," asked Jorgo? "He should be honored to help his prince."

"That's the opposite of what you should say to him," Farava whispered. A figure could be seen on the road now, running in their direction. "It's like you learned nothing after three years in Unity City." She would have taken Jorgo's place but she couldn't leave her friend's side.

The person who approached them was a boy carrying a bag slung over one shoulder and a spear in one hand with a bronze head. He wore a small canvas backpack and a stone knife was in his belt. His hair was brindled brown, and his silver eyes reflected their campfire. Jorgo stood in the middle of the road, both to greet him and bar his way.

The boy spoke first. "We meet in the Light. I am Disciple Phillip the Younger. I offer you my assistance."

"Where did you come from, Phillip?"

"I rent a house nearby. May I have the honor of knowing your name?" His voice was creaky and breaking, undermining the courtesies.

"What's your family name," Jorgo demanded?

"I neither have nor need any lineage to speak of. Do you want my help or not?"

"I don't see why we should let some strange child meddle in our affairs. How do we know you aren't responsible for this ambush?"

"I see you don't want my help. I'll leave you in peace." The boy turned to leave. "By the way, you've lost a man on the left side of the road. Up a tree just there," he pointed with his spear. "Did you know?"

He began to jog away from them.

Leo slapped his friend and secretary on the back of the head. "Idiot." Then he shouted, "Please wait! Let's walk as brothers!"

The boy stopped walking and turned around. He looked guarded and angry.

"My idiot friend's name is Jorgo," he shouted to the boy. "My name is Leo. Please lend us your aid."

"You don't have to lower yourself like that," Jorgo objected. Leo motioned him to silence.

Phillip walked past them both and planted his spear by the back door of the overturned vehicle. He took the long stone knife from his belt and laid it down next to the spear, then ducked into the sideways portal.

"Jorgo," said Leo, pulling him aside, "what was that about?"

"I thought we should know more about him before we let him into the carriage."

"We'll talk about this later. Take Rita and search the trees where he pointed."

Leo saw them off and entered the carriage. Ester and Phillip had Malisa sitting up. Farava had moved to the opposite side of the carriage to give them room to work.

"Malisa, I'd like to take a look at your abdomen but we have to remove your shirt. Is that okay?" Malisa nodded, still struggling to breathe. They removed the guard's leather chest piece and opened her shirt. The healers seemed to see something Farava couldn't.

"She's suffocating from a hemothorax," Ester said, "but my arts won't heal it."

"There's nothing wrong with your arts," the boy said, "the ruptured vessels are already healed. This is the blood that

24

collected before you healed her. It isn't broken, it's not an illness, and it isn't poison."

"So the normal arts don't have an effect. Can you perform a combat heal?" Combat healing was a technique to rapidly restore the body to its ideal condition very quickly, but required more spirit than healers could muster.

He took a black roll of leather from his bag and unfurled it. Inside was an array of surgical instruments made of silver alloy, all slotted into neat compartments. "I can, and that would make the hemothorax vanish, but combat healing is traumatic for the patient. Malisa, what I'd like to do is make a small incision and just let the excess blood out. Then you'll be able to breathe. I'll numb the area so you won't feel anything at all. Ester will be here to heal the incision. Is that okay for you?"

Malisa looked to Ester, who nodded, then she nodded to Phillip.

"Someone bring us a clean, shallow bowl, please? And a second bowl to catch blood in."

"You don't want to heal the incision?" Ester asked, while taking the bowl from Farava and helping to sterilize instruments.

"I can't heal soft tissue very well right now. I'm having to relearn all my fine control. It's neater if you do it."

"Is it puberty?" she asked with real concern. "Is your growth confusing your arts?"

"I really don't want to talk about it." Alcohol poured from a small bottle into the bowl, followed by instruments and the hands of both healers.

While they waited for everything to sterilize, Ester wanted to explore his problem more thoroughly. "It's okay, you know.

Lots of practitioners go through it, especially the strong ones. I had a friend who couldn't pray for light without blinding everyone for the longest time. How long has this been happening?"

Phillip closed his eyes and whispered, "so embarrassing. Please stop talking about it."

"If you stress about it," she advised him, "it'll only get worse."

"I wasn't stressing about it, but now I might be."

Phillip took a cloth and dabbed alcohol over the area he was operating on, then used a prayer to numb the skin. He said the prayer in a rapid-fire string of syllables the lay person would not even recognize as coming from scripture. Ester could sense his spirit working: true to his word, the prayer didn't just numb the targeted area but also half of Malisa's torso. The church had undoubtedly anointed him at such a young age because of his extreme power, but he was right about his shaky control.

Malisa was smiling through her shortened breaths. "You're enjoying my embarrassment, aren't you?" said Phillip. She nodded, grinning but breathing in tiny sips. "Life is so unfair. Can you feel that? I'm touching your skin right now." The patient shook her head.

"Hold up the bowl," he said and, when Ester was ready, inserted the pointed scalpel into Malisa's abdomen and pulled it out again, replacing it with a short silver tube. Bloody fluid streamed from the wound into the bowl and Malisa's breaths gradually became deeper. They collected a quarter of a liter before the stream died down to a mere ooze. Phillip took the bowl and instruments outside for cleaning while Ester healed the incision, and they were done.

When Rita and Jorgo returned with an unconscious and badly injured Nunio, Ester and Phillip divided the work between them. He healed the bones, which required a great deal of spirit, while she focused on delicate soft tissues. After her repeated attempt to use the arts to heal Malisa, Ester didn't have a lot of spirit left and pushed herself nearly to exhaustion. At the end of it, Farava and Rita put Ester in the carriage on a bed of pillows and forced her to rest.

When Nunio was on his feet he gave a report. "I don't know what happened," he swore. "She went berserk and kicked the driver's seat so hard I went flying. That's the last thing I remember until pipsqueak here was setting bones. Thanks for that, by the way," he said to Phillip. "My name's Nunio." He offered the boy a bow, which was returned in kind.

"My pleasure. Has anyone looked at the gurantor yet? Tried to find a cause?"

"We've only confirmed she's dead," Leo told him.

Nunio made a sad face, his wide feline ears folding down. "Poor Bonita. She was sweet, for a gurantor."

Nunio went with Phillip as he took up his spear and knife and approached the fallen beast. She had been a truly magnificent specimen, standing three meters at the shoulder. Bonita's mouth hung open, tongue exposed, and blood seeped from the eyes. There was no obvious cause of death.

Phillip examined the the deceased gurantor, and eventually motioned to Nunio to crouch down next to him, and look at Bonita from low to the ground. "See that wound, under the right front leg? The blood has soaked into the ground right under it."

"Perfectly round. You think a sketterline got her?"

27

"They've been a problem around here lately. There's probably a burrow right under her. It ambushed her from below and ate straight for her heart. There's a bounty on these, too. Three silenz per head. If that's what this is."

"We can't leave it here," said Leo, crouching next to them. "Bounty or not, it's a danger. We should burn the poor girl in place. That would get rid of the sketterline, too."

"Or," Phillip offered, "we can lure it out and kill it. Then you can take some of Bonita as steaks, to remember her by. Your people are going to need big meals tonight. Healing is hard on the body."

"Shame to let her go to waste," Malisa agreed, approaching while donning her armor.

With Phillip's blessing of protection in place, they tapped the ground near the belly of the gurantor rhythmically until the many-legged anthropod stuck its head out to investigate. It's antennae waved around in circles, unsure if it was safe to come out.

Malisa was the first to strike, putting her spear into a body segment and nailing it to the ground. The remainder of the the sketterline poured out of the carcass a meter at a time, attempting to wrap itself around the spear and pry itself free. Swords chopped it to bits, and the sections were dragged into the campfire to burn, making a green flame as the carapaces burned to white ash.

After they had all taken some cuts from Bonita the Gurantor, Phillip purified the meat then blessed the men with strength so they could drag the massive body to the side of the road. He helped them bury the huge gurantor by reshaping the ground. Since their strength was already enhanced, Leo's party turned the carriage right-side up, but had to catch it to keep it from flopping right over to the other side. The contents clattered and crashed.

With the deadly sketterline gone, the group's appalons returned. They were shy at first and didn't want to get too near the pooled blood in the road but they knew they had to let themselves be collected if they wanted to eat. The sole holdout was a creature belonging to Nunio, apparently named Hateful Ben, whose absence seemed to cheer up his owner. "Maybe a sketterline got him," speculated the guard hopefully.

Phillip packed his equipment and prepared to leave. Spear in hand, he spoke to Nunio. "Unless there's some other dire need, I'm heading out. Send your donation to any of the church-run programs in Girona. And try to stay out of trees."

Nunio grinned and was about to say something witty in return, but Jorgo interrupted. "You can't leave us stranded out here. Look around! It's the wilderness! Do you know who our master is?"

"Crown Prince Leonardo Odemira," Phillip said flatly, "soon to be the ninth Odemira to sit the throne of Lavradio."

"And you're just going to leave him here, stranded?"

"Jorgo, was it?" Phillip pointed at the massive carriage with his spear. "You have shelter and a defensible location. You have food, weapons, mounts, money. You have no injuries, and you have a healer." He pointed down the road. "The next town is ten kilometers that way, less than an hour by appalon. You are not stranded."

Phillip turned to leave, sparing only a nod for Leonardo. "Your Highness," is all he said, and then he ran directly into the woods at an easy lope. In a moment he was gone from sight, swallowed up by trees and snow.

"Jorgo," said the prince, "we need to have a conversation about how you talk to people that we need."

The royal party loaded their most important goods onto appalons and headed back the way they had come. The prince's family had a hunting lodge in the area, closer to them than the next town. Ester rode because of her weakened condition, but everyone else walked. That left most of the appalons free to carry baggage: trunks full of the most valuable items in the carriage, plus their food and warmest bedding. It took them over an hour to pack, and most of another to reach their destination.

Their first sight of the lodge came as the winter sun was dying. The two story building was made of fieldstone cleverly stacked then held together with mortar, sitting on top of a course of cut stone at ground level, with a second course of cut stone where the second floor began. The loft was timber, and the roof looked recently thatched. A single chimney was located in the center, rising high enough to avoid catching the roof on fire. To one side was a stable for mounts, and on the other a smokehouse for treating game. The space immediately around the house was paved in stone and marked by a low hedge. By royal standards it was rustic to an extreme, but a commoner would have called it a grand cottage.

What was surprising about the scene was the smoke coming from the chimney and the light sneaking past shuttered windows. The house was occupied.

"I'll talk to them," said Nunio, looking at Jorgo. "We don't need another pointless altercation." The guard checked his armor, in case the reception was poor, and approached the door only to have it open for him preemptively. The boy disciple stood on the threshold, the warm fire inside backlighting him, wiping his hands on a gray towel. His silver pupils gleamed in the shadowed face.

"Phillip" he cried happily, "it's been ages."

"Nunio," the boy replied. His silver eyes narrowed suspiciously. "Did you follow me here?"

"Funny story," Nunio explained, "this lodge is owned by the royal family. We came here to stay the night."

"Well that's unfortunate. I have a rental contract, paid in advance. The house is occupied."

Nunio considered the situation. Surely the boy didn't intend to refuse them shelter. He had already helped them once today, and done so without making a fuss about it. It was only Jorgo who had soured the encounter. The prince's secretary had a general dislike of anyone who couldn't trace their families through five generations of nobility. Even Ester had been subject to his scorn: it had been so bad that the prince intervened to set him straight. The boy might be sore at his poor treatment at the end of Jorgo's tongue.

Nunio bowed with a flourish and spoke in the Unity language's supplicative voice. "Our party is tired and the night is long and cold. We ask you, master of this house, for your hospitality."

"You have my hospitality, unfit for royals though it is," replied the boy formally. The he sighed, "you didn't have to go that far -- all you had to do was ask. You can see where the stable is. Smallest bedroom is mine, divide up the rest as you like." The disciple went back inside, leaving them to their own devices.

Most of the ground floor was a single room, interrupted by the great posts that held up the beams for the second floor. Phillip had installed half a dozen cloth lanterns lit by the arts, which reflected their soft light against the smoothed walls and an immaculate wooden floor. The fireplace in the center added a warm natural flickering to the steady light of spiritual arts. Near the fire was a rough wooden table covered with ingredients prepared for cooking: diced aromatics, root vegetables, sliced mushrooms, winter spices, filets of river trout, and baby greens that had probably been grown indoors using the arts. A stack of eight fine white saucers and cups stood at one corner of the table hinting at the availability of jota, confirmed by the oversized pot steeping on the table.

Phillip kept on with his preparations while prince and party moved in. Appalons had to be stabled and cared for, baggage unloaded and transported into the house, certain items had to be unpacked and the rest stowed neatly on one side of the great room. The party of seven had to decide on sleeping arrangements and move bedding upstairs. There was no real facility for bathing, but their host had prepared a copper pot of hot water over the fire they could draw from using a big wooden ladle. They could put hot water into a basin and then take it upstairs to wipe themselves down. Fresh jota kept them fueled through the whole unpacking and settling-in phases of the night.

Rita was their best cook, so she helped Phillip with the food. The first course would be herbed fish on a bed of baby greens dressed with nuts, honey, and vinegar. That would be followed by meat from the unfortunate Bonita, stewed with roots and mushrooms served in a rich broth. Third course was futobel ribs, braised in winter fruit, served with coarse brown bread to mop up the tangy sauce. Prince Leo promised to provide aperitifs and cheeses for desert.

When Phillip sat at the table during the first course Jorgo tried to object, only to have the boy cut him off and reprimand him. "Don't even start. I'm the host, so I eat at the table. If you're too good to dine with me, then you're too good to eat my food." In his anger, even the whites of the boy's eyes turned to silver. The cloth lanterns, lit as they were with the arts, responded to his temper by growing brighter.

"You can endure my company or you can go to bed hungry. Choose."

Jorgo slammed his hands onto the table and shot up to his feet, ready to put the commoner boy in his place. He was about to declare he wouldn't be treated so poorly, but Leo spoke first.

"I apologize for the behavior of my secretary." Leonardo's voice was gentle, but his glance towards Jorgo was hard. "He truly is talented, but there are some days he isn't worth the bother. You have been very free with your time on our behalf, but I've allowed my man to antagonize you. I had hoped he would recognize his mistake on his own, but his incivility has demeaned us all. I am sorry."

The speech was given in the disciple's direction, but it was largely for Jorgo's benefit the apology was made. Jorgo was so imperious because he insisted everyone else demonstrate the same reverence towards the prince that he himself felt. To have that same prince make an apology on Jorgo's behalf was more painful than a thousand remonstrations from some random disciple.

33

"I accept your gracious apology," returned Phillip. "If Jorgo can confine himself to positive comments, or be silent, there's no need to dwell on this any further. Please, everyone enjoy." As host he took the first bite, and complemented Rita on her skill with the fish. Everyone else joined in, leaving Jorgo standing alone and unheeded. Eventually he sat down and ate, and kept to himself for the whole meal.

There was a lot the royal party couldn't talk about in the presence of an outsider, so they mostly stuck to discussing their time in Unity City. Apparently Phillip had never been there, so he was keen to know more about Enclave, the section of the city that housed the Unity Church, and the Art School especially. The fact he was anointed 'in the wilderness' meant his background would be highly unusual, so Leo wasn't surprised when the boy refused to reveal anything about his past. The quorum that had trained and anointed him included Dean Garsharp, Disciple Leila, and Disciple Mobeen whose moniker was Sacred Blade.

After dinner the guests helped clear the table and put everything away, but it was Phillip who did the washing. He took all the tableware and cookware outside to the courtyard and scrubbed it all in one huge cleansing with a great clattering and some shattering noises. He then remade the several pieces that had broken.

"Only eight breaks," he said proudly to Ester, "I'm getting better."

They entertained each other with music in the Lavradio way, taking turns signing or playing. The royal party had an excellent lap harp they shared, an expensive gilt instrument with impressive resonance. Farava and Leo sang duets, as any affianced couple were expected to do. Nunio chose a

Lavradio classic with his own off-color lyrics added to the originals. Malisa and Rita performed songs they had learned in Gallia, while Jorgo sang old classic tunes that seemed to go on a little too long. Phillip didn't sing a lick, but he had a nickleharp that he played to good effect. Only when the winter moon had climbed high did they call an end to the evening. Phillip was the first to bed down, leaving his guests to set their own watch.

The next morning Leo went downstairs to find breakfast in a pot over the fire ready for serving: porridge and dried meat. The crew was already at table eating by candlelight and firelight. One window was cracked open to let in fresh air and a gray winter light that promised more snow.

"Where is our disciple," he yawned?

"He left before dawn," reported Nunio, "and said he wouldn't be back until at least mid-winter, so we can use the place as we like. 'Just leave it clean,' he said."

Leo sniffed the bowl Jorgo handed to him. Compared to last night's feast, it was the most boring of meals. "Did he say anything else?"

"He said to walk in the Light," reported Ester, "and send your donation to Matrix Lucia."

"That's going to be a problem," said Jorgo, "since we don't know who or where she is."

"Lucia is a retired disciple who ministers to the poor in your bricktown," Ester explained, "so there should be no trouble at all getting a suitable donation into the right hands. You don't approve, Jorgo?"

Jorgo felt safer speaking his mind now that the disciple wasn't around to complain. "I'm surprised he would throw away a royal reward, that's all."

"He's not throwing it away," insisted Ester. "He's using it to continue the Work, which is helping people. Helping people is not a waste. He helped us, even after you insulted him." She turned to Farava, "he must have enough money to travel with, or he would have stuck around." Mendicant disciples and healers had to pay their own way using donations they received. Once they had enough to secure their own needs plus a little security (say, a few month's worth of expenses) the rest of their donations went to the coffers of some nearby temple or towards a church-related activity.

"It still seems ungrateful," complained the secretary. "The next king wants to bestow a reward on him, and he just disappears? He's probably hiding something."

"He's definitely hiding something," Nunio agreed with him, dramatically. "He's a noble son who abandoned the family name to go out into the world and exercise his true talent and perform dangerous heroics. He can't stick around for a bunch of nobles when he has deeds to perform!"

"Enough about Phillip," enjoined the prince, "we need to discuss my entry into the capital. Mother wants us to make a spectacle of it. Since we're already encamped we might as well do the advance planning from here, then move to a staging area a day before the parade."

Crown Prince Leonardo got to work, readying himself to parade in front of his future subjects, and ascend the throne at the solstice.

JOURNEY BEGINS

Lavradio, East Forest

Taylor had escaped from the lodge without anyone trying to convince him to stay. Nunio had a slightly wrong idea about him, but he wasn't far off terms of the level of drama. Prince Leonardo's parents had set out to kill Taylor to collect on a secret bounty offered by the church. At least that was the information Taylor had about their motivations at the time of his death. He had been ambushed by mercenaries in a less-reputable part of the city, but escaped. Then he had run into his own former attendant from his brief stay in the palace, a girl who had been like a big sister to him, and in an unguarded moment let himself be poisoned to death by her.

So Nunio was right: Taylor was hiding behind an assumed name to cover up a dramatic backstory. It just wasn't the one he had imagined. Further complicating matters, to an operatic degree, was the fact that one of the people he was hiding from was Leonardo's brother, Second Prince Estevan Odemira. He and Taylor were friends. Inconveniently, Estevan had some skill at collecting information, especially within the capital city. If Taylor let himself be found by Estevan it would force the prince to choose between fealty to his family or his friend. So Taylor, when considering the worst that could happen (and not being far off the mark, as it

37

turned out) had to procure a safe house that Estevan wouldn't be able to locate.

It might seem strange he would choose to rent a house from the royal family, even under the alias Phillip Young, but the lodge had some excellent qualities. The first was that it was remote. Being well outside of the capital's city limits put it beyond Estevan's normal reach and offered some seclusion while Taylor and his people decided what to do next. The other reason was the property was managed by the royal family's private trust, which was to say it was badly mis- managed by a hierarchy of aristocrats who were not very honest and were in the habit of not reporting certain contracts so they could pocket the proceeds themselves.

Having secured a safe house Taylor had one of his trusted people convert the under-stairs space into a closet. Then Taylor used the arts to seal it as a sacred vault that only he and his fellow fugitives would be able to open. To other people it would look like someone had walled in the area under the stairs, but those with permission would be able to see the door and could access the secret room. As long as the door was closed the insides would be protected from the eyes of the greedy and the passage of time. That was where they stored their cache of emergency supplies: food, clothes, copies of important schematics and recipes, specialized tools, and enough money to start a new workshop.

When he arrived Taylor had found his share of the goods and a letter, left behind by his closest companions at the Pegasus Workshop. On the same night as his murder, Pegasus Workshop had been raided by palace guards in plainclothes. They were attempting to steal money and written methods but Pegasus didn't keep much of either on hand, and what was on site was in a sacred vault. The raiders had put the entire workshop to the torch.

Taylor wasn't worried about the property as much as he was the six permanent employees: Lorena the forewoman, Bao the general handyman/craftsman, Mr. and Mrs. Vale who were the valet and housekeeper, and the young bricktown cousins Mila and Milo who were training to be his followers. The workshop had hired day workers from bricktown on a rotating basis, and he hoped nobody from the palace would track them down and give them a hard time, but it was the contingent of six full-timers who would be attractive targets for revenge or exploitation. According to a letter left behind in the vault, everyone in the workshop had escaped in good condition thanks to a secret back door out of the workshop, built by Bao. The six full-timers had found their way to the lodge, waited for Taylor for the planned three days, then taken their goods and headed east to the country of Gallia to re-establish the business under a new name.

Taylor burned the letter as soon as he was done reading it. If the palace or Leadership caught up with him he didn't want to compromise his people.

The only deviation from the plan had come from Milo. On his way out of the burning Pegasus Workshop he had grabbed Taylor's precious copy of *The Disciple's Guidebook* and slipped it into Taylor's pack. The volume was written on expensive parchment in the hand of his three arts teachers, with the addition of their personal footnotes, as a sort of graduation gift. When he had discovered the unexpected treasure Taylor had silently thanked Milo, wherever he was.

Of course Taylor's guitar had been deliberately left behind as part of the plan. By now all that would be left was cold ashes. Taylor had become famous within Girona for playing the alien instrument and for his singing, so to be Phillip he would have to give them both up. The nickleharp was a common enough instrument that it wouldn't attract attention so they had stashed one in the safe house. Taylor had colored his hair in a brindle pattern using the arts, and his silvery eyes were a side-effect of his resurrection. People would assume these were beast traits, further throwing off anyone looking for a smooth skinned boy.

In spite of having to leave the lodge early Taylor still believed that renting it had been a smart decision. It wasn't Estevan who found the safe house but Leonardo, and only because the crown prince had decided to take a holiday and then gotten himself ambushed by the nearby wildlife. The lodge had only been compromised by stupendous bad luck. Taylor's identity was probably safe: even if Leonardo told his brother about his encounter with an underage disciple there were too many discrepancies between Taylor and Phillip. Still, it was prudent to move on before he said or did something that would stand out as being too uniquely Taylor-ish. He would also be harder to track down once he was out of the country.

All of that explained why Taylor was in the east forest at dawn, already several kilometers from the lodge, traveling north. His two weeks in the lodge had restored him to a state where he was functional, with some odd caveats. He had good command of his spirit, as long as he wasn't doing anything too delicate like making fiber into thread or healing a soft organ. His eyes were giving him trouble: he was sensitive to bright sunlight, and working with large amounts of spirit made him temporarily blind. He also wasn't sleeping well, but if he worked himself hard enough during the day then he would dream less at night and could sleep longer. Overall, he wasn't healthy but he was far from dead.

He was traveling with physical enhancements for strength and endurance. Improving his hearing made the world so loud that every odd sound was a hammer inside his head, so he was going without the sensory prayers Leila had spent so much time teaching to use. Moving as fast as he was, without improved senses, he wasn't that shocked to suddenly find himself on the same patch of forest as a large animal. He was surprised the animal was an appalon wearing full tack, trying to reach for some winter fruit high in a tree and failing. His trunk wouldn't reach the them, even when he propped his front feet on the tree to gain some height.

"Do you want some food?" Taylor said to the appalon. The animal looked at him as if he were stating the blindingly obvious. Which he was. "Let me help."

Taylor put down his burdens and scrambled up the tree to the higher branches, to pluck several of the shriveled fruits and let them drop to the snowy ground. The appalon scooped them out of the snow with his trunk and stuffed them into its mouth, three at a time. Taylor scooped more into his shirt. If he let the appalon eat too many too fast it could get terrible gas. He jumped down and stashed the extra food in his pack, keeping a couple out for himself.

Winter fruit was anything edible that stayed on a tree into winter, but in this case it was a fig-like orb that turned raisiny as the cold season set in. They were chewy, and they had a sweet jammy flavor. Diced, they would go nice in some oatmeal, or in oatmeal cookies. Tenobre didn't have refined sugar but they did have honey and a surprising variety of sweet fruits to rely on. They had a grain that was somewhere between oats and barley (which Taylor thought of as simply "this world's version of oats"), a wheat whose kernels were the size of corn kernels, wild rice, and a plethora of lesser-known local grains.

Taylor had released his enhancements so he could enjoy his brief meal without the tingling, buzzing sensation in his limbs and other distractions that came with the blessings. So when he ended up on his rear end, he didn't know what had happened save that his chest hurt. He looked up to discover the appalon, standing above him, trumpeting. The animal shook his head back and forth (from this angle Taylor could see it was male), shifted his weight onto both right feet, then to both left feet. Then he shuffled backwards several steps and trumpeted again.

The appalon was challenging him.

"Are you feeling feisty, big guy?" The appalon lowered its head and spread its legs wide.

"Fine," Taylor told him, "it's not like I have a job or anything. I literally have all day."

With that the boy charged the animal, collided with it, and wrapped his arms around its head. Both of them put their weight into the uneven grapple. Little by little, Taylor was pushed back leaving drag marks in the snow. Taylor lowered his center of gravity and forced the appalon to put most of weight onto one side. This robbed the animal of some of its leverage, and the much smaller boy was able to push him back a few feet. But it wasn't to last. When the appalon had given all the ground it was willing to, it bowled Taylor over with its sheer size. He ended up in the dirt and snow again, this time on his back. For the first time since coming back to life, Taylor was laughing.

The appalon used its trunk, the most sensitive member it had, to give his face a good long explore making wet noises against Taylor's eyes and nose. Then, it got rather too intimate with his mouth. The beast wouldn't stop, until Taylor pet and rubbed his trunk. "You win," laughed the boy. "Please let go of my face."

The appalon, apparently satisfied, meandered over to Taylor's baggage and knelt down and looked at him. *What are you waiting for?* It seemed to say to him. *Are we leaving this place or what?*

While Taylor was loading his luggage and checking the straps he noticed the tack was engraved with the beast's name, "Hateful Ben". It was the royals' missing mount. Taylor reshaped the leather to read "Magnificent Ben". It was a crude job, embarrassing really, but it was what he could manage.

"I don't blame you for leaving," he told his new acquaintance. "It sounded like they didn't appreciate you at all. You're not a monster! You're just very tactile."

Taylor mounted the animal and directed it to stand up. Then boy and appalon turned south, keeping the distant capital on their right.

Thoughtspace

Mental injury was as real in thoughtspace as a broken leg. A snarl of feelings Taylor couldn't touch were calcifying around a memory. Anything that connected to it had to be treated with care. The knot of memory itself was shot through with such hurt and betrayal that everything it touched was colored by those emotions.

In this memory Micas felt as warm and familial to him as his real sister in Emristar, while she gently poisoned him in a way that robbed him of speech and thus robbed him of prayer. Taylor missed her. Taylor wanted to see her burn.

But, he didn't blame her. The blame was firmly on Queen Diana. He didn't expect gratitude or loyalty from the queen's feckless husband-king, but he hadn't expected the queen to turn on him without explanation. Taylor had worked with her, in a convenient sort of way, to save the capital; to sideline her enemies; to educate her son.

Convenient. That was exactly the problem: he was too convenient. He was too eager to sort out their problems without asking for anything for himself. Taylor liked helping people, that was his nature. But it made him easy to use and thus easy to discard. If it hadn't been a bottle of poison then it might have been a knife in the back, or the smallest push off the edge of a cliff.

He should blame himself, too. On his social graph there was a thick line between the royal couple, a liege-retainer shackle that made the queen a smart puppet yoked to an idiot puppeteer. The king had found a way to profit from his death, and ordered the queen to assist. Whatever hold the king had on her, it was enough to overcome the few shreds of morality she possessed.

Taylor realized he had touched the snarl, and it was making him negative. It was a wound sitting on a nerve, painful to touch and impossible not to. Taylor built a room around the misbehaving part of his brain to make it easier to ignore so he could work. It continued to throb angrily at him, but at least it wasn't actively dragging him down.

There were therapies for this kind of mess, but it required psychoactive drugs and people he could trust. At the moment he was short on both things.

There were piles of work to be done, once he got his mind settled enough for thoughtmancy. The most urgent of which was the discovery that silent casting was possible in Tenobre. Most magic systems that used verbal language used words like guideposts along a well-worn trail: they helped the caster visualize the end result. A practitioner who became adept enough could use the magic without words, and could shape mana without restraint provided they had the will and acumen to achieve their ends.

Tenobre prayers served a very different purpose: they were passwords. Each manifestation of magic was locked behind a long password that made the effect available to the authorized user. If you were anointed and recited the prayer and had the mana for it, then the function became available to you. The password could not be omitted, but it could be recited mentally instead of out loud. That was how Taylor had completed the prayer of Sandim's Return: he had recited it mentally, after his voice had died. The evidence that it had worked was the fact he was walking around thinking about it.

After practicing progressively faster silent recitations of the prayer to protect against poison (because experience had so recently demonstrated the efficacy of paralytics against disciples) Taylor had an insight: maybe the prayer could be mentally recited all at once as a single Word. In theory the idea was the same as the techniques he used to make armor.

When making scales for tirun armor, the practitioner had two choices. The most common was to shape each scale constructively, in stages: Flatten a slug of bronze into the required profile, etch the designs and punch the rivet holes, then harden the scale by degrees until it was finished. The master-level technique was to heat the slug enough to be malleable, then shape and harden it all at once with a single hammer blow. The trick to the technique was to hold the totality of the end product in one's mind, and strike it into existence all at once with the prayer-powered hammer. By maintaining concentration and a steady supply of spirit, scales could be hammered out by the dozen.

After a few hundred attempts, Taylor finally got the technique to work. Learning how to think a prayer as a single word was effectively like memorizing it all over again, only much harder. Soon he had his core repertoire of seven prayers converted into Words. It wasn't reliable at first, but daily practice would make them second nature. Compared to the prayer speed of most practitioners, using Words was instantaneous.

Taylor did not assume he was the first to discover these ideas. There was plenty of evidence that past disciples had extended prayer beyond Numan Battani's explicit intent. For starters, there were were cryptic prayers hidden in scripture: passages that didn't read like prayers but would nonetheless activate an aspect of magic if used properly. Almost as soon as he was anointed, Taylor had accidentally discovered one. He then immediately conducted a thorough search of scripture to find them all. Sandim's Return, the prayer that had resurrected him, was the most extreme example. There was also a cryptic prayer for breathing under water, and another for climbing walls. There was another for copying written materials, which made Taylor think some past disciple had really hated making copies.

One of Taylor's open questions was how, exactly, did one create a new prayer? Scripture mentioned something about how the Chosen, Numan Battani, "raised the stone of origins, and set down the prayers for the faithful." The origin stone was mentioned only that one time, and scripture had nothing to say about what it looked like, how big it was, its purpose, or whether it survived the destruction of the First Enclave. One of the things he wanted to do was climb Mount Yagour to visit the site of the First Enclave, and poke around a while. Maybe he could learn something about how Battani, "set down the prayers for the faithful."

The other gift from his resurrection was his silver eyes. For days he thought his vision was failing: the noonday sun (when it was out) blinded him. Even moonlight could make him squint. Sometimes when he used his spirit his eyesight would suddenly go blurry, or streaks of weird light would obscure everything. It wasn't until he started to regain some control, and restore some of the sense of his own spirit, that he realized what he was seeing: Light of the Spirit. Not only could he see his own Light, but the sun was pouring out a fair amount of it, too. He had noticed that Tenobre seemed to have a lot of extra mana laying around during the day, mana he was happy to scoop up and put to use, but he had never given it a lot of thought.

There were several implications to all of this. One was that Spirit Light could be placed somewhere on the electromagnetic spectrum. Off-hand, he was guessing it would be somewhere in the ultraviolet, but a simple experiment and some trigonometry would tell him for sure.

It also raised the question of the difference between Light and Spirit. The terms were used interchangeably, but what if they weren't the same? Maybe they had the same relationship as infrared radiation and heat. Taylor set to work thinking about ways to test the idea.

It should also be possible to create a fluorescent substance that let one detect the presence of Light as an emission of visible light. It was an interesting idea, but Taylor didn't know what it could be used for. Maybe new practitioners could use it as a bio-feedback system, to help them learn to sense and control their own Light. Likewise, a fluorescent substance that reflected visible light as ultraviolet might be a way to create Light from normal sunlight.

Once again he had too many research topics, and had to prioritize.

Lavradio, South Highway

Routine was key to keeping one's sanity. Mornings began with exercises to enhance strength and flexibility. Then breakfast, packing, and pushing.

Ben liked to push against Taylor in the mornings, even though Taylor was no match for the appalon un-enhanced. Ben would place his head against Taylor chest and the boy would push and strain and, when Ben decided he had earned a little positive feedback, the mount would retreat a few steps. After a few minutes of back and forth, Ben would topple him over, then gambol about the camp site in celebration. After his morning victory Ben would kneel to be loaded up.

On every second morning, Taylor would run part of the day on foot carrying a heavy pack for endurance training, with Ben trailing behind him wondering why the boy was stealing work that better done by appalons. When Taylor pushed himself too hard Ben would kneel down and refuse to move until the boy did what he was supposed to do: put the luggage and himself onto the appalon so they could ride together properly.

The majority of the daytime was spent practicing with his eyes, exercising his spirit, or reciting scripture while riding. Sometimes, if Ben requested it, Phillip would sing to him.

Evenings were for making camp, which he mostly did by shaping the earth to form a temporary shelter for them both. Then he had weapons practice and cooking. As night settled in he would practice the nickleharp and sing. On occasion he would work on new songs, which all came out cynical or angry.

The nighttime was hard because of the rotating selection of awful dreams. In the worst one he was caught in the Queen Diana's carnivorous guard plant, unable to move or speak while she calmly went about her board-clacking administrative work. Micas would come to check on him and, even though he knew better, Taylor would plead with her using only his eyes. She would examine the plant's progress and, if unsatisfied, nonchalantly pour something deadly vile into Taylor's paralyzed mouth. Sometimes it was just a cupful, other times it was a pitcher. Once, she used a hose and funnel to force buckets of ichor into him. Meanwhile, the queen marked him off her to-do list as a finished item by brushing a thick black line through his name.

Other nights he would lay awake, thinking about his people. The Tabua family had taken him in as one of their own and were sorely missed, as was everyone from the workshop. He often thought of Laura Sabrosa, the girl he had taken to sleeping next to in his last days in Girona. He missed the way she liked to link their fingers together while they slept, and how her short puffy tail would swing excitedly when he opened his eyes in the morning. He even missed some of the people from the palace, though not Micas or the queen. He fervently hoped that Prince Estevan wouldn't backslide to becoming uselessly entitled, or evolve into something ruthlessly homicidal.

Lavradio, South Highway

Taylor and Ben worked their way south. They avoided Girona and then, three days later, they avoided Dosal Furst, the capital of Duchy Dosul. From a distance the city looked finely situated at the south end of Lavradio's fertile plains, standing on a prominent hill at the start of a range of mountains. It was a major intersection: to the north where Phillip had just come from was the Lavradian capital of Girona. Skirt the mountains going southeast and you would soon find yourself in neighboring Gallia, a coastal country with a decidedly different view of aristocracy than Lavradio.

The road southwest entered a wide valley between the low mountains of the Navos Altos and the grand peaks of the Interior Range. The valley wasn't flat: it gradually rose above the loamy soils of Lavradio's fertile interior to the high cold wilderness called Fringe.

While climbing up the southwest route it looked to Taylor like an ancient glacier, kilometers wide, had scoured all the loose soil and rock from the two neighboring mountain ranges and carried it away downhill to the northeast. What it had left behind was a gargantuan flat-bottomed trough that the following millennia had just begun to soften and reshape. Most of the plants were widely scattered: low-lying colony trees, vines, and grasses. Anything with a root system that could endure harsh winters and fierce spring winds.

On their way up the valley they passed several narrow side-roads, each labeled with a stone marker bearing one or more destinations. Nearly every name had a narrow board glued next to it with "population 0" written on it. Their destination was Fort Fringe, the southernmost outpost of Lavradio and gateway to the country of Ullidia beyond. According to the signs the fort was still occupied.

The higher they climbed, the worse the noonday sun pressed on Taylor's eyes. He fashioned a (very crude) hat from plant fiber. Without protection, it was like shining a bright light into a dense fog: he had a great view of the fog and nothing else. If he focused, Taylor could suppress his spirit and dim the sensitivity of his eyes.

There was no schedule to keep and their only adversary was the environment. The snow was less than twenty centimeters deep in most places and Ben could eat any of the grasses he found hiding underneath. Like so many mammals in Tenobre, appalons had a trunk he used to feel around the ground and grasp anything edible. For himself, Taylor could hunt small mammals to supplement the rations he had bought from the last tiny farming village on the outskirts of Dosal Furst.

It was tempting to hunt the franango, large ground-dwelling birds that ran the fringe in groups called raids. Taking one would be easy: At a height of a meter and a half, they were only slightly taller than Phillip. But if you took one you might have to deal with an entire raid of thirty or more. They had sharp talons at the end of strong legs and, although they didn't fly much, they could use their wings to get over obstacles and onto high places. They were better left alone unless one wanted to kill and eat a great many of them.

On a whim, Taylor and Ben took one of the side roads to find the town at its end: a mining town that had once been home to fewer than a thousand people, set against the edge of the Interior Range. The place hadn't been abandoned long, less than twenty years judging from the size of the colony trees taking over some of the lots. One day people had packed everything they cared to take with them and left the rest behind.

Instead of camping inside the town, which would require clearing out a long-abandoned house, they made their usual camp in a sheltered crevice of the hillside. Taylor played the nickleharp and sang, until the sun was fully down and and the world cast in complete darkness. Looking up from their tiny crevice they could see an irregular line of stars, traversing the sky from one ridge to the other in less than an hour.

On that particular night Taylor wasn't too inclined to sleep. Sleep only brought painful memories, or longings for his real home in Emristar. On a good night he dreamed of the people in Girona he missed, only to wake alone to a cold morning sky. So on this night he stayed awake listening to the night animals hunt and evade each other, bowing strange sounds from his instrument to answer the wind among the rocks. For some time, as the night grew late, he sat with the instrument quiet in his lap as the last dying lights of the three Tenobre moons faded from the sky. Only the stars were visible, clean and sharp.

Ben knew something was coming before Phillip did. The appalon raised its trunk and sniffed deeply, then looked at the human. *This is your problem. I carry stuff.*

All around himself Taylor could feel sources of spirit. These weren't practitioners. Humans with spirit were like generators that threw off complex waves. What he was feeling now was small point sources, hundreds of them, steady little lights that didn't waver. As Phillip spread his senses wide his eyes became sensitive to spirit, and picked up the sources as tiny shining specks scattered along the rock wall of the crevice.

He almost stood up and went out to investigate but he remembered Ben's warning. Something was out there, and soon he could hear it: claws in the shallow dirt. A lithe body scampering across the ravine. It was scratching at something, moving on, then scratching again.

Eventually the animal came into view: a mimica. They were a predatory species with small heads, long mustelid bodies, prehensile tails, and fur that could change color. Mimicas mostly ate small mammals and birds, but they weren't above filling up on beetles or other insects. They normally didn't grow longer than a meter but this one was over two: a monster.

Disciple's Guidebook was clear about monstrous creatures: they should be killed whenever the opportunity arose. There was a theory that animals became monsters when they somehow absorbed more spirit than an animal should. If allowed to live, the monstrous specimen could mutate or, in the worst cases, become cursed. The guidebook proposed many theories about how animals came to possess so much spirit but Taylor now knew at least one method for sure: the mimica in front of him was going from one light to the next. As the creature put its mouth to the lit areas of the rock the light was transferred from the rock to the creature in peristaltic waves that made the creature glow. Taylor couldn't be sure how much of what he was seeing was normal visible light and how much was his weird new vision, but his sense of spirit was keen enough to understand exactly what was happening. Something in the rock was storing mana, and the animal was eating it.

Taylor killed the mimica cleanly by crushing its head with a thrown rock, causing the light within it to begin to fade. He gutted the monster and hung up the body to cool in the frigid winter air, steaming and dimming as the last of its spirit died with the creature's cells. That done, he turned his attention to the strange phenomenon in the rocks around him.

The light, he soon learned, was coming from tiny crystals embedded in the rock. He dug them out one after another, then remembered he had a prayer that could separate any material from any other. Using his new understanding of the water purification prayer, he separated all of the crystals from about a hundred cubic meters of rock. That yielded a double-handful of what he was pretty sure was low-grade gemstone.

None of the crystals were bigger than a sesame seed or clear enough to be considered a gem, but they were all full of mana.

Where had that mana come from? Was it absorbed from the sun? Why hadn't he detected it until so late into the night? How many other minerals could perform the trick of storing mana?

After some hesitation, he used the prayer of shaping to merge them all into one large piece which he held in a fluid state, encouraging it to crystalize. Gradually, it formed itself into a hexagonal rod terminated at each end. By dawn he had one massive gemstone, four centimeters wide and twelve long. Unfortunately it was riddled with bubbles and feathering. Since the surface was unpolished the stone was opaque. Most people wouldn't recognize it for what it was.

He would need to test it to make sure, but Taylor guessed what he was holding was beryl with enough manganese ions to color it bright red. He had no idea what the value of it was in Tenobre, but in some worlds the gem in his hand would be among the most rare: a huge red emerald. But the value wasn't what interested him. The stone's ability to store mana, then give it up later, was what he found interesting.

He was unlikely to be the first to discover the phenomenon, yet there had been nothing in his training about reactions between unshaped mana and physical objects. That could mean any of several different things. The knowledge might simply be undervalued, or it might be genuinely useless. More likely, the knowledge was forbidden by the Unity. Church doctrine said that spirit was a property of living things, so the idea it could be found in rocks might be heretical. Studying the phenomenon could be apostasy.

Phillip made a lightweight wooden box and packed the crystal snugly into it for later study.

FRINGE

Lavradio, Barony of Fringe

Morning of the ninth day found Taylor and Ben at Lavradio's border with Ullidia, admiring the lay of the wall and fort. The border wall spanned over a kilometer across a chokepoint in the valley, but was more of a formality than a serious defense. The barrier was just over two meters high, barely taller than a man but wide enough that the patrols could be seen walking on top of it, three abreast. Like most soldiers, their blessings skewed towards obvious combat advantages like claws and thickened skin. Wide, heavy wooden doors bound in bronze barred any travel between the counties, unless one felt like detouring into the hills.

The fort was more impressive, being situated on a hill on the east side of the valley. Its walls were higher and fronted on a steep incline. From an attacker's point of view there was fifteen meters of climb, unless they approached by the raised roadway which passed within a stone's throw of the city walls. The curtain wall of the fort connected to the border wall, allowing reinforcements to arrive from the city.

The disciple had bathed in freezing water and donned his regalia that morning, the better to pass through the gate unquestioned. He would have used the cleaning prayer, but in spite of his training it continued to knock him off his feet. At least it didn't scour his entire campsite any more. Practice was paying off.

Taylor also took the time to wrap a thick scarf around his face, leaving only his eyes exposed. When he was first summoned to Tenobre, he had spent a summer at the royal palace eating at the same table as the local baron's three children and his mother, the Dowager Baroness Fringe. Although Taylor and the baron had never met, Taylor's face was known to several of the man's underlings. With any luck he would only need to show is face once at the gate. He wondered idly if his friends were in the fort, still sleeping and unaware he was passing by. Taylor was breaking a promise to them, sneaking through the border this way without visiting.

Disciple and appalon waited by the side of the chilled road, a hundred meters from the gate, observing the pacing guards and a detachment of cavalry descending from the castle. Then he felt it: the approach of another practitioner. From the strength and direction of their spirit they were a healer riding with the approaching soldiers. It seemed he would not pass through today unnoticed. He turned Ben to face the oncoming cavalry without using his hands and waited, spirit unfurled so his fellow practitioner might sense him.

"Good morning, I am Phillip the Younger," he practiced. It had been days since he last spoke to a human. "We meet in the Light," he tried again. After a few more attempts he managed a well-modulated greeting.

The party that approached was a hundred strong, outfitted in hardened leather reinforced with bronze plates. They were equally divided between those bearing polearms, and those equipped with bows. Nearly all of them carried sturdy short swords and wooden shields. Not cavalry, but mobile infantry. The leader wore a helm with a silver wreath embossed across its brow, indicating nobility.

This was going to become inconvenient.

The leader signaled a stop and walked his mount up to Phillip with another rider by his side, dressed like a healer with the addition of soft leather armor. The detachment behind him put up a cloud of breath in the brisk cold of morning.

"We meet in the Light," Phillip greeted them, his voice muffled by the scarf.

"Let's walk as brothers," the healer replied hastily. "I am Healer Julius, posted in these borderlands. May I present Rodrigo Monforte, Baron of Fringe?"

"I am Disciple Phillip the Younger, mendicant. This is Ben." As they seemed to be in a hurry he skipped any further pleasantries. The minimums had been met. "Are you hunting men or monsters?"

"Monsters," said the baron. "Will you lend us your aid?" He was a thinner man than most of his soldiers, but judging from his forearms he was well muscled and wiry. His face reminded Taylor powerfully of his two sons, especially Gonzo Monforte: it was the clever eyes and the whiskers.

"I will. You can tell me about it on the way." He turned Ben to follow the baron.

"Bifurdactica," said Rodrigo as they were riding north the way Phillip had just come. "Do you know them?"

"Only what I've read in books," Taylor replied. "I've been trained in their calls, but I've never met one to try them out."

"You're going to meet several today. Our scouts tracked down a nest. We're lucky you happen to be passing by."

Bifurdactica looked like a snake with fur, but was really a very long mammal with tiny vestigial legs. The males could grow to two meters, and females had been recorded at over four. The females also had a fake head on their tail: the lump of flesh with a face-like pattern of coloring wasn't convincing to a human but to some predators it was an effective diversion.

When a female wanted to mate she would find a cave or burrow and invite the males in to fertilize her en masse. The males would feed and guard her until after she gave birth and the pups were old enough to leave the den. If the males failed to provide enough food their mate would eat some of them. It wasn't personal: the babies had to be fed. When they left, each surviving male would take two or three of the pups with them to raise for a year before the pups set out on their own.

The babies tended to re-settle within several kilometers of the den and proceeded to deplete game and livestock in the area. If the surviving female pups matured and mated, the next generation could be a major disaster for anyone living nearby.

The extermination party moved several miles north then took one of the turns towards an abandoned town. There they picked up a scout who was waiting for them, tucked away in the Navos Altos hills. They spent another two hours following a game trail, then led their mounts up a hill. Phillip offered to bless the entire company with strength and endurance to get them up the hill, but the baron said to save his strength.

Monforte passed some of the time by giving Taylor tips on hunting the snake-mammal. The males were scary because of their numbers, speed, and sharp teeth. The females were scary because they were strong and hard to pierce. She could crush an appalon and then rip it to pieces small enough for her pups in a few minutes.

Julius questioned Taylor closely about his fighting and healing skills, but wasn't very sympathetic about his control problems. "Everyone gets that to some degree," he said when he was almost done laughing, "but you're going to have it rough. A light like yours must be hard to wrangle at the best of times. What's your cleaning prayer like?"

"If you don't stop laughing you're going to find out," Taylor grumbled.

Passwords were exchanged and the infantry joined the scouts on the hilltop to set up camp. The appalons knelt in rows and felt around in the cold earth with their trunks searching under the snow for food.

Introductions were made with lead scout Didica and a few of her people. Taylor didn't recognize any of them, so his secret was probably safe. Nonetheless, he decided to keep his scarf in place until he had seen everyone's faces.

Didica took the baron, Julius, Taylor, and the officers down the other side of the hill to a vantage point where they could see the monsters' den.

"We have to do this today," said the baron while several males worked together to pull a large animal into the burrow. "We can't have them finding us at night."

"I can build earthworks in a few minutes if you want them," Taylor offered.

"I would rather have enhancements on as many of my pikemen as you can manage. They're going to take the brunt no matter how this plays out."

"I was offering the earthworks in addition to the enhancements."

"Let him do it, Roddy," Julius told him. "Phillip has more than enough light."

They planned for a while, then broke up to brief the soldiers. Taylor made a hut for himself and Julius to sleep in, and an adjoining stable with a water trough for Ben. He checked his combat load, which was his weaponry and other bare essentials strapped securely to his body, and went to the final briefing.

The plan was to seal the den using the arts, build a pit in front of the den with a short wall around the rim for the pikemen to fight behind, and some elevated shooting platforms behind them for the archers. Phillip made the platforms by shaping the deadwood into simple shooting stands. He gave a benediction for everyone, then said the prayer for protection from harm and touched all one hundred fifteen people present with it, including himself. The pikemen also received strength, and the bowmen received a small increase in movement speed. The enhancements didn't take very much spirit individually because none of the soldiers were experienced bulwarks. It didn't pay to over-enhance someone who wasn't used to it.

With all prepared, Taylor re-opened the den and ran back behind the pikemen. The lead scout made a bifurdactica distress call, as if one of the den mates was signaling a threat to the den. Within a minute, dozens of furry snakes poured out of the hole and into the bowl below. The pikemen worked in pairs: one would separate a snake from the group and another would kill it by chopping its head off. The goal was to kill them safely while preserving the fur for export: it was a valuable commodity in Tenobre. They worked like that for over an hour, rotating the men to keep the front line fresh. Whenever they ran out of animals to kill, they called again. There were hundreds of the things.

One of the officers said, "She's gotta be pissed by now, right?"

"Let the disciple try calling it," said the scout. "He hasn't had a turn yet."

Phillip stepped to the edge of the bowl, behind the hastily erected wall, and uttered the bifurdactica challenge. They needed to end this soon: the sun was starting to disappear behind the mountain. Phillip called again, and then a third time more stridently.

They heard it before they saw it: Whatever was coming was moving earth to get to them. The den's hole was a meter wide, but it wasn't big enough. The hole broke wider, two meters at least.

The sun and moon went out. Then the shouts of alarm began. Something moved among them in the dark, easily more than a meter thick. Something that lashed at them, sent them flying like toys.

Huge jaws grabbed Phillip and pressed, unable to pierce his enhanced skin but perfectly able to crack his hip bones. It tried to re-adjust its bite, maybe to swallow him whole, but he dug the fingers of his left hand deep enough into the head to reach bone and got a good grip. He dropped the spear in his right hand and drew his stone knife and began to stab at the monster in the dark, looking for its brain.

It was cursed.

❖ ❖ ❖

"You're mostly invulnerable to monsters," Mobeen had told him. "As long as you have a bulwark and don't get overrun by sheer numbers, then you're not going to die. The biggest threat to you is your own arrogance."

Mobeen had given him that speech over a campfire, while a leporid of a hundred and sixty centimeters roasted over the fire. They had chased the jackrabbit-like creature on foot, and Taylor's tutor had made him kill the thing bare-handed by wrestling it to the ground and snapping its neck. The monster was herbivorous but its teeth and sharp little horns were something fearsome. It could bite a man's hand clean off, but against Taylor's enhancements the beast was powerless. That was the point of the lesson.

Mobeen continued his lecture. "The exception is cursed monsters. They're the only real threat to a strong hunter disciple. Don't ever take one lightly, not even small ones. Prepare multiple lights ahead of time. Wear your armor. Enhance everything. Bless all your weapons. Protect yourself from poison. Hunt smart, and don't hold back. If anything out there is going to kill you, it'll be a cursed monster or other people."

"So why is there only a paragraph in the *Guidebook*?" The book had suspiciously little to say about cursed monsters:

> *Cursed monsters carry darkness with them wherever they go. Their bite is poison. Their skin is hard as metal. Their hate for Light runs deep. To counter their darkness you must fight them in the full sun. Failing that, you may hope to ward off their darkness with the mightiest prayer for light you can invoke.*

"The *Guidebook* was written a little before the Alignment," explained Mobeen. "It's just over two hundred years old, and it hasn't been updated much. Cursed monsters hadn't been seen since scriptural times, so the people who wrote that paragraph were passing on some rote advice they themselves had never needed. Then about fifty years ago a Disciple Casimir claimed to kill one in the wilds of Hyskos. Nobody believed him. Now we get several every year."

"Do we know what causes them?" asked Taylor.

Mobeen shook his head at Taylor while he sliced a strip of crispy meat from their prey. "That's someone else's problem, so don't let your curiosity distract you. Focus right now on how to find cursed monsters and kill them without ending up as someone else's dinner."

"Disciple! Light! Light!" The baron's voice broke through the mayhem and Taylor's daze.

He silent-prayed the Word for light and, for a lack of anywhere else to put it, enchanted his knife. Every time he struck at the head he gathered more and more light, plunging the battlefield into darkness and then back to ever-brighter light again and again. It burned like the surface of the sun in his hand, yet the snake did not die. While he did that, he mass-protected the company from poison. He followed that up with an audible prayer for regeneration, which he shouted at the top of his lungs while stabbing at the creature's head. He was pouring his spirit over the soldiers like water.

Not this time you monster, he thought spitefully, thinking of Micas, *I will not go quietly. You won't have any of us today.*

The eyes and nose he was stabbing at were only fur, he realized, colored to look like facial features. The books had never mentioned the female's fake head could actually be dangerous, but Taylor's fractured hips and broken femurs said otherwise. The real head was trying to bite him too, but someone had thrown a rope over it and people were tying it down by looping the other end against a tree. The beast couldn't run, but that didn't prevent it from trying. It coiled a part of its fourteen-meter body around the tree and tried to push itself away hard enough to break the rope, but its muscles were better adapted to squeezing than pushing.

The disciple's broken bones could be dealt with later: adrenalin dulled the pain to a, "that's going to hurt so bad later," level. The real problem was they still weren't winning. The soldier's weapons bent and broke against the monster's hide and Phillip couldn't reach anything important from where he was.

"Use my sword," he said as loud as he could, and flung it among the soldiers. One of them, a young officer, scooped it up and stabbed at the monster's lungs and heart again and again while dozens of men strove to keep the thing from slithering away. Didica found Taylor's spear and attacked from the other side of the bifur. When they had made enough holes in enough places, the beast finally died.

Taylor couldn't remember how he got out of the bifurdactica's fake mouth, or how he ended up in his shelter. He just knew everything had stopped trying to eat him, and he wasn't freezing. He explored his body, flexing muscle groups to figure out what hurt. He was very systematic about any kind of body-acquisition incident.

Everything seemed whole and functional, except his body was insanely tired. He was under a felt blanket folded to double it up, and there was a small fire in the fireplace. That explained the warmth.

Someone was here.

"You're something else, kid."

Taylor's voice came out in a whisper. "What day is it?"

"It's tomorrow," said the soldier. One of the archers, blessed with reflective eyes that spoke of enhanced night vision. Taylor didn't recognize him.

"You're supposed to eat." He help sit Taylor up and put a bowl of something warm in his hands: a white soup with chunks in it. Winter tubers, dried herbs, appalon milk, and meat. Fresh, not from jerky.

"Bifur meat?"

"Excellent guess," the archer grinned, "we have a lot on hand."

"We're so lucky." After investigating the bowl thoroughly with his nose, Taylor took small sips even though his body clamored for the food. He ate the solid parts, a little at a time, then drank the rest of the broth. The soldier waited without comment, letting him finish at his own pace.

"Actually not terrible." Feeling a little stronger, he handed the bowl back to the archer. "Who are you?"

"Rolo Tyreum, at your service."

"Phillip the Younger," said the disciple weakly, "pleasure to meet you."

"You're supposed to drink this, too. Healer's orders." Rolo handed him a wooden cup that smelled medicinal.

Taylor recognized the recipe by smell. "No." He waved the cup away.

"Julius says you need to sleep to fully recover. And you do not sleep well, my friend. Not well at all."

The boy was clearly afraid of it, refusing to even touch the cup.

"Julius says, and I quote, 'Tell Phillip that if we wanted to poison him we would have done it already. Drink the medicine, get better, and stop being a bad patient.'"

Taylor drank the potion. Ben stuck his head in long enough to sniff at Taylor to verify he was still alive, and then Taylor was asleep again.

"What would you prescribe for someone with your symptoms?" Julius insisted. "Would you recommend ignoring the screaming in the night, unstable spirit, and deep bags under the eyes?"

The command tent had been cleared for this meal. Maybe it was breakfast or maybe it was early dinner. The gray winter sky looked the same all day long, so Taylor had no clue what time it was other than 'not night'. There was more bifur soup, a tureen of beans and sausage, and mulled wine. A tiny bronze stove in the center of the table kept the massive central pot of soup hot and radiated enough warmth to allow them to remove their outer coats. Baron Monforte, Julius, Rolo, Didica, and Phillip were the only attendees. Even the servants and guards had been sent out of the tent, and Taylor had been asked to set up a privacy barrier.

Taylor tried to think of something to say, but he knew the healer was right. However, the kind of treatment needed for his condition required a partner he could trust, someone who could guide him while under the influence of a mind-altering drug.

"I would recommend two weeks of rest," Taylor said finally, "followed by the gamanda protocol." Gamanda was a hallucinogen derived from a fungus. The drug could break someone out of a pattern of trauma or addiction, but it had to be taken with a trustworthy guide. "Two treatments minimum. Four would be better."

"And?" Julius looked at him expectantly.

"And that requires someone I trust to guide me. All of you seem like decent people, but I'm not ready to put my brain into your hands."

"You're going to need to trust somebody," Julius reasoned with him, "sooner or later."

Taylor scoffed at the idea. "Trust is what got me into this mess."

"What happened?" asked Didica. The way she asked was so matter-of-fact, as if to say, "yes, it sucks when you get hurt badly. How did it happen for you?" The Fringe was not a safe barony, and these were not people who lived safe lives. If anyone could understand, it would be them. But there were a lot of things he couldn't tell.

"I got poisoned," he said at last, "by someone I trusted, for just a moment. They left me for dead."

"Would this be the 'Micas' person you yell at in your sleep," the baron asked?

Taylor found he couldn't look at them, or else it would all come out. He stuffed the words back down his throat while looking at the table.

"You should forget you heard that name." His warning was whispered to the stove glowing redly on the table. "It's the kind of information that could put your family in danger." The stove smoked and pinged.

Healer Julius decided to pull the conversation back on track. "So, what will you do about your treatment?"

"I hadn't planned to do anything right away. I wanted to make a pilgrimage to Mount Yagour, and see the site of First Enclave."

"That's a terrible idea," Rolo said bluntly. "The paths to Mount Yagour are under several feet of snow this time of year, and winter has barely started. Even a disciple risks his life making the trek now. If you wait until summer I'll take you on the pilgrimage myself, if the baron allows."

Baron Monforte was emphatic in his agreement, pointing at Rolo. "Rolo is my best long-range scout, and he's been to the region several times. Don't be a fool. Listen to him."

Phillip thought of Ben, trudging through kilometers of snow drifts, uphill. "Gallia, then. It'll be easier on Ben, and there's people there I can trust. I hadn't planned to see them until spring, but ..." Phillip thought of his employees and followers from Pegasus Workshop. Now that he had allowed himself to consider it, seeing them again felt urgent. He was worrying about them every day, so maybe catching up with them now was a good idea. "I'll go to my friends in Gallia. They can help me."

"My house is going south for the coronation in two weeks," invited the baron, "you could journey with us partway."

If he traveled with the baron's family then it would be impossible to keep Taylor DeLanion dead: he had worked too closely with the Monforte children and the dowager baroness. Without knowing the palace's official position on his death he didn't want to risk letting the palace know Taylor was alive.

"Now that I've decided," he told the baron, "I'd rather leave from here. One or two more nights of bifur soup and sleep potions, and I'll set out. I can catch the regular gurantor train in Dosul Furst, and relax."

His new acquaintances didn't seem entirely satisfied, but they were mollified enough to start dinner.

Taylor recalled another question that had been bothering him. "Can I ask about all the towns in Fringe that are deserted now? Were they ever full?"

"In the first Monforte's time most of them were thriving," noted Didica, "or that's what we're taught."

"And? What happened?"

"Some of them were mining towns," replied Rodrigo, "whose mines went dry. But most were abandoned because we couldn't protect them. We just don't have enough people to protect so much area. There's more monsters today than there used to be."

Phillip removed a small book of paper and a wooden writing utensil from inside his jacket and made some notes, then flipped through several pages. He had made the paper and pencil himself using the arts, because he was tired of using clunky boards.

"I've been passing a lot of dead downs, not just in Dosul but even around Girona." He counted a list of something in his book.

"Here's a theory: The forces of civilization are losing. Humanity is retreating. Thoughts?" He wasn't seriously proposing the idea. It was the kind of proposal his family in Emristar would wrangle over, as a form of dinner edutainment

71

Baron Monforte choked on his wine. "People prefer living in cities, don't they?" He dabbed his front with a napkin. "Or near them. People have been migrating to cities for generations. Only the odd or the dutiful live in places like our wild and beloved Fringe. We aren't exactly normal nobility, are we?"

Rolo looked pensive. "You get so used to seeing ruins, you don't question them, or ask what it means that they're everywhere. There are more ruins than there are settlements."

"To really examine the question, I would need total population numbers," said Phillip, "and the sizes of various cities over a period of time. Supposedly every prelate has at least a hundred years of that close at hand. And if he doesn't, the nation's government does."

"What are you going to do if you're right?" queried Rodrigo. "Let's say you prove that humanity is dying out. What will you do then?"

"That depends on the cause, doesn't it?" Taylor smiled, as if he hadn't just posited the decline of humanity. "Maybe we learn there is nothing to worry about. I doubt we're in an urgent crisis, or the church would know about it. I can't worry about a remedy if I don't know what the problem is. Assuming there even is one."

Baron Monforte looked at Taylor hard enough to make him nervous. "That's not an answer, young man. What would you do if there is a crisis?"

"I would probably take the information to Leadership or the Deans," he told the baron, "get confirmation, and press them to take up the problem. I'm just one person. I'm not going to try to save the world all on my own."

After dinner they all took turns singing, as was the Lavradio custom, with Taylor bowing the nickleharp on his lap for accompaniment. Learning the standard Lavradian repertoire had been a good investment of his time: everyone sang, but not many people played an instrument so he was always a welcome addition to any party. When it was his turn to sing Taylor instead played them a new composition from his time exploring the ruins of Fringe, a song of empty skies and vast landscapes where the night was endless and bright. The table was so silent after his song was done, he wondered if they hated it.

The baron seemed especially affected. "Our wild and beautiful Fringe," he toasted, gulping down the last of his wine. "May I purchase the song, Phillip?" He was asking for more than a physical copy: he wanted permission to claim the song as an emblem of his house.

"Take it as a gift," Phillip replied without giving it much thought. "Consider it a token of friendship." Too late, he realized how forward that was. He might as well have walked up to a child in the schoolyard and said 'let's be friends, okay?'

"So be it," said the baron.

Lavradio, Dosal Furst

Five dawns later, Phillip was in Dosal Furst with some days to kill. The hilltop city of ten thousand offered fantastic views of the surrounding mountains and the expanse of farms running north towards the capital. He had tried to rent a room in the Agate Hotel, more for the sense of security a high-end hotel could provide than the luxury, but was offered a suite for free when the clerk found out he was a disciple. He practically had to force the clerk to accept any coin. Apparently the news of his encounters with the crown prince and bifurdactica were already circulating. The hotel would probably spread the word they were hosting a disciple to draw people to their amenities, like the dining room and bath house, in hopes of getting a look at him.

He had spent two more days in the hunting camp, fueling up on bifur soup while watching skinners work their way through the mountain of corpses. The low temperatures were a blessing, and Phillip had added a prayer of preservation over the dead animals so none would go to waste. The female was especially valuable. Not only did she provide a vast pelt, but her bones were an iridescent material that was a prized material for artists. The laminated structure that made the bone shine so beautifully was also what made the monster so tough to kill. The bone was tough, and difficult to work even for a disciple.

The baron had sent him off with a stack of silver bullion, several square meters of the female's skin salted for preservation, ten of the female's best ribs, and voluminous well-wishes. Phillip had given him a copy of *Our Wild and Beautiful Fringe*, with the lyrics he hadn't sung, carefully transcribed onto paper using a waterproof ink and permanently marked on the back with Taylor's disciple mark. His mark was a futobel under a sky of four stars. The animal was a six-legged boar-like creature with scooped antlers and a long, mobile snout. An adult would grow to about 150cm. The four stars above her symbolized the four tenets.

It took all of two seconds for Julius to start ribbing him about having such a weird animal as his symbol: most male disciples would prefer something more fierce. Taylor didn't mind as much as he pretended to because he had wrestled with the animal several times. The futobel was odd to look at but she was strong and wily. The little beast tossed her antlers in challenge while the stars shone on her from above. Not many disciples could mark something permanently, but Taylor had more spirit than he could get rid of.

Before he left the hunting camp, Taylor had flipped a brass triangular coin at Julius: a token payment between healers. "Some day when you're old enough," teased the healer, "let's get a drink. Until then, walk in the Light."

Since he had promised to take the relaxing carriage train into Gallia, Phillip and Ben were obliged to explore Dosal Furst for a few days. Mostly, they saw to their grooming and gear. They both got a wash and trim, although in different facilities. The hotel staff gave his two good outfits, long stuck at the bottom of his baggage, a proper clean and press. They visited a saddlery to buy bags worthy of Ben the Magnificent.

Taylor used to own an armored vest of excellent cut, but the palace had stolen it along with everything else. Replacing his armor was a top priority. In Fringe Taylor had gotten into a fight with a cursed monster while underprepared, which had been stupid, and he wasn't going to repeat that mistake. He found a leatherworker to create a coat long enough to cover him to the knee and suitable for his purposes. Getting someone to make a custom jacket on such short notice would normally be impossible, but disciples paid well and the work was considered an honor. Once the coat was finished he would rivet bronze armored scales to the insides to make brigandine armor.

The local temples received a gift of iridescent bone. Phillip had planned to give them bullion, but then he was told about a project to add a new mural to one of the smaller temples. With three of the ribs to work with they would have material for inlay work, plus a large quantity left over to sell for operational funds. While he was in the main temple, Taylor resisted the urge to check the local copy of *Luminous Histories* for his own name.

Most of the second day was spent in a forge, making tirun scales to be riveted into the jacket. A journeyman armorer handed Taylor one measure of heated bronze after another, which he shaped and enhanced in a single blow of a stone hammer. The smiths gathered to watch in envy as one perfect scale after another was produced: each one as thin as parchment and more durable than laminated plate. They were the size of a man's palm, decorated with a tiny futobel and stars, and had small holes for rivets.

When Taylor asked to buy rivets so he could finish his armor, the shop wouldn't hear of it. They insisted on picking up the jacket for him and finishing it before his departure, even if they had to work through the night. To compensate them, Phillip paid for materials, blessed the shop with a benediction, and hardened a great many of their tools. The master smith's hammer not only received an intense level of enhancement but, at his request, an engraving of the futobel-and-stars on one side. The master, an imposing man with a profusion of muscle and not a single hair on his body, shed tears of gratitude for the gift as he hugged the tool to his body. He promised to cherish the hammer, pass it down to his successors, and never allow a mere apprentice to lay so much as a finger on it.

Phillip thought that was more gratitude than his several minutes of work was worth, but was glad to see everyone so happy.

Breakfasts and lunches were always somewhere in town but dinners were had in the Agate Hotel dining room, where inventive sauces made a nice change from the previous bifur soup diet. Phillip skipped the after-dinner entertainments to practice and to tend his thoughtspace.

Now that he was getting sufficient sleep, things were calmer inside his head. The tangled area of his mind didn't hurt so furiously as before, but it wasn't truly healing either. But, the smallest things could open that wound.

The Agate had an attendant service, a desk where you could make special requests. They were impressively useful, and helped Taylor find his leatherworker and smithy. Taylor always avoided it when one particular young woman was on duty. She was too young, too pretty, too professional, and too impassive. She was too much like Micas, and Taylor couldn't go near her without fighting an urge to stab her before she could stab him.

Taylor wanted to believe he was fine now, and there wasn't any reason to be concerned. That everything would be fine in time. Another part of him knew he would pay dearly in the long run if he didn't handle this.

Early in the morning on the day Taylor and Ben were to leave the city, the armor smith and two of his journeymen arrived with his completed order. They delivered a jacket of vivid blue leather, punctuated with bright brass rivets. On the inside it was a coat of gleaming bronze scale covering the torso and thighs. Phillip liked the new armor so much he put it on immediately and wore it on his way to the carriage depot.

Ben got to ride in the rearmost of four carriages with the luggage and several other appalons, while Phillip rode with people in the first car. For the next few days they didn't have to do anything but sit, as the gurantors pulled them from one town to the next.

TEGEA BY THE SEA

Gallia, Tegea

Tegea was a town of twelve hundred, the last depot in the north of Gallia. They fished the nearby seas, grew tidemellon in the shallows, and terraced the nearby hills for barley and root crops. Their main export was giant cypress, brought down from mountains to the north. The locals were experts at felling and transporting the gargantuan, centuries-old boles using guarantors and specialized sleds. The wood was in high demand, but Tegea limited the harvest each year to keep prices high and their forests viable.

To the south stretched several miles of low-lying delta too bracken for normal crops. In that area the village maintained halophyte forage plants and breeds of grains. These weren't exactly farms, but landscapes irrigated by the tides they groomed to attract a wide selection of wild grazers and migratory birds. They were excellent hunting grounds almost year-round. In the autumn they could harvest grain and fiber. It was the opposite of the intensely cultivated terraces, a minimal effort for the food produced.

Following the procedures laid out in *The Disciple's Guidebook*, Phillip's first stop after disembarking the carriage was to find the local temple. It was late in the day, and the patrix was settling down for dinner in his parsonage with all the shutters closed tight against a frigid wind that blew in from the ocean. A housekeeper, surprised at the sudden appearance of a disciple, let him in and announced his arrival.

The patrix was named Primos Myos. He was in his mid-twenties, unexpectedly young, with tufted ears and a chest full of tawny fur that exploded from his wide-open shirt. Since body fur counted as clothing, Taylor wasn't supposed to consider him underdressed.

The patrix, though surprised, welcomed him enthusiastically. "Olyon bless, but you're young! I'm afraid I don't have a spare bedroom," he said, "but you're welcome to share my bed for warmth. Let me have Pipa set a place for you."

"There's no need to put yourself out," Taylor said, shaking the man's hand in the fashion of Gallia. The physicality of the touch shocked him, and he yanked back his hand like it had been burned. It surprised them both.

"Sorry," apologized Taylor, rubbing his hand. He hadn't let anyone touch him since Micas, at least not while he was conscious. He hadn't realized shaking hands was going to be a problem. "My spirit has been doing weird things lately."

"It's about that time of life for you," observed the priest. "I remember some of the practitioners at art school were late bloomers, and they had a tough time of it. I'm guessing you're in for quite a ride."

"That's what everyone tells me. Look, I just came to introduce myself and ask where is the best place to stay. The fellows at the depot have their favorites, but they aren't always the best. I'll need to stable my appalon, too."

Primos grimaced ruefully, "Smart of you to ask. I've been burned a few times by the depot favorites. The place you want is up the hill: it looks like a grand mansion but the owner lets out rooms to travelers. Most first-timers don't know about it, and this time of year she always has room." The patrix insisted on having Phillip for dinner.

"So, Phillip. Are you on assignment, or working mendicant?"

"Mendicant," said Taylor, warming his hands around a bowl of soup. It was marsh deer, wild rice, herbs, and root vegetables: the local analog of beef-and-barley. "I need a quiet place to train over the winter. Of course I'll pick up any work that's handy, as long as there isn't too much of it."

"Our only healer is Ferange, and we share him with two other towns. We have him two days a week, if we're lucky. Fishing is dangerous work, so there's always an emergency around the corner. You sure you're not hunting monsters?"

"I've had my fill recently," answered Taylor wryly. "A cursed bifurdactica nearly bit me in half last week. Fourteen meters," he added to the priest's astonishment. "Why, are there any around?"

"Fourteen! We don't have anything like that here," said the patrix, shaking his head. "Sometimes we get hunters who assume we're overrun with monsters just because we're the last depot on the line. North is all forest and mountains, but it's quiet as can be. South of us is where things get lively, but that's mostly in the summer. You should have yourself a nice quiet winter, if that's what you're looking for."

After dinner they walked the half mile, uphill, to Hylee House with Ben trailing behind.

Though the wind made the trees bend and twist wildly, they still managed to get some conversation in. Primos had only recently taken over from the previous patrix, who had retired and headed south to gentler climes. He had no expectation of further promotion or transfer to any better place, nor did he want for one. He was proud of the temple's sanctuary, which was unique in being framed entirely in local cypress. It had seen two hundred and twenty winters, with few signs of serious wear. Phillip promised he would attend morning services so he could see the sanctuary in the daytime.

Hylee house looked like, and indeed had been, the residence of some local aristocrat before they got tired of making the trip uphill and settled closer to the shore. The proprietress, Livia Hylee, was waiting for them when they arrived and opened the door before they could knock. Her teenage son Atticus unloaded Ben and took him to the stable, with promises to treat him well.

"We are honored to host a disciple," she said when she welcomed him, "but I have a rule about weapons inside the house. Please leave them here in the entryway." Livia was not only statuesque and beautiful, but gave him the feeling she was at peace with everything around her. Now that he was close enough, Phillip could detect a soft glow of spirit around her. Her reddish-brown hair became short fur over most of her face and neck, set off by gold dappling and indigo eyes. A black stripe ran from the crown of her head down her back.

Phillip was meant to lean his spear by the door and hang his stone knife on a hook by the door, but it was proving difficult to let them go. They were both hardened to the point they could not only pierce cursed monster hide, but could not be shattered by any normal means. Just leaving them near the front door seemed strange.

"I promise you," she told him, "nobody will touch them. Not even another guest, since you're currently the only one." His traitorous face must be giving him away. Again.

He finally let go of the stone knife and let himself be shown to his room. It was outfitted to be the most comfortable place he had stayed so far. The bed was a thick pile of wooly skins, with a closely woven sheet on top. Compared to the bed the rest of the furnishings (which were nice) didn't matter, nor did the second dinner (which was delicious): it was the best bed Phillip had slept in since he had come to Tenobre.

They were at it again, kicking him out of the carriage and driving off without him, their voices fading as the carriage moved away. Now that he was dead, the women were talking about what dresses to wear at the next dance. He lay in the cold ditch where they had left him, growing colder by the minute. Snow began to collect on his paralyzed body. Nobody would find him there by the side of the road under a blanket of snow. The wildlife would get to him first, frozen in his edible state, and drag him away to a den for storage and convenient consumption.

He could feel one approaching him now, its indigo eyes appraising him cautiously. It wouldn't take a chance with prey that wasn't already dead unless it had to. It would wait until he was cold, just to be sure.

Taylor couldn't even muster the usual outrage this time. He had let Micas kill him, and that was the truth. He earned his death by trusting someone he knew wasn't on his side at a moment when he should have been at his most cautious. She earned her victory by earning his trust, and he had died as a result. And now those indigo eyes watched him, waited for his body to cool.

Taylor was tired of this dream. He stood up and shook off the snow. Instead of winter he wanted autumn, so the season changed. He was in Girona now, walking the streets with his tool bag over his shoulder on the his way to the union to earn a little coin. Working as a healer was great, but sometimes he really just wanted to make something with his hands. The skill and attention required to craft something as simple as a spliced mitre joint was a tonic for his attitude.

The eyes continued to follow him. When it occurred to him that they might not be part of his dream Taylor forced himself fully awake, eyes open, and leapt out of bed. He invoked the word for protection before his feet even touched the ground. The feat might have been a lot more impressive if he could remember where he was, but the room he found himself in was completely unknown to him. Wood construction, nice furniture, plastered and painted walls. He was facing an animal he had never seen before, and could not recall from literature. It was a reddish-brown streak of fur, with long limbs and a tail that ended in short spikes. The limbs ended in four long claws and an opposable claw. Its eyes, disconcertingly human, were set back from a short snout featuring short, sharp teeth. A black stripe ran down the animal's head to the end of its tail, punctuated by white and straw colored spots.

His unwanted visitor must have weighed a good twenty kilos. It looked arboreal, and had probably climbed in through the open window. With those limbs and claws, getting into the second story window would be no challenge at all. The intruder was backed into a corner, chittering at him in rapid staccato barks.

Taylor relaxed his posture from the fighting stance he had assumed, and moved his gaze away from the creature. That seemed to calm it some, but it was still crouched in the corner.

Taylor moved away from the window. "Go on," he told it, "you can go." But the beast only had eyes for the door. Taylor gently pushed aside the chair he had wedged under the handle and opened the door for it. As soon as he moved away to give enough room, the long-limbed creature jumped for it, taking a single bounce on the bed and sailed through the exit ... into the waiting arms of Livia Hylee.

Indigo eyes. Dappled spots over dark hair. Fully awake now, Taylor could put it together.

"One of yours?" he asked his host.

"My youngest," she said, shifting his weight onto one hip in a practiced motion. "His name is Carl." She spoke directly to the giant squirrel. "I told you not to disturb our guest while he is sleeping."

The arboreal animal child had its limbs around Livia, and its face was buried in her neck.

"I'm sorry, mama. I was only looking."

It talked! Of course it talked. If it was Livia's child then it was sentient, and it shouldn't be surprising that it could speak. The really surprising part should be that humans were not alone in Tenobre. None of his lessons, nor the beastiaries he had read, mentioned anything about non-human races.

But, were they non-human? Livia obviously had a human form, and Carl might too. Probably he should ask rather than just speculate. But first...

"Carl, I know you didn't mean any harm. But my head is not a safe place for you. There are things in my head that are dangerous to know, and they could hurt you or your family. Stay out of my dreams, OKAY?"

"Yes, sir." Taylor wasn't entirely convinced. A child that would climb through a second story window to satisfy its curiosity wasn't going to be warned off so easily. He would have to lock and ward all entrances to his room before sleeping, just like when he was in the wilderness.

"An hour 'till dawn. No point in going back to bed now. Do you mind answering questions?"

"We'll be in the kitchen." To her child, Livia said, "come on mister, you're helping with prep this morning."

"But mo-o-o-om, the sun isn't up yet."

"But you are, and so am I, and so is our guest. And whose fault is that?"

"Mine," sighed the squirrel-child.

"So who has to live with the consequences?"

"I do."

Taylor closed his door so he could dress.

In the kitchen, over cups of warm spiced milk, Livia told him of her people while Carl cut and peeled vegetables for the day's meals.

"Our people call themselves the kilabora." She folder her hands around her cup and looked into its surface. "In ancient days there were many tribes like the kilabora -- people who had two forms: the human form and an animal form. Now there are only a few such tribes left, and we are one of them.

"When the ancient civilization fell it became impossible to maintain a population of purebreds, so we began to gather together in mixed settlements. Living together resulted in cross-breeds. These could not change their forms, but they were adaptable in other ways."

"You're saying today's humans are the result of the ancient dual-form tribes cross-breeding. Someone with a kilabora's claws must have an ancestor that was a purebred kilabora clan member."

"Exactly. There are only a few two-natured settlements left in Tenobre, and one of them is in the Old Forest near here."

"So how is it you came to live in Tegea? Is there much socializing between Tegea and your people? How many people know about this?" Now that he was awake the questions wouldn't stop. "Have there ever been problems between the Unity and the kilabora? How long do you live? I assume you're arboreal. Do you live in the trees?"

Livia's smile was relieved. "You're taking this very well. Some people get very upset when they learn about our existence. Especially church people."

"Never assume the church teaches everything there is to know. Scripture is less than five hundred years old except for Beginnings, and that reads like myth. And Leadership definitely has a habit of destroying knowledge. I've pretty much been waiting for the next surprise for a while now."

Taylor took a mouthful of the drink, filling his nose and sinuses with the smell of spices, leaving a cool sensation that contrasted with the hot liquid. He was able to identify all of the smells and flavors, so it probably wasn't poisonous.

"During the alignment there was an attempt to wipe out all the two-natured tribes, but we have our own spirit abilities. We survived by moving to places the church couldn't reach, not even with an army. When that patriarch died, the old policy of acceptance was restored. Of course some bad blood remained, but that was two hundred years ago."

"But people don't forget so easily, which is why most of your tribe lives somewhere in the mountains where they're hard to reach." He finished for her.

"It is also why my family has run some kind of business in Tegea for several generations, as sort of ambassadors. The more experienced foresters know about us, and so does the local lord and alderwoman. The tribe hunts monsters and brings harvested parts down for trade, which is good for the town."

"And a reminder that without you, Tegea would be less safe."

Livia nodded. "Some of our young like to live here for a few years, but most of them return to the tribe. Eventually."

Taylor felt a weak beam of winter sun sneaking in through the shutters. "The day is breaking without me," he told his host, "I have to train."

As he stretched, Taylor wondered what other important facts the Unity was hiding. They weren't currently on an extermination binge that he was aware of, and they weren't going out of their way to demonize the dual-natured tribes. The church was quietly ignoring their existence. Maybe that was the best way to protect a minority that could blend in with the majority: let them get on with their lives without making a fuss. As long as the few people who knew were benign then it was fine.

They're not just destroying ancient technologies, observed Taylor, *but hiding modern knowledge, too. Maybe I should start a list.*

Taylor availed himself of the garden in back of the house for meditation and exercises. He said hello to Ben and verified he had been properly brushed and fed. After washing up it was time for breakfast with the Hylee family. Atticus stared intently, while pretending not to, as did his little sister Fabia but without the pretense. Somewhere there was the third child, Cadu. Taylor pretended not to notice all the staring, and ate his meal (with seconds) without inviting any questioning. Livia engaged her two children in conversation without once giving an obvious opening to address their guest, or ask any questions about him. The guest excused himself to don his regalia (stole, star, knife) to visit the temple.

He loaded Ben with the minimum: the nickleharp and a small pack of essentials for a day spent plying his trade. His brigandine jacket would protect him from most unexpected threats. To all of this he added a pair of gloves. He couldn't bear to touch people, so to get around that he would try wearing gloves whenever he might be required to shake hands. If anyone asked, he would just tell them his spirit made him very sensitive. Together, Taylor and Ben went down the hill to the town's temple to see it in the daylight.

Like most Unity temples the sanctuary was round, topped with a tall dome. The altar in the middle held a seven-pointed star on a fine cloth. The specific colors could vary by country, season, and local habit. The dome was truly a remarkable edifice: a complex stack of ascending wooden arches bent towards a lofty center, where a candelabra hung below the oculus. Primos explained that, instead of painting the dome directly they suspended canvases facing down to the congregation. They could be changed seasonally, or brought down for maintenance without erecting a scaffold that would interfere with services.

Taylor accepted the duty of giving the benediction for all seven of the day's services: three in the morning, one at noon, and three at night. Daily services were only twenty minutes: long enough for the congregation to receive a daily reading, sing a hymn, and receive a benediction. Eighthday services were longer and involved a sermon, perhaps a choral performance, community announcements, and gatherings afterwards.

His giving the benediction was a normal part of his visits to any community: a chance to be blessed by a practitioner didn't come around every day, especially in a small town like this. Healers couldn't do a benediction. But Taylor had an ulterior motive as well: word got around fast when a disciple was handing out blessings. He expected that, by the end of the day, his people would know he had arrived.

After morning services Taylor and Ben explored the town's shops, watched the ships in the small harbor, and generally observed the functioning of the town. He took a cup of jota at an inn with a good view of the main road. The town looked like fishing villages anywhere: squat stone houses braced against the wind, giving way to cheaper pine structures near the shore. People lived uphill, and built the shoreline buildings cheaply enough to replace.

After the noon services he had lunch in the parsonage with Primo, where he ate the first seafood he had had since being unceremoniously summoned into Tenobre: squid in a wild rice sauté. He spent his afternoon generally exploring the town and getting to understand its economy. Tegea was a very affordable place to live, but most of the work tended to be seasonal. Most families had more than one profession so they could put together a living throughout the year.

After evening services Taylor and Ben retreated uphill to the Hylee House where he warned Livia that he might have visitors and needed a space to meet them. She gracefully turned over a small salon to him, to use as an office and drawing room. She even gave him a bell, to summon Atticus should he need anything.

Taylor was happily making an annotated copy of scripture from memory onto paper when his first visitor arrived: alderwoman Sophie Rosa. She managed the town on behalf of the local lord. She was middle-aged, thickset, and sharp-eyed. Her voice was a soprano that soared and swooped over the least bit of excitement. Atticus showed her in without knocking first, or announcing her properly. It was all very sudden.

"As the alderwoman," she said after introductions, stringing high notes together in her vowels, "I should have been informed when a disciple arrived with a mission. It is the town's responsibility to aid the church in a crisis so we can face difficulties together." She ended her speech on a happy note, as if everyone in the room were suddenly great friends.

"I am aware of the protocol, your honor, but in this case it does not apply. There is no mission." He offered her a seat and hoped jota would be coming. "I'm working on a project of my own at the moment, so I'm strictly mendicant."

91

"You mean you have no job?" she queried, as if it were unheard of.

"I wouldn't say that," he responded, "after all ..."

"Won't Leadership complain if one of their valuable assets is so underutilized?"

"Actually it's the deans who manage the disciples," he began, only to be interrupted again.

"I'm sure we can find something constructive for you to do." The town alderwoman looked around her, searching. "Has Livia run out of jota?"

"I have no trouble finding work," Taylor told Sophie, whom he now considered an intruder. "There is always someone who needs healing and there is never an end to training."

"I have never heard of you, you know," Sophie said, her focus back on the disciple.

"I'm not surprised. I've only been a disciple a short while."

"How do they decide to let a person as young as yourself out of the academy?"

"My teachers were eager to put me to work," he replied, growing annoyed. "Perhaps I was a bother to them?"

"Well! I have other people to visit tonight before I can take my dinner. Good evening to you, Phillip. We will speak more anon!" Sounding chipper but apparently frustrated by the lack of jota, the alderwoman left.

Taylor managed three more pages before his next visitors arrived: a man and his two children, who had pulled their mother all they way up the hill in a cart. Her leg had broken and now she was unable to work. The father was a Feller both in name and occupation: his main work was seasonal logging but he took other odd jobs when he could. Other income came from his wife's work as a midwife, which was impossible with a broken leg.

This time, jota arrived quickly.

Mrs. Feller's broken bone hadn't been set properly, and in the last several days had started to heal crooked. To heal her, Taylor put her into a deep sleep so he could re-break the bone and set it properly. While he was working, he quietly erased the signs of a budding cancer.

When the father stumbled over the donation Phillip told him, "whatever you can easily afford, and no more than a day's wage in any event. I also," he whispered, "accept edibles of all kinds."

"Ahhh," said Mrs. Feller, "I have just the thing for you. Now that I can walk again!" The family hugged him profusely (which made him desperately uncomfortable) before walking down the hill together, the children pulling the now-empty cart.

"That was kind of you," Livia said, entering to tidy up the room. "This is a lean time of year for the Fellers, but she's very proud of her tidemellon preserves. Margorie's preserves are considered the best in town."

"Then I have something to look forward to," said Taylor.

There were two other visitors after the Fellers, also looking for healing services. With Tegea's healer available less than one week a month, injuries often had to wait days to be treated no matter how serious.

The last visitor of the day was a messenger bearing a gift basket. The boy waited for a response while Phillip investigated the contents: familiar poultice packets, tiny clay jars of liniment and lotion, and a stoppered clay carafe of a liquid that turned out to be shampoo. The scent was reminiscent of the Pegasus Workshop's signature products: cedar and citrus. The basket was filled out with evergreen branches, fresh tidemellon, and farmer cheeses in a variety of flavors. It came with a nice note:

Dear Phillip the Younger:

It is the great pleasure of Penguin Workshop to welcome you to Tegea. It may be the last stop on the north carriage, but ours is a wonderful town filled with friendly people and much to recommend it. We hope your stay is both peaceful and productive.

Eleanor, Proprietress

"Where is this Penguin Workshop?" Phillip asked the messenger.

"Up Blueridge road," said the boy. "You go down the hill then south and back up Blueridge. Or you can cut across using the hillside path."

Phillip took a blank board and brushed a response, expressing a general interest in medicinals and asking for a tour of their facilities. "My schedule is quite open for the next several days," the note concluded, "excepting temple services." As soon as the ink was dry enough he sent the boy off with his fee and a little extra for working so close to dinner time.

He handed the foodstuff to his hostess but kept the other products and the basket of fragrant branches for his room. After dinner he played nickleharp for the Hylee family, then took a dreamless potion and slept like a rock sunk in the bottom of the sea.

Taylor's plan was to stay in Tegea until the spring equinox, then tour around Gallia and Ullidia until summer. Then he could climb Mount Yagour with Rolo for a guide, if the scout was still willing. Until then, Taylor needed a place where work could find him. The parlor at Hylee house was comfortable, but it would be a strain on Livia to use it for business every day.

Healer Ferange's clinic was in a building between the harbor and the commercial center of town, in a building owned by the church and run by the local temple. Patrix Primos offered some unused space to Taylor in the same building at a reasonable rent. Taylor could see emergency patients, and the rest of the time he would have room to do as he liked. The first task was to buy a large slat of wood and set up a sign with his mark on it, the futobel under four stars. Below the divine mark the sign read:

Phillip the Younger, Mendicant Disciple.
Tool Enhancement
Construction
Monster Extermination
Emergency Healing
Mornings, 2nd to 7th day

Below the writing was a row of ideograms for the illiterate, which was the majority of the population. People gathered around just to look at his sign all afternoon, as the futobel pranced around and shook its antlers at them. Taylor spent that time setting up his office. Primos had some used furniture stashed in the basement and enthusiastically lent a hand rummaging about: with the application of the arts and some good-quality finishing wax they discovered the pieces weren't at all bad. Most of them were local cypress of unknown age, but a maker's sigil carved on the underside of one chair claimed it was a hundred and thirty years old. The chair felt as solid as if it were new.

Taylor and Primos were working all afternoon getting the office ready, then some more after evening services. It was only Taylor's second full day in Tegea but it felt right to be properly industrious after a month of training and traveling. Livia sent her daughter Fabia down the hill to him with dinner in a basket.

"Mother says not to expect meal deliveries as a regular service," she recited.

"I'll remember that," he said, poking around in the basket, "and I'm grateful. I completely forgot about dinner."

"We thought so," she nodded sagely. She looked at the row of spirit lamps he was using the light of office. "You have a lot of those."

"They're just a bit of cloth, string, and a rock." He unpacked the food and gestured for her to sit across from him. Livia had packed an earthenware crock with hot roasted vegetables, and another one with spiced meat over wild rice. Fabia declined his offer to share the meal.

"Have you killed a lot of monsters?"

Taylor shook his head. "I'm pretty new. I've killed a cursed monster, and a few smaller ones. And my teacher took me on some hunts."

Fabia's indigo eyes looked him over carefully while he ate.

"You don't look like you can hunt monsters," she said at last. "You're kind of small."

"If you do it properly, you don't fight them alone. The disciple's best strategy is to make others strong, and fight as a group."

The kilabora girl did something then, with her spirit. Taylor couldn't tell what exactly she did, and she didn't explain herself. She just started giggling.

"It's rude to use your spirit on someone without permission, you know."

The girl was still giggling, "I didn't mean to. It just happens sometimes. I'm going now." She skipped out of the office, still giggling to herself.

Taylor was in business for a quarter of an hour when his invitation to the winter solstice ball arrived, attached to the hand of Alderwoman Sophia Rosa. The ball was a major yearly event in Tegea open to everyone, so an invitation wasn't actually necessary. But Sophia apparently made a point of delivering invitations anyway. She had a little basket full of them.

"I love what you've done with the place!" She gave the statement thrice the enthusiasm it deserved. "I've never heard of a disciple setting up a storefront. How unorthodox."

"I've never heard of anyone else doing it either, but it's an option suggested in the guidebook." Phillip pointed to the expensive parchment book in question, open on his newly-polished desk. "It seemed interesting enough to try. I apologize for not offering you jota, your honor, but as you can see I'm still getting settled."

"It's no matter," she trilled, waving away the non-offer. "I love your lighting! It is simply divine. Where did you get it all?"

"It is divine," he said, feeling impatient with her, "as it is lit with prayer."

"Next week is the solstice ball. You must come, and bring your lights with you."

"I'm not much for dancing, Alderwoman."

"Nonsense," she declared in a swooping soprano voice. "You must come. Why, nobody would trust a disciple who thought so little of the town that he refused to attend the ball. I can find someone to teach you the Gallian dances. You only have to learn a few to get by. I can teach you the rondel right now: I am an excellent teacher."

Phillip had to agree to bring his lamps to the ballroom for the lighting ceremony, or else the woman wouldn't leave. He could see why she was valuable as the alderwoman: it seemed to be in her nature to arrange other people to her own liking.

After the alderwoman came a string of people wanting their tools hardened or sharpened. Every single one of them bemoaned the fact he was seeing the town in winter. Winter was cold, spring was wet, and fall was frantic with the felling of trees. Summer, on the other hand, was slow and balmy and glorious. The opinion was universal that he should stay at least through summer. There was even a "kite festival" at the summer solstice, where the whole town would compete for the most elaborate kite.

His last visitor, just before closing, was a familiar and welcome face: Eleanor. She showed up just as the previous client was leaving.

"Disciple Phillip, it's a pleasure to meet you." She stuck out her hand, as if they were meeting for the first time. The departing client didn't notice anything amiss. "I'm Eleanor, proprietor of Penguin Workshop."

"She of the fine liniments," said Taylor. "A pleasure." When he shook her hand she noted the gloves but didn't say anything. "I have an interest in medicinals. I was hoping we could get together and compare notes."

"Come to lunch, after the noon service," she invited him. "The Penguin would love to have you. Our cook is quite good.

"I look forward to it."

Eleanor had come right into his office, in front of other people, and introduced herself to "Phillip" and invited him to lunch. Either she felt that a mutual interest in medicinals was grounds enough for the invitation, or she was just impatient. When Taylor found the workshop his heart was beating so fast he thought it would run away from him. They were all there, healthy and whole. Mr and Mrs Vale, Eleanor, the laconic Bao, and Milo and Mila.

Their first order of business after introductions was the tour. They had a good-sized house for living quarters, and a pair of buildings for the workshop proper. Most of the workers were women from the town who spent their days preparing and packaging poultice kits, lotions, liniments, and shampoo. Notable by its absence was the highly refined castle soap that had made the Pegasus Workshop so much money in Girona. Selling the soap would give away their origins, but shampoo should be a similarly lucrative business.

After the tour they cloistered themselves in the dining room and set up a privacy barrier, the dropped the pretense of being new acquaintances. They ate at the table together, which was how Taylor liked it best. His friends' eyes were all over him, taking in his changed appearance.

"They weren't very subtle about it," said Eleanor over Mrs. Vale's excellent luncheon. "They dressed in civilian clothes but they were obviously Palace Guard. They didn't wear masks or anything. They even called each other by name. They barged through the courtyard gate and started roughing people up. The day workers ran out the front, while we went out the back."

"Nobody was hurt?"

"A few bruises, from being thrown to the ground," said Mr. Vale. "The greater worry was your two followers. They wanted to fight the palace guard. Mistress Eleanor had to be quite firm with them." He cast a wry look at the bricktown cousins, Mila and Milo. They were fifteen and sixteen years old. It was easy to imagine them wanting to fight instead of flee.

"What did they want?"

"They said they wanted money and formulas." Eleanor sighed. "But they didn't look very hard. They set fire to the workshop too quickly to give it a good search. They just wanted to destroy all our hard work. Some kind of punishment. That Janocas fellow really hates you. We escaped through the secret gate, as planned."

"Noble jerks," spat Milo. "They kept calling us scum. If you had been there we could have knocked them all into the gutter where they belong. But I picked up your guidebook on the way out. Did you get it?"

"I did, thank you. It was a very nice surprise, getting that back. What about after your escape?"

"Nobody bothered us," reported Eleanor. "We took our appalons from the hostelry, left the city by the north gate, then circled east. We waited at the safe house for three days, then came here."

"It didn't take you long to get set up here. What did you tell people about your background?"

"That I've come from Lavradio to get away from my family, who didn't like my mercantile ambitions."

Taylor nodded. Strictly speaking, the entire statement was true. It just omitted that she had ben run out of the capital city. "Everything okay on the business front? Do you need anything?"

Eleanor waved away the question. "We're fine. It would be nice if we could sell castle soap, but that would expose us. We don't know what the situation is in Girona. Are they looking for us? Has everyone forgotten? It takes news a while to make it this far away, but I'm working on that.

"What we all want to know is, what happened to you? The last time we saw you, you were making deliveries in the labyrinth." The labyrinth was the red-light district of Girona.

"The delivery was a setup by Frenzio. He had mercenaries waiting to ambush me and make it look like a mugging. After I was done with them, I ran into Micas. She pulled me into a carriage, cleaned me up, and told me that the Unity had offered a bounty. Frenzio and the king were trying to collect.

"And that," he said dramatically, "was when she poisoned me."

"Micas?" said several of them at once.

"She's one of the queen's ladies in waiting now. Apparently the ladies do a lot more than keep the queen company. Remember when Alex Ramada was rescued from kidnappers? Micas was missing all that week. She wasn't with me, and she wasn't with the queen either."

"I can't believe it," said Mila, stunned and revolted. "I liked her."

Taylor gave a bitter laugh. "I did too. That's why the queen used her. They buried me on a hilltop way out on the edge of the coppiced woods. It took me two weeks to find my way back, more or less. Before you ask me about the other side: I don't remember anything from being dead." He explained Sandim's Return, and what he could remember of his first moments returning.

"Anyway, it was unpleasant, my eyesight is all weird now, and I'm still recovering."

"The royals killed you," repeated a shocked Milo, "and then you came back from the dead."

"Or, Olyon sent me back. But yes, that's the general idea."

"Huh," said Bao. It was the only syllable he would speak all afternoon.

"That's obviously not for public consumption. It shouldn't ever come up as long as the Phillip identity holds. If it does, just say the palace injured me badly."

"You can't be killed! Not even by kings!" Milo was awed by the prospect.

"It would be arrogant to assume that," Taylor told him. "I don't know how the prayer works, or if it would work a second time. So let's not assume I could do it again, okay?"

"But, you're immortal!"

"Seriously Milo, stop saying that."

Eleanor addressed Taylor in a more sane tone, "what are your plans now?"

"Winter here in Tegea and train with my bulwark." Taylor indicated at the cousins. "Tour Gallia and Ullidia in spring, then make a pilgrimage to Mount Yagour in the summer."

Mila's spines stood up in excitement. "We're going to see First Enclave?"

"Whatever's left of it, sure. Have you been keeping up with your training?"

"We've been trying to," said Milo, "but it's hard to find teachers out here who are willing to spend time on us. There's a gymnasium, but hardly anyone uses it. There's not even a garrison up here, so there's no soldiers to train with."

"Then let's meet up regularly in the gymnasium to practice. It's a natural way to strike up a relationship. People are less likely to think we knew each other from before. When I take you on as followers, nobody will be suspicious."

Mr. Vale interjected. "Aren't you forgetting something, Master Phillip? The Unity put a price on your head. Are you sure you want to continue working as a disciple?"

"We don't know if that's true," Taylor pointed out, "it's just something that Micas said. If it's true they offered a bounty then it was for Taylor, and they kept it very quiet."

"I hope you're not staying with the church out of some sense of loyalty," advised the older man. "As far as we're concerned, you have no obligation to them." Everyone at the table seemed to agree.

"My loyalty is to the divine, and my guide is the four tenets." Taylor picked up his nickleharp and began to tune it. "I'll keep working with the church as long as it helps me with the Work. If they become a hinderance ... I'll find another way."

THE DELANION AFFAIR

Enclave, Hall of Guardians

"Lavradio invoiced us for what?" Guardian Maia thought it sounded like a bad joke.

President Phrenos handed her a fine white parchment, scribed in an elegant hand and embossed with an elaborate gold-leaf seal. The woman paled as she read the King of Lavradio's demand for one ton of gold, for the service of ridding the church of an unwanted disciple.

"This was never discussed in the full council," Maia said angrily.

"Nor was it discussed in any council," confirmed Phrenos.

The Unity Church's Guardian Council had twelve members, collectively called Leadership. They elected one of their number president by a majority vote. The guardians were appointed by the hierophant, Matriarch Noora, to handle the executive functions of the church so she could focus on more spiritual matters.

Leadership had just recently arranged the marriage of a prominent daughter to the next king of Lavradio in an attempt to bring that kingdom more into alignment with the church. A scandal would have been bad enough, but targeting a disciple amounted to a major incident. At times like this, guardians insulated Her Holiness: they would handle the problem, and take the blame for any turbulent side-effects.

Maia put down the invoice. "What does Her Holiness say?"

"'It is best to find the truth before committing to a course of action.' If the invoice is genuine, the King of Lavradio believed he was authorized to eliminate a disciple and he expected to be paid for the service. We would like to know why."

This was the first notice that anything was amiss with disciple DeLanion. He had been very young but highly promising. Leadership had advised the boy be sent to the School of Spiritual Arts for further cultivation, but the quorum sent to look at him had anointed him and put him to work immediately. If Dean Garsharp's reports could be believed, the boy was a phenomenon in spite of not being descended from the first family bloodlines. His only impediments were his age and size.

"I'm sending you to Lavradio to determine the facts," declared the president. "Take a disciple and bulwark team with you. Her Holiness has authorized a recession, if you feel it's warranted." Maia had worked her way into Leadership by troubleshooting problems for the church, but in her thirty years of devotion this was the first time she was given power to remove all church resources from an entire country.

"Does Garsharp know what's happening?" she asked. "He was DeLanion's mentor. He might know something important that isn't in the reports."

"Go talk to him," agreed President Phrenos, "but don't take too long. I want you on the road within three days." He passed her a stack of boards authorizing personnel, travel, funds, and other necessities.

Lavradio, Royal Palace

Vacation was over for Crown Prince Leonardo. King Joaqim's idea of a transfer of power to his nephew was to have the prince take all his meetings while his majesty idled away his final days as monarch at a pleasure estate, thirty kilometers away. It wasn't so much a transition as it was a complete and early abandonment, with little documentation and no enthusiasm from the ministers who would be replaced. Leonardo and his chosen staff were trained for this, but that didn't mean it was easy. Some of the current ministers had obviously been chosen for the purposes of making alliances more than for their competence.

Chief among the incompetents was one of the men who stood before him now: Prime Minister Julio Marvao. The man looked the part of prime minister, with his thin dignified appearance and large scintillating eyes, but he was thoroughly mediocre in every other respect. Such a talentless person had no business holding one of the most difficult jobs in the kingdom.

The other man before the crown prince was the prime minister's cousin: Girona's City Minister Carlos Marvao. Queen Diana, Leonardo's mother, claimed he was exceptional. The capital city had been on the verge of disaster and this man had put it onto the path of recovery. He had repaired the poisoned wells, punished corruption, restocked the grain warehouses, reduced rents, repaired the city's budget, and improved the economy. The bricktown slum was shrinking, thanks to this man's efforts. He had accomplished all of that in less than half a year using a band of teenage nobles as his secret weapon.

The three of them met, attended by a platoon of guards and secretaries, in the large council room. A banner was spread out before them, reading "WHERE IS DISCIPLE DELANION". The sign was decorated with a pegasus, for citizens who didn't read. Thus, the illiterates knew at least who the sign was about and could ask others what was written on it.

It was the ninth such sign the city's peacekeepers had taken down. On the eve of the prince's ascension any signs of unrest were unwelcome. The crown prince had seen the first of them during his procession into the city, a grand parade that was meant to both welcome him home and remind the people of his pending coronation. There was a group of angry commoners near the sign chanting something, but they couldn't get their voices together enough to be understood.

Prince Estevan, who was acting as City Minister Marvao's aide in this meeting, had surprised Leonardo with his actions. He had abandoned the safety of a royal carriage and plunged into the crowd with only a single guard to protect him. He spoke with the crowd, and even placed his royal hand on some of their shoulders. By the time he left they were all kneeling respectfully, grateful that the palace had heard their pleas.

When Leonardo had asked him about the incident Estevan said, "I told them DeLanion was my friend, and that I missed him greatly. I told them his deeds in the city wouldn't be forgotten, and we are still searching for answers."

Leonardo had praised him. "That's perhaps too personal a response coming from a royal. Still, it was neatly done, brother."

"Not quite neat enough," was Estevan's response. "The instigators slipped away, and our agent lost them in the crowd. This is another one of Frenzio's plays. We just don't know what he wants."

The banners kept appearing, but never in the same place twice. Short of posting the entire force of peacekeepers throughout the city all night long there was little chance of preventing more, or catching the perpetrators.

"They're stitched together from many bags that used to hold various commodities," explained the city minister. "There are traces of shop sigils on the back sides, but they are all widely available goods. The makers could have gathered them from trash heaps, or found a stack of old bags in a basement. Even the ink is cheapest available. It could be anyone."

"The king wants this handled," intoned the prime minister with the utmost gravity. "We all know what that means: you declare DeLanion the villain and arrest anyone who questions the palace's position. But instead, you called him a friend of the kingdom!"

"Wasn't he?" asked Carlos. "He healed hundreds of people, started a school, and wrote popular music. Need I remind you of his many accomplishments?"

"Infamy, more like," insisted Julio.

"Only if you listen to Duke Frenzio and his minions. Everyone else admired the boy."

Julio glared accusingly at Carlos. "You blamed a noble for his disappearance. You chose a noble over a commoner."

"Nobles were absolutely involved in his disappearance. Worse, they were seen acting against him. And there was hardly anything common about DeLanion," scorned Carlos.

"If you want to tell a public lie then invent something believable. He did too much good too publicly for too many people. His teachers ensured it, for exactly this reason. The palace doesn't have nearly enough credibility to spread dirt over his name. I doubt you understand this, but the common man doesn't trust nobles at all.

"Also," Carlos' voice grew hard towards his cousin, "the king never instructed me to lie. He said to handle the situation, and we are."

"You aren't doing anything," Julio complained. "Arrest anyone who makes a disturbance over the missing disciple. Shut them up."

Carlos turned to Leonardo. "That would be the worst possible course of action, Your Highness. It is exactly what the organizers want: for us to resort to violence and stoke anger in the city."

Julio tried to interrupt, but the crown prince motioned him to silence. "Explain, Minister."

"Right now, the signs only say, 'Where is Disciple DeLanion'. It's not an open accusation of the palace. It's not a call to arms. It's just a plea that we find out what happened to him. If the palace reacts with violence then it confirms our guilt and makes us the enemy of all commoners. We won't be able to settle little incidents with words any more. It will be fire and blood all the time. The situation is a trap.

"This is being run by agents from outside the city," continued Carlos, urgently. "We have skilled agents in the peacekeepers, people who helped expose the Colares family. They know some of the organizers by sight and try to follow them, but the suspects keep disappearing in west town. We think the opposition is using ancient artifacts to evade capture. This is a prelude to something else, but unless we can capture an opposition agent we won't know what until too late."

"And you think the opposition is Duke Frenzio," Leonardo mused. "Where is the duke now?"

"The duke returned to Nurr, Your Highness," informed the prime minister. "He begged the king's leave to handle an unusual number of monster attacks. He is very loyal to the kingdom, Your Highness."

"Then we can't question him right away. I presume he left an heir in his place, to attend the coronation?"

"Juliana Frenzio," said Julio. "Lovely woman. She would of course be honored to assist the next king of Lavradio in any way she can."

"Juliana is indeed lovely," Carlos agreed, "and has a head full of pender fluff. Cuelar is no more likely to confide anything important to her than he would a complete stranger. She's his heir in name only."

"That will do for now." Leonardo put an end to the topic. "Prime Minister, schedule Juliana Frenzio for a public audience. As a duke's heiress I should take her measure in any event. City Minister, continue as you see fit but keep me informed. I think you are wise to avoid violence as long as you can."

As the meeting was breaking up, Prince Estevan asked his half-brother a favor. "Leo, can you get the Audit Bureau access to military records? I need force summaries."

"For what purpose?"

Carlos Marvao stepped closer to listen.

"We've always assumed Frenzio wanted to destabilize the city so he could save it, then as a reward he could have one of his clients appointed as city minister. As things stand right now that can never happen. Nearly all of his clients in Girona are dead, destitute, or stricken from the noble register."

"Or all three," agreed Carlos with a satisfied show of fang.

"So why is he still making trouble in the city? What if controlling the city was never his intent? What if the harm is the end goal?" Estevan paused to let them think about that.

"That fits the theory that all of this is groundwork for something grander," said Carlos, gesturing at the banner. "If he can disrupt the capital city then it weakens the whole country. But that only makes sense if he intends to take the throne," Carlos said, "or secede."

Estevan finished the thought. "If Frenzio is our opposition and he aims to rebel, a top priority would be building his military. Instead of training raw recruits he could convince soldiers and knights from Nurr to go home at the end of their contracts. I'm looking for evidence that he's draining talent from the army."

Leonardo had Jorgo write the authorization so he could sign and seal it. "You should begin immediately, brother. There's less than a week until my coronation. Minister, I'll need another moment of your time."

When Estevan was gone, the crown prince looked to his city minister. "I'm surprised at the changes in Estevan. I've always liked him on a personal level, but I was concerned he wouldn't mature. Did something happen?"

Minister Marvao allowed himself a small but satisfied smile. "Queen Diana put him to work under someone who had no patience for nobles."

Girona, West Town

Cuelar Frenzio, Duke of Nurr, had a good view of Royal Avenue from his perch atop a shabby five-story tenement. It was a distant view, but it was good enough to measure activity in the palace. Every wagon load of supplies and every noble carriage train had to move along the same wide street. Massive quantities of high-value goods went in one direction; empty carts and smug palace nobles came out the other. The palace sucked blood and money from the rest of the kingdom over that road, and gave nothing useful back.

When Girona starved, it took food from Nurr. When King Joaquim picked a fight with Ullidia, his best knights had come from Nurr. Every festival, ball, and tournament at the palace was a drain on the lifeblood of the entire kingdom, but most especially Nurr.

The story was different when Nurr needed its king. Then they were told, "we expect our duchies to manage their own affairs," or ,"the border is yours to protect," or, "all our allotted healers are too busy to travel." When Nurr protected the north borders of the kingdom, it did so alone. Likewise when monsters attacked from the mountains in the west. When his daughter was sick with the red pox Cuelar had been told to bring her to the capital. The king avoided any expense, knowing the church would eventually send healers and disciples from Unity City. But they were too late for his daughter and hundreds of others. Cecilly had been the best of all his children, and she had died to line the king's pockets.

The tenement Cuelar was using as a base was permanently stuck in a half-remodeled state, occupied mainly by those too poor to afford anything decent but too proud to descend into the bricktown "slums". Residents had to navigate stairs without railings and gaping holes in the floor. Piles of materials clogged hallways, ever shrinking and shifting without progress being made. It wasn't quite the gang-ridden hellhole Cuelar had feared, but neither was it nice.

Unlike his fellow nobles, Cuelar didn't feel the poor accommodations hurt his pride. Rather, they enhanced it. Every day he told himself, *I can handle this much, for a kingdom of my own.*

The disorder gave his people cover to move in and out, acting as if they were common laborers struggling to find work. In truth they were agents, running around the city, gathering information and spreading rumors. His people held the top two floors, legitimately rented from a landlord desperate for cash. The small space where he ran the operation included a secret room where he slept and, if needed, could hide from unwanted visitors. He did the bulk of his work from memory: anything written down became fuel for the stove as soon as he finished reading it.

Nothing had gone exactly to plan, but he had nearly reached his objective. The poor were angry and the palace was on the verge of using violence against them. The king had shocked the Unity Church with his absurd demand for money. A sizable fraction of the nation's military had been slowly siphoned off to his own "local defense forces". Anyone in Girona who could testify against him was dead.

Soon enough he would be free of this apartment, this city, the palace and its king, forever. They had bled him for long enough. His realm would be his own. Without the burden of the king's taxes, the king's petty squabbles, and the king's useless person, Nurr could thrive.

But before that could happen, he needed to tip the city into chaos.

Cuelar went inside his headquarters and checked the message box: a flat box carved of black soapstone, almost a meter square and ten centimeters tall. Once per day it would exchange its contents with an identical box in Unity City. It was large enough to pass documents, small objects, and valuables. The timing of the exchange was a little random, so he checked it several times each day.

Eagerly, Cuelar took the message he found there and worked through the decoding process: "grd maia dispatched dpt 3 day team unk recession auth". On the one hand, the news wasn't great: Leadership was moving slower than he wanted. He wouldn't be able to execute most of his plan until after the coronation. On the other hand, he was granted extra time to work with. He wouldn't let it go to waste.

Cuelar burned the message and began encoding several of his own.

Girona, North Town

The burrow-born were seldom welcome anywhere, even in places where they were useful. Their fused fingers ended in long curved claws that made normal tasks awkward. To most people this was a grotesque beast trait. Their pale eyes were creepy, and their thick brown quills were just plain ugly. A burrow-born could only find another of their own kind for a mate, so their blessings varied little from one generation to the next, continuing the cycle of isolation and disenfranchisement.

In Duke Frenzio they had finally found an ally: he not only gave them steady work but ennobled some of their own to govern them. Burrowers from all over Tenobre had moved to settle in Nurr, where they were treated as equal citizens. Oh sure, a burrower might catch some nasty glances from surface people in the street, but anyone who actually tried to harm them would be punished.

"Mole" was becoming less and less of an epithet. The young ones even took up the label with pride. They were the underground strength of Nurr and proud of it.

Moles weren't simply used as miners, to dig in the most dangerous places for the duke's wealth. They were proper delvers now, exploring ancient installations and cataloguing whatever they found there. There was no-one who understood the ancients as well as the delvers of Nurr, though any good delver would say they had barely scratched the surface of that great civilization.

The duke had won their loyalty with loyalty of his own, and all he required from Chansu was a simple task: dig tunnels to the appointed places and wait until he received further orders. Chansu was no fool: he knew what those orders would be. The tunnels he had dug were too narrow and poorly ventilated for anyone not burrow-born to use, so it wasn't an invasion. The shafts simply ended instead of fanning out, so it wasn't sapping. That left arson or sabotage. When the small barrels of oil arrived, along with a stone crate containing a fiery ooze, it only confirmed his suspicions. The ooze was dormant now, long starved into a state that allowed easy transportation and storage. Given a little food and a few hours to recover it would expand, divide, and go in search of more flammables to eat.

Chansu dug mostly in the daytime, when the surface noise would cover his steady scraping of soil. The narrow shafts, barely wide enough for his thin frame, were dark and damp. He had no need for light, and little need for fresh air. He was the most gifted of all the delvers of Machki, the underground city in Nurr populated mainly by delvers.

He had filled a vast warehouse full of tailings. It wasn't all clean dirt either: some of it was contaminated with seepage from the city gutters, workshop runoff, and strange smelling mycelliums. Those parts he had covered with cleaner soil, to make his extended stay easier to endure. He had done all the digging himself, with a crew to help move and pack the earth inside the warehouse. The crew was gone now, all except a lone messenger who dropped off food and other necessary things daily, and kept telling him to wait and wait. It was almost like waiting for rescue in a cave-in of his own making, except that when word arrived he would be going into danger instead of coming out of it.

Today's message was not the same: it said there was time to dig one more tunnel. If he started a new branch off of an existing shaft, there wasn't even that far to dig. The bigger problem was not having a crew to pile the dirt for him. Chansu replied with an encrypted request for helpers, then began to plan the new dig.

Ullidia, North Frontier

Guardian Maia's carriage train was two cars: a carriage for a dozen people, and a wagon for luggage and appalons. Their gurantor could pull both cars, fully loaded, fifteen hours a day. From a distance he might have seemed lumbering but he was moving too fast for appalons to keep up. They went swiftly through Dace, then Ullidia, and were approaching Lavradio.

Maia brought with her an assistant priestess, Sister Susana, and Disciple Mobeen. Mobeen's retinue was an apprentice disciple named Edos and eight elite soldiers turned out in the yellow star over blue background that was the Unity's colors. Their armor was all tirun scale, and the weapon of choice was enhanced bone longswords. The cadre of disciples and their bulwark were worth a battalion of heavy cavalry. They worked in shifts of three: one driver with two guards riding post.

The driver notified them about another carriage broken down up ahead. That wasn't so uncommon on its own, but it was reason for caution as they got closer. What was surprising was the explosion of blood and flesh inside the car.

It happened with an awful tearing sound: Something large passed through the car, punching through the front and back, taking part of Maia's face with it. Her head was bursting with pain and an unbearable ringing sound. Somewhere, people were shouting but she couldn't understand them through the ringing, and her eyes were too covered in blood to see. She could feel smaller impacts hitting the top of the car. Mobeen was on the floor, head mostly severed, drenching the floor in his blood. Most of the ringing noise stopped when Susana had screamed herself to exhaustion. Maia could hear well enough to recognize what was happening now: one of the bulwark was entreating Edos to bless them so they could fight, shaking the younger man roughly to pull his eyes away from Mobeen's corpse.

"Benediction, Edos! Remember the benediction!" The soldier started saying the first line of the payer himself, to get Edos started. Several times he started the prayer, until finally the young man spoke the words with him. Chaos and pain receded a little as the prayer took hold and the bulwarks' courage filled them all. Edos rapidly followed that with enhancements for protection, strength, and speed for each of the five fighters still in the car. It took time to say all the prayers, even in the disciples' rapid patter. The men outside were already blessed because they had been on duty when the attack began. The five piled out of the carriage and charged the ambushers, leaving Edos behind with the three external guards to protect Maia and Susana and the mounts.

Edos rattled off healing prayers for the two women, and he wasn't gentle about it. Her jaw reset itself just as fast as it had been broken, while the flesh forcibly grew back with an itching sensation so intense she had to fight against an urge to claw at her own face. There was nothing to be done for Mobeen.

Maia could tell when the guards left behind deployed their slings. They were standing on top of the carriage, and every time they launched one of the big hardened stones the entire car would jerk. The stones made loud buzzing sounds as they passed through the air and, more often than not, a distant cracking noise when they hit their targets.

Edos closed and barred the shutters and told the two women to get down. Maia grabbed Susana and knelt on the floor, her knees touching Mobeen's blood. Edos leaped out the door with his sword in hand. There was brief fighting near the carriage, but then he returned with his sword slick from someone's blood. "Stay here, your grace." Then he closed the door and was gone again.

Sister Susana pointed above them at the ceiling: arrowheads intruded into the cab. It shouldn't have been possible, unless the heads were enhanced with the arts. The bronze bodkins were as sharp and clean as if they had come fresh from the forge. There was a hole at the front of the car as wide as her hand, where Mobeen had been sitting, a cone of blood spread out from it painting most of the interior in a crimson spray. Clear shapes on the walls showed where people had been sitting when Mobeen died. Maia took a blanket, she didn't know whose, and covered him. His face was still smiling, even charming, over the wreckage of his neck and shoulder.

Whatever had killed Mobeen had passed straight through the car, grazed her own face, and made a similar hole in the rear, then entered the second car. Maia could see through the holes into the wagon, where at least one appalon lay dead. The disciples' and bulwarks' beasts were trained for battle and barely fussed, but hers and Susana's trumpeted fearfully and kicked the sides of their transport. Looking out the hole in front, she saw the guarantor was dead.

Maia thought about reminding Edos they needed some of the bandits alive, but decided it was pointless and tried to help Susana instead. The young priestess was hyperventilating under a bench. The sister had never seen this level of violence. In fact, it might be her first time venturing out of Unity City and its surrounding area. She kept muttering, "they killed a disciple, they killed a disciple" over and over again. There was little to be done, other than have Susana breathe into her hands and try to hold her breath.

There was a quick triple knock on the door, and then it opened. Bulwark Altheas told them they were chasing down stragglers and it would all be over soon. She spared a glance for Mobeen's body under its makeshift shroud, reminded them to stay put, and closed the door again.

Guardian Maia tried to marshal her wits and think about what all of this could mean. Their attackers had killed a disciple, and very nearly killed a member of Leadership in the bargain. Anyone so well equipped should be able to tell from their colors they were church officials, so these weren't simple bandits and this wasn't a random attack. The ambush was for them specifically, which meant their presence was anticipated.

Then there was the timing of the attack. Even if news of their mission had leaked the moment it had been decided, how did a rider get this far so fast and organize it all? It would only be possible if the resources were already nearby, waiting for word that it was time to deploy. That suggested some very advanced planning.

They were also in Ullidia, just shy of Lavradio's border. No nation would be foolish enough to attack Leadership unless they were ready to fight the church itself. As far as she knew, Ullidia had no reason to start a war with the Unity: they had been well-aligned for decades. It was Lavradio who was lax in their religious duties and resentful of church influence, but their (now former) king was hoping to be paid so an attack made no sense coming from them. DeLanion's death had set off a chain of events that brought Maia's group here to be ambushed, and the timing was too neat to ignore. Some devious mind was behind all of this, and they would plant false trails everywhere. Whomever seemed at fault was probably the witless dupe.

To Maia, the situation smelled like somebody was trying to start a war. Throughout her career it had been normal for the kingdoms to attempt to use the church's power for their own ends, but it was unheard of for a kingdom to start a war with the Unity itself.

The bulwark fighters knew their job: eliminate threats and don't let anyone get away. At last the fighters returned with the enemy's gurantor puling a sled piled high with bodies and a ballista. Maia would have berated them for not keeping any of them alive, but it was obvious from their blackened faces that some of the dead had taken poison. Other than not wearing uniforms they all had the look of soldiers about them. Their hair was nearly the same, they were all fit, and their hands all showed signs of regular weapon training. Their underclothes were identical, sourced from a shop in Dosul Furst, Lavradio. A cursory search didn't turn up any messages, but a more thorough search could be done later.

Maia thought about her next move while cleanup got started. The carriage (and people) had to be cleaned, two dead appalons had to be buried, and corpses had to be preserved and stowed for later examination. The instrument of Mobeen's sudden death was a ballista bolt enhanced with the highest level of art. It had flown through a massive gurantor, two armored walls, Maia's face, and two appalons. Maia didn't know which profoundly irresponsible idiot had made such a thing and left it lying about, but it had a maker's mark so she could find out. She was expecting that trail to lead to Lavradio too, the same as the ambushers' clothes.

Maia's stomach turned at the sight of fifteen corpses, lined up so Edos could preserve them with the arts. Edos preserved Mobeen first, then his bulwark wrapped the corpse tightly in furs and stowed him in the front carriage. He would ride with them. The attackers' bodies were stacked like cordwood in the cargo wagon.

In the carriage with the sobbing Suzana and the corpse of Unity's most celebrated monster hunter, Maia understood the goal of her adversary: to isolate and weaken Lavradio. They were a long way away from having any satisfactory answers, but the church had to exercise its authority and all of the fingers would point to Lavradio.

The holy party exchanged their dead gurantor for the enemy's living one, then set out for Fort Lean.

Fort Lean faced its counterpart, Fort Fringe, across a kilometer of narrow valley populated by colony trees and little else. The two towns could have been designed by the same mind: the same low wide walls ran the width of the valley, and similar compact towns perched at one end of the walls. The main difference between the two was that Lean had been carved out of the rough granite mountains to the west, while Fringe was situated on top of the lower, more rounded hills to the east. The matched fortresses were a physical manifestation of the Treaty of Alignment, a two-centuries old pact brokered by the church that had frozen international boundaries and put a stop to most thoughts of conquest. Her Holiness wielded a big stick in the form of the continent's practitioners. Those borders had barely moved in the centuries since, but that didn't mean nations stopped vying for supremacy. There were still skirmishes from time to time, typically over water rights and other resources, but the general shape of the Alignment-agreed borders had held firm.

Out here at least there was little to fight over. The pass between Ullidia and Lavradio wasn't exactly fertile, and the silver mines had long since dried up. Baring the unlikely discovery of a new vein of metal-rich ore there was nothing here to tempt anyone.

When Maia's train turned off the main road to climb the switchbacks to Lean it must have set off alarms. Her train was met by a military general and a civilian wearing the formal sash of a city mayor. The lord of the region was nowhere to be seen, nor had he bothered to send a representative. Possibly he wasn't in residence.

"Your Grace," greeted the mayor, as they both placed their hands over their hearts and bent slightly at the waist. Ullidians didn't indulge in the excessive bowing of their neighbor in the north, a little tilt would do.

"I am Mayor Carabast, and this is General Gustave, commander of the northern army. We are honored by this unexpected visit."

"Guardian Maia," she said curtly, but allowed them to kiss her holy symbol of silver set with blue stones.

"We require a house," Maia demanded without further preamble, "large enough for eight, plus a cold room to store corpses." The general eyed the state of her carriage and went around to the back car to look at the appalons and cargo.

"That's a difficult request, your grace," complained the mayor. "We are a compact town, as you can see. There aren't so many houses large enough, and they are all occupied."

The general returned from his inspection and interrupted the mayor's useless whining. "They can use my house," he said. "Does your grace require the use of my servants, or do you prefer the house to be empty."

"Empty it," she demanded, knowing what an inconvenience that would be. Not only would he need to find lodging for his family and servants, but he would need to remove any sensitive or personal documents, plus sufficient clothing and other goods for an indeterminate stay away from home. "You have our thanks, general."

"Please grant me a little time to arrange it. While you're waiting, allow us to provide dinner for you and your men. I know a place nearby we can commandeer. And if you feel like sharing, we will be happy to help in any way we can."

The place General Gustave had in mind was a tiny restaurant barely large enough to hold the dinner party of thirteen. The two patrons who occupied the place were doing more loitering than eating, and they melted away once the general tossed a silver coin at the proprietor. Food came out of the kitchen quickly, to feed the fighters' unseemly appetites: their respected colleague was dead but they were digging in as if nothing had happened, taking shifts so a pair would always be at the door. Even Edos, who had apprenticed with Mobeen for over a year, didn't hold back. Maia could barely touch her food.

Once the dishes were cleared and drinks poured, Gustave prompted Maia for her story. "Leadership was attacked on the road. In Ullidia," he said to start her off.

"But not by Ullidians, surely!" exclaimed the mayor. "Nobody would be stupid enough to attack her grace on their own land."

Maia fixed him with one of her more piercing stares. "That remains to be seen. Assuming Ullidia had nothing to do with the attack, you nonetheless allowed a band of a dozen skilled fighters to operate within your borders and ambush a church vessel while on a mission. With a ballista, no less. We're not talking about concealed kitchen knives or camouflaged farming tools. They parked a gurantor carriage in the road with a siege weapon mounted on it. Some of the responsibility will fall on Edge."

"But, that's not fair!" complained the mayor. "You can't hold us responsible for something we didn't do!"

"That said," interrupted the general, "you will have any assistance that is ours to give."

"I'm pleased to hear it. The enemy carriage is several kilometers south of here. Track it. Find out when and where it entered your territory. Gurantor carriages are not something you just sneak into a kingdom. There will be records. Bulwark Altheas will observe the investigation."

"Yes, your grace." The general was visibly relieved to have something tangible his people could do.

"And summon your healer. I need his help with the dead men."

"He's not in town today," said the mayor. "We share Healer Julian with Fringe. You'll have to wait a couple of days until he's on rotation."

Maia sighed inwardly over the mayor's attitude. Either he was being passive-aggressive, or he was just passive. "Sister Susana, write a summons for Healer Julian. Edos will mark it. We'll send it with a bulwark pair, and enhance them for the journey." Having a pair knights in Unity colors show up in Fringe with a summons for the local healer was sure to raise both questions and anxieties. Let them be worried. It should make them cooperative.

"All right, general. If your people are ready, I'll see this house of yours. You don't happen to have a large cellar where we can store the bodies, do you?"

The general's home did have a large basement under the entire house, which they re-arranged so half of it was empty except for a pair of butcher's tables. That gave just enough room to stack the enemy bodies and conduct examinations two at a time. Healer Julian and Disciple Edos together were able to determine who had died of injuries, and who had died of self-administered poison. They catalogued distinguishing features, clothes, possessions, and other observations. Most importantly, they were searching for messages.

They finally found what they were looking for on the body of someone who had tried to escape using an ancient artifact. The device had failed. Instead of making him faster, his legs and spine fractured. When he realized he was about to be captured the man took poison. He died without saying a word, but he was carrying a series of coded messages on his person.

By day three of the investigation the mayor had stepped aside to let the general represent Ullidia. Guardian Maia and General Gustav met twice-daily in the general's dining room. Sometimes Disciple Edos and Bulwark Altheas were included.

"It's a Lavradian code," confirmed General Gustav. He held one of the strips of silk gently, with gloved hands, to look through it in the light of the makeshift morgue's spirit lamps. A sequence of letters were written on it, but they seemed random. "From the size and shape of the cloth, it's one of their lightning codes. If these were all coded with the same key, there's probably enough here to decode them."

"How long?" asked Maia.

"A day. Maybe two. But the fact we can read these messages is highly sensitive information. If you weren't Leadership, I wouldn't be offering."

"Hence our meeting alone this morning," said Maia, understanding. "I won't use any of the contents without a plausible explanation of where the information came from. What did you find out about the carriage?"

The general put aside the tray of delicate message strips for an aide to copy later.

"Not very much," he said, handing Maia a stack of boards containing the report. "It came through the frontier gate the same day you left Enclave. It was never seen again until they attacked you. They hid in the Edge, waiting for you. We found their campsite, and their observation post."

"Observation post?"

"Think about the situation from their point of view. They obviously knew you were coming, but they didn't know the exact day or hour. It would be suspicious if our daily patrols saw the same broken-down gurantor train in the same spot every day. So they have to position themselves near enough to the road to set up the ambush in a hurry, but stay out of sight from patrols."

"Someone has to watch the road," said Maia, getting his point, "and see far enough ahead to have enough time to warn the assault force to get ready."

The general drew a rough map on the slate between them: the road Maia's team had come up, with a few mounds for the eastern hills and jagged peaks for the western mountains. He marked a location with a triangle, "there was a two-man signal team on a rock formation we call the Neck. It's an ideal spot: they could see far enough down the road to alert the ambushers with plenty of time to spare." He put an x down the road from the triangle, next to the road. "The main force's camp site was shockingly close to the road, but well screened. Every day that our patrols passed by they had to be holding their breath, to not give themselves away. Damned nervy of them."

"Did you find the signal men?"

"They're long gone, but I can tell you they were experienced mountaineers."

"Could they be from Fringe?"

The general stroked his beard nervously. "Fringe has people like that, good ones too. But I've known the man across the way since we were both pups. He could arrange something like this, but he's not someone who decides on his own to skirmish with Leadership. It's a stupid fight to pick, and stupid doesn't last long out here."

"Then how do you explain the mayor?" Maia was indulging herself a little, needling the general about his useless mayor.

"Temporary," countered Gustav, with a slight smile. "Lord Peroz lets the town nominate a bumbling citizen to be mayor. When things get serious and they turn to the lord for action, he fires the mayor and solves the current crisis. Then they nominate someone else to be mayor, and the cycle repeats. There's little harm done because the real work of running the city is handled by a team of city managers."

"That's just," Maia had to search for an appropriate word, "nefarious."

"High praise, coming from Leadership."

Every dead man got a board, with his face on the front (Sister Susana was remarkable with an artist's charcoal) and identifying details on the back. Once the bodies were all catalogued they were transported to a pit outside the city and burned. Maia had Edos purify the general's basement thoroughly, and ensured a significant sum would be set aside for borrowing the man's house and filling it with corpses.

The coded messages didn't contain anything revelatory. One was an order to enact the plan, without saying what "the plan" was. A few more were about logistics, mainly provisions. It seemed they had set out with only a few days of provisions and needed a resupply. The last message was encouragement, assurance of victory, and a reminder not to be taken alive.

"This is all scrap-loaf," declared the general. "You're meant to find this. It doesn't tell you anything you couldn't guess on your own."

"It was written in a Lavradian code," Maia reminded him.

"A code we in Ullidia recognize. If we know how to break the lightning cipher, then someone else might have figured it out, too. So they write these messages to make you think Lavradio is involved."

"Or, you are reluctant to see your counterparts across the way get involved in a conflict with the church."

The general didn't try to deny it. "It's a fair suspicion, but here's a better one. Why did your guy have these messages?"

"They were his messages," she said.

"They were encrypted messages, about a covert operation. Any sane security protocol says you destroy sensitive messages as soon as they become obsolete, but this guy is keeping week-old ciphertext about resupply runs that have already happened. There's no reason to keep any of this. So why does he have it?"

Maia took a few seconds to catch up with him. "You're suggesting that he was carrying the messages, but they were meant for us. We found them in the pommel of his sword. He might not have known he had them."

"Right. Or he did know, but didn't know what they said and was told to deliver them to someone else, after his mission here was complete."

"He's expected to die," she realized, "and we're supposed to search him. He would have gotten away, but his ancient device malfunctioned."

"Or it functioned perfectly, breaks his back, and he takes the poison like a good soldier."

"I take back what I said about Lord Peroz being nefarious. Propping up useless mayors is small ale, compared to sacrificing your own agents."

Once the messages were decoded there was nothing else to learn by staying in Edge. Maia let her people know they would be leaving the next morning.

BURNING NIGHT

Lavradio, Girona

As soon as he arrived on the scene, Fire Marshal Hutisho knew it was going to be a bad night. The first two fires had started in the dead of night, between the hour when sex workers went to sleep and the early delivery men came awake. A pair of tenements were burning on Brown Street. The fact they were across the street from each other and two such fires had broken out at the same time was a sure sign of arson. In one of the buildings everyone had escaped without serious injury. In the other, nine families had perished, some of them from jumping off the top floors. They had chosen a quick death over burning alive.

Those fires in turn spread to nearby structures in the west side of the city, traveling across clothing lines and makeshift wooden walkways strung between the close-packed buildings. The fire crews were able to limit the loss to only three blocks, thanks entirely to city planners who sectioned even the poorest parts of the city with wide avenues. They both improved transportation and acted as fire breaks. As long as he kept his people in the area, the fire shouldn't spread.

While all hands were attending the Brown Street fire another conflagration sprung up near the north gate. All eight of the large city-owned warehouses were completely engulfed before anyone could arrive.

The marshal commandeered all the peacekeepers he could lay his hands on, but it was barely enough to fight two of the blazes. Lacking any instructions about how to prioritize the buildings, he directed his makeshift crews to focus on the two smallest fires. It was a decision that would earn him years of scorn from the public, because he had unknowingly put storage space rented to businesses over the food storage for the city.

It was while they were in the throes of the warehouse blaze that he received word of a new fire: Plaza Hall. It was a shock because, not only was it their third major fire of the night, but the building itself was made entirely of stone.

Hutisho pulled twenty men from the warehouse fire and rushed to the plaza on his weary appalon, picking up volunteers along the way. He arrived to the sight of a dozen men stumbling down the grand steps covered in soot, faces and clothes singed. They were peacekeepers, assigned to guard the building at night. Smoke poured out of the lower windows, indicating the fire was in the basement. He found the one who seemed least hurt.

"Tell me," Hutisho demanded.

"The fire is in the archive. We used all the sand in the bunkers, but the fire won't go out. I think," he hesitated, looking at his fellows.

"Something is alive in the fire," said another, a woman holding up the left side of a barely-conscious and badly burned peacekeeper. "The sand didn't even slow it down."

"Start a bucket brigade until a water engine gets here." They tried to protest. There were sand bunkers in the archive because water was never to be used there. "The archive is lost," the marshal told them, "the best we can do now is save the rest of the building, and that's not going to be easy."

With their two available water engines deployed he sent several people to the apartment fire with orders to redeploy one to the plaza. Citizens came out with their buckets to help get water from the nearest well to the plaza and douse the walls of the building. Heat stone for long enough and it failed. A quarter of Plaza Hall could be lost.

Hutisho sent mounted messengers to the garrison to fetch fighters, to the minister's mansion to fetch Marvao, and to the Chapel of Compassionate Light. "Tell Matrix Lucia we need her here urgently. There's some kind of fire monster to be handled." That done, he put a nearby lieutenant in charge and entered the building himself. He was highly resistant to fire and knew how to move quickly while crouching low. He took the stairs down, then entered the archive's anteroom. Even here, the wood furnishings were beginning to smoke. The archive door was open, but the room beyond was empty of everything except a white ball radiating a forge's intense heat. Spread all around it was sand from the bunkers, glowing red.

The archives were considered so valuable that even the door was made to resist fire: treated fire-resistant wood sandwiched between two sheets of a mysterious temperature-resistant metal. It was said that the metal panels had been found in an ancient ruin and the door had been built to fit them. The first crew had opened the door to fight the fire. With nothing left to save, the best thing Hutisho could do now was close it and hope they had better success at keeping the fire inside the archive than they had at keeping the fire out. With heavily gloved hands, Hutisho dived at the door and pulled it closed as fast as he could. The skin on his lips blackened and his gloves caught fire, but the door would hold for a little while.

He used his axe to break down the anteroom table with a few well-placed swings, dragged the potential fuel down the hallway, and followed that by tossing out the chairs. When he felt his lungs start to crackle he ran out, staying low as he went up the stairs and down the hall and down the grand steps to the plaza. He shucked his still-flaming gloves and smoldering outerwear then doused himself in water. The expedition had cost him his shouting voice and some facial skin, but the information might be worth the pain.

He started giving orders in a raspy voice. "Get a crew into the basement and pull out all the fuel out you can. Just push it to the other side of the building. You there, did you deliver your message?" The marshal got back on his appalon to gain a better view, from where he could see the plaza was full of people either watching or trying to help. Water was coming from a second well, three blocks away.

City Minister Marvao arrived, sooner than could be explained by messenger. He must of come on his own accord. To his credit, he didn't ask any stupid questions or demand a detailed explanation.

"What do you need?" shouted the minister, as soon as the carriage pulled up next to Hutisho.

"Fighters," croaked the fire marsal over the din, "there's some kind of fire monster in your archive. I've sent for Matrix Lucia, but she'll need spears. I sent for help from the garrison, but they won't follow my orders."

"What else is burning?"

"Brown Street tenements, and the city's warehouses. All of them."

The minister's face turned white. "I'll get you what you need."

They ran their respective staffs, the minister from his carriage and the fire marshal from atop his appalon, practically side-by-side. One of the fire engines arrived, and a pump crew soon had a stream of water flowing to three hoses. Meanwhile a crowd of people pulled every last stick of furniture and other fuel from the basement and first floor offices. Hutisho had the hose crews focus on the interior and exterior walls around the archive. His biggest immediate worry was the structural integrity of the building: that much heat for so long could cause the structure to collapse. Massive plumes of steam rose from the building and into the sky.

Matrix Lucia arrived with her entourage of husband-priest, a pack of teenage students from the school, priestess Lorena, and a posse of healers. At about the same time, a complement of soldiers marched up led by a green-looking lieutenant. Hutisho briefed them on the situation as succinctly as he could.

"What I need to know," he rasped at the matrix when he was finished, "is will this thing burn itself out? Is doing nothing an option?"

"What shape was the ooze?" she yelled. "Was it flat like a puddle, or was it round like a ball?"

"It was round, white. Just sitting there. And the sand around it looked ready to melt."

"White and round and doing nothing means it's going to divide. The little ones are very energetic, impossible to catch. The whole city could be lost."

"Then you'll have to take a team and kill it," said Minister Marvao. "Can you do it?"

"With respect, Minister," said the lieutenant, "that's not going to happen. You are not in our chain of command. You can't give us orders."

"This is an emergency, lieutenant! Half the city is burning, and we're going to lose the rest if we wait."

"I have to wait for appropriately authorized orders, sir."

A shout went up from the pump team: the well had run dry. It would be several minutes before they could pull so much as a bucketful from it. Hutisho ordered them to move the engine to the rear entrance of the building, where there was a second well. Even as he said the words, he could feel the first creeping sensations of despair in his chest. This could end up as something worse than a total loss: it could be the end of the city as they knew it.

Prince Estevan arrived with a colonel and half the palace guard in tow. To arrive now, they must have mounted up before the plaza had caught fire.

"Minister," shouted Estevan, to get his attention.

"Your Highness," he said. "Please tell the officer to lend a hand, or send him away."

It was the colonel who responded, in a voice that rang clear over the din. "Lieutenant, take your men to the warehouse fire and follow the commands of the head of fire suppression there. Double-time!"

The soldier saluted and led his men away at a run, while the colonel detailed six palace guards to the matrix.

"Use these six as you see fit," he told her, "they've worked with disciples before."

Lucia placed a wide-scale blessing of benediction over everyone, then told the guards, "I'm blessing you with fire resistance, strength, and toughness. I will also bless a spear from each of you. The seven of us will enter the building. We will open the archive door and throw spears at the monster, two at a time until someone lands a solid hit. I will create a barrier to keep the fiery ichor from turning us into ash. Don't be alarmed if I fall unconscious: just pick me up and haul me back." She said her prayers then, in rapid-fire back-to-back fashion that made it all sound like one impossibly long word.

The disciple and her makeshift bulwark disappeared into clouds of steam around Plaza Hall. Mika, her husband of many years, stood silent and still at the foot of the stone steps for a time, staring through the doorway that had swallowed her up. Lorena organized the healers into teams and sent them to different sites according to the casualties reported so far.

The fire marshal felt a pang of sympathy for the old priest. He had just watched his elderly wife run into a burning building to fight a deadly monster. The priest pressed his star fervently to his lips. Then, he got to work organizing food and water for the injured and volunteers. If it had been Hutisho, he wouldn't be able to tear his eyes from the font door, but those two had doubtless worked so many crises that Mikas understood there was nothing he could do to make his wife safer right now. The best he could do was help with the mission.

Some instinct told Hutisho to send the order to withdraw, relayed through runners. Either the matrix would succeed or she would fail. In either case there was no point to having people inside the building. Before another minute had passed, as the last of the fire teams and volunteers ran out of the building, the foundation began to break.

The sound of cracking stone rang against the facades around the plaza. The crowds hushed and stared at the distressed building. That was followed by a sudden sagging of the corner of Plaza Hall that sat over the archive.

"Pull everyone back!" he tried to shout, but his voice was gone. The fire fighters nearest him took up the shout.

"Pull back, pull back," they shouted, "Move the line back to the prince!" The prince, who just happened to be the right distance for safety, became the line.

"To me!" called the prince, picking up the call, "get behind me!" The crowd moved, weaving their way around the prince and the palace guard on their appalons.

The hall made a series of noises like boulders being smashed together, or a giant cracking its knuckles before performing an awful sleight of hand. Then a quarter of the building gave way entirely, the floors falling flat onto each other, crushing the contents of the building into dust which flooded out in a hot choking cloud. The colonel in charge of the palace guard commanded a right face, and two ranks of appalons and riders to put their sides to the incoming debris, shields up, in an attempt to shelter some of the crowd from the worst of the scorching ash.

Hutisho had just enough time to admire the colonel's presence of mind (and close his own mouth and eyes) before he and his appalon were alone in the hot suffocating void.

Blind and deaf he waited, eyes closed and a wet cloth over his mouth to keep hot ash from adding to his internal injuries. His mount turned away from the ash, but didn't bolt. When the air finally stilled, the animal and Hutisho shook themselves together, and he cracked one eyelid to venture a peek. The cloud thinned as it spread over the entire plaza and beyond, and started to settle to the pavement. A few scattered people were screaming or crying, but not as many as he would have thought. Or maybe that was just his hearing, returning slowly one panicked voice at a time. He used the last of his canteen to clean his face and mouth, and the face of his mount. The old beast had seen fire before, and wasn't put off by a blow of ash. Some of the palace mounts weren't faring as well, sketching to one side or trying to bolt, but the guards were keeping them under control. Only one had run off and left their rider behind, groaning on the pavers.

The marshal still couldn't see as far as the building, but the entry team ghosted in from that direction, ashen from head to foot like everyone else, hardly discernible from the air around them. They carried the matrix between them. People ran up to take her, while the rest approached the command center of prince, colonel, marshal, and minister. The minister was miraculously clean: he had shuttered the windows in his carriage just before the cloud had overrun him. He had the distinction of being the only non-gray person on the scene.

"The ooze is dead," reported one of the palace guards. "When the building started to come down, we went out the north exit. The matrix collapsed from spirit exhaustion. No other injuries. When we speared the ooze it sort of spilled all over the place, and drained out a hole in the floor. I think someone tunneled under the city to get to the records room."

"Why the records room," wondered one of the palace guards.

The city minister growled, "to make the city impossible to govern."

"I got a good look inside the archive before the collapse," the reporting guard added, "and there's nothing left in there but sand. And that was before the collapse."

"What about the rear hallway," asked Estevan urgently, "did you see if it was damaged?"

"We came out that way. It's smoke damaged, but not burnt."

Estevan spoke to Minister Marvao, "we need to empty the map room, get those slates somewhere safe."

"Not so fast, Your Highness," countered Hutisho, with his vanishing voice. "I'll send some building inspectors first, and if the rear of the building is safe then you can enter. I'm not losing a prince tonight, on top of everything else."

Lavradio, North of Girona

Cuelar Frenzio, Duke of Nurr, waited in the shade of a copse of trees beside the river Tramagul. The men and women with him were darkly dressed and crouched low. Their appalons, all chosen for their excellent training and dull coloration, knelt beside them. The moon Crevist shined brightly on the river. Over the distant city of Girona, clouds were lit from above by ashen moonlight, and from below by angry fire. The timing hadn't been perfect, but it would do.

One of his agents approached. "Sire, the delver is late. We have to go soon or we can't finish."

"I'm aware," said Cuelar, "but we are going to give him a little while longer." Cuelar could hear the man's approach from afar, ragged breathing and stumbling steps betraying the man's desperation not to be left behind. In a few minutes the rest of the group could hear him too. Chansu eventually appeared, clambering out of the irrigation ditch he had used to stay hidden, and stumbled in their direction. At Cuelar's word the perimeter guards allowed the delver in unchallenged. He collapsed before the duke, on his knees. "My Lord, it is done." He smelled of wood smoke and earth.

"We are quite satisfied," Cuelar pronounced. With his own hand, he gave the man a skin of water and waited patiently for him to drink, already opened so he didn't have to manage the stopper with his awkwardly fused fingers. "Drink and rest. We leave in ten minutes."

Whole and rested, Cuelar's band of spies and saboteurs mounted their appalons and followed the green belt northeast, taking sheltered paths wherever they could and exposed routes when they had no choice. He regretted the tracks they were leaving behind, but there was no helping that. To hide their exact numbers, they traveled in single file. He wished it would snow, but the sky was not that cooperative.

They traveled for the rest of the night, and made a cold camp during the day. They traveled like that, heading north by northwest, for two more days and two nights, skirting towns and farms. Nobody followed them.

At the Urtigosa river they found boatmen ready to ferry them, even though it wasn't an official crossing. It took half the night to get the party to the north side of the river, and afterwards the ferrymen floated downstream as if they had never been there.

Their journey paused where the Urtigosa basin rose into some hills, at a lone farmhouse. The house was abandoned, but the adjacent fields were planted. There was a tense moment while signs and countersigns were given, then a party of twelve emerged from the landscape. The leader's voice was familiar to the duke.

"We're putting in the last of them down now, your highness. Would you like to see?"

"Show me," said the duke.

The leader took them to the margins between two fields, where a woman lowered a fifteen centimeter wide sphere into a wide hole. It wobbled like gelatin. If it had been daytime they would have seen smaller ovoid shapes beneath the translucent skin of the sphere: an egg sac of the dreaded magulo, a pest of the first order. A normal sac was only one or two centimeters wide, but this one had come from a monstrous specimen. The sac was placed in the hole, on a thick bed of grains to feed the young. The whole thing was covered with a layer of "monster ore".

Cuelar's people didn't know why the powdered rock promoted monstrous mutations, but it undeniably worked. Finally, a thin layer of dirt was scattered over the area and the carefully removed ground cover was replaced. The spot was between fields sown with winter wheat. Just as the fields began to head in late spring these eggs would hatch. Nourished by the buried stores of food and ore, the nymphs would excavate themselves to gorge on the nearby fields. Already monstrous by nature, they would swiftly become unmanageable. They would molt several times, growing over a meter long, becoming more and more carnivorous as they matured. The normal maguro only preyed on grain and other bugs, but the monstrous ones would go after meat bigger than itself. Cuelar's people had planted dozens of these sacs, each bearing hundreds of eggs, all along the northernmost fields of Lavradio's central territory. The maguro would eat their way south as they became increasingly vicious, wiping out crops and people as they went.

That alone would have been enough to make the project worthwhile, but the addition of powdered beryl escalated the threat by an order of magnitude. Feeding ore to the already monstrous insects not only made them larger, but ensured a small fraction of them would become cursed. Cuelar's people didn't know exactly what the cursed beasts were capable of: in their experiments they had killed the cursed ones immediately rather than find out. But they were sure to add a new dimension of terror.

"Any problems?" asked the duke.

"We had one casualty, an accident."

"What did you do with the body?" Having one of his spies found would compromise their plan.

"We buried her deep, sire. She had nothing to identify her except this." He handed over a leather thong bracelet braided in Nurr colors. A pretty ceramic bead was woven into it. It was the kind of keepsake a spy could get away with: specific enough to remind them of someone or somewhere, but innocuous enough it could belong to anybody. There would be no name or label on the bracelet, but Cuelar didn't doubt the family would be grateful to have it returned.

"And the crates?"

"Kindling."

Cuelar nodded. "Follow in single file. We don't stop until dawn."

"Yes, your highness."

When King Leonardo demanded Nurr's help, Cuelar would refuse. He had let too much Nurrish blood spill for the Odemira family. Too late, they would learn what they had been taking for granted.

INQUISITION

Lavradio, Girona

The damage in Girona was apparent from half a day away. As her train approached the city, Guardian Maia and the other passengers could see a pall of smoke squatting on Girona, trapped by a winter inversion. Not only could they see it, they could smell it, more acrid than a wildfire. So much smoke rose from the city that the sun was eclipsed. Only a wan brown light lit the streets, barely enough to see a block at a time.

As their train picked its way carefully through the streets people emerged out of the haze, hunched under their morning burdens as they tried to get to work around the rubble and ashes. A great many of them pointed at the ornate car and made comments to their fellows. Some applauded and cheered, thinking the church had come with healers as reinforcements. They faded just as quickly as they appeared, lost in haze as Maia's train passed them by.

When they pulled into the plaza they discovered city hall was partially destroyed and drifts of wet ashes sat where the gutters should have been. The gurantor heaved its train of two carriages in front of the Basilica of Magnificent Light and slowed to a stop with a prodigious grunt. They had driven the beast captured from their attackers as far as Dosul Furst, swapped animals, and driven this one to the capital without rest. She knelt in the street unbidden. Sir Quinton, the leader of Maia's bulwark, was the first out of the carriage and examined the gurantor.

"She's done, your grace," he said with a concerned look on his face. He spoke to her through the window of the carriage. "We'll have to bring her food and water, and hope she recovers on her own."

Guardian Maia thought about having Disciple Edos revive the beast with the arts, but one look at the shaky young man put that thought out of her mind. He had kept the beast moving at full speed all day. He was as finished as the gurantor.

"See to it," Maia agreed. "There's supposed to be a market on the northwest end of the plaza: send two people in plainclothes to gather news and buy food. Edos will stay here and rest." Among her party Mobeen was the only person who had ever been to Lavradio, and he was supposed to be their guide. With him gone the plaza and its surroundings were all they knew about, and that was second hand. At least the basilica had been easy to find, being right on the plaza.

Maia gave her guards a minute to organize then stepped down from her transport to make the walk into the basilica, flanked by Sir Quinton and Sister Susana. People were scattered around the small paved courtyard between the plaza and the steps, waiting. Inside, the foyer was packed with hundreds more. Workmen and house wives mainly, with a smattering of merchants and scribes, all packed together.

"Make way for the guardian," commanded the bulwark. The crowd turned, saw Maia in her silken Leadership robes, and parted to form a clear path to the sanctuary door. Now that the crowd was quiet, she could hear singing from the other side.

"Isn't it a little late for morning services?" she asked the foyer.

One well-dressed woman, some kind of scribe or bureaucrat, came forward to speak. "It is, your grace. Brother Javach said he would keep giving services for as long as people wanted them. It is a time of great need."

"Then I will wait with you," she proclaimed, taking a place directly by the sanctuary door and instantly making everyone slightly uncomfortable. This scene was unexpected. Lavradio was supposedly the least devout nation on the continent. Maia would expect some extra worshipers in a crisis, but not so many to keep the morning services running close to noon. It sounded as if the courtyard was filling up too, in anticipation of the next service. Her original plan had been to impose a recession immediately to force the cooperation of the new king. While she had to unravel this mess about DeLanion, her ultimate goal was to uphold the authority of the Unity. Abandoning the city right when the populace was most invested in the church might be a poor way to accomplish that goal.

Maia motioned to the woman who had spoken up before, who approached and introduced herself as Nella of Westside. Maia learned from her most of what had happened the night before.

"You seem very well informed," she praised Nella.

"I work in Plaza Hall, your grace, as an archivist. It was a terrible night for us, but it would have been a lot worse for everyone if Matrix Lucia hadn't shown up when she did. If the fire monster had multiplied, it could have destroyed the city. I hear the effort nearly killed her. Prince Estevan was very concerned."

This was also news to Maia. Members of royalty were close enough to clerics to be personally concerned about them.

When the doors finally opened the foyer crowd let Maia and her attendants enter ahead of them, right into the surprised face of Brother Javach on the other side. His mouth silently opened and closed twice before he got ahold of himself and made the proper greetings. Behind him, worshipers filed out through one of the wings so the next group could enter from the foyer unimpeded. The priest was running his sanctuary at full capacity, one service after another.

"I need to see your prelate," Maia declared. "The matter is urgent." Javach quickly passed her off to a junior priest who guided her through the sanctuary, into the administration wing, then upstairs to the prelate's apartments.

Along the way, Maia got a good look at the famous basilica's sanctuary. The uppermost level of the dome was inlaid with lapis, lit by the Fragment in its oculus. Statues of the Chosen and various saints lined the colonnade beneath, and under them were painted scenes from scripture. The Fragment lit it all in a graceful coruscating light that blessed the sanctuary. Worshipers arrayed themselves in the circular room, standing around the altar where a priest would perform the twenty minute service. Whatever he had paid, DeGray had gotten his money's worth. It wasn't the largest temple in the world but it was among the most beautiful. And, thanks to the Missing Disciple, he had a Fragment of Sun as a holy relic.

And unlike the Fragment in the Enclave's basilica, this one was real. That realization was enough to stop Guardian Maia in her tracks, snagged at the threshold between the sanctuary and the administrative wing, watching the people seek solace under Olyon's star. She didn't tear herself away until the service began.

The prelate's apartments were only a little less impressive than the sanctuary. They occupied the entire third floor of the administrative wing, with rooms enough for a family and servants. The kitchen and dining room were in the opposite wing however, since those spaces were also used for church-related meetings. At mealtimes the prelate and his guests would have to parade through the entire basilica, but maybe that was the point.

When Maia was shown into the prelate's private study she found herself facing not Prelate DeGray as expected, but Sister Karsyn. She had been dispatched to take over the ambassadorial role from the disgraced Brother Serano, who had been recalled. Karsyn and Maia were of the same age and had attended the School of Spiritual Arts together, so they were glad to see each other. But Maia had pressing issues to discuss.

"Where is DeGray?" she asked, not even bothering to say hello.

"He's been dead for weeks," said Karsyn. "Didn't you get the notices?"

"It seems not," Maia said, off balanced by the news.

"It's good to see you, too. Sit," Karsyn motioned to the comfortable seating in the room. "I'll get a fresh pot of jota. We can at least do that much in this wing." She struck a small chime mounted on the wall and a servant appeared to accept instructions, then left.

Karsyn's beast trait was orange spots on her skin. They weren't functional but they were beautifully arranged, tiny across her nose like freckles then growing bigger as they crossed her neck and arms. Today she set those against a midnight blue walking skirt and jacket, over a blinding white shirt. The jacket featured a wide embroidered lapel, and her ambassadorial badge was a star with seven points instead of the usual eight. It was a carefully coded outfit elegant enough for the palace, austere enough for the church, and incorporated a stole and holy symbol in its design. It was too cryptic for most people, but the veteran clerics and diplomats for whom it was coded would understand.

"It must be dire, to bring you here. How big is your party?"

"Eleven total. We need housing. Can you put us up at the ambassadorial estate?"

"That would not be to your liking," smiled Karsyn ruefully. "The estate is tiny. You should take these apartments, instead. There's plenty of room, I'm barely using them, and the servants are getting bored. I sleep at the estate, so you're not putting me out in the least. Just let me hide here in the study a few times a day."

"It's a deal," agreed Maia. They talked of inconsequential things until the head servant returned with jota and pastries.

"Dayma, the guardian and her ten companions are taking up residence here. Consider her the primary resident from now until she leaves."

"Understood mam," said Dayma, bowing. "Are there any special instructions at this time, Guardian Maia?"

"Quite a few. Susana, would you?"

Susana left with the lead servant and shut the door firmly behind them. Quinton remained behind to take up a post by the door.

Maia went first. "Tell me about DeGray."

"He was found dead one morning, in his public study, on the first floor of this building. Healers say it looked like natural causes and there was no poison found in the room. Nobody was surprised he died because he had gone a bit sideways in his last days. He didn't like that people kept coming to admire the Fragment and remember Disciple DeLanion. Edmond was raving about commoners in the sanctuary and how the basilica was his great achievement, nobody could take it away from him, and so on.

"That was two days before I arrived. Head Priest Javach claims he filed the notice, so I assumed the message passed by me on the road. But I included his death in my initial status report, which you apparently did not receive."

"We've had nothing from you at all," Maia told her. "I thought you were procrastinating your paperwork. Again."

Karsyn sighed. "I broke that habit when I was a teenager. As you should well remember. Let it go, already."

"Anything else I should know?"

"The old king didn't receive me. As soon as Leonardo returned home, Joaquim unofficially retired early. I had to wait until after the coronation to officially take up my post. Also, DeGray kept a secret 'repair fund' that only two other priests knew about, in a sacred vault that only the three of them could enter. Most of it is missing. The priests swear on the Fragment they didn't take it, so maybe DeGray embezzled it before he died."

"Do you believe them?"

"Absolutely," said Karsyn. "This Fragment isn't like the one in Enclave. That's a fake. This one does not let you lie. There's a reason they hoist that thing all the way up to the oculus: any lower and people would be caught in its effects without realizing it. You should try it at least once while you're here."

"How much gold," asked Maia.

"About a ton, according to Javach."

Maia put down her cup with some force. Missing messages. Missing money. Dead disciples. Dead prelate. Arson in the city. The child disciple's death was only one of many cuts.

"Maia," asked Karsyn, "does that amount mean something to you? Maybe you should tell me why you're here."

Maia tried to respond in even tones, as if the whole matter was only mildly interesting.

"We received an invoice from the former king, demanding one ton of gold. He was billing us for a very peculiar service: killing disciple DeLanion. He seemed to believe he was working at the church's behest."

"And a ton of gold is missing from the repair fund," continued a shocked Karsyn.

"Which Joaquim never received, or else he wouldn't have been so foolish as to invoice us. But there's more. I was sent to investigate, but we were ambushed by an impressively equipped force. Disciple Mobeen is dead: We had to inter him at Fort Lean. The evidence we found on the attackers says they took their orders from Lavradio."

"Sacred Blade is dead?" Karsyn looked shocked. "People here really liked him. They said he was the strength of a hundred men."

"I had planned to issue an immediate recession, to punish the country and force the king's cooperation, but seeing how devout the people are I'm not so sure it would give the right message."

"It wouldn't," Karsyn agreed. "The city had four disciples running around for months when DeLanion was in training, and the faithful loved it. People talk about last summer like it was a golden age of renewed faith. To be honest, I'm a little tired of hearing about it."

Karsyn made a concerned expression. "Listen, Maia. A recession would go over very badly with the anointed here, too. Every last one of them is here because they are at the end of their career. Either they retired here, or Leadership retired them here. They're all smooth skinned, or lack family connections, or crossed someone who had better family connections. Only a few made actual mistakes and ended up here for a reason. But they're dedicated to the Work like nowhere else I've been. The general feeling is that Leadership isn't nearly as loyal to the anointed as the anointed are to Olyon. The practitioners here won't obey a recession order, and some of the priests might risk expulsion if they thought the faithful really needed them. And right now, the faithful need them."

"I didn't realize this was such a difficult posting," said Maia.

"It isn't especially difficult, it's just one you can never leave. When you get assigned here, you are told in no uncertain terms that this is the end of the line for you. The

Assignment Committee is very deliberate about putting all of the undesirables and dead-enders right here. Not a single cleric here has received a special billet or training in Unity City in twenty years. This is the designated last stop of everyone's career, except maybe mine. There was some hope that Larava's marriage into the royal family might signal a change."

Maia wasn't on Assignments, and so hadn't known about Lavradio's status as the end of all dead ends. But she knew the members of Assignments, and it sounded just like them to have a designated hole where they dumped anyone they didn't like. If the loyalty of the clerics here was damaged then she had lean on their dedication to the tenets. It was harder than simply giving them orders, but she could manage. She was Leadership's best trouble shooter for a reason.

"I need to send some messages," Maia said, pointing at a nearby writing desk, "do you mind?" Soon she was hard at work.

Maia had only just finished composing her messages when a message arrived addressed to her. She hadn't even summoned a carrier yet, and there the envelope sat before her embossed with the city seal. Minister Marvao had invited her to lunch at the Vargos-Avelar hotel which had, if Karsyn was to be believed, nearly as fine a restaurant as any to be found in Unity City. In the city of Lavradio it was without peer.

"What do you think," she asked the ambassador. "Is it worth going?"

"Definitely," said Karsyn. "Does it say you can bring a friend?"

"I mean, is it worth attending for any reason besides the food?"

"Definitely," Karsyn repeated. "The minister and the Missing Disciple worked hand-in-hand to tear down the Colares faction and save the city. One of the many reasons he was so admired. Prince Estevan will be there, probably. He was more than a good acquaintance: he and the disciple were good friends."

"It says nothing about extras. If you're helpful I'll treat you after I have a handle on the situation."

Susana returned to say everyone was getting settled and the animals were being cared for. Edos was sound asleep in his assigned bed. Maia detailed Susana and Quinton to attend her at the Vargos-Avelar, along with one other guard to be chosen by Quinton.

The guardian's luncheon party crossed the vast plaza by appalon, several minutes tardy, and dismounted at the grand portico where liveried footmen took their mounts around to the side of the building to be stabled. Doors opened before them as if by enchantment as they crossed from portico to lobby to restaurant to private room unimpeded. As expected, Minister Marvao and Prince Estevan were waiting for them. Marvao could be identified by the deep rows of ridges along his thickened forehead. Estevan had his family's trademark mane of hair that ran vertically from the top of his head down his neck.

Un-expectedly, former queen Diana was there too. With her full body covering of silver-blue fur and almond eyes, she couldn't be anyone else. Maia couldn't see exactly what was happening, but she worried she was being outflanked. It probably didn't matter because Maia was Leadership and the new king was supposed to be in Alignment. Still, she preferred to have the upper hand even when she didn't need it. Graceful wins were better than messy ones.

Introductions were made. Dishes were enjoyed. Small talk was had. Susana sat at the table with Maia, the same way Estevan sat with Marvao. Apparently, the young man had a useful position in city government working under the minister. They must have judged disaster planning and the rebuilding effort to be safe topics, because they went into quite some detail about them and how hard they were working to outsmart the profiteers.

The one time Maia caught a true facial expression from Diana was while Estevan was speaking passionately about some school foundation he headed. Within a year they expected to receive their first apprentice scribes from the school into Plaza Hall. There was a lot packed into that fleeting look: love, pride, relief, hope, and guilt. That was the moment when Maia knew, her mission would drive a wedge into the Odemira family.

So she picked up her wedge and hammered it into the crack.

"Susana," Maia said over the finishing course of jota, "the invoice if you please." Susana produced the roll of parchment and handed it to Maia, who offered it directly to Prince Estevan. "This is the document that brought me here. I'm curious to receive your opinion."

The prince unrolled the parchment, noted immediately the grand royal seal of his father, and began to read with the minister looking over his shoulder. The dowager queen occupied herself with enjoying her jota and watching her son. The prince didn't shout or exclaim or otherwise make grand gestures of displeasure: he kept himself mostly to himself. Most people wouldn't have seen it, but Maia had been at this for a long time. Watching the young man's face was like seeing an onion peel itself layer by layer, all the while trying to pretend it was doing nothing of the sort. The document had even more meaning to him than it did to Maia. Judging from his constantly evolving expressions, it must have explained a great many things.

The minister, on the other hand, just gave a grunt like it simply confirmed what he already knew and sat back down. Estevan slid the parchment to his mother, who did little more than scan it. Maia observed the three of them, waiting for someone to explain. Nobody said anything until the dowager queen gave Minister Marvao the barest of nods.

"DeLanion had enemies," the minister explained, "most obviously the Colares family. They were sabotaging the city in multiple ways, and the disciple took the lead in uncovering all their plots. As far as I'm concerned he should have received at least two notices in the *Luminous Histories* for his work, but he asked for his involvement not to be publicized.

"The Colares family were claws for Duke Cuelar Frenzio of Nurr. They worked at his direction, and the duke was quick to eliminate a Colares whenever we were about to interrogate them."

"Poison," Estevan added, "and fire."

"Then there was Prelate Edmond DeGray," continued the minister. "Edmond spent over a decade turning a decayed temple with a cracked dome into the Basilica of Magnificent Light, but he couldn't have achieved even a fraction of that feat without Cuelar's help. The prelate and the duke were allies, and the prelate did not get along well with Disciple DeLanion. They weren't enemies exactly, but the two of them avoided each other. It's not hard to imagine Cuelar turning Edmond against the disciple: the seeds were already there.

"I have known Cuelar for most of my life, and I assure you he has a singular talent for persuasion and subterfuge. If he convinced the prelate that DeLanion was a threat to his life's work, then the two of them could go to the king and ask for the palace's help in return for a hefty reward. King Joaquim didn't like working with the church, except when he was getting paid. Then he liked it very much. But, the lady Odemira would know more about what happened next."

"It's true," said Diana, "DeGray approached King Joaquim, with Frenzio in attendance. DeGray claimed Leadership put a bounty on DeLanion's head. Frenzio offered his 'help', in the form of a mercenary team he conveniently happened to have on-hand. I was not in attendance, but the king came to me afterwards to manage certain aspects of the task."

"You could have said no, Mother," said Estevan, trying his best to sound conversational but failing. "Didn't it ever occur to you to simply not do it?"

"If you're asking if I would disobey my king, then the answer is no. But I argued against this plan, in the strongest terms. I told him it would weaken the kingdom, that he owed DeLanion a debt, and so on. It was a shockingly bad idea for many reasons, and I told him so. All he could see was the gold. He gave his orders, and I did my duty."

"I don't suppose he fell off a cliff somewhere," the prince said softly, "or tumbled into a river. Body not recovered?"

"My people are better than that," said the former queen, with sympathy. "He was buried well, I promise you, but don't ask me where. The only person who knows the location of DeLanion's grave retired and left the city. She did her duty, but I think the task broke her loyalty."

"Inez," said the prince, without any explanation offered for Maia's benefit. The queen simply nodded in response.

"You should know most of the rest from our report," said the minister. "Obviously, the palace never received payment, which prompted the invoice."

"What report?" asked Maia, sensing a pattern.

"We compiled a full report of all the events of that night and sent it to Unity City. We assumed," said Estevan irritably, "Leadership would care that a disciple was attacked and had disappeared. Are you telling me you didn't bother to read it before coming here?"

"We've had very little from Girona all through the fall and winter. And before you bark at me again, young prince," she warned him, "there are a few more facts you should know." Maia told the stunned nobles about the attack against the caravan, the death of Mobeen, and the evidence against Lavradio.

"This has my uncle's stink all over it," said Diana with distaste. "He's trying to use the Unity against the king at the same time he's put the city into crisis."

"I need more than speculation and second-hand conversations," Maia told them. "The council was already irritated over DeLanion, but they knew Mobeen and will want revenge for him. If you want to avoid a full recession, we need evidence that anything you've told me is true."

The room was quiet, until Estevan broke the silence with a high lecturing voice. "A set of givens. First, the prelate was convinced of his own importance. Second, the thoughts of such an important man should be recorded daily. Third, the prelate was not a negligent man. Therefore, the prelate kept a diary. We should read that."

"It's almost like he's still with us," the minister said wistfully. "The more annoying parts of him, anyway."

On Kasryn's advice, she and Maia attended evening services together with their various guards and attendants and assistants. They took the last service of the evening, the one meant for devout families who worshiped together after dinner. Again the sanctuary was nearly full. Maia had traded her Leadership robes for a nice civilian outfit so she could stand among merchants and minor nobles unremarked. As before, the worshipers were mixed: clerks and craftsmen and working families next to merchants and minor nobility, greeting each other across the supposedly rigid social lines of Lavradio.

"This service isn't quite like the others," Kasryn murmured to Maia as they stood at the edge of the sanctuary. "You see the that tall, thick-skinned family, with the gorgeous mother? They're the Tabuas. He called them family." Maia could only assume they were talking about DeLanion, again. "There's the city minister and the auditor prince. They rescheduled the palace train so they could attend this service every night. You can see they brought most of the auditors. The striped-haired girl is the minister's daughter Zanda, and the auditor next to her is the next Baron of Fringe. They're recently married. They taught him to play netball. See that clutch of

161

old tradesmen, talking to Fringe? They're from the unions. He did occasional day-work as a union man. Now they want to repair the plaza fountain this spring and dedicate it to him."

Kasryn continued to scan the sanctuary as it slowly filled up. This service seemed to be on a looser schedule than the others, to give everyone some time to socialize. "The man with the elegant tail is Alex Ramada, who had three of his fingers regrown. There's the Sabrosa wives: very rich importers. They have a daughter who was his bed-friend, but I haven't seen her in a while. About a third of everyone here was healed by him at some point. The glamorous woman in silk is a matron from the labyrinth. The women talking to her and laughing? They used to work in his factory, making soap and poultices."

"So they all come here at the same time just to remember their missing disciple?" asked Maia.

"Not exactly. Having him in common made it easy for them to worship together. But then something happened. You'll see."

The two of them stuck to the edge of the sanctuary closest to the administrative wing, participating in the short service. It was all entirely normal until the closing benediction, which was sung by the worshipers instead of being recited by the priest. It was the same song Maia had heard through the sanctuary doors that morning. Maia couldn't sing along because she didn't know the tune, but the effect was unmistakable: her fatigue from the day lifted. As she looked around for the practitioner, she felt the love and hopes of the people around her. Like the prayer said, there was no darkness so deep they couldn't face it together.

Shaken, she looked up at the Fragment high above the congregation but the blessing wasn't coming from there. It was coming from everywhere, all at once. It was a nice feeling, but Maia had come to bring judgement and discipline to these people, not to be one of them. Staring up at the dome was making her light-headed, and her heart began to race. Her knees shook and she had to reach out to her assistant for support. As soon as the service was over Maia retreated to the prelate's ground-floor office, aided by Susana. They found her a chair where she could sit and put her head between her knees.

"What's happening?" she asked the floor. "What happened to me?"

"You resisted a powerful benediction," said Kasryn from above her. "Which was pointless, by the way. The effects are temporary if you're only blessed once in a while, so you should have just accepted it and saved yourself the trouble."

"I didn't see a disciples," Maia said between breaths. Priests and healers couldn't give benedictions with any real power. Only a disciple could do that.

"There wasn't one. And it didn't come from the Fragment, either. As long as you have enough people and an anointed priest singing along, the song works. Most services in Girona are like that now. It's spreading to other cities, too."

Kasryn put a goblet of something alcoholic on the floor between Maia's feet, but she didn't feel like she could sit upright to drink it without fainting.

"What? Kasryn, what's happening in Lavradio?"

"What's happening?" she repeated, sounding incredulous. "People are worshiping daily, making the temple a central part of their lives. They gather together no matter their wealth or rank. Even the king worships here on the odd eighth day and sings the same as anyone else. Olyon's power is manifested in the lives of his people. It's only a matter of time until temples in Gallia and Ullidia do the same."

"You mean this is spreading?" Maia gasped.

Kasryn sighed. "After all these years talking about it, I'm a little shocked. I really thought you would recognize Alignment when you saw it."

"See that she drinks that," Kasryn told the servants, "it will help. And get her to bed soon. The guardian has had a very long day."

By the next afternoon, Guardian Maia found herself in a room with a mass murderer. He didn't look like a mass murderer: he was a bald, affable looking man in once-fashionable speaker attire now threadbare and billowing around the prisoner's thinning frame. Bright blue eyes twinkled in the convict's intelligent face. Calloused skin around his wrists spoke of the frequent trips out of prison in shackles to give advice to Plaza Hall.

Six months ago Jojo Serta had been running the largest, and deadliest, real estate scam of the century on behalf of the Colares family. These days he offered his cunning in exchange for better accommodations. He had his own cell, enough fuel to stay warm, and enough food to avoid hunger. Best of all, from Jojo's point of view, he occasionally had something to whet his mind against. As long as Plaza Hall kept bringing him suspected grifts and cons, he didn't much care that he was in prison. He could have used a new set of clothes, however.

Although a convicted fraudster and mass poisoner, Jojo was in Plaza Hall because the prelate's diary had yielded some unwelcome surprises. It claimed that King Joaquim had threatened to destroy the basilica if DeGray didn't hand over gold on a regular basis. The king then killed DeLanion because the boy found out about the extortion. Aside from being simply unexpected and unwanted, the story went against the old king's character. According to those who knew him best, Joaquim was too unimaginative to come up with such a scheme and too lazy to risk angering Unity in the process.

With the investigation at an impasse between the dead prelate's diary and the dowager queen's testimony, Minister Marvao suggested they bring in an expert. To spot a con, hire an accomplished con artist.

The interview room was nearly bare: a bright light of spirit arts, courtesy of Edos; a table and chair, occupied by Jojo Serta; two chairs against the wall, occupied by peacekeepers. On the table between Maia and Jojo were stacks of boards, packed into a covered box with leather loops for carrying handles. Estevan had insisted the box was important.

"Mister Serta," she began.

"Please call me Jojo," interrupted the prisoner, gesturing in his manacles. "As you can see, I'm not a mister anything any more." He spoke to her like he had been invited to tea.

"In front of you is a diary," she continued, resisting his attempts at friendliness. "Some of the entries may be forgeries. Your task is to identify the false entries, if they exist. These two men will observe you, to ensure you do not damage or misplace any of the boards."

"The box is for your benefit, isn't it?" Jojo offered her a conspiratorial smile, which she declined to return. "You know which entries you want to be fake, and don't want to tip me off, is that it? The Outlander Double-Blind routine."

"It was Auditor Estevan's idea," she told him.

"And he learned it from Outlander." He rubbed his hands together, making the chains rattle. "The minister brings me the most interesting things. I'll get started, shall I?"

When she didn't leave immediately, he continued to stare at her and refused to open the box.

"I've been a confidence man all my life," he finally said in beautiful, buttery tones. "If you so much as glance at the part of the diary you're hoping is false, I'll know. If you avoid looking at it, I'll know. Those who know the answer cannot be present for the test. You have to leave before I start or the results are compromised. After all, this matter is very important isn't it?"

Maia reluctantly turned to leave. "Watch him," she said to the guards.

Maia made her way back to the Map Room, where Auditor Estevan (as the prince was known in Plaza Hall) and his team were working on their massive map of Girona. The space was large enough to host a ball, but the floor was covered in square slates. Every lot in the city had its own slate, with key data chalked on the front and back. The squares were arranged according to their position in the city, topped with gambling tokens to represent the number of residents, jobs, and recent taxes paid. At at glance she could see where people lived, where they worked, and where most of the money in the city was being made. Wells, public carriage routes, and other important features had their own tokens in the city.

Down the hallway from them, on the far side of Plaza Hall, the building was blackened and collapsed from the recent fire. All of the city's records on property ownership and taxes were destroyed. The Map Room was the city's only record for vital information.

As Maia watched, the slates' contents were being copied one by one into new ledgers. Auditors and archivists worked in pairs to prevent mistakes and unauthorized changes. Maia and the peacekeepers detailed to guard the room were relegated to specific areas outlined in red, again to prevent unauthorized changes or damage to the slates.

A few enterprising citizens had already tried to take advantage of the situation by presenting false documents to the records clerks, claiming ownership of what was not properly theirs. Their attempts had failed, thanks to the map room, and they quickly found themselves in jail. The auditors fully expected more such attempts.

An archivist entered the room, to tell Maia and Estevan that Jojo had finished his task.

Guardian Maia, Sister Susana, Auditor Estevan, and Minister Marvao gathered in the interview room with Jojo. The peacekeepers had been sent out of the room for this discussion. Jojo had three stacks of boards in front of him, almost evenly high, and a smug look on his face.

"That was fast, Jojo," said Auditor Estevan, "what did you find?"

"What did I tell you about spotting forgeries, Auditor Estevan?"

"Look at the materials," responded the prince, apparently not offended at being lectured by an infamous criminal. "The wood and ink all seemed the same to me."

"Look at the materials *from all sides*," emphasized Jojo. He rotated each of the three stacks one quarter turn. "Tell me what you see now." The edges of the boards had been almost perfectly uniform in color, but from the new angle there was a clear discrepancy. In the third stack there were two bands of lighter color.

Once they had had a good look, Jojo deftly separated out the offending entries and presented them with a flourish. "Are these the entries you were looking for?"

Maia could confirm with a glance they were the damning entries, the ones that claimed King Joaquim had tried to extort money from Prelate DeGray. Her heart both rose and fell at the same time: Lavradio had not decided on its own to kill a disciple, but a high Unity official had. The queen dowager's account was most likely the truth, and her king had been too blinded by the offer of gold to check the authenticity of what he thought was a request from Leadership. Duke Frenzio was probably, but so far unprovably, the mastermind behind the boy's death.

"Tell us everything you've learned," demanded Estevan, as if what they had wasn't enough.

"These are not your typical clackers. They are quite thin, very fine grained, and smoothed to a nice softness on both sides. Of course a man of the late prelate's great distinction would only commit his private thoughts to fine materials and only use one side. Every day as he sat down to write, the prelate pulled a board from stock that he's had for a long time, but the forger bought new boards in an attempt to match them. The end grains all look the same because they darken with age quickly, but the side grains darken much more slowly. When you look at the stack from the long-grain side, the age difference is apparent as a lighter color on the new boards.

"The ink DeGray used was also very high quality, but ordinary. That is, until he received the Fragment from Outlander. Then, the prelate started mixing in black mica powder to give his writing a little extra sparkle. I doubt you can see the difference except in sunlight and," he pointed meaningfully at the light above them, "spiritual light. The forgeries lack the mica."

"Do you have anything besides materials," asked Estevan?

"The writing," said Jojo with an approving smile, "is very good. The line height, the slant of the letters, even the voice are the same. But the forger had a weakness." He pointed to an unusual letter combination, "see these three letters here?"

All three of his audience peered closely at them in turn.

"I don't see anything wrong with them," the minister declared.

"Now, look at the other examples, in his other entries." Jojo passed around a couple of selected boards.

"The prelate runs the three letters together," Maia noticed. "Every time?"

"Every time I've found so far," confirmed Jojo. He pointed out a few more discrepancies, where the forger's letters looked identical to the late prelate's but, on closer inspection, the brush had moved in the opposite direction.

"We can also infer a little about the person you're looking for," added the prisoner. "You're looking for someone close enough to the prelate to know where he keeps his diary, but not someone with unrestricted access to his supplies. The forger would have used the priest's own boards and ink if he could have, but had to buy new materials instead. The forger also has a collection of letters from DeGray's own hand, but not enough of them to sample all his idiosyncrasies. I suspect your mastermind had to be selective about which samples he could give to a hired forger.

"So the forger was hired, by a friend or conspirator of the prelate" Jojo concluded. "The forger was themselves not a secretary or protege who worked every day in same space as the prelate."

"Thank you Jojo," said Auditor Estevan, directing his staff to pack up the diary. "While I have you here, let's talk about how people are likely to try and take advantage of the archives situation."

Maia and the minister left Estevan to his interrogation and retreated to the minister's office.

The city minister was visibly relieved. "Guardian Maia, may we report to King Leonardo that Joaquim was deceived and Lavradio will not be subject to a recession?"

"Unofficially, you may. Officially, it's time to arrange our first formal meeting."

"There is a writing desk, with everything you need. And, I'm keeping a royal runner on standby so your message will be received promptly." Maia wrote her request for an audience, and Susana produced the council seal from her bag. It was a relief to have one big uncertainty out of the way.

There was still a lot of work to be done. It would take weeks for all the reports to be written and copies made. There were details to be verified and several open issues to be addressed. Most of that could be handled by Susana and the ambassador's staff, working with their counterparts from the palace.

The king could now focus his attention on the rebellious Duke Frenzio. Leonardo would almost certainly try to pull the church into his conflict with the duke. Maia needed to decide if the church should go along with it, or not.

From Maia's point of view, the most troubling matter now wasn't Lavradio's retired king or the Duke of Nurr. She was most worried about Leadership's mail service. Someone was selectively intercepting messages from Lavradio, and she needed to find them.

Lavradio, Royal Palace

"So now that we know what happened to DeLanion, what do we do about Frenzio?" The small audience chamber held King Leonardo and Queen Larava, Marshal of Armies Earl Aleutis, Minister of State Lolanda, and Prince Estavan. Estevan wouldn't normally be included in a meeting at his level, but he knew more about Duke Frenzio's actions within Girona than anyone else in the room. The Unity Church was represented by Guardian Maia and Ambassador Kasryn. A gaggle of secretaries and functionaries for both sides filled in the edges of the room.

Most of the room was focused on Maia, because everyone wanted to know what the church's position would be. In theory the Unity Church could rally a multinational response if it wanted to. In practice, convincing nations to commit armies to another country's civil conflict was complicated. It was also expensive, in all sorts of ways.

Maia let Kasryn speak for her. That was the woman's job.

"The Alignment forbade nations from changing borders by force, and it has been a tradition for the Unity to become involved in those sorts of conflicts. However, the Treaty of Alignment does not apply to internal conflicts. The church can not involve itself in every dispute between warring nobles in the same state.

"As much as it pains us to leave the deaths of two disciples unavenged, their deaths were incidental to your own internal politics. And it is Unity policy not to interfere with internal matters. Doing so now would invite future requests for us to intervene in the internal affairs of other countries, or even invite attacks against our people under false colors. It is also unclear to us how you will resolve your current situation with Nurr.

"That said," the ambassador sighed dramatically, "we are convinced of his involvement with DeLanion's death. Leadership will advise practitioners to avoid the Duchy of Nurr, and will not assign anyone there for the foreseeable future."

Aleutis, a man with thick pointed horns and a short fur over most of his body, spoke with a rumbling voice. It was like listening to a sack of rocks. "What about aid, if there is fighting between the crown and Frenzio. If we had some disciples then we wouldn't need foreign armies."

"That would count as interfering, Marshal Aleutis." Kasryn's denial was firm. "We can provide minimal healing, ten kilometers behind the front lines." That was the standard "aid" the church offered to all sides of state conflicts. They performed the healing required to preserve life, but the wounded had to travel several kilometers to get it. Many soldiers and civilians died on their way to the field hospitals, and those who arrived alive were often left with scars or disabilities because of the limited healing. It was a policy that let the church claim the mantle of mercy while keeping their own people safe and the cost of conflict high. It was Leadership's position that if enemies could fight with minimal casualties, they would fight more instead of less.

"Thank you, Ambassador Kasryn. Guardian Maia. You have made the church's position clear." The two church women bowed their heads slightly in the Unity manner and filed out of the room with their aides in tow. After the Unity representatives were gone, Leonardo addressed Minister Lolanda. "Have we heard from the duke?"

"We have. His response to your summons was this." She handed over a piece of parchment that appeared to be blank, except for the ducal seal. The new king looked at the parchment, turned it over to see if anything was written on the reverse side, then turned it over again and looked at the seal.

"I see," he said, and passed the parchment to Marshal Aleutis. The marshal glanced at the seal and passed it on to Estevan, who had his turn then handed it to an aide to ferry to the queen. What caught all their attention was the ducal seal of Nurr, an arkto standing on its hind legs accompanied by various other heraldic elements. Surmounting the seal was a crown, which was a forbidden heraldic device to all but the king.

"So is this a coup or a secession?" asked Estevan.

"Secession," said the king, "or he would have used the Lavradio seal. That doesn't mean we should believe him. He might change his mind and want the rest of the country."

"Your answer has to be the same either way," the marshal declared. "A king that won't keep his country together won't remain king for long."

"It still makes a difference," interjected Estevan. "Knowing his ultimate goal matters."

The marshal nodded. "Nurr has damaged all the roads between itself and the central region. As of a few days ago they started turning away merchants and other traffic. It began as soon as he received the summons. Frenzio seems to believe he can be self-sufficient, or run all his trade through the north road to Moldonia."

"They can't feed themselves," said Lolanda. "Maybe in a very good year they could supply all their own food, but they need trade. That's a weakness we should be able to exploit."

"What is the disposition of our army?" asked the king.

"Degraded," admitted the marshal. He had taken the job from his predecessor just a few weeks ago, but he was still responsible for the state of the army and didn't like giving bad news. Much of that bad news actually came from Prince Estevan's analysis of personnel records. "For months, Nurrish soldiers have been returning home instead of reenlisting, and recruitment hasn't kept pace. Nearly all Nurrish officers resigned in the last months of the previous reign. Regular forces are only a fifth under quota, but our officer corps is down by a third, and elites are down nearly half from where they should be."

"And they all work for Frenzio now," finished the king. "How long will it take to rebuild our ranks?"

"Years, to do it properly. You can train a new soldier in six months, three if you hurry. But then all you have is a green soldier. Your Majesty, what you're suggesting is we should maintain the old army size based on a smaller population. That will create some new difficulties."

Leonardo shook his head at the mess they were in. They needed to retake their own land, and the defenders would be their own ex-troops. Because of the troop loss they didn't have enough to invade Nurr, so they would have to rebuild their forces. They had the added burden of needing to buy food from other countries just to get through the winter. It was astonishing that Duke Frenzio had compromised their war fighting so badly before hostilities were declared.

"Hold the previous marshal for questioning, and perform a search of the military archives. Find out if anyone noticed what was happening, and how it never came to the attention of Joaquim. Arrest Juliana Frenzio, and hold her in the Tower of Regrets. If Frenzio does not come to heel, her life is forfeit. In fact, take all of the Nurrish nobles in residence and put them into the tower."

The Tower of Regrets was an entirely ordinary tower, used as a prison to hold nobles accused of crimes or, like Juliana, official hostages. The entire point of having nobles or their heirs reside in the palace for one third of the year was precisely for this reason: in the event of a rebellion they became instant hostages. When Duke Frenzio rebelled while leaving Juliana in the capital as his designated heir, he had knowingly forfeited her life. Killing her would serve no useful purpose, yet that was the most likely outcome for her now.

"There are very few Nurrish nobles here in winter," observed Lolanda. "Only five. And two of those are adopted from branch families. The rest are third or fourth children."

Estevan, a third child himself, looked queasy. "Disposables. Why didn't they just recall them?"

The marshal looked grim. "That would have been noticed."

The young king, only a few weeks into his rein, found himself facing a civil war and the prospect of executing nobles. It wasn't at all what he had imagined he would be doing.

"Frenzio has revealed himself as an enemy, so let's start treating him like one: we don't need to follow the same legal policies with respect to him now. Strike him and his descendants from the noble register. Let the people know he's responsible for Burning Night, and the deaths of Mobeen and DeLanion. Get me better intelligence from inside Nurr." The king waved them out impatiently.

Everyone but Queen Larava and a few guards left.

"It's about what we expected," he told his queen, "but it's still hard to believe the church is going to shrug off two notable deaths. If a normal country lost two of their best they'd invade for revenge."

"Leadership's concern is to keep the first families happy, and the first families want the church to survive with themselves at the top. The outcome of this affair doesn't matter to them, so why should they stick their necks out?"

Larava put a hand on her husband's arm. "Leo, I know you're still angry at your mother for what she did, but she's loyal and she's competent. We are blind in Nurr without her network."

"She murdered a boy without cause."

"At the command of her king. And she told you about it the day you ascended. She didn't try to hide it from you. She thought it was the most important thing to tell you on your ascension, and she was right. Compared to most of your step-father's helpers, she's outstanding. Can you really afford to leave her on the sidelines right now?"

"I'll consider it."

Farava smiled. That phrase usually meant she was going to get her way.

Guardian Maia was thorough. By the time she was done with an incident it was clear what had happened, why it had happened, and the conditions under which it might happen again. That meant gathering statements and reports.

The old king would not himself testify. It wasn't that he objected to questioning, but he was off hunting somewhere. They had to question his secretary, then have that statement endorsed by Joaquim whenever he bothered to showed his face again.

Maia sent Quinton on that unpleasant errand, tracking down the old king and making him sign and seal the parchment. Ultimately the old king, now the new Earl of Arrantes, agreed to sign only if Quinton would give him a bout. It seemed Joaquim didn't give one bit about the mayhem his errors had caused, but was happy to get pummeled by an expert swordsman. The former king got his bruises, and Quinton got the man's signature.

The auditor prince was much more helpful. The city's reports filled in all of the details around DeLanion's assassination, including the links to Frenzio. Prince Estevan seemed to know everything that was happening in the capital city, down to which ale house the Red Fang mercenaries liked to frequent.

Maia could have filed her final report without the endorsement of anyone else. She was, after all, trusted enough to be the council's investigator. But having the sign-off of the current king and Disciple Lucia added credibility, so she made use of them. The king was no real trouble. He took a few days to read the final report and then gave his endorsement.

To get the matrix's endorsement, Maia had to visit the DeLanion School of Math, Scripture, and Music. The buildings were simple structures, piled up from the same bricks as the adjacent bricktown slums. With Lucia's health fading, her husband Mika gave the tour so she could save her fading energies for the one class she taught each day.

Art students' ages ranged from eight to thirty, all of them candidates. They were less than candidates: some of them were only just beginning to learn to read. And yet Lucia had them spending time every day reciting the simpler prayers and learning to apply their spirit.

Her teaching guide seemed to be a scribbled set of exercises left behind by DeLanion himself: nonsensical to Maia but apparently meaningful to anyone practiced in the arts. The local healers, who aided Lucia in tutoring the candidates, assured her the training regimen was far better than anything they had received in Enclave.

The strangest sight was the game room, which Mika showed off with pride. It was a large room with wide tables covered in hexagonal grids. Students from both the arts and scribe classes gathered around two players, with short stacks of boards in front of them. Some boards were lined up, face up, featuring elaborate drawings and rows of letters and numbers. Tokens were placed on the grid, being moved about in turns.

For any two players there were several spectators.

"We call it Monster Hunt," Mika told her, "and as you can see it is very popular. Each board defines a monster, disciple, bulwark, implement, and so on. Players deploy them to defeat each other. One side plays for the monsters, the other plays for the disciple. It's so popular we have to limit the hours of play."

Some of the table sections had more than just hexes on them: they featured terrain as well. As they watched, a teenager's disciple and four-man bulwark was losing against a nine-year-old's swarm of monstrous rabbits.

"What happened here, Nicolas?" Mika sounded amused.

"I let myself get lured into the open. I'm going to lose some bulwark unless I get lucky."

"This is interesting," said Maia, "but are you sure this is how your students should be spending their time? Shouldn't they be practicing their reading?"

"To play they have to read, add, and subtract. They have to learn the use of different prayers, budget their spirit, and understand the needs and abilities of monsters. The game mechanics are based on some of DeLanion's ideas, but I assure you the materials are based on years of experience. It's very educational. I'll give you an example. Molly, what should Nicolas have done differently?"

"He should have waited," said the girl. "Monster bunnies have to eat a lot. If he had stayed behind the village palisade then I would have to come to him by the next day. He would have had the advantage."

Nicolas seemed to disagree. "An attack on the village gets civilians killed, though."

"Maybe it gets people killed, maybe not," reasoned the girl. "But out here? This is a fight you can't win. And after I nourish my bunnies on the blood of your bulwark, the village is all mine."

"The scenario is based on a real town," Mika told the guardian. "Every year they have blooms of these rabbits. They've learned the hard way to fight from behind their palisade".

Back in the rectress' office Maia didn't bother to hide her doubts. "Why are you teaching them spirit work," asked Maia, "before they can properly read?"

Lucia, in her wheeled chair, turned her clouded gaze on Maia. "Because the one has nothing to do with the other. Many people read without having any talent for the spiritual arts. Talent for the arts appears even if one does not know how to read. Taylor's talent was manifest before he knew anything about our language at all."

"You really think you can make practitioners out of them?"

"I do," insisted the rectress seriously. "You seem doubtful."

"It's just .. They're all so ..." Maia stopped herself. Nearly all of the church's disciples came from first families, for whom religion was the family trade. They learned at least the alphabet before stepping into a school of any kind. They entered Enclave's art school at fourteen to sixteen years of age, when they could pass tests in literacy. Most of the Girona students wouldn't have the wherewithal to get over that high bar. Some of them weren't even children. Was Lucia planning to send a thirty-year-old to art school?

"Too poor?" suggested the matrix. "Too old? Too far removed from Enclave? Insufficiently cultivated in the ways of the church?"

"Yes, to all of it," Maia said irritably. There. Now it was said. "It isn't polite to say so, because we're supposed to 'love without borders', but they will never pass muster with the school."

The rectress continued to press the guardian, patiently. "Why not? Taylor's first scholarships went to a pair of teenagers straight out of bricktown, and they were coming along very well until the palace drove them out of town. If they had had the luxury of three whole years to learn, they could have passed the entrance exams to be bulwarks, or even priests. With ease."

"Finding a few people with a knack for scholarship is one thing," agreed Maia, "but talent for the arts..."

"... can appear anywhere, and should not be lightly wasted." Lucia was growing emphatic. "Every art student here is a disciple-class talent. These eyes of mine don't see the way yours do any more, but I still have the gift of seeing the light of the spirit. There is more in Lavradio to be found, much more if we only look."

"But the first families," complained Maia.

"Have grown complacent and entitled!" Lucia practically spat the words. "They laud the talent of their children but fight, fang and claw, to keep them in Enclave. We don't train nearly enough practitioners as it is, and many we do train can't be deployed. These students," she gestured in the direction of the school, "have no expectation of being coddled. They expect to work for their place, to serve others with their light. We need them, far more than we need another useless generation of self-satisfied legacies."

The speech seemed to have winded the matrix. It occurred to Maia then that the disciple's actions on Burning Night had broken her, and now she was fading into her final days. Maia wondered if she had known, when she set that barrier, that it was the last serious working of spirit she would ever make. Did she know she was dooming herself and leaving her husband behind?

"That's not very tactful, Matrix Lucia."

"I'm out of time for tact. The church is in crisis, guardian. Any active disciple knows it's true. Dark monster attacks were up again last year, yet we fielded fewer disciples than we lost. We're losing."

"We've trained them at a steady rate," Maia tried to argue.

"But the monsters aren't steady, are they? There's more every year. And half the disciples we train are never fielded. A disciple without works is just a priest who reads well. We need working, fighting practitioners who live to share their light, not sit at home in Enclave bragging about how they have so much of it."

"I hope you're not putting that in your reports."

"What would it matter? Nobody reads them!"

"You truly intend to raise disciples, here. With scribes and musicians down the hall."

"Until they're ready for Art School, yes. When the time comes, you will find the novices from Girona to be superior."

"You're next to a slum! Your temple is tiny. Your buildings are ugly. Your students are poor."

"Irrelevant," said a tired Lucia. "Not a single bit of that matters. Character, talent, and training are relevant.

Everything else can be thrown away. The only thing we need that we don't have is a great arts teacher, for an extended assignment."

"I'm not giving you Garsharp or Leila. We're using Leila, and Garsharp is into some useful research right now. Assignments will never agree."

"I'm not asking for them. I want Phillip the Younger."

"Who?" Now the guardian was truly confused. Disciples were few in number, and Maia thought she knew the names of all the notable ones living.

"He's a wilderness find of Garsharp's. He is as superior as DeLanion was. Garsharp says he will make a great teacher."

"I'm not on the Assignments Committee," Maia reminded the matrix.

"But you are on special interdiction, so you can order it. We've had superb results teaching from DeLanion's notes, but the students will benefit from a strong spirit user to guide them. It will put them well ahead of most students entering the Arts School."

"You're breaking a lot of unwritten rules, Lucia. You're talking about sending students to their entrance exams barely literate but already trained to apprentice level. That is not the way it is done."

"The way things are done is failing us. Catastrophically. Anyone who reads *Histories* and counts would know this. Which is why I want a talented wilderness disciple. He won't have preconceptions about what the school should be like. He will train the students he's given."

The conversation had tired Lucia so much, her voice was reduced to a whisper. "Maia, we're out of time. We need them as fast as we can make them. And we have to make them better. The first families have failed us. They've done worse than fail us: they've doomed us. We have to change. Now."

"If I requisition your disciple I can't guarantee he'll come. You know how difficult disciples are."

Lucia nodded. "He'll come, but he's mendicant. We have to find him first."

"Fine. Now endorse my report."

Mika walked Maia out toward her waiting appalon, with Sirs Quinton and Altheas a few paces behind. Maia kept her pace slow, to favor the older man.

"I'm sorry to see her so badly off, Brother Mika. I heard about Burning Night, and what she did."

"Thank you. She's been fragile for years, but now it's only a matter of time before her spirit fails completely. That's why she's so desperate. This is her last chance to put things on the right track, and make sure there are enough disciples to protect the faithful."

"So you believe in these dire predictions about the future, that the monsters are going to overrun us? We've been hearing about this from some disciples for years now, but the Governance Committee isn't concerned."

Mika clasped his hands behind his back as he walked in a classic lector pose. With his white hair and priestly vestments, he could have just stepped out of Enclave's Art School. "It's not really a matter for believing or disbelieving. It's a matter of doing one's homework."

"Homework," repeated the guardian, skeptically.

The priest nodded, and leaned towards her confidentially. "As you are a Guardian you can delegate this homework. I promise not to tell."

"And what is this homework?"

"Reading and counting," he said. "Read *Luminous Histories* backwards. Year by year, count the number of monster encounters and dark monster encounters. Count the disciple anointments, deaths, and the number of active disciples. Go back at least ten years, or better yet go to twenty."

"I get the annual summaries on my desk," she said, annoyed now.

"But have you looked at them, side by side, spanning a decade?" He didn't press her, but just walked with her half way across the little campus. The numbers he was talking about were buried in a larger report, which found its inevitable end as kindling when the new annual report arrived. The library kept copies, but nobody would dig in the archives for every annual report for the last twenty years.

The older man held the appalon's bridle for her while she mounted, giving the beast an affectionate rub along the nose.

"Did you know that fifty years ago there were no cursed monsters? It had been so long since the last sighting, people thought they were myths. When they started appearing again, nobody would believe it. For the year just ended, the count will be in the teens. It's all in the *Luminous Histories*. You just need to read and count." He released the bridle and stepped back, so the appalon could rise from kneeling to standing.

Doubtful, Maia and her guard rode back to the basilica.

"Ah," said Kasryn when Maia brought it up with her that night, "you want the yearlies. Don't let the old man con you into reading the histories yourself, it's deadly boring if your name isn't in it. I quit after two years. Some scholarship students did all the annual summaries as a project, going back fifty years. They're in the crypt, a permanent part of our collection now. I'd say 'enjoy yourself'," she added while pouring brandy into a pair of tiny glazed cups, "but it's grim stuff."

Once again, Lavradio was putting Maia off her stride. It seemed like this assignment was just made of surprises. "It sounds like you think Matrix Lucia is right, about us running out of disciples. Why is this the first time we're talking about it?"

"You're leadership," Kasryn said simply. "I assumed you knew. Your lot is in charge of governance and long-term plans, right?"

"I'm not on Governance," complained Maia, "or Education or Assignments. I fix problems and clean messes."

"Then this should be up your alley." Kasryn toasted her. "The faithful getting eaten by monsters is a big, dirty problem."

DODONA

Gallia, Tegea

The night before the solstice ball, Hylee House was awakened by a pounding on the front door. Patrix Primos had come with a messenger, sweaty and cold from a long ride. The final climb up to the house had almost been too much for the woman.

Too winded to speak, she handed over a sealed leather pouch containing several boards. Taylor brought her into his sometimes-drawing room and read through the stack while Livia served jota. Her son Atticus warmed up some leftover dinner. Primos waited quietly to learn the news.

The first board was a plea for help: the town of Dodona was afflicted with giant toads. It sounded funny at first, but the largest of them could swallow a man whole. Normally a squad of soldiers or professional hunters could handle a problem like that, but among the toads was a cursed monster.

The remaining boards were drawings and detailed reports. The cursed toad had eaten several men and much livestock. Now, it squatted in the center of town. Darkness surrounded it most of the time. Weapons broke against its skin. Those who touched it with bare skin and survived suffered from poison.

Most citizens had evacuated the town, and many of them were coming to Tegea.

"Will you come," asked the messenger? In spite of her anxious expression she had waited until he was done reading to ask.

"Of course I will come," Taylor said off-handedly. "It's only one cursed creature, and only as big as a house."

"Patrix," he continued more seriously, "I think you should wake the alderwoman and arrange a welcome for the refugees." Taylor handed him the message bag, minus the detailed report on monster behavior. "Maybe she can round up some carts to go out and pick them up, so they don't have to walk the whole way."

"We'll take care of them, disciple."

"Atticus, prepare Ben with the pre-packed bags and four days worth of those oat cakes. I can't be sure I'll find feed for either of us where we're going." The oat cakes in question were good for mounts and people.

Atticus, following the patrix's lead, gave him a "yes disciple" and set about his work with energy.

"Livia," he began.

"I'll take care of the messenger," she said serenely, "and Fabia will pack you some real food. The disciple should have something besides animal feed."

"Thank you. I'd also like you to send Carl to Penguin Workshop and wake the spiny-haired cousins who live there. Mila and Milo. If they're up for the work, they can muster at the depot."

Inside thirty minutes Taylor was dressed, armored, armed, packed, loaded, provisioned, and on the road. That time of night, when the land and sea were the same temperature, the air was still. Crevist lit the world in its ghostly light as Ben paced easily to the far edge of town where the depot building stood, its only visitors two teens waiting next to their appalons.

Taylor, Mila, and Milo found refugees south of the tidal flats, landward of the road, making a miserable camp of three hundred souls crouched among a stand of gnarled and windswept pines. Several approached Taylor, so he made light to greet them.

"We meet in the Light," said a middle-aged woman.

"Let's walk as brothers," said Taylor, "I am Disciple Phillip the Younger. I offer you my aid."

"We have little to offer," said the woman, "but we're glad you're here. My name is Sandra. I guess you could say we're all refugees from Dodona."

"I'll help you with shelter, and make sure you have water. That should keep you together until carts get here from Tegea to take you north."

"Now just a minute," said a beefy man. Judging from his nose he was a habitual brawler. "If you're heading to Dodona to kill the monster, we can just turn around and go home." The gathering crowd began to look hopeful.

"No." Taylor had to crush that hope quickly, before it took hold. "It could be days before we kill it," he told them, "and there still won't be anywhere to live or anything to eat. Go to Tegea as planned: they're preparing for you. More news will arrive."

"What if we don't to!" shouted the man. "Our whole lives are back there. And who are you to tell us what to do. You're only a child!"

Taylor had Ben kneel and gracefully dismounted animal. Mila and Milo were already on foot, spreading their arms out to make space around the loudmouth, pulling people back from the pending altercation.

"I am a disciple," Taylor said. "I can't order you to do anything, but if you go back to Dodona and get hurt, I won't heal you. I won't fix deliberately stupid mistakes."

The man tried to loom over Taylor and intimidate him. You could almost hear his, "Now see here," preamble. Instead of letting him act out the usual theatrics, Taylor touched him and he collapsed. A few seconds later he began to snore, loudly.

"Much better," Taylor said with satisfaction.

For the next hour, with the cousins' help, Taylor made enough shelters and water for the people who didn't have any. Mila gathered the seriously wounded for healing. Milo made sure everyone had access to a tent or one of Taylor's earthen huts. Then they moved on.

Dodona was worse than he had feared. The entire center of the village was flattened and smoldering. Half of the town hall stood, and a few other buildings kept one or two of their walls. The rest of the town center was rubble.

The fires, Taylor learned, were from the corpses of the few giant toads the locals had managed to slay before their cursed king had joined the fight. Setting them on fire had turned in to a hazardous proposition, because the bodies melted and bubbled, then sprayed globules of flaming goo all around.

Dozens of fresh graves were lined up on a hillside cemetery, some filled and others still waiting. The people he could see were moving under the burden of the wounded, the dead, or defeat. Even the dawn air was listless, unmoving, letting the carrion smoke sit on the town brown and stinking.

Taylor found the outpost of soldiers, near a picket line of fifty appalons. They were camped in a cluster of houses at the west edge of town, with a few men stationed on the roofs to keep watch. He made two shelters for his party, one for people and the other for appalons, then went in search of someone in charge. Inside the houses the soldiers were all over the place, on any horizontal surface that could accommodate a sleeping person. Taylor checked the houses until he found one that was being used as a command post. He caught up with a sergeant acting as officer-in-charge, standing on the roof. The sergeant's head and cheeks were blessed with a rich brown fur, long enough to wax and shape into an extravagant wave. The bags under his eyes told Taylor they had marched hard to come here, only to fight and lose against an enemy they had underestimated.

"We meet in the Light," the man said, barely looking at Taylor. "I'm Sergeant Albia."

"Let's walk as brothers," Taylor relied and introduced himself. "Is your commander dead, or sleeping?"

"Sleeping," said Albia, "do you want me to wake him?"

"Let him sleep. He's going to need it." The rooftop was a good location: Taylor had a thorough view of the devastation from there. It was even worse from on high. "From the report I read last night, it didn't seem so awful. What happened?"

"We force marched from Kourion, took fresh appalons from Miletos, and arrived here last night. The alderman told us to wait for a disciple, but Commander Urban ordered the attack last night. He said the toads would be less active at night, so we would have the advantage. We divided into two groups, beaters and the defensive line, but the toads were not afraid of the beaters and instead of running away they attacked. The defensive line tried to close in and support them, but ran into the cursed monster. Fifteen dead. Most of them, we won't get their bodies back."

"What was your plan to deal with the aura of darkness?" Taylor asked him.

"The commander said if we used enough torches..." He let the sentence die with a shrug.

"Yeah, that wouldn't work." Taylor scanned the town. "Where are they now?"

"Buried. Squatting." The sergeant pointed out a few of the toads, which had buried themselves among the rubble with only their eyes and a part of their backs above ground. Once you spotted one it got easier to find the others. Taylor and Albia counted nine.

"The big one doesn't care what happens to the rest," Albia told him. "It didn't start fighting until our line got close. It's in town hall, in the basement we think. There's old storage rooms down there, according to the alderman."

"Where is the alderman? I should speak with him."

"Dead. His son is acting, but he's sleeping this shift." The sergeant shook his head. "These people are so fucked. Even if we kill these things they have no homes to come back to. Pardon my language."

"I would say the evidence supports your sentiment," Taylor told him. "But let's keep their hopes up. We're going to kill the cursed toad and all its lackeys. Then we can figure out where everyone will live."

Albia looked Taylor up and down, at the way he held his spear and wore his stone knife. "Are you sure you can do this? You're not even a mouthful for these things. The dark one could eat ten of you."

"We can do this," Taylor assured him. "You need a light strong enough to drive back its darkness, and weapons that can pierce its skin. I can give you plenty of both, plus protection against poison and physical damage. And you need a better plan. Can I talk to a few more of your people? I want to know how these things fight."

Toads, Taylor learned, hung around together but didn't seem to actively like each other. They congregated like this because once a male found a good source of food it sent a mating call which was answered, in the main, by more males moving into its territory. The males couldn't get too close together without fighting amongst themselves. This activity culminated in large field filled with male toads all waiting to pounce on the first female that came to investigate.

As competitors, a male toad wouldn't come to another's aid unless it felt personally threatened. Its most fearsome weapon was the tongue, which could reach a third of its body's length and snatch a man right off of his feet and swallow him whole. Toads could also crush attackers by jumping at and ramming them. When a monster is large enough all it has to do is land on someone to kill them.

Commander Urban woke with this shift at mid-morning looking like he could use another two full days of nothing but sleep. His men weren't in much better condition, but at least the unit had food and water enough for a few more days.

Acting Alderman Pierson, Commander Urban, Sergeant Albia, Healer Ferange, and several functionaries held their planning meeting the in the kitchen of the appropriated command post.

"You want to experiment?" The commander was not impressed.

"Yes, I want to experiment. I want to give them something to swallow that will be harmful. We make a decoy, cover it in barbed edges, and dangle it in front of the most isolated toad and see if he takes it. If eating one or two stops him from using his tongue then your men can approach within spear range without being swallowed and suffocated.

"This isn't an original idea," Taylor tried to reassure them. "My teacher was Disciple Mobeen. Maybe you know him as Sacred Blade? He recommends the tactic." There were nods around the table. Anyone who studied monsters, even a little, should know the name.

"And if they all attack us again?" asked the alderman.

"We'll be geared up for a full battle, just in case" Taylor reassured them. "I need to enchant your best weapons to pierce the cursed toad. The attackers will have a full stack of blessings for strength, protection, and poison resistance. We can test the idea this afternoon, and if it works we make more for tomorrow."

"What about the darkness," the alderman asked? "That was the worst, being attacked and not being able to see."

"I've taken care of that already." Taylor laid four small silver disks on the table, each with a hole in the center so they could be conveniently tied to a person or an object. Each one shone bright enough to blind everyone present. The company groaned and complained, covering their eyes.

"Tie these to poles and have someone carry them to light the way for everyone else."

The decoys weren't great: they were rather small, were only vaguely humanoid, and Taylor would have preferred longer spikes with more barbs. They were really just a selection of sticks jointed together with rope to form the world's most crude marionettes. He couldn't help but notice they were exactly as large as himself. The rationale was they needed to be small enough to mount on long poles so two people could hold it forward and shake it a bit to bait the toad, but it made him feel like he was the one being dangled in front of monsters.

They picked the most isolated individual and approached, shaking the dummies to entice it. The toad, large as a coach and mostly buried with its eyes closed, didn't seem interested until one of the scouts threw rocks at it. Then the beast exploded from his hiding place and sucked down one of the dummies in in a blink of an eye. It seemed to have trouble managing the awkward treat, but didn't stop trying to swallow it. The baiters withdrew leaving the second team in front with Taylor next to them for protection (it was his idea, after all) and the toad took the second dummy.

That was when things started to get interesting. The toad obviously didn't like it, but kept trying to eat it anyway. The pikers moved in for the kill and pierced it several times in the head and and chest, but it refused to die. The toad leapt directly at some of them and threw them several meters away. The second line of pikemen finally killed it, mainly through blood loss.

On Taylor's orders they dragged the specimen away towards the camp. No other toads seemed to care: less competition for them. Commander Urban came off his rooftop post to shout at them all for such a messy kill, yelling himself blue in the face about how poorly they had performed and didn't know where the vital organs were. The soldiers stood at attention and took the abuse, but after a full two minutes of shouting the commander seemed ready to keep going all evening.

"Excuse me, commander," interrupted Taylor, loudly. He would have preferred literally anyone else put a stop to this but it seemed he was the only one with enough authority. "It looks like these idiots need a remedial course in toad anatomy. Let's dissect the one we have, and show them where the heart and major arteries are. Maybe next time they get it right."

"Sergeant, arrange it."

"Yes Sir!" Sergeant Albia saluted, but the commander was already retreating to his bunk.

"I'm sorry," Taylor said out of the side of his mouth, "for calling your people idiots."

"I get it," Albia said, "and I'll make sure the boys get it, too."

"See if you can pull whoever is left in the village to help with making more decoys. And get some sleep, Albia."

"I'll sleep when you do, sir." Taylor couldn't tell how serious the sergeant was about that, but resolved to get at least six hours if at all possible.

When the sun went down the toad song rose. First just one started trilling, loud enough to vibrate the walls of the command center. A few minutes later a second joined in, harmoniously. Then just as suddenly, all was quiet ... for six seconds. Then a whole chorus started trilling back and forth in a dissonant call and response that shook the dust from the rafters.

The moment the soldiers started to crack jokes about lullabies, the toad king had his say: a rolling avalanche of noise the pealed echoes off the hills. The vitreous humor in their eyes vibrated so badly they couldn't see straight.

Taylor stormed out of his little shelter that he shared with Mila and Milo and shouted a prayer of solitude at the top of his lungs towards the town center. It was the angriest, most impatient recitation of prayer anyone in attendance had ever heard.

Blissful silence reigned once again.

"Hey," yelled some smart-alek, "I was listening to that!"

Like all such battles, the troops were prepared with a benediction, and various enhancements and protections were layered on top of that. Of the eight remaining toads, they were able to isolate six and kill them singly by using the baiting method. Mila and Milo acted as the spears for the first one, to show how it was done, and the next five were taken out entirely by the soldiers.

The last two were close enough to the king toad's hole in the town hall to worry them.

Commander Urban proclaimed, "I will solo the king," while adjusting his sword belt.

"You won't reach its heart with the sword," Sergeant Albia told him, "take one of the enhanced spears, Sir."

"The spear is not a noble's weapon," he sniffed.

Albia looked at Taylor, pleading, and took a little distance. That left Taylor alone with the commander.

"Have you ever killed a cursed monster before?" Taylor asked the commander, not waiting for an answer. "They're huge. It won't matter how good your form is if your blade is too short. I've actually made that mistake, and I was lucky nobody got killed. You can use my spear," Taylor urged the commander. "See how there's no crossbar, and the blade is slightly wider than the shaft? You sink the spear right up to the butt, if that's what it takes to reach the heart. Don't fight solo, and don't fight with a short weapon. There's no honor in dying while trying to look great."

"That's not the noble way," spoke Urban. "Mine will be the name people remember here. Not yours."

"Is that what this is about? I only care about what goes into the *Luminous Histories*. Whatever you put into the reports for Gallia is your problem."

"That's enough," ordered Commander Urban, "I order you to stop interfering."

"I'm not in your chain of command," Taylor reminded him. "But, it's your funeral."

For the last skirmish they broke into three groups: A and B for the toads and C for the cursed toad king. If the king stayed where he was, all well and good. If he joined the battle then the third team would be responsible for intercepting it. Taylor refreshed the enhancements and checked the lights were in place. When all was ready Commander Urban signaled the start.

Teams A and B baited their targets and fed them the dummies while luring them away from town hall. By now the squad knew how to kill them cleanly. Mila and Milo were each attached to a team, but by this time they weren't needed. The toads were killed and their corpses dragged away from the town center.

Waking the king toad didn't seem to get them anywhere at first. The squad had mounted the lights all around the ruined city hall, and started shouting and throwing rocks in the general direction of the king. There was a moment when Taylor feared they would have to dig the monster out of the building's basement, but they were spared the trouble. The remainder of the building collapsed as the entire basement erupted. The true monster on the field crawled up out of the pit. Five meters tall and wreathed in an aura of darkness that visibly wrestled against the light from the enchanted lanterns. Poison glistened damply on its skin.

"Decoys forward," Albia called.

"Delay that order," the commander countered. "Don't interfere!" He drew his sword, saluted his enemy, and charged the cursed toad. With the enhanced speed and strength of Taylor's arts he was able to close the distance in only a second.

The king toad followed Urban with one of its eyes but paid him no mind until the commander stepped into it and stabbed deeply into its body. His aim was true but the reach of the weapon was far short. The toad scuttled sideways a few meters, the kicked-up bricks and rubble scattering over a large area. Commander Urban, suddenly alone and holding his bloody sword, got to take three steps closer to his foe before the toad's two-meter long tongue flicked out and landed on him like a carriage full of bricks. He lost his sword in the shock of the impact, was flattened to the ground beneath the slimy tongue, then got dragged up and away as the king folded its massive appendage back into its mouth.

When a toad swallows it closes its eyes and draws them into its head, to pressurize the sticky spit into a liquid. If they didn't do that, they wouldn't be able to release their prey from the tongue. It took nearly three seconds for the king toad to swallow Commander Urban, during which time the man was pressurized enough to destroy his ear drums.

"Decoys forward," Albia called again. With the commander off the field there was no one to countermand him this time. Three teams of two men, each paired up to dangle a decoy at the end of a long pole, advanced. The jiggled the mannequins, as if they were walking jauntily along the square without a care in the world.

Taylor and Albia nodded to each other, and Taylor said his prayer to be overlooked in rapid syllables. As soon as he moved, Albia lost track of him.

Taylor sped around behind the king toad and waited for its next attack. When it ate the first dummy with a great clattering of wood and tried to swallow it Taylor ran up its sticky noxious back. He found the slight depression well behind the eyes that indicated where the pith should be, and stabbed his spear deeply into it until the head of the spear and fifty centimeters of the shaft had disappeared into the skull. The shaft of the spear snapped in his hands.

The king, in mid-swallow, cocked its head as if it were curious. Taylor had to grab the broken haft with one hand to keep from being thrown. He dropped the remaining shaft with his other hand and drew his stone knife. He had one more strike, or maybe two, before the toad made up its mind and threw him.

Taylor summoned a great deal of spirit and, with the Word of strength spoken in his mind, struck the toad's skull with the pommel of his knife. These were breaking blows, powerful enough to split boulders or break fortifications. At the first hit, the toad king shivered. At the second hit, it slumped forward to rest its face on the ground.

"He's stunned," Taylor called to them. "Finish it off!"

"Sergeant," yelled one of the soldiers, "what's it doing?"

"Keep baiting it! Give the disciple his opening."

"It's not working," another soldier yelled. "He won't move!"

"I pithed it already," Taylor tried to tell them, shouting. "Come kill it!"

"Should we get closer," yelled a third?

Taylor remembered his overlook prayer was still working, and removed it.

"It's Phillip!" shouted one of the men. Cheers went up among the whole detachment.

"It's stunned!" shouted another, "Let's finish it!"

Together, ten of the men (all with enhanced strength) were able to turn the monster onto its side and pierce its heart until all signs of life left it. Quickly, they cut it open using the enchanted blades and excavated their commander. Urban slid out of the toad's innards slimy and burned from the stomach acids. His mouth moved like a gulping fish, filled with a sticky slime that retreated into throat every time he tried to inhale then bubbled out when he tried to exhale. His face was a ghastly blue.

Taylor uttered the shotgun syllables to purge the commander suddenly and violently. Everything inside him that wasn't him was ejected with force, from every orifice, for several seconds. The result looked a lot like the aftermath of Taylor's own unpleasant resurrection. The entire detachment was gathered around the commander, and saw everything.

"Everyone hold tight to your weapons," Taylor warned them, "I'm going to cleanse us all." He said the prayer for cleaning, at normal human speed this time, and used just enough spirit spread over a wide enough area that nobody was knocked off their feet.

Taylor wasn't sure what the sound was that was coming from the Commander Urban, but he might have been crying.

"He has relatives in the House of Lords," Albia explained over lunch. They ate plain soldier's rations, augmented with the last of the town's bread smeared with liberal amounts of Margorie Feller's tidemelon preserves.

"There are open seats right now, and he's desperate to get one. His whole family is political, so if he can't get at least a minor position he'll be considered a failure."

"That's why he acts so asinine," realized Taylor, "he's desperate."

"The local lord is his older cousin," added Pierson. "He requested Urban to lead the extermination, probably as a favor so he could add to his deeds and get his own territory. Of course it's the aldermen who run the towns, but I would pity the citizens stuck with him for a lord."

"Can anyone become a lord?" asked Taylor.

"In theory," Pierson said, "but most seats go to people from well-connected dynasties. There's always a few self-made lords on the benches, so the system is better than Lavradio's."

After lunch, Taylor had no trouble convincing Albia to detail seven soldiers to him. They followed the toads' trail to their origin, a marshy area twelve kilometers to the west, wedged between hills. There weren't any toads left in the marsh, but there were plenty of signs their large bodies had been there, packing the snow and making deep depressions in the ground.

After a few hours of hunting he found what he was looking for: a shallow placer deposit bearing a variety of crystals, near the edge of the marsh. He was able to excavate enough of it to yield a small sack of rough crystals: some with traces of mana in them and others without.

"Is that what you came up here for?" asked a corporal.

"Not exactly," Taylor explained. "I think there's a connection between some minerals and cursed monsters. I'm trying to learn what that is."

"Of course there is," said the corporal. "I could have told you that! If something's valuable, it's dangerous to get. That's your connection right there."

The corporal eyed the young disciple, suspicious of his motives. "So, what are you going to do with those pretty rocks?" he asked.

"After I'm done examining them, I'll find out if they're worth anything. I'll have to turn them over to the local lord, but I'd like to route some money to your fallen."

"Don't let Urban see them," he said without hesitation, "he'll just keep them all for himself."

DANCES

Gallia, Tegea

Thanks to the Dodona incident, the solstice ball was delayed by two weeks while food and lodgings were found for the refugees. The town might be lost permanently. Most of the displaced had decided to move south to Miletos or even farther, to the trade hub that was Kourion. A few would stay in Tegea, especially those cherry-picked by the ever-industrious alderwoman who had a nose for the useful and talented. Taylor used the time to write his report and practice his dancing, since he couldn't sing in public.

All were welcome at the ball, locals and refugees alike, in the grand meeting hall. There was food enough to sink ships, room enough for dancing, and a sea of people to fill it all. The building was ancient: a double-walled monstrosity fit to endure hurricanes. The roof was new, "only" seventy five years old. It was made of local cypress, built in a year when demand was so low they chose to keep two of the great trees for themselves rather than sell it for next to naught.

Taylor put up his lights and circulated for a while until he found the Penguin Workshop clique. At this point he didn't care if they all looked overly friendly with each other. Everyone understood they had taking a liking to each other and expected the cousins to become his followers.

His main target for the night was Lord Bardam, the principal of Dodona. He was surrounded by the local principal Lady Puabi, Alderwoman Sophia, and Patrix Primos. A small distance separated that group from the rest of the gathering, a scant half-meter that spoke volumes about peoples' unwillingness to intrude on their betters. Taylor crashed through the distance with the intent of introducing himself but the Patrix saw him coming.

"Lord Bardam, here is Disciple Phillip, who appropriately styles himself 'the Younger'. Phillip, Lord Bardam."

The principal was surprisingly young, maybe thirty at the outside, dressed in black and white: expensive options. A cravat the color of lapis lazuli adorned his neck. At first he thought the lord might be smooth-skinned, until he spotted the man's tail: a bushy and expressive affair of black with a white underside.

Lord Bardam stuck his hand out at the same time as Taylor. "An honor, Disciple. I am grateful for everything you did for my people."

"All part of the Work. How long will you be in town, your lordship?"

"Please, call me Bardam. I am here for two more days, and depart on the third. I have citizens spread out over three towns right now. You can imagine the headache."

"Call me Phillip," said Taylor. "Can I have some of your time before you leave?"

The patrix laughed nervously, "I hope you're not going to squeeze the lord too hard for a donation, Phillip. He has an entire town to rebuild."

"I am well aware. I have information that may help. The sooner you know the particulars, the better. Do you know Hylee House?"

They agreed to meet the next afternoon, for one of Livia's excellent luncheons. Taylor was surprised the principal didn't push back on the idea of coming to Taylor instead of the other way around, but maybe that was out of a sense of gratitude. Or, he wanted to escape his staff for an hour or two. Regardless, Taylor preferred to control the venue for that meeting, given the topics.

"Enough business," said Sophia in her excited way, "More dancing! We are short on younger men. See?" She waved at a gaggle of girls about his own age. As he turned to look the whole lot of them stood taller.

"I don't know any of them."

"That is why," trilled the interfering alderwoman, "we have public dances. But, I'm confused. I was informed you had been practicing for the occasion." The alderwoman looked to the west side of the hall where most of the Penguin crew was assembled. Eleanor gave him a friendly wave.

"If you don't dance it makes the church look bad," warned the patrix. "The hero of the hour can't be churlish."

"Then who are you dancing with?" Taylor accused him. "If the disciple has a duty here then so does the local priest."

"That's true," he said, and downed the remainder of his cup. He walked directly at a group of unattended women, asked one to dance, and was on the floor just that fast.

Across the room, Eleanor, Bao, and the Vales all waved at him again. "Thank us later," seemed to be the intended message.

Groaning only a little, Taylor summoned his courage and got on with it. They couldn't be any worse than a bifurdactica, and if he kept his gloves on he probably wouldn't panic or startle. And, if he was dancing then nobody would ask him to play.

His first partner was so eager she stepped in front of all the other girls to be chosen. But then she tried to steer him around the floor so strongly they had to negotiate. She could lead for the first half if he could lead for the second. His next partner was so shy she could barely speak, but it was a group dance so there was no harm done. The third took some offense at him wearing gloves, but seemed mollified by the explanation that his spirit arts made him highly sensitive to the touch.

During the break after song four, Taylor tracked down Eleanor and accused her of meddling.

"It was a team effort," admitted the proprietress, smoothing his hair affectionately with her finger. "You need a little meddling, now and then."

Taylor brushed her hand away. "I do not," he insisted, "stop that." Bao arrived with drinks handing one to Eleanor while keeping the other for himself. He only smiled, enjoying the show.

"Yes, you do." She adjusted the penguin pin she wore, making sure it was straight. "You need a lot of interfering. For example..." She nodded to someone behind him.

Taylor turned around but all he saw was the same press of people... until they parted. Facing him was a familiar figure, a fixture of his insecurities and nicer dreams. The rest of the room fell out of focus, as his entire attention was directed at the girl with the tall soft ears and a scut tail. She was wearing a bright green dress with a tasteful amount of cherry-red embroidery and red flats to match. He didn't remember moving, but he was standing in front of her. The raucous hall was beyond them, or had died off of its own accord -- what did it matter to him?

Laura curtsied as if they were still in Lavradio. "Disciple Phillip, I am Laura Sabrosa."

She was being uncharacteristically demure. It was more than suspicious, it was an affront after her intense pursuit of him in Girona where she had mustered all his associates to her cause. There were too many things he wanted to say to her. Among them were "I liked you better when you were shoving bugs in my face," or, "you look amazing," or "I have screaming night terrors so you can't sleep with me."

What came out of his mouth was, "how are you here?"

"Gurantor train," she said, clasping her hands behind her back. She was probably holding her tail to keep it from fanning the room.

"That's not exactly what I was asking."

"Since we don't know each other, you will have to ask more clearly."

Taylor took a step closer to Laura so they were eye to eye, or would have been if she wasn't five centimeters taller than him. "What I meant to ask is, what brings you to Tegea?"

"Oh!," she feigned surprise, "I'm a Sabrosa, of the merchants Sabrosa. I'm traveling Gallia in search of opportunities. All very routine."

Her spear-shaped ears, the tips of which rose well above her head, were rotated to point directly at him. She rocked back and forth on her heels for several seconds while Taylor started at her.

"She sent you samples, didn't she?"

"You mean Eleanor? We received a box of lovely things from her. Naturally, I sensed an opportunity. Sabrosa, remember?"

"How could I? We only just met." They stared at each other awkwardly while the band tuned up for the next set.

"This is the part," she whispered, "where you ask me to dance."

"In Gallia," he informed her, "the second set belongs to the girls. So this is the part where you ask me to dance. That is, if you want to dance."

She had him for three numbers, then took pity on the girls who hadn't had a partner yet and gave him up a few of the group dances.

They took the next break outside, at the edge of the hill overlooking the sea. Laura never asked about the gloves, and she didn't even hint about bedding together that night. She had definitely been briefed.

"Where are you staying?" Taylor asked her.

"The inns are all full, so I'm renting a room at Penguin's workshop dorm. They're putting up some of the Dorona folks, too. It isn't ideal because I'm also in negotiations with them, but the food is good."

"I thought someone of your stature would take a room in Hylee house."

"I'm here on my own budget. A girl has to make a profit, you know."

"And will you?"

"You don't need to worry about me," she said, "I will do very well. Penguin products are fit for nobility. They won't be able to make enough to fill demand. A Sabrosa girl is born for this."

Laura hooked her arms into his and pulled herself close. He reflexively pulled away from her, then got control of himself and allowed the familiar gesture.

"You should worry more about yourself, mister disciple. Did you know, when you stare hard at people, like you did to me earlier, it hurts?"

"What do you mean? I don't hurt people," he insisted.

"You don't intend to hurt people, but when you focus on them it's like having a hundred hot needles poking your skin."

"I'm sorry, I didn't realize."

"That's not all," she pressed on, "there are bags under your eyes, and your heart isn't beating well. You're not eating enough. You're so paranoid you won't even shake hands without gloves on. You tell everyone you're fine, but you don't seem fine to me."

She leaned her head against him and sighed. Taylor tried to think of something to say, but he couldn't argue against her: she had her facts in order. That was one of the things he liked about her. He couldn't explain all his reasons to her, but mostly there just hadn't been enough time to work on his personal problems. He barely had his local practice up and running.

"There are a lot of things I need to do. Things that maybe only I can do."

"That's why you need to to take care of this now. So all the things only you can do aren't left undone, just because you wouldn't take a couple of weeks off.

"There's another reason to care care of yourself, too. So we can keep being friends."

He pulled away from her and looked hard into her eyes. "Are you trying to blackmail me into getting treatment?"

"Ouch," she said gently, and covered his eyes with her hand. "That hurts."

Taylor closed his eyes and looked away, while she resumed hugging him. The cold was biting, and his bifur-lined cloak was warm.

"I'm going to tell you a story. When I was a little girl, my favorite uncle was Uncle Felix. He was a genius: he would walk into a room where nobody could agree on anything, and by the time he left everyone was making a profit. Whenever he came through Girona he would stay with us for a whole week, and tell me stories of where he'd been and the things he'd seen. He was so funny, too. His letters made me laugh so hard, I would read them over and over. I still have them.

"One day his carriage got rammed by a gurantor. Healers were able to save him, but his lover died. A few weeks later, Uncle Felix was back to work and everything seemed fine. He was a little quieter, and not as funny, but we thought he just needed time.

"But time didn't make it better. At first it was just a little too much drinking so he could sleep, but that didn't help much. He was afraid to travel with anyone else, in case they got hurt again, so he went alone and tried to do everything himself. He was too exhausted and too hurt to connect with people like he used to, so he wasn't the brilliant deal maker he used to be. The more his business suffered the more he tried to make up for it by squeezing every last bit from every contract. The kinds of opportunities that had made him successful all dried up. The man who used to make deals everywhere couldn't find one anywhere.

"He blamed other people for all his problems. Another merchant needed too much commission, or some farmer lied about the harvest, or a craftsman failed to make enough product. The more things fell apart, the more paranoid he got. He fired people he used to trust, hired new people, then fired them at the least hint of trouble. Working for him was a nightmare, and pretty soon not many people would do it.

"He stopped coming to see me, but he still sent me letters. They weren't the charming, funny stories he used to tell. At the end, they were just long complaints about how everyone was cheating him at every turn, and how all the kings in Tenobre had him on a secret hit list, and he was going to get revenge on all the people who had harmed him.

"The last time I saw him he was in our living room yelling at my moms. He threatened them, to try and force them to loan him money. He said we were colluding with the kings to destroy him and he was going to burn down our house. He was so awful, I didn't recognize him.

"He died alone, in his bedroom, and nobody found him for a week. They had to batter down the door with a ram because he had it triple barred. Healers said his heart failed in his sleep.

"It wasn't just himself he destroyed. Everyone around him suffered in all kinds of ways. It wasn't just business. He used to make everything better wherever he went, but after the crash he hurt a lot of people on his way down. When I think of everything he could have done instead, everything he could have been ... there aren't any numbers for that, you know?"

She pulled away from him so she could look into his eyes. "That's why you have to heal what's broken inside of you, so you can do all the things that only you can do. I won't have another Uncle Felix in my life."

"I assume everyone else is in on this. How did you draw the black lot?"

"I volunteered," she said proudly. "Everyone else works for you. The cousins are your followers, Penguin is owned by you, and the patrix is below you in the church hierarchy. The alderwoman and those lords aren't going to do it, they just want things from you. I, on the other hand, am first and foremost your friend. My principal interest is that you get better.

"I have already made the appointment for you with Healer Ferange: he'll be at Hylee House for breakfast. No training, no work, no adventure, and no delaying."

"But I have a lunch with Lord Bardam tomorrow."

"Then that's perfect. You can have breakfast with the healer, lunch with the lord, and dinner with me. You can tell me all about your treatment plan."

The morning after the ball, Taylor was examined by Healer Ferange, who gave him the same lecture that Julius had but at greater length.

"When you train, you put stress on your body and it gets stronger as a response. But, you only grow and get stronger when you are resting. Your body needs rest and food. Am I boring you?"

"I know this already," said Taylor.

"Well you aren't acting like it, Phillip. You're training too hard for the amount of food you eat. You're breaking yourself down instead of building yourself up. The same goes for your spirit, too. I can feel your morning practices from all the way down the hill, but your spirit is turbulent.

Try feeding your spirit for a while, instead of just working it to death."

"I know, I know," Taylor groused, sounding like a twelve-year-old for a change.

"Healers make the worst patients," sighed Ferange, shaking his head. "You're not going to survive to sixteen if you don't take care of yourself. You're the most talented practitioner of your age, but you're dying of self neglect. That is, quite literally, the stupidest death I can think of.

"Two weeks of rest," Ferange insisted, "I mean it. The only exercise you should be getting is to ride Ben down to the wharf to stuff yourself on chowder. Stop trying to move all the light in Gallia every morning. No more rucking your own body weight up and down the hill.

"If you're good, and I mean very very good, we can start your trauma treatment."

"That puts me out of commission until spring!" complained Taylor. "That's forever!"

"Not that long, but I understand your concern. There's a special treatment, only available here in Tegea, that takes less than the usual four weeks. The downside is that it can be strenuous, packing several sessions into a few days. If you're rested, well and truly rested, I'll approve the treatment. But you can't go if you are malnourished and have bags under your eyes. Eat a lot, and take your sleeping potions."

"What's this treatment," he asked, curious. "Why haven't I heard of it?"

"It's only available here in Tegea. There's a forest of special trees, up in the mountains, that live for thousands of years. These trees are all one organism, connected to each other through their roots."

"Are they conscious?" Taylor asked with excitement.

"Not exactly. Or, maybe. It's hard to be sure. But they definitely remember. You can think of it as one huge plant, that remembers."

"So how does a not-exactly-conscious tree help me?"

"I'm getting there," Ferange said. "You drink the same extract as normal, and then we put you in contact with the roots of this tree. For a while, you're part of this much larger thing. I'm not explaining it well. With the tree's support it is easier to heal, like putting a cast on a broken bone helps support it.

"People here use the ritual for handling grief, alcoholism, trauma. All the old feller families know the ritual, and quite a few others, too. It's a common practice here."

"But not universal," suggested Taylor.

"Not everyone wants or needs mental treatment," Ferange countered, "but in Tegea this is the preferred method. Gallian nobles pay good silver to spend a week up here, just for this. The results are solid."

"So you're telling me," summarized Taylor, tossing him an eight-bit coin, "if I eat drink and make merry for two weeks you'll arrange an arboreal mind-meld so I can get back on the road?"

"Yes. That is exactly what I'm saying."

Lord Bardam arrived for lunch on time, with minimal staff: just a secretary and a pair of guards. Livia had prepared the drawing room for them, and compelled the guards to leave their weapons at the door.

The first thing Taylor did, after everyone was settled, was spill a fat pouch of rough-cut gemstones onto the table between them. Beryls, sapphires, and varieties of garnets scattered across the tabletop. Many of them looked like little more than rocks, with a bit of bright color showing. Others were obviously crystalline but rough cut and unpolished.

"Where did you get all of these?" Lord Bardam looked at the double-handful of stones suspiciously.

"I found them in a high marsh in your territory. A few of these are even valuable." Taylor was aware that taking the gems without permission amounted to theft. Mining was a licensed activity, and he hadn't exactly filed for a permit before hiking up in the hills with his little expeditionary force.

"I'll explain," he said.

"I'm all ears," said Lord Bardam. He examined a pale green stone in the sunlight, one of the cleaner examples.

"I've been working on a theory, that certain minerals collect spirit. Some animals have the ability to absorb spirit from the rocks, and they become monsters.

"After killing the king toad in Dodona, I took a few men and tracked the monsters back to what used to be a lake. It's all filled in with silt now, so it's wetland. I was able to locate a weak source of spirit, started digging, and found these. They were under about eight feet of silt."

Bardam picked up the stones, a few at a time, and turned them over in his hands. His face was neutral, but his palms were sweaty. He rubbed a bit of tea onto some of the sides to get a better idea of the color.

"This is an excellent find, Disciple. Thank you for bringing it to my attention." He was going to make Taylor ask for what he wanted. Taylor leaned back in his chair, sipping hot jota carefully. He knew the quality of gems he had dug out of the lord's marsh, and had a general notion of their market value. He had shown the lot to Laura and, while she wasn't a specialist, she assured him there was more than a gold crevist worth of gems here. That was five years of income for a skilled worker. Not a tremendous amount by noble standards, but as a taste of what was lying in the hills it was enough to tempt people into very bad behavior.

Taylor also knew that Bardam's status as a lord depended on rebuilding his sole settlement, which would be a strain on his finances. He would need to restore the roads and other public facilities at his own expense and at the same time provide loans to help citizens rebuild.

"The soldiers have already reported the location of the gems. If you want a finder's fee, I can arrange a few boraz for you."

It was an insulting offer, but Taylor had gone and dug up valuables on his territory without permission. Bardam probably felt like he was being robbed by a church sanctioned pre-teen run amok.

"I'm not asking for anything for this information. All the stones here are yours by right. I'm not going to attempt to make you pay for what is already yours."

Bardam waited, knowing there had to be more.

"That leaves the matter of your donation for my assistance. I'm currently asking for two boraz a day for assisting nobles. Four boraz will settle all the issues before us." To a noble, four of the fat silver coins were only a little more than pocket change. To Taylor it was a month or more of operating expenses, depending on how rough he was willing to travel. To a professional artisan it was at least three months of income.

"You're offering to close all the business between us, for four silver?" Bardam definitely didn't trust him, which made Taylor wonder what the man had been told.

"It's a donation, so you can give more if you want. But it's too small a sum for you to quibble over, Lord Bardam. Especially when seventeen soldiers had already died by the time I got there, and none died after. The church is happy to lend aid when people are in need, but we do have to pay our expenses."

Bardam nodded at his secretary, who counted out four large coins of nearly pure silver and lined them up on the table. They rang nicely as they touched down on the wood. Taylor picked them up, letting his pleasure show, and pocketed them. Disciple or not, he loved getting paid. He thought back to the first money he had in Tenobre, a sack of mixed coins King Joaquim had dropped in his lap via messenger, just to see what he would do with it. Getting what he had earned was ten times better than receiving a king's thoughtless cast-offs.

"That concludes our current business," Taylor said. The secretary reached forward to gather up all the stones, but paused when Taylor added, "Now let's talk about future business."

Bardam waved his secretary back. "What business?"

"You have a problem you maybe haven't thought about yet, and that's the threat represented by some of these gems." Taylor pulled two of the stones away from the rest: red-orange garnets. They weren't the most valuable stones in the lot, but he had cleaned them up the most while studying them.

"These stones are the ones that act as storehouses for spirit. As long as there is a deposit of them near your village, you will be more susceptible to monster attacks. A second attack by a cursed monster will be the end of Dodona, for good.

"You could drain and excavate the entire area, spending months or years to recoup your startup costs and run your operation on credit in the mean time. That is the usual way, I believe."

"It is," the lord said, then he ventured, "Are you from a merchant family, by chance?"

"My background is as interesting, but it's my own." As a wilderness disciple, Taylor could get away with not explaining his past. "The other way is to let me help you. I have advanced training in construction. I can drain the swamp and pinpoint the location of any stones that contain spirit. I can even excavate them. This reduces the threat from monsters and will give you a big financial boost right when you need it. But this job is commercial in nature, so the renumeration is more than a few pieces of silver."

"You want the spirit gems," Bardam said, relaxing a little now that he understood Taylor's desires. "You think you can buy my goodwill with these, and then angle for a share of the mine."

"Is it working?" asked Taylor.

"Keep talking."

"I'll offer a week of labor. That should be enough to drain most of the swamp and dig up all the 'spirit gems' as you called them. In return I want two considerations. First, you set up a fund to pay a pension to the families of the soldiers who died, for the next twenty years."

The secretary spoke. "Why should he do that? They were soldiers. That's the risk they take." Lord Bardam nodded in agreement with his henchman.

"Because your cousin, Commander Urban, got them pointlessly killed. He deliberately chose a company of junior recruits to make his victory look better. He refused to wait for a disciple just so he wouldn't have to share the glory. Then he got himself swallowed because he wanted a solo victory against the king toad. We had to cut him out after the fight to save his life."

"Our report said he stabbed the king's heart with his sword," sad the secretary. "Are you saying the report is a lie?"

"Oh, he made a very fine thrust directly at the heart of the monster," agreed Taylor, making a dramatic thrusting motion with his arm. "It would have been a victorious blow, too, if his sword had been longer by a full meter. Everyone told him to use a spear but he refused to listen."

The secretary regarded his master carefully. These were new facts to them, yet they didn't seem surprised. Maybe Commander Urban had fudged his report worse than expected.

"My second requirement is I want twenty-five percent of the gems I dig up, by value. Priority is to be given to the spirit gems."

"That's a tremendous amount of money for one disciple. Especially such a young one."

"I'm not going to keep it," said Taylor, scoffing at the idea. "I'm already well-funded. I want to study the gems. When I'm done they'll all go to the church. Some will stay here in

Tegea, to fund the church's expenses caring for your refugees, and some will go to rebuild the temple in Dodona. Most will be earmarked for other church-affiliated programs I support."

"Are you saying," said the secretary, "that you don't want a percentage of the ongoing operation?"

"That's exactly what I'm saying. I don't want an ongoing concern that I have to think about."

Lord Bardam looked even more suspicious than before. "What do you want out of this?"

"Get the spirit gems away from Dodona," Taylor counted on his fingers, "fund some charities I care about, outfit a couple of new followers, and ensure Leadership knows I'm doing my job."

"And the Urban report?" asked the secretary, "will you sign it?"

"I will if it's true. But if it's the travesty I think it is, then don't expect me to endorse it. The report I care about most is the line that goes into the *Luminous Histories*. 'Phillip the Younger assisted soldiers of Gallia in Dodona. From the time of his arrival they killed ten monstrous toads, one of them cursed, with no casualties.'"

"I would be willing to agree to all of your demands if," said Bardan, "you were to endorse Urban's report unconditionally."

For a few seconds they faced each other. If Lord Bardam was trying to elevate his cousin to the peerage, then showing a good record as an officer was a step in the right direction. Taylor hadn't seen the commander's report, but he had heard about it from Dodona's acting alderman. Apparently, it pinned all the commander's failures onto other people, mainly Sergeant Albia. Urban's errors weren't the result of enemy action or a lack of information. He had gotten people killed because he was vainglorious. Taylor didn't want anyone to keep giving Urban dangerous assignments because they thought he had done a great job in Dodona. There was a real danger the idiot would get promoted without ever learning his lessons or taking responsibility.

Taylor leaned forward and began to push all the stones into a pile, sweeping them together with his palms. Then he scooted the pile as far away from himself as he could, to the lord's side of the table. Bardam and his secretary watched curiously.

"No."

He stood up to signal a pause in their discussions. "Lunch will be ready soon. I hope you brought an appetite, because Livia's cooking shouldn't be missed."

Taylor and Laura met up, well after dark, in a simple wooden building near the center pier. It catered to the owners and captains of the fishing and trade vessels that called Tegea home, so it was a few steps up from the common seafarer's establishments. The tables were polished, and were lit by expensive oil lanterns instead of open wicks in bowls of cheap oil.

They had taken a private space for their date, but calling it a 'room' was stretching the facts. It was more of a booth with a door. The chowder was amazing. It was full of a lobster-like meat, starchy roots, savory spices, and served with a thick slice of hearty brown bread.

"So you let him leave without a deal?"

Laura sounded so critical, Taylor felt like he had to defend himself. "He wasn't interested in any arrangement where I didn't endorse his cousin's libelous report. And I wasn't interested in any arrangement where I did. There wasn't any deal to be made. The money barely mattered."

"That was a lot of money to walk away from." Her face had soup on it. That, and her wide eyes, made her look her real age of fourteen.

"I'm not saying it didn't hurt," he admitted. He used the last of his bread to steal a little of her chowder right out of her bowl. Shocked, Laura pulled the precious vessel against herself and protected it with both arms. Taylor ate the bread with her soup on it, while she glared at him jealously.

"It hurt a lot," he said after consuming the purloined food, "but what could I do? There was nothing on the table that was worth my integrity. I actually use that. And I have enough money for now, so walking away from it all was the best move for me. He'll just have to build up his operation without me, like he was planning to do anyway. How are things with you?"

"Fine," she said, "except my date is stealing my food." She tipped the bowl to her lips and drank the rest of the broth in one go. Taylor wondered how much trouble he would be in for if he swiped her remaining bread and used it to scoop her dregs and eat it. He was fast enough to pull it off, but probably not charming enough to get away with it. From the way she was watching him, she knew exactly what he was thinking.

"Eleanor and I will ink a deal this week. You'll be happy to know the DeLanion school is getting royalties from all of the methods. They'll be able to expand again."

"The what, now?" Taylor could guess she was talking about the school he had started, then left instructions for in his will, but he never meant for them to name the place after himself. Of course, if they thought he was dead then naming the school after the founder was a natural thing to do.

"Eleanor was a great find," Laura went on. "Putting her in charge was the right call on your part." Taylor refilled their cups with cider while she talked. "She's even bringing in a perfumer from Kashmar. It's a huge get for the Penguin. Some of the pegasus products sell for absurd amounts of money. Do you remember the his and hers soap you made for Eternal Blossom?"

"I do. Two different scents that smell exciting together. There was a batch of it curing when everything went sideways."

"It sells at auction for five silver a pair. Custom scents was a brilliant idea: nobles in Lavradio used to go all the way to Kashmar for that. Being able to design your own is a great way to crack open markets.

"I'm heading out on the next train after our deal is signed. I'm doing the Gallia tour, then Ullidia, and back up to Lavradio. I would have offered to carry your gems for you and sell them on consignment in Kashmar, but it looks like I'm out of luck on that front. I'm buying fragrant wood in the south, wool in Ullidia, and I'll sell it in Fringe for monster bone. Then back through Lavradio and repeat."

"Sounds gutsy," he said. "I would be afraid of getting stuck with stuff that nobody wants. I'd rather make things I know people are going to want. It feels safer to me."

"You have your gifts," Laura said, popping the last piece of bread soaked in the last of the chowder broth into her mouth. "And I have mine."

The two of them occupied the room, taking seconds and then thirds of everything until the place closed. Afterwards, he wrapped Laura in his bifur-lined cloak and let her ride behind him on Magnificent Ben. They took their time, plodding up the hill to Penguin Workshop. Ben knelt to let them dismount but Laura complained she was too tired to do it herself. Taylor carried the girl, who was taller than him, to her bed and laid her down. She laughed, and pulled his face down so she could kiss him on the lips.

"Get better soon," she whispered, "so I can sleep over at your place." Then she rolled up in the bifur cloak without offering to give it back, and went to sleep. Taylor could feel her lips on his, all the way to Hylee House.

Thoughtspace

"Magic makes people stupid." That was practically a mantra for Yr Mostru, Grand Master of Evocation and Taylor's mentor four lifetimes ago. Of course he wasn't Taylor back then: he was a different person in a different body. But Taylor still remembered Yr vividly. That old man looked like a farmer who should be knocking back mugs of ale at the grange after plowing his back twenty hectares. But Yr had had a keen mind for thermodynamics and most other forms of natural law. And, he had a point. When all you needed was a few words and an exercise of will to raise a pillar of ice or turn stone into lava, then there was no need to think too hard about how the universe normally worked when you weren't using magic on it.

Master Yr wasn't a feared wizard because of his stunning resources of mana and vast magical repertoire. He was a terror to his enemies the world over because of his ingenuity, which sprang directly from his ability to leverage natural law using spell craft. He dropped a thousand square kilometers of dry land into the ocean by lubricating a tectonic fault. He disappeared a thousand-year-old fortress into a sinkhole by diverting a tiny underground stream by just a few meters. His thermobaric explosions were the stuff of legend. He was able to perform a hundred mythic feats because he didn't let magic make him stupid.

Magical theory was errant nonsense. That's what Taylor was learning after reviewing everything he knew about magic from twelve different worlds. The truth was, nobody understood much of anything about mana or magic, aside from what they could personally feel. If you were strong enough in will and imagination, then you could change the world around you. Prayers, appeals to spirits, mystical signs, it was all a crutch: mental frameworks invented to help people focus their intent or explain away phenomena they didn't want to think about too much.

It was only after he had given up on all of magical theory that Taylor started looking at material sciences, and that was where he found his first clues. There were several types of gems and other substances that had identical uses across multiple worlds. Their use as sacrificial elements was unimportant: in some magical systems, anything could be used as a sacrifice if it was important enough to the user. But these substances were used in other ways besides sacrifice: as mana storage, conduits, or detection. As soon as he started combing his mindspaces for the intersection of magic and materials, he started collecting promising leads.

Magic had made Taylor stupid. He possessed a massive red beryl, a substance that was capable of storing mana not only in this world but in several others. He had been putting mana into it every day for weeks just to see what would happen, but hadn't bothered to think about it in his quest for generalized knowledge. The same was true of the chrysoberyl "spirit gems" he had turned over to Lord Bardam: they were also prized on multiple worlds for their ability to store mana. He had no choice but to laugh at his own folly.

Now that Taylor recognized his ignorance, he knew what tools to apply to become less ignorant.

His two weeks of imposed rest would be put to excellent use.

Gallia, Tegea

One could not be ignorant of her approach. Her voice pierced wood, stone, and bone from a block away. The dramatic swoops and trills of her speech triggered emotions of alarm, danger, delight, and excitement in nerve-wearing alternations. Her auditory assaults were daily, her appetite for jota was endless. She was getting closer, even now. Alderworman Sophia Rosa.

"Please Phillip," begged Healer Ferange, "you have to distract her. She's going to insist talking to me for an hour, and I have patients waiting."

Taylor understood. It was winter and the man only had two days a week to spend in Tegea. If he got behind so early in the day, he would never catch a break.

"Stop feeding her jota," he advised his neighbor. "That's what Livia does. She goes away if you don't have any."

"That's still a twenty-minute minimum, while she sits there and waits for it. Noisily."

Taylor took pity on the man. He was a good healer, and had a heavy workload. "All right, I'll waylay her."

Whatever internal plan was driving the alderwoman that day brought her to the disciple's door first, so there was no need to intercept her. All he had to catch and hold her for a while. The moment she entered his office Taylor put up a privacy barrier to contain her noise and started a pot of jota.

"Well! You haven't done much to the place since our last visit, have you?" The alderwoman didn't look disappointed or disapproving. She was just talking. She seemed to do that a lot.

"I like it open," Taylor told her while brewing, "and I don't have to accommodate a lot of people at one time like Ferange, so I don't need a bunch of furniture." His front room was a few chairs around a square table, a miniature stove in the corner that vented to the outside, a writing desk, and a few shelves. His back room was a long workshop with workbenches along one side, and several different projects laid out. They were all his own inventions, the kinds of things he enjoyed that didn't require a lot of spirit work. As far as Taylor was concerned it all counted as "resting".

"What kind of bow shoots an arrow like this?" The alderwoman was holding a shaft, a hundred and fifty centimeters long, with raised vanes in the rear like an arrow. "It feels too wobbly to be a weapon."

"It's odd isn't it?" Taylor picked up a stick with a reversed knob on one end, and fit the knob into a divot in the butt of the shaft. "You throw it with this device. Line up, step forward with this foot, and throw. Give it a try. Aim for the red circle on the back wall."

"Oh I couldn't!" she said, grabbing the assembly and lining up on her target. She missed her target by a half meter, but the dart hit the back wall with a satisfying thunk.

Taylor handed her another dart. "Put your hips into it, madam alderwoman. These are just lightweight prototypes. They should break with a good throw. Don't hold back."

"Really!" Her next throw came with an unnecessarily dramatic "Hyaa!". It was still off target, but the shaft fractured audibly.

"This is quite enjoyable, Phillip!"

"Have another, Sophia. Put your whole body behind it. You're doing it right if it smashes to bits."

With a little more practice the alderwoman was hitting her target, and soon all his darts were shattered to pieces. By that time the jota was over-steeped yet the alderwoman didn't seems to mind. Some of the excessive energy seemed to have left her voice.

When they finally settled down at the table she sighed contentedly. "What an odd project, Phillip."

"I've been thinking about our toad hunt in Dodona. We always end up putting someone directly in front of a terrifying monster armed with blessings and a pointed stick. What we really need is a ranged weapon with really great penetration. I'm hoping this will be a solution."

"Why not use a bow? Hunters use them all the time!"

"Disciples and bows don't have a great history together," he explained. "Bulwarks fight with massively increased strength, and to make use of that with a bow you need something that's as strong as your typical ballista. It requires a lot of skill to make a bow like that, and they tend to break frequently. Often the arrows will snap, too.

"Don't get me wrong: they're highly effective when they work, but the reliability issues are very real. The disciples who use them spend a lot of time on them."

"I understand," said the alderwoman. She reached into her purse and produced packets of sandwiches wrapped in waxed cloth, a dense brown bread full of dried fruit and nuts called march cake, miniature tuns of butter and jam, and winter fruit. She indicated he should help himself, while she chose a half-sandwich. "You have only each other and your arts to rely on."

"Exactly! So, simpler is better. If we can kill a cursed monster from a little distance, even just ten meters, it could make a big difference."

"Even I could make a ten meter throw with this! But," she said critically, "your darts could be more consistent."

Taylor thought about that while he sampled the winter fruit. It was tart and a little spicy. Something they didn't have in Lavradio.

"A jig," he said eventually. "It would be easy to make them all the same with a template. A hole for shaft size, triangular cutouts for vanes, and so on."

"It would have to be possible to replace the jig itself, in case it was lost or broken."

"I can arrange that, too." He hadn't expected such useful contributions from the alderwoman. "A schematic would be useful, if I can keep the geometry simple enough."

Sophia looked very pleased with herself. "I am a very practical person. Speaking of which, I came here about something important. Lord Bardam wants your endorsement for Commander Urban's report. He seems to think you're holding out for some kind of consideration."

Taylor unconsciously made the Lavradian hand sign for frustration and grumbled, "that just proves he isn't listening to me. I'd sign Urban's report without any consideration at all, if it wasn't a stack of lies."

"Well!" The alderwoman pulled a stack of boards from her purse. "Why don't we go through it together and you can point out the errors to me."

"Just give me the chalk," Taylor told her. "And while I do that, you can compare it to my own report." He pulled his own three-board report from his desk and handed it to her.

It didn't take long for Sophia to see the problem. "These are very different reports." Then she looked at the sections in Urban's report that Taylor had drawn through with the chalk. The first two boards were half-covered by chalk. "Irreconcilably so." She watched as Taylor lined out a block of text, shaking his head.

"We agree the weather was good for the time of year," Taylor said at last, when he was done obliterating most of Urban's nine boards, "and that too many people died. And the king toad was impressively large. That's about all."

"I suppose it's no good looking for Ferange's endorsement? He's already signed on yours, I see. And Sergeant Albia, and Alderman Pierson. This doesn't bode well for Commander Urban's record of achievements, does it?"

"He was pretty awful. And now he's trying to pin all his own failures onto other people. Like I said, consideration isn't the hold up here. It's Urban."

"Well! I'll put this aside until Urban writes a report his witnesses can tolerate. I should drop in on Ferange to see how he's doing."

"Sophia, about that..."

"Here's a lunch basket, courtesy of the alderwoman. She says, 'remember to take care of yourself'. That's all."

Ferange flipped him an eight-bit coin. "You're a genius."

Grinning, Taylor snatched the brass triangle from the air and pocketed it. "I have my days. And, I made this for you." He handed the healer a red stone lozenge.

"Is this one of those spirit stones you were talking about? From Dodona?"

"This one is from Lavradio, so it's slightly different. It's full, too. If you run low today, draw from that. I can show you how, if you can't figure it out."

"You're supposed to be resting, Phillip."

"I am resting," insisted the boy. "I'm resting my butt off over here. I could use a break from it. Let me know if you need bones mended."

"Actually, I have a waiting room full of sick and impatient children. If you could bring over your nickleharp and keep them occupied..."

"Consider it done."

JYMTANDI

Gallia, North of Tegea

Taylor, Mila, and Milo rode their mounts behind their assigned guide who was on foot, an older kilobora man named Twoluck. He had the same striped and dappled hair as Livia and her offspring, but of a lighter color. Ben seemed happy to be out on the trail again, reaching out with his trunk to touch the branches every now and then. The trees changed as they climbed north, from the lowland birches to tall thin conifers.

As they reached a plateau they found themselves among giants: the massive cedars for which Tegea was famous. The Cedar Plateau was a special, rarified habitat: just the right altitude, kilometers of almost level ground, watered by ever-shifting creeks that tricked down from glaciers to the west. In spite of the creeks, the majority of water was blown in by sea breezes during the hot summer and fall seasons. As the moist air pushed over the boundary hills in the east and came into the cooler valley it became a thick fog. The water was taken up by the canopy, the copious mosses that grew on the east-facing sides of the trunks, and the ferns on the ground level.

They rode through successive stages of the grove, where the trees became progressively smaller and smaller, until they were in a field of saplings among stumps. Then suddenly the trees were massive once again. The fully mature trees were a minimum of two hundred years old, hundreds of feet tall, and their lowest branches were twenty meters from the ground. Twoluck described how only a limited quota of mature trees were taken each year, all from the same area, to create a sunlit space for new growth. Cutting this way let them manage the forest in perpetuity. It had worked for at least four hundred years: feller shacks tucked away in the forest had the carved names and dates of expeditions going back at least that far.

Twice, Twoluck armed himself with a pair of wooden devices that looked like hollow batons and banged them together, shouting in a language that wasn't Unity. Both times, something huge and ursine detached itself from the shadows of distant trees, and ran off deeper into the woods.

"That old Roger," said Twoluck, "he curious but best he not get too close. He get hungry, he think you feed him. Then you have big problem."

Milo put his hand nervously on his short sword. "What kind of problem?"

"How to feed three hundred kilogram of Roger." Twoluck cackled. "He mad if you feed him but not have enough."

Past the zone where Tegea fellers plied their trade was the Old Forest, kilometers of untouched old growth. When a tree fell in the Old Forest the kilabora would take some of the wood for themselves, cut a path through the fallen trunk if it was in the way, and use the rest to cultivate mushrooms until the trunk was too deteriorated to be worth farming. The kilabora lived beyond the Old Forest, past a cleared firebreak, and nestled their village against the barrier hills. Uphill and slightly east was a large south-facing slope they had terraced for crops. The rest of their diet consisted of of whatever they hunted or foraged from their sky-scraping neighbors. In their animal forms, kilabora were superb climbers and often brought down delicacies from the canopy: birds eggs, honey, pine nuts.

The village houses were stacked stones roofed in bent timbers thatched with reed that didn't seem to grow in the area. Taylor thought he could detect the use of the arts in shaping the roof timbers and some of the stones, and recalled what Livia had said about her people having their own spirit arts. The denizens of Kilopoli were not all in their human forms. Quite a few were in their animal form, and it tickled the visitors to see humans and large animals conversing casually with each other.

Taylor appreciated the chance to get a good look at a several individuals. There were plenty of differences in coloration and markings. Some were only striped while others were mostly dappled, and fur color ranged from dark brown to red to nearly white. The most constant feature was the central black stripe that ran down the neck and back and tail of all kilabora. Some of them showed gray at the tips of their tails, and he guessed it was a sign of advanced age.

They were barely in Kilopoli long enough for Taylor to whet his curiosity. Another party of four were waiting for them with two pack appalons and extensive provisions. All the animals carried baggage while all the people went on foot. The five kilabora, including Twoluck, changed to their animal form and led Taylor's party northwest into the mountains.

The kilabora set a hard pace for the climb. Taylor, Mila, Milo, Ben, and the other appalons only kept up with help from Taylor's arts. They left the giant cedars far behind and below them, and they passed among thinning pine stands. Near the summit they found themselves walking crouched under a low canopy, stepping carefully along thickly-tangled roots filled in with debris and ground cover. These were the jymtandi trees, contorted by the high-altitude winds and grown together to shelter each other. Their tops were woven so densely that little sunlight could find its way in, and the roots made a tangled mess under their feet. The kilabora had built a path of planks through the forest, not for themselves but for visitors and their appalons.

The entire top of the mountain was covered with the jymtandi. Taylor estimated they passed the crown by a hundred meters and turned north for a few minutes until they found the camp. It would have been hard to miss, composed as it was of a wooden deck built over the roots. In the middle of the deck was a hole, and stairs went down into it.

One of the giant arboreal squirrels, the one with the most gray on his tail, spoke in Twoluck's voice. "You get clothes off now and get in hole."

"What's in the hole?" demanded Mila.

"Roots," said Twoluck. "Also mulch. Keep Phillip-Priest warm. Tree embrace the mind so thoughts can heal. Make skin, let's go. Soon begin, soon end!"

Taylor stood at the top of the stairs, looking down into a pit full of wood mulch, reconsidering his choices. He trusted Twoluck because Ferange trusted him. Taylor trusted Ferange because he was a fellow practitioner and they had worked well together. He couldn't say he really knew Ferange, but he liked what he knew so far. Livia knew of Ferange too, as did the Patrix, and Taylor had some amount of trust in both of them. Both of them also knew what he had come here to do, and had approved.

"Phillip, you don't have to do this," Milo reminded him. "The standard treatment will work. You could take the normal treatment and just stay in Tegea for a while longer."

"And be out of commission for another month," sighed Taylor. "Or skip it all and suffer. I don't think so." He began to strip. If his followers wanted to turn their backs they could, but he didn't expect that courtesy from the kilabora. It was universally true that shape-shifters had a different sense of modesty than creatures with only one form. He let Milo take his weapons, and Mila take his star and stole. Everything else got dropped where he stood, and he descended the stairs into a pit large enough for three people to lie down.

Spying a dug-out space with a barley-husk pillow at one end, Taylor laid down in the trench and let Twoluck cover him in wood shavings using a crude rake. Once only his head was exposed, Milo came down the stairs bearing a fired clay flask. Taylor had prepared it himself, and several more doses just like it.

Twoluck sat cross-legged next to the submerged Taylor, and spoke to him in his raspy voice. "Drink the dream tea, and dream with the jymtandi. Twoluck will keep you, followers will guard you. Phillip-Priest must join, and learn. Learn to be healed."

Taylor nodded that he was ready, and Milo tipped the drink into his open mouth.

Thoughtspace: Jymtandi

It was thoughtspace, but not his own. Taylor had barely settled his mind, and found himself among the trees. Here, they were different from their tangible counterparts. The shortened, contorted trunks were pillars of smooth wood glowing in the colors of sunset. Their tops spread far above him, and the roots spread far below. The roots and leaves touched their neighbors to make millions of connections between them.

The forest was finite, numbering fewer than two thousand pillars. Taylor wasn't sure what to make of the space. It was like being inside someone else's mind, but without the sense of another consciousness.

"What are you?" he asked the trees. In his own headspace the objects were packed with knowledge and memories that could be unpacked, but these entities seemed solid. There was nothing to unpack: just a single, solid now.

Then the tea started working, and Taylor disappeared.

They remembered.

They remembered everything.

Every breeze that brushed their needles, was remembered.

Every bird that perched in their branches, was remembered.

Every drop of rain that fell on them, slid down the branches and trunks to soak into the soil, was remembered.

They remembered the long cycles of years that had passed by on the mountain. They remembered storms and sun and snow and heat, year after year. They remembered every logger, kilabora, every noble, every cleric, every person who had lain down with them to share minds, their faces and forms passing by like fireflies.

They remembered an age when the sun beat down with storms of spirit and monsters prowled the edge of their colony. In those days the kilabora lived in its roots, protected by the shade and the blood-sucking needles sharp enough to pierce monster hide. They shared their memories with the jymtandi, and were protected in return.

They even remembered when the kilabora first came, scared and dwindling in number, looking for a place they could survive the predation of monsters fed by spirit storms. Jymtandi had been bigger then, covering far more than just the top of the mountain. It pushed up shoots wherever it could find enough sun and water, extending into what was now (which now was that?) the Old Forest.

The first kilabora came before the peak of the sunstorms. Those first few survivors gathered more and more of their kin over time, until three hundred had found shelter and a second generation began to be born.

They recalled even older memories. Still days, like these days, when the sun did not storm and the jymtandi kept to itself on the mountain top. There were people then too, but they came only to be healed -- they did not stay. Some were two-shaped, and some were not. They laid down in the roots and shared their memories, which jymtandi soothed and smoothed as it read them.

Back and back the memories went, to another age of a storming sun. There were no people then and no memories shared. There was only the blood of dark creatures to feed upon. Nourished by the spirit-rich liquid of cursed monster blood and the sun's light, the jymtandi covered most of the mountain.

There were older memories still, sun and rain and receding storms, to when the jymtandi was much smaller. Smaller and younger it became until it was a single sapling atop a barren mountain top.

At this time there were people, all smooth skinned, dressed in shiny fabrics of unnatural hues. They spoke in a language that was not Unity.

"It's growing," said a woman with glasses.

"It should," said the man next to her. His head and face were smooth from the use of a depilatory. "It has enough nutrients. We had to airlift his body up here."

Indeed, jyntandi did have ample food then. The corpse of a human was decaying under its roots, generously large compared to the others. The rich bounty let the tree grow quickly, and its strong roots were already turning nearby rock into soil.

"It's hard to believe we'll never come back here," said another man, older than the others. "I came up here every year with him. Twenty years we've done that. And now..." Tears welled up in his eyes but did not spill.

"We're not even sure how often we'll get to see sunlight," said the woman.

"One day soon they'll close the doors for good," said the first man, who was maybe in his teens. "I don't even like the outside so I don't mind. Monsters. Sunstorms. How did you survive out here?"

"It used to be nicer," said the oldest, a woman. "Monsters were rare, and dark ones didn't exist. But you've grown up underground. This must seem scary to you."

"The no-roof thing is panic-inducing," admitted the young man, "but it's not so bad if you keep looking down." He had kept his eyes fastened to the ground the whole time.

"It's getting cold," said the woman with glasses. "We have to get off the summit before sundown. Trust me on this. Anyone have last words?"

The two older people, the man and woman, looked at each other and, by some unspoken signal they agreed the woman should speak. "Nobody worked harder to save the human race than Jim Tandy. But he always said the underground was for the next generation - he was a child of sun and sky and wanted to be buried in a place with plenty of both. Several hundred years from now, our descendants will be children of sun and sky again and they will be alive because of Jim Tandy.

"And so, for the last time, we say good-bye to our friend, our teacher, and our mentor. We put him here as he requested, with his final and most mysterious project."

"Damned if we know what it does," pointed out the older man to general laughter. "But it's growing, like everything else Jim did."

Each of them said a goodbye, shorter than the speech just given, and the people hiked away. They left their friend and his last creation on that mountaintop together.

Gallia, Jymtandi Mountain

"How far back have you gone, Twoluck?"

Taylor was eating ravenously. The jymtandi had taken most of his spirit, and now he was starving from his few hours in thoughtspace.

"Worry about yourself, Phillip-Priest. Twisted things must be made straight again, so they can be strong. Big works need a strong heart."

"My heart is coming along fine," Taylor insisted through a mouth full of beans and jerky stew. "I checked. How soon can I go back in?"

"Sleep first. Drink tea and sleep. When spirit is full Phillip-Priest can go again. Twoluck sleep too. Let bulwark keep watch."

"We should have brought more people," complained Mila.

"There is no one else," Milo reminded her. "I'll take until morning. Silenz is out." Silenz was Milo's favorite of the three moons.

After he was full, Taylor wasn't quite ready for bed. Milo brought him his nickleharp and he began to tune up.

"Twoluck, if I sing will you keep it a secret? Most people don't know I can sing."

"Jymtandi sharing is sacred ritual for kilabora. All here is your secret. None here will tell. But jymtandi will remember. Anyone who shares can remember."

With the canopy as their roof and the roots as their floor, the edges of the world could not be seen. The interior of the strange tree colony felt safe. So Taylor played and sang *Our Wild and Beautiful Fringe*, the piece he wrote in the lonely uplands of Lavradio. He had tried to evoke the abandoned places, stark mountains, and sudden storms of the place. He had played it for Baron Fringe, but this was the first time he had sung it for anyone.

"I know you don't like it, but I'm going to hug you!" Mila cried. She and Milo both rushed him, and held him as if he might get away from them.

"We're always going to be with you," Milo choked out.

Twoluck was back in his animal form. "Ayala! Old Jim Tandy should like that one. Play some more while you are here, Phillip-Priest. My people will come and remember, always. But play tomorrow. Tonight, drink tea of the dreamless." Twoluck set an example by curling up into a ball on the deck next to two of his kin and closed his eyes.

Gallia, North of Tegea

Jymtandi had done its work well. That didn't mean Taylor was all better, but he could start to get better. Trauma had a way of twisting a person's mind around on itself, trapping them in a loop of suffering they couldn't escape. What the jymtandi had done was untangle the skein of memory and pain, freeing Taylor from constantly reliving those moments in his head. His dreams weren't fearsome every night, and he could shake hands without gloves.

Now when the thought of Girona and the palace, what he felt was angry. He was right to be angry. He had good cause. Unbidden he had helped them, and in return they had killed him. They deserved his anger. They had earned it.

"This is better, Phillp-Priest," insisted Twoluck in his animal form. In spite of the last few days of close contact with the kilabora, it still felt weird to be taking mental health advice from a sixty kilo tree squirrel. "Much better than where you started. Do not be stuck in anger: know it without feeding it. This is your danger now Phillip-Priest, to let anger be your master."

"Twoluck, I've been meaning to ask you," said Taylor, changing subjects, "is Unity your only language, or do your people speak something else?"

"Unity is our only language! We speak it different from the low landers. Why ask this? Does Phillip-Priest think to teach us proper Unity?"

"No Twoluck," he laughed, "I'm not out to change your people. I was only curious."

"Twoluck is curious too, little priest. You should be asking, what about your people? Kilabora have jymtandi to give them shelter. What do your people have?"

"Good question. If we don't change our ways, we won't have anything at all."

Milo was ahead of the group then, checking the path ahead. Mila looked curious, but chose not to ask what they were talking about. She would question him later.

"Will Phillip-Priest keep our secret? If others know then kilabora is in danger."

"I understand, Twoluck. They won't hear it from me. Has no-one else gone so far back?"

"Kilabora can, some of us. Most outsiders we help can only remember the recent past. Never do I know an outsider who can see the beginning. I work many years to know so much."

The kilabora elder regarded Taylor, as it trotted easily alongside Ben.

"I just wish," said Taylor, "I had something I could show others to prove the cycle is real. Or, at least to support the idea."

"When we get to my village I will show Phillip-Priest something he has not seen."

What Twoluck had in mind was the Kilopoli council chamber. It was just a circular building with a single room, built around the stump of a truly ancient tree. Nearly the entire village had been built from the wood of a single bole, and the stump of that tree was the floor of this house which they had built around it.

The stump was highly smoothed and polished, well enough to show the rings. The twenty-five hundred rings were red and brown in the center, shaded to white, then to red, then to white again, then part-way to red. One could count the cycles as easily as counting the rings.

Taylor produced one of his paper notebooks and started writing.

"Twoluck, I estimate about eleven hundred years between cycles. Does that match your count?"

"Eleven Hundred Nine," answered Twoluck. He was back in his human form and wearing a robe that someone had produced.

"When was this tree harvested?"

"When the village is built, in the year of alignment. Unity begin hunting us, so we build here. Close to jymtandi."

"That leaves us less than a lifetime," murmured the disciple. Exasperated, he closed his book with a forceful snap. "Unbelievable."

Taylor knelt on the floor and examined the rings again, focusing on the bands of near-white.

"Twoluck, I have a big favor to ask of you."

Twoluck only saw them to the border of the Old Forest and said goodbye as they turned towards Tegea. For a while they rode in silence, across the Cedar Plateau, before Milo couldn't take it any more.

"So are you going to tell us what's going on, or do we have to guess?" Their appalons' feet padded quietly on the deep layer of needles covering the road. They could ride three abreast here, because the road had been cut to haul hundred-foot sections of tree trunks. Fellers kept the road clear of saplings and debris, and once a year the church sent a disciple to repair problem areas. A hundred years of that had made the road very pleasant to travel.

"I'm going to make you reason. Consider this part of your make-up for the lessons you've been missing."

Taylor indulged in a wicked grin as the older cousin groaned. "I promise you, it's interesting. What did you notice about the stump we were looking at?"

"It was big," said Milo.

"Come on, Milo," Taylor scolded him, "do better. Close your eyes and remember. Really look at it. Describe it."

Milo, spurred by his master's rare rebuke, closed his eyes and trusted his appalon to keep pace with the others.

"About five meters across, sanded smooth, and coated in laquer or some other finish. I didn't touch it. The rings were different colors, from dark red to nearly white."

"Were the different colored rings all mixed up randomly, or was there a pattern?"

"The colors were grouped together, dark, then light, then dark. And," he threw in before Taylor could criticize him again, "the color changes were gradual. And the pattern was regular."

"Better. Let's do an experiment," Taylor told them. "What do you think we'll find if we look at other cypress stumps?"

"The same thing," Milo said, "dark in the center fading to white, then back again."

They detoured to where the year's cut had taken place. Taylor made stone tools for them, and ordered each to smooth a section of stump on a different tree. To make the work easier he mildly enhanced their strength and hardened the stone tools. Milo picked the biggest stump he could find, while Mila chose a more middling-sized one. He wanted them to each smooth a pie-slice of stump well enough they could get a good count of the rings. That task took took a good part of the afternoon.

Taylor used the opportunity to have a good long think, free of Jim Tandy's memory tree. The longer he thought about what he had seen, the more the implications stacked up. This world had a way of springing big surprises on him.

Up to now Taylor had been very restrained in his behavior. He had been careful about the few pieces of technology he had introduced, and had barely spoken about his life in Emristar. Now he was thinking that had been a big mistake.

Mila and Milo returned to him, sweating. Together, the three of them examined the rings from two trees: a two-hundred year old specimen that was most typical of the fellers' harvest, and a five-hundred year old giant.

"What did you observe?" Taylor prompted his followers.

"Mine is about five hundred years old and is medium in the center," said Milo, "becomes dark, then almost medium again."

"While mine," said Mila, "was only two hundred years old, was darkest in the center, and was the same medium color on the outside."

"Any conclusions?"

"The tree doesn't just grow that way," Milo said. "It depends on when they were planted."

Mila posited a new theory. "Maybe something outside the trees are affecting them. All of them at the same time in the same way. Didn't Twoluck say the meeting stump was cut at the alignment? That was a dark-ring year."

"Yeah," agreed Milo, putting his finger on about the right spot on his tree, "both of our trees show their darkest rings at two hundred years ago."

"They're responding to the environment," Mila added. "Maybe it's some kind of adaptation."

Milo nodded excitedly. "Like the way gurantor fur turns black if they spend all their time in the snow."

Taylor couldn't help himself from feeling proud. Six months ago these two couldn't have managed a feat of inductive reasoning. The money and effort he had spent on them wasn't being wasted.

"That's my theory, too. Your gurantor example is a good one. Any guesses as to why the gurantor makes a darker coat in the show?"

"To stay warm," said Milo, "and they turn white in the desert to stay cooler."

"It's all about the sun, isn't it?" said Mila. "What happens to the sun, to make all the trees turn white?"

"For now it's a theory. Summon the mounts," Taylor ordered. "We're going to travel fast. It's getting cold out."

Part way home during a rest break, Taylor grilled them on the book *Beginnings*. He asked them what they could recall about the few verses about the ancients. Mila had the best grasp of scripture, so she summarized for the both of them.

"The ancients grew powerful, and turned their backs on the sun. They hid in their fortresses of stone. Only a few of the fortresses survived Olyon's wrath. Those who survived returned to the sun. When they were beset by monsters, Olyon blessed them with the form of beasts. Even so, they nearly died out until the Chosen gathered them together in the worship of Olyon."

"And gave them the book of *Prayers*," finished Milo.

"Good enough," said Taylor, "except for the phrase 'turned their backs on the sun'. What does scripture say, exactly?"

"They denied the sun's power," quoted Mila with a sigh. "Are you going to tell us it doesn't mean what everyone thinks it means?"

"Like the word 'borders'," Milo added, citing the best-known such example. When the Chosen said to love without borders he was talking about wealth, status, and similar lines people draw between themselves and others. But the meaning of 'border' changed, so modern people often thought the phrase 'love without borders' meant people shouldn't make war on other nations. It was a perennial subject for sermons.

"So-o-o," wondered Mila, "what do you think it means?"

"That's your combined reading, writing, and scripture lesson for the next few days," Taylor told them. "Go to the temple and find every occurrence of the word 'deny', and explain its meaning in context."

"I knew it," groaned Milo.

"I knew it!" cheered his cousin.

"When you're done with that we'll resume this conversation. But in the mean time, here's one other thing to think about: Why do we know so little about history before Chosen?"

TEGEA DAYS

Their detours meant Taylor had come in late. Milo and Mila had taken the hillside road over to Penguin Workshop, so it was just Taylor and Ben arriving at Hylee House in the night. Livia had been waiting at the door to welcome him with a light meal and warm spiced milk by candlelight. Meanwhile, Atticus unloaded Ben and stabled the beast, ensuring he was well-brushed and fed. Taylor was grateful to fall into one of Livia's excellent beds.

Carl was in his dreams again but Taylor found it hard to admonish the child for his curiosity. The boy obviously had an innate knack for thoughtmancy, because he followed Taylor through his dreams, tagging along in a weird sort of dream-squirrel form with a human head. He was awed by the visions of Emristar and kept asking questions about how much of what they were seeing was real. Taylor humored him for a while, but eventually had to kick him out to get some real rest.

"This is fun, but I'm really tired from the jymtandi," the told the human-headed rodent, "and you should ask for permission instead of just barging in here." He ushered the child out of his dream and set a low-grade barrier around his mind. It wouldn't drain Taylor much, but it would remind Carl he wasn't welcome back unannounced. Taylor would have to talk to Livia about the kid's ability and whether he should receive accelerated training.

Taylor had arranged a late start with his followers the next morning, so he was able to take a leisurely breakfast of herbal tea, porridge with dried fruit, and a stack of message boards that he read from oldest to newest. Laura had departed, excited for what the road might bring and hoping they could connect again in some distant town. Lord Bardam's board asked if he would reconsider endorsing Urban's report, which he put aside to answer in the negative later. The alderwoman had written to ask if he would set up in Tegea as his permanent base, and her board went on top of Bardam's. Somebody named Lord Kanun wanted Taylor to improve the road to his mansion, and in compensation offered the pleasure of his company and the chance to sleep in a bedroom once used by the founder of Gallia. That too went onto the growing 'no' pile.

There were two requests for healing he could handle right away, and various bits of news from Patrix Primo. The last board from Primo, which was the newest message, was the problem.

"A woman calling herself Inez Trancoso, late of the Lavradio Palace Guard, has come seeking confession with Disciple Phillip the Younger. She is staying at the Speckled Eel, and awaits the disciple's call."

At first Taylor felt surprise, but it rapidly morphed into fury. They were insane to track him this far and then claim to only want confession. The last time anyone from the palace had talked to him she had lied about being his friend then poisoned him to death. If he wanted, he could pull down the whole palace before they even realized they were under attack. He could be there in four days if he pushed Ben to his limits, or seven if he decided to relax on the gurantor train while he plotted his attack. The whole matter could be settled within days, and the lame palace full of idiot nobles would cease to bother him. If he was clever enough, he could probably kill everyone in the central palace. The mayhem and power struggles that followed would keep them all too busy to worry about him.

"Phillip!" yelled Livia, "Phillip! Stop it! My children are crying!" From another room, Taylor could hear Carl wailing and another voice trying to console him, also in tears.

For a while Taylor had to simply follow his own breath. Control the breath, control the body. Control the body, control the emotions. The fury burned lower and lower, a little at a time, until he was near some approximation of normal. His eyes were semi-blind from the light of his own spirit, and the entire episode left him with a headache at the base of his skull.

He almost sent Atticus to run a message to Penguin Workshop, if Inez wasn't friendly he could be putting the boy in danger. He couldn't afford to put Livia's family in harm's way. Nothing from Primo had indicated foreign soldiers or unusual church personnel had been lurking around town, but they could just be hiding under an overlook prayer. He would have to fetch his followers himself.

He was tempted to tackle this problem alone, but the *Guidebook* cautioned against your bulwark at home. It said so quite often, in fact. There were even stories in scripture about early disciples who had left their bulwark behind only to suffer dire consequences. Leaving the bricktown cousins out of the situation could also count as a betrayal on Taylor's part. They lived together, or they died together. Maybe it was just the daily benedictions talking, but Taylor decided his first step was to join up with his followers without anyone being the wiser.

"Atticus, saddle Ben but leave him in the stable. Livia, have there been any rumors about strange people hanging around? I mean besides people from Dodona."

"There hasn't been anyone. What are you going to do?"

"That depends entirely on if someone tries to kill me today, how many there are, and who sent them. Or, maybe I'll just hear a confession. Hard to say."

Taylor dressed, packed a few meals worth of oat cakes, and recovered his weapons from their place by the front door. Protected by layers of enchantments he mounted Ben and took the hillside road to Penguin Workshop. With the both of them under the same Overlook prayer they made it to the workshop unobserved, although they had to step off the trail a few times to let people pass: if they didn't there would have been a collision on the narrow lane. They circled the workshop, looking and listening and smelling for anything out of the ordinary.

By the time Mila and Milo took their mounts and left the workshop, Taylor was pretty sure there was nobody around who didn't belong in Tegea. If there was an ambush it would be somewhere else. The cousins rode downhill towards his office where they were supposed to meet for the day's work, unaware he was ahead them by only a few meters. Taylor expanded his spirit to include them and their mounts, effectively making him appear suddenly in front of him while causing them to disappear to anyone else who was watching.

"Nice trick," Milo said while pretending not to be surprised. "What's going on?"

Taylor pulled them to the side of the road, so nobody would run into the trio while they were talking, and told them about Inez.

"It sounds like a trap," mused Milo, "offering something you really want. They could be waiting for you."

"Or she could be remorseful," countered Mila, "and needs to confess her wrongdoing."

"Or it could be a trap."

"If it's just her," Taylor thought out loud, "and she starts a fight the three of us are enough to kill her. The best she can hope for is to fight us to a draw. We just need to search her thoroughly first, to make sure she isn't carrying enhanced weaponry."

"Let us scout the area first, with Overloook and Eyes of Night," Milo offered. Eyes of Night was a prayer that gave one night vision, but it did so by letting the recipient see into the infrared spectrum. In the daytime it was still useful for spotting hidden people.

Mila nodded her agreement. "If it really is just her, we should be able to handle her safely."

A survey of the area around the temple found nothing except the patrix and his housekeeper cleaning up after the morning services, and one old lady who had come by to pray while her two grandchildren played noisily in the courtyard. After she left, they entered the sanctuary and revealed themselves to a startled Primo. He was happy to send Pipa to fetch Inez from the Spotted Eel.

"Do you have something you use as a confessional?" Taylor asked him.

"All we have is a wooden plaque," said Primo. "I'm told it was carved from the heartwood of the same tree as the dome." He went to fetch what turned out to be an ornately carved placard of a scene from *Disciples*, the edges worn smooth from centuries of penitents and priests touching it.

They removed the star from the altar so it couldn't be taken as a weapon, and decided that Mila would be visible and weaponless when Inez arrived and conduct the search. Milo and Taylor would be invisible during the search. In case things turned violent, all of them would be enhanced. During the confession, the bulwark's job would be to guard the sanctuary. If they had to escape, Taylor would create a hole through the back wall of the sanctuary. Primo would not be present because there wasn't any reason to pull him into their problems.

"She showed up two nights ago," Primo said, while they were waiting, "looking for you. Came in on the train, working as a guard to pay her way. Do you know her?"

"We know of her," said Taylor, "but I'm not sure how well we know her. I know we can't afford to trust her blindly."

Primo looked concerned about how things were developing. "Phillip, you look ready for bloodshed. I can send her away and tell her you'll never see her."

"She's one of the palace guard's best fighters, and the palace is implicated in the death of a friend of ours. So yes, we're taking her very seriously."

"This isn't about the Missing Disciple of Girona, is it? What does that have to do with you? Or her?"

"That's what we're going to find out. You should give us the room." If Inez was in earnest then the confession would be private. If she was not, then things would get bloody. Primo saw the wisdom of retreating to his residence.

Inez herself seemed satisfied at the arrangements when she arrived and was instructed to drop her overcoat and anything she was carrying outside of the sanctuary. Mila searched her thoroughly including the hairline, between the thighs, under the arms and breasts, and even felt along the seams in her clothing. Inez had entered the sanctuary with empty hands and empty pockets.

"Is your disciple in this room," she wanted to know, "ready to pounce?"

"Fuck around and find out," said Mila, pushing her down into one of two chairs facing each other by the altar, using her prayer-enhanced strength. The only item on the altar was the confessional. Mila stood behind Inez, ready to pop her head like a grape if the situation called for it.

Inez put her left hand on the carved placard next to her. "I've come to confess," Inez announced to the room, "to the events surrounding the death of Taylor DeLanion."

Taylor, who had been sitting in the second chair, disbanded his Overlook prayer to appear before her. "Hello Inez. What a surprise."

Inez started with an intake of breath, and scanned his face with greedy eyes. From this distance his brindled hair and shining pupils couldn't hide who he was. "I've come to confess," she said at last, quieter this time.

"Confession to a priest is a solemn ritual, meant to unburden a heavy heart," advised Taylor. "Confession to a disciple is something else. It's a trial. You cannot lie. You cannot speak half truths. You cannot hide. You can either talk until you're done, or you can break off the confession. It can be a cruel ordeal for someone who isn't ready to face their actions. Are you certain you want to do this?"

"I want to confess," said the tall woman again, "to the events surrounding the death of Taylor DeLanion, beloved disciple of Girona. Your death. Please, hear my confession."

Taylor placed his right hand on the confessional and said the prayer to open hearts and bind them to the truth.

Inez began to speak.

Inez

I come from a long line of knights. For us, it's the family business. My brothers, my father, his brothers, and their father are all knights. Some of the women, too. "Serve the realm with honor," is the family motto. I grew up looking at it carved on the mantle. Most of my life, I've been able to live by those words.

I was always proud of my service to the palace. Someone from a nobody family like mine has to be twice as good as everyone else to be a Palace Guard. Most of the time the work was dull but honorable. Even when the things they made me do weren't very honorable, it was always in service to the kingdom. My own honor could take second place as long as I was serving the good of the realm. That's how I was taught.

When Queen Diana told us you were to be killed I couldn't believe it. I was about to resign on the spot, but she said the Unity had put a bounty on your head, and for the good of the kingdom you had to be ... 'Removed' is the word she used. We figured you had gone the way of Juca DeSintra, full madman heretic, and that was why they wanted you dead. So I did what I always do, which was whatever they told me to.

My task was to keep tabs on the Red Fang, those mercenaries hired by Duke Frenzio, in case they tried to do something stupid with your body like dump it in a sewer. It was important that you disappear without trace so nobody would know what happened. The church and the palace both wanted you gone, but nobody wanted to take the blame. You would be gone, nobody would know what happened, and they could claim you went off and got eaten by a monster or something.

Of course, Nurr sabotaged that part of the plan by including Janocas. The minute he knew you were dead he tried to raid Pegasus Workshop in revenge for his family. He was identified, naturally, because he is inept. So now the palace is implicated. There have been demonstrations, almost riots. Did you know that? The city is ready to come apart because of this. Which was probably Nurr's intent all along, to make everything unsettled again because he failed last time.

I decided I had to be the one to bury you on my own: I didn't trust those harpies from the queen to do it properly. I put you in a nice east-facing hillside, with Deshiron's knife, and built a mound over you. But you probably know that part.

After, nothing was the same. They were all such vultures. They took everything you had on you, and they emptied your vault. If you hadn't put Prince Estevan in charge of the school they would have taken that, too. I felt sick, every day, watching the palace nobles tear each other down and vie for position in the new regime. The harpies acted like nothing had happened, they just kept dancing and flirting with the nobles. That's their main job, you know. It isn't waiting on

259

the queen. It's pumping the court for information. Dances, pillow talk, gossip, everything is a source of information for them.

The worst was standing guard for Estevan. He was looking for you, his friend. He was literally the only person who was looking for answers, and I had to pretend the whole time I didn't didn't know you were dead and buried. He tracked down Red Fang's residence in the city and linked them to Frenzio, but he couldn't prove with certainty he was behind them.

One day, I'm guarding the king, and he's complaining about how Lavradio hasn't been paid for killing you. The country's debt when he retires affects his pension, and Frenzio was supposed to cancel some of the national debt when he got the gold from the church, but Frenzio claimed he never received it. DeGray was dead, found in his office by one of his priests, so the only way to get the gold was to go to Leadership. So I was there when King Joaquim wrote Unity an invoice for killing you: One ton of gold. That was the reason. That gold-grubbing lazy sack of a king had killed you to fatten his pension. There was no bounty from the Unity: Cuelar Frenzio had played DeGray to use the basilica's money, killed him, and probably ran off with the gold, too. It's all very elegant, in a Frenzio sort of way.

I think that was the end of it, for me. You hadn't done anything wrong. You weren't a threat to the kingdom. The unity didn't want you dead. But I helped them kill you, and every day I would look in the mirror and wonder who I was looking at. Where had all that sense of honor gone?

When Leonardo arrived he started telling this story about an under-aged disciple who saved Malisa's life. Estevan was so hopeful, but other than the age it didn't sound at all like you. Brindle hair, silver eyes, poor spirit control, didn't sing, surly. Yes, they described you as surly. It didn't sound at all like his friend, so Vani never looked deeper.

But I couldn't stop thinking about it. How many under-aged disciples can be running around loose in Lavradio? The idea wouldn't leave my head, even though I knew for certain you were dead. On my next day off I took an appalon and visited your grave. I don't know what I was going to do when I got there, I just knew the palace was a bad place for me and I wanted to be somewhere else for a day. So there I was, on the hilltop, looking for a missing grave. I think I went a little mad then. There's no other word for it. I laughed, and turned over rocks like there would be pieces of you I could pick up to prove it had all happened. I wondered if the queen found your body and moved you. I thought maybe I had buried you somewhere else. Then I just rode aimlessly until it was dark out and finally headed back to Girona. The poor appalon was footsore by the time we got back.

I came in through the north gate, so of course I thought of bricktown and Lucia. I must of been frightful to look at because people were avoiding me like I had plague. Matrix took me in, gave me food and served me jota. She said, "is this about Taylor? Then you have to find Phillip the Younger." I tried to confess but she refused to hear it. She said the only person I could confess to properly was you. I had to track you down first. Once I had a name it wasn't that hard to follow you, starting from the *Histories*, but it took a while.

I can't change what I did. There's nothing that can make it right. Everything you did for them was meaningless as soon as they could make money by killing you. I thought I was so honorable, but all they had to do was give me an order and I was willing to murder an innocent. And it didn't make the kingdom safer. Leadership will come down hard on them. Nurr will sit back and enjoy the show, then execute whatever plan he has while the palace is occupied with sucking up to Leadership.

And I'm here. I can't stand any of them any more, so I'm here. They'll get some of what they deserve, and I won't be there to help them through it. They made their own problems, so as far as I'm concerned they can clean it up on their own.

I think that's everything.

Gallia, Tegea

Taylor removed his hand from the confessional. "So what do you want from me? I'm not sure I'm ready to forgive anyone yet. I'm still pretty mad about the whole thing."

"I don't want anything," she said. "I don't have the right to ask for forgiveness or absolution. All I wanted was to tell you what I did and why it happened, and that I'm sorry. Maybe knowing why it happened will help you, somehow. That's all.

"If there's something you need from me, though, all you have to do is ask. I owe you. But I'm not here to get anything from you."

Taylor had thought getting answers would make him feel better, but instead he felt empty. He knew he should have questions about the whole matter, but he couldn't think of what they were. He had bigger things to concern himself with now, anyway.

"Stick around for a few days," he finally said to Inez. "I might think of something."

"So, what are you going to do about Inez?" The question came from Primo during afternoon jota three days after the ex-guard's confession. Taylor and his followers had taken up their usual schedule, starting each morning with physical training, followed by disciple office hours. In the afternoon the cousins pursued their latest assignment in the temple's small library the while Taylor continued his experiments with the natural laws of spirit.

The patrix had found him in his office, next door to Ferange's clinic. Mrs. Vale had packed an extensive basket for lunch, and Mr. Vale had brought it down to the office and was serving jota and miniature sandwiches from it. Primo was poking around at his various apparatuses, trying to figure out what they all did.

"I'm not obliged to do anything with her," said Taylor. He wasn't sure what had happened to his fury from three days ago that had so frightened Livia and her children, but now he couldn't find it in himself to be any more than passingly irritated at Inez. The way she had buried him said even more than her confession had. He had bigger problems than Inez to worry about right now anyway.

"You could do worse than a former palace guard for a bulwark, you know," Primo suggested. "You said you were looking for better martial training."

"Did she ask you to say that to me?"

"No. It's just an observation. And you've told me more than once there isn't anyone suitable in Tegea." He opened a wooden box and gasped. "Is this a giant ruby?"

"No," Taylor told him with a tinge of mischief, "it is something much more rare. It is red emerald."

"I didn't know there was such a thing! Where did you get it?" Primo picked up the long, double-terminated crystal and held it to the light.

"I made it. It stores spirit, kind of like a waterskin. If you have extra you can pour it in, and if you run short you can take some out."

"How much does it hold?" he asked.

"Well, now you've hit on a very difficult question. We don't have a well-established way to detect spirit except to be spirit sensitive. And we don't have any standard measures for spirit, either. You might as well ask me how much starlight it would take to fill this cup." Taylor drank from the cup for emphasis.

"So all I can tell you is 'a lot'. The rod can hold a full week's worth of my excess spirit, however much that is. Don't drop it. I don't know what happens if you damage a full spirit stone. Probably nothing good." While he was thinking of it, Taylor made a note in a nearby notepad to test that very thing.

Primo carefully replaced the rod and closed the lid on the box.

"What's this?" He picked up a board the size and shape of a plate that had a coil of metal pinned to it, and the loose end had a red pointer attached to it.

"That detects the light of spirit. Watch the point." Taylor shaped some of his own spirit around the board, and the

264

needle moved to the right in a smooth arc. When he removed his spirit, the needle retreated to its initial position.

"That's impressive. You should put numbers on it, so you can read it like a gauge."

"That's the problem I'm working on now. How much is a unit? How do we define the quantity in a way that is universally reproducible? How do we ensure the devices can be properly calibrated? Once we solve all of those problem, what do we call them?"

Primo smiles beatifically. "I can help you with the last question. Call them youngs."

"I was thinking lumens, or maybe ergs."

"Who is Erg?" asked Promo. "Did he help you with all this?"

"There is no Erg, it's just a word I made up so it wouldn't be confused with anything else."

"It's a terrible word." The young cleric shook his head, making his tufted ears flop back and forth. "People who invent things get them named after themselves. It's common sense! Mr. Vale," he appealed to the butler, "ergs or youngs?"

"Youngs, sir. Quite obviously. The master's followers feel strongly about it, too."

Taylor sighed and gave up on convincing them. It made him happy to have so many people in his corner, but he didn't think taking public credit was such a great idea. When the youngmeter started giving bad news the world was sure to blame its creator. Naming it after himself made the inventor too easy to find.

"We're back," called Milo from the front room. "Bless you Mister Vale. We're starved."

"We can take over service, Mr. Vale. We have to give a report to the disciple."

"I'm quite capable of making a new pot, young Mila."

Taylor interrupted them. "They're trying to be tactful, Minho. Their report is church business."

"I understand," said the butler. "I'll return to the house."

"Thank Mrs. Vale for me, too."

"I will, sir."

"Should I leave?" asked Primo.

"Only for your own peace of mind. But I am curious about your reaction. Your choice." The patrix chose to stay.

Milo busied himself with the jota and the small stove in the corner, while Mila began their presentation.

"The assignment was to catalog all uses of the word 'deny' in scripture, using context to decide what it meant at the time. These boards are a complete catalog, but I'll offer a verbal summary. In *Beginnings* and *Chosen*, to deny something meant to push back or struggle against an attack. It wasn't until the middle of *Disciples* that people started using the word as a negation of an idea or defiance of authority. By late Disciples the original meaning was no longer in use at all, at least not in scripture."

Mila went on to give specific examples, while Milo wolfed down his share of the sandwiches in the back of the room where he thought no one but Mila could see him.

Milo refreshed their cups and plates when she was finished and took over so she could eat.

"When scripture says the ancients denied the sun, the modern assumption is they did something wrong and the reason their fortresses didn't survive was because they were punished by Olyon for their sins. But what *Beginnings* really says is that the sun was attacking them and they were trying to protect themselves.

"If you want to hide from the sun there is one obvious place to go, and that's underground. And that's why," he said triumphantly, "you never hear about ancient ruins above ground. They took their civilization underground. Some of them survived, and when the sun stopped being so dangerous they returned to the surface."

Mila jumped in, "and then the cycle repeated. But this time their answer was to become two-formed. Instead of building their way to survival, they changed themselves. And it must have worked, because people survived. Eventually the different tribes met and interbred, giving us the blessings we have today. We've lost our second form, but the population was probably very low after the sun storms so interbreeding was a necessity."

"Sun storms?" asked Primo. "What do you mean?"

"We mean," said Milo, "a long period of time when the sun is dangerously hostile. It makes too many monsters, and the world is too dangerous to live in like we do now. It happens on an eleven hundred and nine year cycle."

Primo was looking ill, which Taylor took to mean he was paying attention.

"This is why we have so little history," said Mila. "Every cycle comes close to killing everybody, and we have to rebuild from almost nothing. It doesn't help that the church is going around destroying everything from the ancients."

"Yeah. It's pretty dumb, throwing away knowledge," said Milo, effectively scolding Leadership in the presence of a priest and a disciple. "What are they thinking?"

"They're protecting the Enclave," Taylor told him. "The ancients have their own kind of art, and if people learned how to put that to use it would undermine the church's power. You see that kind of behavior a lot in large institutions. Sometimes they prioritize their own survival or primacy, at the expense of their core mission. I wish I was more surprised."

"Excuse me," interrupted the patrix, "but this is all just theoretical, isn't it? All you have is a bit of textual analysis, and a novel interpretation of scripture. Where does the eleven-hundred year cycle come from?"

Mila shook her head. "We have tree rings, and the lore of the kilabora. We could look at tree rings from other parts of Tenobre and see if they follow the same pattern and timing. And we can get in touch with other two-form tribes. We can ask if they have lore about their own origins and how they survived the last cycle."

Milo joined in. "And we can look in *Luminous Histories*, and count sightings of cursed monsters. If we're right about the timing, it should be lowest around the alignment and growing since then."

"And I would like population summaries from all of Tenobre," added Taylor. "I have a hunch the last fifty years haven't been good for humans, and the Unity is not saying anything about it. If we're wrong then it's good news."

"And what if it's not?" asked Primo.

"Then we have a very limited time to prepare for a world that is hostile to human life," answered a thoughtful Taylor.

"How long?" insisted the priest.

"If we're not ready by the time these two die of old age," Taylor told him, pointing at his followers, "then we're too late."

"You can't tell any of this to Leadership," Primo warned them, "it upsets everything. You need backing before you say a word of it. The deans might listen, but the council will use everything it has to crush you."

Taylor now had more problems than he could manage on his own. He had theories that needed data, inventions to refine and deploy, and ideas that may or may not be deemed heretical. He desperately wanted advice from someone he trusted who was highly placed in the church. More than once, he had to remind himself that the fate of the world was not entirely his responsibility: he had been kidnapped here, then murdered. Anything he did for these people was something he chose to do, and if they died it wasn't actually his fault.

In spite of his lingering grudges he was going to try to do something, and right now he needed to be doing it from Unity City, in the Enclave. It was a long journey, it was winter, his entourage was too small to handle real trouble on its own, and he needed a guide.

"Inez," he asked the woman in front of him, "have you ever been to Unity City?"

"I have, Phillip," she answered. They were seated in Livia Hylee's drawing room. "I was there for three years when Prince Emilio was attached to the embassy there."

"And what about the Art School grounds. Are you at all familiar with them?"

"Very. It's common for embassy assistants to take a few classes at the school, even if they're a little older than the other students."

"Then I have a proposition for you. You said I could ask you for something. I would like to employ you as a follower on a short term basis. Say, six months. You will do the usual guard and attendant duties, plus martial training. We need your experience.

"In return, you will share the roof over my head, the food from my table, and the light of my spirit. As soon as I'm able, I will equip you appropriately. There is also an insufficient stipend for this position. What do you think?"

"Are you sure you want me as a follower? After what I did?"

"I think I have a good idea of what you're made of, and the world needs more of it. I realize it's a step down from guarding royalty, but I would be an idiot not to ask while I have the chance."

Inez had to clear her throat to speak. "It's not a step down. It will be my honor to call you my disciple, and help you bring Light to the world."

"I'm glad," he said. "Now the first thing we need to do is go fishing."

Gallia, Tegea Coast

The *Red Bird* was a small fishing vessel that prowled the waters near Tegea with either nets or traps, depending on its prey. In summer it sometimes took charters from parties of rich merchants, or nobles come up from Philius looking to get drunk away from the House of Lords and catch a few big ocean fish they could lie about the rest of the year. A winter charter was a rare chance for the *Red Bird's* captain to not fish during the harshest part of the year and kick back with a few lines instead. A guaranteed income was better than the uncertainty of paying deck hands to haul nets and maybe come up empty.

Captain Leboc was already familiar with Phillip the Younger. The disciple had healed one of his men's injuries for a very reasonable sum, and strengthened the boat's hull and keel. It was worth every silver he had paid to the boy, but he was glad to have a chance to earn some of it back. The charter was guested by Patrix Primo, Healer Ferange, Phillip, and his three followers, all wrapped up warmly against the chill.

While the others fished, the disciple asked dozens of questions about the fisheries, the seasonal effects on different species, and whether anyone kept records of the catch. He also asked questions the captain couldn't answer, like if there were any underwater vents that blew hot air or water into the sea. Leboc's answers were written down in a small book, which seemed like too precious a treatment of a mere fisherman's knowledge. It was the disciple's book, however, and he could write in it if he wanted to.

The other odd thing Phillip did was drag a contraption behind the *Bird*. It was a little like a midwater trawl, cone shaped and set to a depth of just a few meters below the water. It was set too shallow to catch anything, and the net ended in a small cup, too small to hold any fish worth keeping. The disciple seemed perfectly aware of all these shortcoming.

Whenever Leboc furled his sails and let his passengers put out their lines, Phillip pulled in his net and examined the cup. What he found there was a variety of small life-forms, but among them was tiny flecks of metal. The charter stopped at three different locations, places where Leboc spied the sea birds diving for young mackerel that rode the upwelling waters close to shore. They would catch a few of the rich oily fish, grill them quickly on the ship's stove, and snack on them with a milky grain alcohol before moving on. At the third stop they found what they were looking for: big sailfish hunting the small mackerel.

Leboc kept their hooks baited for the smaller specimens of sailfish. They caught and released a few that were about a meter in length, until Primo hooked one that put up a real fight. Just a few minutes into it, the priest begged Phillip to enhance his body. The boy laughed and strengthened his line and pole instead. This was sport, he said, and anything more would be cheating.

From then on the priest and the other guests had to struggle together against the fish. They took turns supporting Primo or, just as often, fortifying him with alcohol. When they finally landed the beast, a sailfish over two meters long (not including the meter-long bill) Inez killed it deftly with a single blow to the head using a belaying pin.

It didn't take long for Milo to filet it into chunks for the cooking pot, with the head and bones going into a second pot for stock. The ship's tiny galley had been stocked ahead of time for this exact purpose, and the smell of stew was soon raising their hunger.

For the rest of the evening Primo was proud as a king. He insisted the crew be served from his catch instead of the usual dried store, and jota was brewed strong enough to wake the dead. They feasted and sang, as the little ship made its was to the delta so Phillip could try his device there. Leboc tacked the *Bird* back and forth across the mouth of the delta until Phillip pulled in his last catch of the night: two kilograms of dull shiny metal flakes.

"Is it silver?" asked Leboc from his wheel.

"Manganese," said the boy, coming closer so he could see. It was a word none of them had heard before. "Much more common than silver. It comes from the rocks in the hills and dissolves in the water. With the arts and a little creative artifice you can extract it."

Healer Ferange came up behind him to look. "Why are you so interested in this manganese?" Between the drinks and the rocking of the ship Leboc worried the healer might fall overboard. With night and a cold wind on them, it was safer to have them in the cabin for the journey home.

"The metal can be alloyed with bronze to improve it. It's the secret to Moldonian bronze, but their manganese probably occurs naturally in their tin mines."

"I don't know of a prayer that lets you separate metal from water," said Ferange.

"A lot of prayers have deeper meaning and more uses than we're told. The next time I'm in the north of Gallia, I can teach you some things that might be useful. If you want."

Once the passengers were safely stowed in the cabin the *Red Bird* sailed home, festooned with spirit lamps and trailing music in its wake.

MENDICANT

Taylor took his time reaching Unity City. He made a lot of excuses to himself: he had too much to think about before he arrived; he needed to finish parts of his research; there were record searches they wanted to do in Gallia's capital; they encountered requests for aid. The real reason for the slow trip was that he was having a good time. Seeing new places and helping people deal with disasters and monsters was his current idea of a perfect life. There was even the occasional wondrous sight to behold. He could live a lifetime that way, if the world would cooperate enough to let him.

Their first stop was the trade city of Kourion, at the intersection of the Lavradio road and the north-south spine of Gallia's main highway. There he purchased the cheapest copper he could find and rented time at a forge that looked underemployed. With his followers' assistance he used the arts to separate out the impurities and create a series of alloys until he found a good balance of strength, spirit response, and acid resistance. They selected two alloys, one for weapons and one for armor, and spent a week making spear tips, short swords, and armor scales. The swords all received grips of lustrous bone from the cursed bifurdactica, which Taylor discovered by accident enhanced the duration of enchantments on the blades.

The scales were incorporated into brigantine armor. For helmets they had some decidedly unimpressive leather caps with thin layers of enhanced bronze on the outside and a thick lining on the inside. Taylor also commissioned bifur cloaks for all three of his followers, exhausting his store of fur but effectively putting them all in uniform. Anyone who saw them would know they were together as a team.

Those preparations left Taylor nearly broke, but his cadre was thoroughly equipped. It was fortunate everyone had their own mounts already, because he couldn't have afforded three appalons on top of everything else.

Thus outfitted, they toured every town between the city Kourion in Gallia, through the outskirts of Kravikas, ending at Unity City in Dace.

Now that Taylor had a proper bulwark, monster hunts were both fun and profitable. But there were only so many monsters that needed hunting so he made his day-to-day expenses by holding healer holidays. He would heal anyone and everyone in a town of any injury or malady, all for the same low rate per person. Often, the local lord or alderman would pay for everyone out of the town's funds. Room and board were always free to the disciple's cadre in those towns, so the silver began to accumulate.

They stopped in Philius, The capital of Gallia, for a week so they could survey the population records kept in the main temple. They also took in a few concerts, allegedly for the sake of the cousins' cultural education but mainly because Taylor had a craving for new music.

After Philius, they crossed the border south into Kravikas, where they skirted the big central desert until they came to the great center of trade and culture that was Kashmar. On the city's outskirts they hunted a mimica bigger than an appalon, and then a mutant bog spider with so many legs it made even Inez ill to look at it. The spider put up a serious fight, even after Milo put a spear through some of its eyes, and they ended up denuding it of its many legs before they could kill it.

Camped on the shores of the Vaidas river and wrapped in an Overlook prayer they chanced upon a tribe of shy two-formed people. Silently, the cadre observed them morphing from seals to humans to come ashore and climb trees to pluck the winter fruits. Taylor's party watched from their shelters as the naked people stuffed their finds into net sacks and disappeared into the river. They drifted downstream in the cold waters, resuming their animal forms at their leisure. The language they spoke was definitely not Unity.

Did they live entirely apart from normal society, or were they just on the margins like the kilabora? Were they fresh water swimmers, or did they live in the ocean too? Taylor regretted not asking them questions, but he knew they would have run if he had shown himself. It was probably best to leave them in peace.

In Dace they took a cursed monster hunt. The main complications came not from the beast itself, but from the people who hired them: a village of hunters and farmers called Mariusto. They had submitted the request directly to the church, and when Taylor tried to contact their local lord he was turned away. The lady in question was notoriously reclusive and neglectful of her domain, so being rebuffed wasn't unexpected but it did make the situation delicate. They would effectively be hunting on her land without permission, and getting away with it only because Taylor was a disciple and killing a dark monster was doing her a favor. Taylor wrote the lady a notice declaring his intent, and invited her to send him away or negotiate if she wanted different terms.

The hunt itself was anti-climatic. The found the arkto, a huge ursine creature, upwind of them meandering along a greenway that bordered two farms, pulling down trees and gouging the drainage canal as it went. From a distance it was just a mass of darkness that left random destruction in its wake. It would have been hard to miss, even without a pack of trackers and hunters guiding them. They approached using Overlook and once they were close enough for their prepared light to illuminate the arkto, the beast rose up on its hind legs to threaten them: over three meters from foot to snout. Mila used the atlatl to send a dart into its skull and clean out the other side. The hunt was over.

Between the effective group tactics learned from Mobeen, the power of a spear thrower, the new alloy, and Taylor's spirit arts, a run-of-the-mill cursed monster wasn't a great challenge. Taylor recorded all their monster encounters, in keeping with the Mobeen method. He looked forward to the day he could show off his growing collection of hunts to his former teacher.

The villagers had little to pay with except their labor, so they insisted on skinning the arkto. They wanted to carefully preserve the head and paws and turn the entire thing into a massive trophy rug, but they could only do this if they had better tools. Taylor improved their tools enough to handle the cursed monster hide, which incurred a new round of negotiations about how they would pay. Taylor didn't need anything else from them but the *Guidebook* was adamant that some kind of value should always be accepted for a disciple's work. They settled on having the local hunters tutor Mila and Milo for the duration of their stay. The cousins would improve their tracking and game processing techniques, Inez would guard Taylor, and Taylor would enjoy some dedicated research time.

Taylor's cadre stayed in Mariusto for over two weeks, training by day and enjoying the company of the village people at night. The nights were exceptionally cold. More than once Taylor awoke in a neighbor's living room among a heap of bodies, where everyone had gathered together to stay warm. In the short time he spent in Mariusto, he wrote two new songs and made notable progress on his research.

The arkto rug was magnificent, a blue as deep as night with a rippling sheen of indigo. The paws and head were stuffed to resemble their original shape, with the claws and teeth all intact. The upturned tusks were so sharp that Mila was afraid someone might trip and fall on one and die, so Taylor fashioned sheathes of brass for them, with blunted points. The trophy was so large it had to be transported by cart, which wasn't an imposition because they also had a load of the arkto's best bones to carry. Taylor left some of the bone behind for the villagers, and a quarter share he sent to their lord as a tax.

The village chieftain accompanied them to the nearest depot town to certify the completion of the task to the temple. The proposed summary to be added to *Luminous Histories* was, "Disciple Phillip the Younger and three bulwark killed a cursed arkto, saving the village of Mariusto. No casualties." To Taylor the simple, undramatic entry was perfect. If he spent a lifetime piling up such mild acclaims he could count it as a life well lived.

The next day they boarded a carriage train to Unity City with appalons, trophy rug, and seventy kilos of top-quality monster bone.

ENCLAVE

Dace

Taylor's first view of Unity City was from afar, on the road
that came over the Lamia Hills before descending into the
plains around the city. Some enterprising person had built a
rest stop on that last hill, with a road house for the foot-
weary travelers and table service at a perfect spot from which
to observe the distant city. It was really a full day's walk, but
the city's architecture was so grand that even from such a
distance one could identify specific domed buildings tiled in
vivid blue, rows of white rectangular buildings roofed in red
clay shingle, and a large central park. Those central features
were surrounded by an impressive wall, forming the Enclave.
The remainder of the city, its buildings the size of children's
toys by comparison, spilled around the Enclave for miles in
all directions.

It was the largest and most beautiful city Taylor had seen
in Tenobre so far.

The travelers took hot jota on the tavern's chilly but
stunning overlook. The train stopped just long enough to let
them browse a small store of snacks and commemorative
pottery stamped with the road house's name, "Pandosia
View", featuring an image of the Enclave's great basilica.
From Pandosia it was only a couple of hours by carriage to
the city. It was a classic tourist trap: to not capitalize on such
a location would go against human nature.

Taylor's copy of the *Disciple's Guidebook* was special for a few reasons. Instead of thin wooden boards, it was written on parchment so it was easy to carry. The book had been hand-scribed by three of his teachers and presented as a kind of graduation gift, and each of them had added personal notes to the text. And, importantly for Taylor, it included an entirely original chapter by Disciple Leila about how to get around in the Enclave. The last chapter covered many things Taylor would have known if he had grown up in the church and spent several years at the Art School. He spent most of his time at Pandosia View re-reading the last chapter.

The party of four and their appalons entered Unity City and took lodgings at the Knight's Cup, a Leila-approved boarding house that catered to the transient church personnel who always seemed to be moving in to and out of the Enclave. The place wasn't cheap, but it included meals and stabling and a private bath house. They also had a concierge service that could summon anything you needed: hairdressers, event tickets, messengers approved to deliver inside Enclave, and so on. It was also only a few blocks from a gate into Enclave. They took a suite, where they unrolled the trophy rug in the common area to impress anyone who happened to visit, or just to roll around on because it felt awesome.

With part of the day still left to burn they bathed and took the time to groom off whatever wilderness had stuck to them. Appointments for hair and nails were made, and a messenger was summoned to run a letter to Dean Garsharp letting him know Phillip was in town. These were all routine matters to the staff of the Knight's Cup. The Enclave was the church's equivalent to palace grounds so one did not normally enter in a state of dishabille.

Their first morning in the city was spent on repairing their appearance, which put them at the main gate well after lunch. The gate warden was a tough-looking woman in her sixties who, according to Leila, was not to be taken lightly. The wardens memorized every name and face native to the Enclave and, it was rumored, had a mysterious power that let them eject anyone who needed to be removed. When Taylor approached the warden, in her red jacketed uniform, she silently handed him a board to be marked. Taylor said the prayer out loud and placed his futobel under four stars onto the wood so vividly it looked ready to walk off.

"Disciple Phillip the Younger anointed in the wilderness, with bulwarks Inez, Milo, and Mila. Welcome to the Enclave." It wasn't surprising to him that she had their names. Disciples registered their followers the same way they did their works, through whatever local temple was handy. Those notices were copied and forwarded to the Enclave. It was more surprising she had their names memorized. Maybe the wardens had noticed his message from the night before and knew to expect him. Any messenger would have to pass through one of the gates and show the address on the message.

"This is your first time entering," she said. It was a statement, not a question. "If you need assistance or direction, anyone wearing a red jacket similar to mine is available to you. Within reason." Her name tag, a strip of embossed silver, read 'Helen'. The silver indicated she held a supervisory role.

"Thank you, Warden Helen. Which way to the library? And, is there somewhere we can acquire a map?"

The cheapest way to get a map turned out to be copying one from the library, so they followed the warden's direction to one of the largest buildings in the Enclave: a three-story marble building with an enclosed courtyard. The courtyard smelled strongly of incense, which was mysterious because there was none visible.

Taylor knew better than to go looking around on his own in a vast unfamiliar collection. He would surely get distracted. Instead, they located one of the most under-appreciated resources in any world: the library's reference desk.

The reference librarian looked surprised to see Taylor and his three followers.

"I don't believe I know you," he said when Taylor introduced himself, his feline ears flicking back with annoyance.

"I was anointed in the wilderness, and this is my first time in Enclave," Taylor explained, not for the last time. "But I can prove my identity easily enough, if your histories are up to date."

The librarian sighed. Taylor thought he must have interrupted something, but the reference desk was utterly clean of anything except a stack of blank boards, an inkwell, and a brush.

"Let's have it then," he said, and handed over a board.

Taylor marked it, but neglected to say the prayer out loud.

"You use silent prayer," he noted. "The last reliable user of silent prayer was Juca DeSintra. Are you by chance related, Phillip the Younger?"

"I doubt it. In fact, that's probably impossible."

"You do realize the phrase 'probably impossible' implies the possibility exists."

"True," said Taylor after a moment's thought. He smiled at the new game, "But it is not possible through any set of circumstances that I am aware of. Maybe we should call it 'unlikely, to a high degree of certainty.'"

"That's not any better," said the librarian archly, his long tail tapping the table with impatience. "It means the same thing."

"Then let's settle on a firm 'no'."

"That was a most troublesome 'no', Disciple Phillip Out Of The Wilderness. Are you going to be a Problem Patron?"

Taylor pretended to be alarmed. "I hope not. I've barely arrived here. I was aiming to at least learn the library before alienating the reference librarian."

The man admired his silvery futobel, prancing and tossing his antlers in a challenge. "He's very cute. I'm Lector Herod. Do you have a work to report?"

"We're all caught up, thank you. What we'd like is summary population figures for all the nations in Tenobre since the Alignment. Secondly, we need a map of the Enclave useful for navigation."

"I'll show you." Herod took them to the second floor, where polished brass plates reflected the sunlight onto tables set out for studying boards. "We haven't had a candidate in today to light the hand lanterns, but I'm sure you can manage?"

"Of course," said Taylor, who had already been lighting every spirit lantern in passing. People were peering at the shelves, squinting in the dark, or trying to reflect light from the study area down into the isles. With working lanterns they wouldn't have to squint.

Herod showed them where the annual reports on population and trade could be found, pointed at the large framed map of the Enclave on a nearby wall and reminded them of the rules. Absolutely no fire. Food and drink were only allowed in the designated break rooms on each floor. The break rooms were even equipped with small charcoal stoves and kettles for making jota or tea. Once made, the drinks had to stay in the break room.

Each of Taylor's party took a yearly volume and parked as a group in the study area to see what they were up against. Most of the reports were about trade and agriculture, with only a passing discussion on population changes.

Taylor's little research team made their way through all two hundred years since the alignment in under two hours, but were unhappy with the data they had.

"I think this is suspicious," said Mila. She and her cousin had learned to read while running daily errands to the commodities exchange and city hall in Girona. "In the early years they reported year-over-year differences in population, births, and deaths. Then they suddenly stopped reporting the year over year numbers as soon as they leveled off."

"They're hiding the fact we've stopped growing," agreed Milo. "You won't know unless you look at multiple reports at a time, like we're doing now. How much you want to bet the news is even worse than that? There used to be summaries by region for each country, but now there isn't. And they've stopped reporting total grain harvests. It's all per-capita now."

"Useful, but derivative," said Mila. "You can tell if the harvest was good or not, but it conceals the fact that total harvest is flat because population is flat."

Milo dug out the report from twenty years ago. "I bet it's declining and they're flat out lying. Look at this: 'New methodology includes estimates of rural population not enumerated by national census.' Am I crazy, or is this a fancy way of saying they assume the monarchs don't count everyone and just add in whatever numbers they feel like?"

Taylor took the book and read the notation himself. "I think that's exactly what the means."

"And every year," noted Mila, "they estimate just enough people to keep the population level."

"I smell scrap-loaf," grumbled Milo.

When they asked the reference desk for the original census reports from the kingdoms they got a firm, "I'm sorry, but those are unavailable."

Taylor attempted to get a clarification from Lector Herod. "What precisely do you mean by unavailable? Does that mean the reports don't exist, aren't here, or I'm not allowed access to them?"

Herod's response was deadpan. "That information is also unavailable."

"Then let's try something else," said Taylor. "Can you tell us how many dark monsters have been fought by disciples for each of the last twenty years?"

"That summary information is unavailable." This time, the librarian looked sympathetic.

"Then what about the original records of the *Luminous Histories* for the last twenty years? The long form reports are all kept here, correct?"

"Please follow me to the third floor." Finally, they found something Herod was allowed to help them with.

The *Luminous History* archive was tightly spaced shelves, each packed with boards. Occasionally, a painted board demarcated the months and years. At a glance you could find exactly the month you were looking for, which helped if you were searching for records by date. Taylor lit several waiting spirit lamps and did a quick survey. The records went back over two hundred years, but he noticed something odd.

"Lector Herod, is it just me, or is the number of reports declining for the last fifty years?"

"I don't believe your perception is at fault."

"Have reports always been limited to one board each?"

"They have," he said, "with a rare exception for major battles. It was the Chosen's policy, to prevent disciples from attempting to accrue glory by words alone."

Taylor made an approving sign with his free hand. "The more I learn about the guy, the more impressed I am by him. Okay everyone, split into five year sections."

While Milo prepared a reading table with writing implements, Taylor turned to Herod. "Have we been a terrible burden to you today?"

"Oh, not a terrible one," he said.

"Phillip," called Mila, "I don't understand these abbreviations."

"Do you mind advising us for a little while, Lector? We won't ask you to perform any tabulation yourself. We just need a librarian's advice on interpreting the reports."

The lector's face did something Taylor couldn't follow. His pupils expanded and the corner of his lips twitched upwards, at the same time his nostrils flared and the tip of his tail froze as if in the presence of danger.

"I am due a break now," he said, "and am known to use the third floor room because it is quiet. If you should happen to ask me questions while I am having my cup, I won't turn you away."

The original reports, like the one written by the Mariusto chief, were kept at whatever temple they were delivered to and were generally simple narratives. One of the patrix's jobs was to ensure each board was copied into the format required by the library, which started with the date, location, and practitioner's name. The second line was a dense sequence of symbols that summarized the contents of the report: number of people healed, monsters killed, roads built, and other such quantifiable information. The next line was a filing number set by the library, the temple where the report was filed, and who performed the transcription. The rest of the board was the copied narrative from the original.

Mila asked Herod, "is there a book or catalog that has just the filing numbers and the abbreviated summaries?"

"I'm sorry," he said with his ever-increasing sympathy, "but that information is not available."

"Poor guy," she whispered to Milo, "I think he really wants to help us."

Once they understood how to decode the second line, thanks to Herod's instruction, paging through the boards became easy. They pulled just the dark monster attacks, tallied them, and sat down to read them. Cursed monster sightings were rare, but they were devastating. The cursed bifur in Fringe was unusual in that nobody was killed. Dodona was a more common case, with a whole town destroyed and nearly one hundred people dead. In the most year there had been fifteen cursed monsters, and two disciples had died fighting them. That didn't surprise Taylor one bit. If you weren't prepared for the darkness and the tough hide, then a dark monster could easily overpower a disciple. The bifurdactica had fractured his hips with its fake head. If the real head had bitten him, Taylor might not have survived.

The cursed monster attack reports, lined up in yearly stacks, make a perfect graph of the last fifty years: sporadic appearances of one every few years, then one or two every year, and a steep rise over the last several years.

"I see you've found your answer," said Lector Herod, emerging from the break room. The five of them looked at the sequence of stacks in silence. It wasn't a large enough sample to predict how big this year was going to be, but Taylor felt like last year's fifteen was going to be an easy number to beat.

"Does anyone want to bet," Milo offered, "that if we go back to the Alignment we discover zero cursed monsters for years on end, and a very low number of normal monsters. And I mean, maybe a tenth of what we have today."

"No bet," said Inez.

"Me neither," said Mila.

"A good question for tomorrow," said Taylor. "Lector, do you prefer jota, herbal infusions, or tea?"

"I am most fond of tea, but it's hard to obtain in the city lately."

Inez picked up what Taylor wanted. "When we passed through Kashmar we picked up a good variety of teas."

"Somebody went a little crazy at the bazaar," accused Milo, looking at Mila.

"The master said he wanted variety and quantity," she said proudly, "and I delivered."

"And that success has left us in a quandary," explained Taylor. "If we should have guests we don't know what to serve them, because we don't know the current style in Enclave. The next time we can take a break together, would you mind enduring a tasting? We'd love to have your opinion. We'll provide food as compensation, of course."

"It sounds enjoyable," said Herod. "But can we do it away from the library? And can I bring a friend?"

"Sure. We're at the Knight's Cup. Let us know when you have some time off and we'll arrange it."

The Knight's common room was crowded that night. Taylor met three healers who were traveling as mendicants but had been summoned to Unity City for assignment.

"Dey don't let you run around loose forever," said a thirty-ish man named Trifon. His tusks gave his speech an odd inflection. "Dey like to pin you ta one place eventually. Tis different for a disciple, o'course. All da best ones are mendicant. De first families make disciples, den keep em at home."

Most of the fifteen guests, besides Taylor's group, were students at the school. Students from first families were billeted in Enclave, in reportedly luxurious dorms. Students from second families were were placed in housing just outside the Enclave, like the Knight's Cup, again at church expense. Anyone else had to provide their own housing or have a sponsor on staff.

"I was anointed in the wilderness," Taylor explained, not for the last time, "so I'm surprised. I hoped the Art School would be more egalitarian. Or, meritocratic at least."

"Kid," explained another healer, and old guy named Mendelos with swollen knuckles and cocoa-colored skin, "you're very earnest, so its best you hear this early on. There's two kinds of practitioners. There's the ones who believe in the Work, and the ones who are just in it for the status and free meals. The workers are mostly out there," he waved at the whole world, "doing the Work and keeping civilization alive. The other kind never leave Unity City. They can barely evoke a candle's worth of light, never mind fighting monsters. They tell each other tall stories about their lineage, but really they're freeloaders. Leadership lets them get away with it because it's their children, and they don't want their precious heirs going out into the world and getting killed."

"Mendelos, look what you done," admonished Trifon, "you crushed the boy's heart."

"It's my own fault for getting my hopes up," admitted Taylor. "I actually know better, but the disciples I've met so far were such great people. I should have expected it all to be, I don't know, more disappointing on the inside."

"That's no way to talk," said the old healer soothingly. "The useless nubs here can't keep you from doing right out in the field. You just keep living by the tenets and don't let the Enclave dwellers interfere with you."

"Leadership knows they're useless, dear" said the woman next to Mendelos, "they just get their free room and board, and nothing else. Nobody confuses them with real working practitioners, except each other."

A gust of cold air blew in from the door as someone let themselves in and started stomping around. Loose flakes of snow drifted in with them and melted in the warm air.

"Where is Phillip?" shouted the new arrival. "Phillip the so-called Younger. Where are you, work-thief?"

"Here I am," said Taylor, raising his hand. "Did I do something to offend you?"

"Did you? You lit the library lanterns! Not that it matters to some rich kid, but some of us need to work to eat!"

The woman was near twenty, with dark hair that hung damply. Her pinched face and bare hands didn't show any signs of beast traits. If she was smooth-skinned then most people would assume she was talentless and low-born. Just looking at her Taylor could tell she was gifted, but her light hovered near her skin. Most gifted people had more of a nimbus around them.

She strode up to the table, at the space across from him, and pounded both of her fists against it in anger. Inez had her in a submission hold before most people could blink, and the cousins had their swords drawn. One was facing the interloper, while the other watched the door for any friends of hers that might have tagged along.

The smooth-skinned woman was on her knees, forced there by Inez's grip on her hand and wrist. The room stayed silent, expectant, while Taylor looked her over. Threadbare robes, insufficient layers of clothing for the climate, and a sunken look about the cheeks told him he must be looking at one of the unfavored students. She likely had no stipend and no support.

"My name is Disciple Phillip the Younger. These three are my bulwark. I hope you will forgive their enthusiasm: You wouldn't be the first person to try and kill me. And you are?"

"Oh shit," the woman whispered. "Oh shit. He didn't tell me you were a disciple. He just said you would be here. But of course you would be a disciple."

"Inez, loosen your grip. I think she's forgotten her name."

"I'm Candidate Khali. I'm sorry I barged in like that. I wasn't going to hurt you I swear, I was just trying to make a point."

"Have you eaten, Candidate Khali?" When she shook her head, Taylor motioned the proprietress to bring a meal. Inez deposited Khali into a chair across from him.

"I only lit the lanterns because it was past noon and the stacks were dark. I never meant to steal your meal, but I admit I may have gotten carried away. Be my guest, and let me make it up to you."

The woman glared at him, probably trying to divine his true goals, but Taylor signaled Mila to fetch his instrument. Taylor tuned up while soup, meat, and bread were plopped in front the hungry Khali. Taylor suspected she wouldn't eat if he kept staring at her, so he took song requests and played for various singers. Eventually Khali relented and ate, then at Mila's urging had seconds. When she seemed sated, Taylor put his instrument away and let someone else take over. The singing moved to the other side of the room, mostly.

"So, what happened today, to keep you from your meal?"

"It was my advisor," Khalil said. "She's supposed to bless my star in the mornings so I can work, but she's not exactly an early riser."

"And she doesn't feel you are a high priority," concluded Taylor. "Give me your star. I'll bless it for a full day so you can work tomorrow. What does she normally give you access to?"

"Just light." Khali handed over her symbol of Olyon. "I'm still having trouble with it."

"Really?" Taylor was surprised. Her reserves were significant, so she shouldn't have any problems. It had to be her technique. He said the prayer to bless her holy symbol and gave her permission for light, shaping, and water purification. Those three were considered essential starting prayers.

"Let's test to make sure I did it correctly. Bless this spoon with light, please."

As Khali said the Prayer for Light, her spirit barely budged. The spoon shone a little. Wood wasn't a good material for the light prayer, but her real problem was her technique. She didn't have any.

"Would it be okay if I gave you some pointers?" The spoon's light was weak, and seemed to be growing dimmer by the second.

"I'm saying it wrong. I know I can fix it. I just need to practice more." The public demonstration had stressed Khali.

"What? Your pronunciation is more than good enough. What I want to know is, what are you thinking about when you pray?"

"I'm thinking about saying the prayer perfectly, just like I've been taught. Day after day I say prayers hoping to be blessed, but only light ever comes. And barely that." The tears were welling up in her eyes and Khali looked ready to bolt up and flee into the night.

"Let Phillip help you," suggested Mila. "He's an excellent teacher. The worst that can happen is you waste a little time."

Khali nodded, she would stay.

"Is this typical?" he asked the table. "They put you in a room and you say the prayer until something happens?" The healers all nodded.

"It can take years to be blessed with all the healing prayers," said the old woman, "a lifetime might not be enough."

"Khali, I want you to try something. Close your eyes and imagine the sun, the blue-white source of infinite light. Imagine you have a piece of it, right here in your hand. It's heavy. It's so bright, the light pierces flesh, and it is right here in your hand. It's going to live in the spoon for a while. The spoon is made of stardust, like all of us, so this is perfectly natural. Can you feel the light in your hand, how it has weight and shape?

"Say the prayer now, and keep that image in your mind. Unite the spoon with the sun."

Candidate Khali said the prayer, and her spirit collected inside the spoon and set it alight. It was so bright, the whole table had to shade their eyes.

"You can open your eyes now," he told her.

"Ah! Did I make that?"

Without giving her a chance to consider what she had done, he passed her a series of small objects to enchant. A few coins, a clean bowl, a candlestick, and a stone bead. He watched while she prayed over each one.

"I don't understand," she said. "How does that make it so much easier? And brighter? Why didn't Lector Sulpiono ever teach like that?"

Mendelos offered an explanation, giving Taylor a look like he had done something improper. "Visualization is an intermediate technique," he said, "only taught after the basic form of the prayer has been achieved. Disciple Phillip is jumping ahead, teaching it before you're ready."

"Visualization isn't some special technique," scoffed Taylor, "it's fundamental. Prayer doesn't even work without it. Pronunciation has nothing to do with it. Once the words are good enough it doesn't matter how much better you make them. The important part is what's happening in your mind, not your mouth."

The elder practitioners shook their heads. "That isn't so, Phillip. The prayer will fail if the words are not spoken to near-perfection."

"Let's test that," said Taylor. He said the prayer for making a disciple's mark, slurring the words and drawing out the vowels to a comical degree. At the end, a brilliant futobel was glowing from the surface of the table, under the four stars. He trotted from one end of the table to the other, challenging everyone.

"See?" Taylor signaled for a round of drinks for everyone, sticking to fruit juice for himself. The healers argued among themselves good-naturedly.

"If words don't matter," demanded Mendelos, "why do we have them at all?"

"The words do matter, just not in the way you think. The prayers are a supplication. You are asking Olyon to bless you with a power, but it is still up to you to put that power to use. Saying the words is only one step, a key that opens the door. Once that door is open you can't just stand at the threshold and do nothing. You must wrestle with the power behind that door.

"The second thing you must learn," he continued with Khali, "is spirit control. That really is a hard one. You have to feel your spirit, which is only learned by attempting to control it, which is practically impossible if you can't feel it. Getting started can feel like pulling yourself up with your own bootstraps. But I can show you what I mean."

Taylor spoke the words for light out loud, so he didn't have to explain silent prayer. He suspended the light in mid-air, shining but disembodied. Then, he shaped it into a disk, then a thin line, and then expanded it again so large that it covered the room in soft diaphanous light that came from everywhere. Then Taylor condensed the light into a dozen pinprick stars which he set about his head.

"As you learn to shape a prayer you will become aware of a sense of spirit, dim at first but growing over time. Like a muscle, it must be worked on a regular basis to become strong. As you gain fine control, you can do more art with less spirit."

Taylor looked at Mendelos, hoping he would take over.

"Quite true, quite true. A good healer learns to shape their spirit to the area being treated. Otherwise, one wastes precious energy attempting to heal what is not broken. But Phillip, we teach this as an advanced technique. We don't teach the sensory and control aspects until most of the healing prayers have been learned up to the intermediate degree."

"That's all backwards from the way I was trained," Taylor told them. Khali already had a fat gob of light, pulsing and wobbling like pudding. It was growing more oblong as they watched. "Visualization and control are not intermediate and advanced skills. They're basics. They are the daily practice of every practitioner, from candidate to master. You might as well tell a novice swordsman not to start calisthenics until his second year."

"But she can only do this much because she already knows the light spell," complained the old woman. "That proves our point."

Taylor smiled. "Khali, put that away please," he told her as if he were her regular teacher. "We're going to do something more challenging."

"What?" Khali's light pudding disolved into thin air.

"How far have you gone with shaping objects?"

"Nowhere," she shook her head.

"Not even a crack or a wiggle? Not ever?"

"Never," she said, looking hopeful.

"Mila, can you fetch the..." But he stopped when she handed him a lump of obsidian. They had found it in a market and Taylor had bought it as a curiosity. It shaped beautifully, flowing like glass and capable of making edges sharp enough for surgical instruments with ease.

"Good," said Taylor. "I want you to try again now. Don't worry about pronunciation. But while you are praying I want you to imagine this rock becoming fluid and turning into a puddle. Imagine that as vividly as you can, while saying the prayer. Close your eyes if it helps."

Khali forgot her earlier nervousness and closed her eyes. Everyone watched her, and watched the glassy black stone. She said the words of the prayer beautifully, as if praying for her own heart to be shaped by Olyon into a better, purer form.

And the obsidian melted, like an ice cube left out on a hot day. The transformation stopped with only half of the rock puddled around a smooth center lump. The candidate was sweaty but happy. The healers were congratulating her: shaping was one of the milestone differences between healers and disciples.

"Master Phillip," whispered Inez, kneeling next to his chair, "I would advise caution. The Art School is very set in its ways, and the advisor might take offense at your meddling with his student."

"I'm offended by his poor teaching, but I see your point. Thank you, Inez." Taylor signaled the hostess for another drink for Khali, who looked like she could use it. He leaned into the center of the table, which pulled everyone else into a conspiratorial huddle.

"Mendelos, how long has the school been teaching prayer this way? Putting them in rooms until something happens?"

"Ever since the founding of the second Enclave, I believe. Certainly it was true in my father's time, and he said it was the same in his grandfather's day."

"Did it ever seem to you like certain families were especially talented?"

"Oh, certainly. Leila Fortuna comes from one of those families. Then there's the Namalous, the Pearlcamps, and the Donglars and Karolos. The first families always produce talented children who rise fast."

299

"There are many secondary families," said another, "whose children are endowed with spirit but the way to mastery is more difficult for them"

"Is Sulpiono from one of these families?"

"He's a Karolo," said Khali. "You don't think he's deliberately refusing to teach us, do you?"

"I think," he said carefully, "the first families are doing what privileged people usually do. They advance their own, and let everyone else fend for themselves.

"I also think you should practice every morning. And, if you can find a few other disaffected students who believe in the four tenets, form a little study group to share notes with in the evening. It doesn't have to be long. Even a half hour every day would be enough to make good progress. An hour is better. And, there's no reason to tell Lector Sulpiono about your methods unless he asks directly. He only needs to see the results."

"What if he does ask?"

"Tell him you've been practicing morning, noon, and night," suggested Milo. "It'll be the truth."

"If he really digs, you can't lie to him," agreed Taylor, "but make him ask. He probably won't care enough to bother. As soon as he can pass you off onto someone else, he will."

Taylor touched Mila's arm, silently enhancing her with protection and strength. "See she gets home all right. I'll see you in the morning. Milo, Inez, I'm turning in. Good night everyone." The whole table stood for his exit, which Taylor acknowledged with a wave and a faint smile. Climbing the stairs was a chore. Milo helped him slough off his brigandine which had weighed nothing in the morning, but had gained mass with each new disappointment of the day.

"Master Phillip, do you really think Leadership is undermining the disciples?"

"Milo, the Second Enclave was founded on it. When Saint Bahram built this place he insisted all disciples be based in Unity City. There were about forty who refused, and they all disappeared from the *Histories* within a year. Controlling the disciples was his top internal priority."

Milo was silent while he went about his business of preparing Taylor for bed. Taylor wasn't entirely comfortable being tended to like that, but Mr. Vale had convinced him of the results. When you were well looked after it showed, and people treated you accordingly. His followers' pride was bound up in his presentation as much as his own, so he submitted to the nightly nail cleaning, twice-daily face scrubbings, occasional mid-day clothing changes, and every other valet-induced chore. Because there was no denying it made him look great. If only it was enough to make Leadership change their ways. But they had their own valets, who were literally bred and raised for the task. And, unlike Taylor, they believed in the superiority of their birth.

Eighth day was a rest day. Taylor's bulwark gleefully imposed a no-training, no-work moratorium insisting he instead "feed his spirit." That usually meant a leisurely walk around whatever town they were in during the morning, or by appalon if the animals were getting restless. There was usually a relaxed meal or two, and temple services. Depending on where they were, they could even take in a bit of entertainment in the evening. They had seen variety shows and grand concerts in several cities so far.

This morning the spirit was hungry for pastries, so the cadre visited a row of bakeries, jota shops, and other storefronts that catered to the worker either on their way to or back from their place of work. They loaded up on warm breads stuffed with non-bread things and a jug of spiced jota that was popular in the city, and made their way down to the riverside park that ran along much of the southwest side of the city. They found a table, one of dozens, probably shaped from stone by some long-ago arts students. Inez fed the appalons oat cakes laden with dried fruit while Milo laid out the food and Mila kept watch. When everything was ready they prayed for benediction together, catching the appalons in their little web of community.

As they dug in to breakfast Taylor couldn't help but note how happy they all seemed, talking about nothing important, positioned to watch each others' backs, laughing at in-jokes and teasing. Even the mounts were happy, pushing against each other head-to-head. Ben had taught the other appalons his favorite game and now they played it every day.

When a pair of peacekeepers passed by, swinging their batons and nodding at the happy group, Inez chased them down with a pair of muffins in her hands. She spoke with them for several minutes before returning.

"Anything interesting?" asked Mila.

"The older one is named Fernando," she informed them, "is widowed, lives alone, and is very handsome."

"Anything interesting for us?" asked Milo.

"I think it's interesting," objected Mila.

"All of this," Inez indicated the park, "is the preferred party spot for arts students. It's far enough away from Enclave that the deans don't usually come looking for them here. That's a summer activity, obviously."

They took their time getting back to the Knight's Cup, where they stabled the animals and changed clothes into their eighth day best. Hitching posts were scarce around the basilica so the four of them plus the healer party and a few of the priests in training piled into a public carriage train.

"Seating is segregated," Inez briefed Taylor, "with deans and leadership in front on the east side. Directly behind them are disciples and prelates. Oldest are in front, youngest in back."

"So we're on the east side, last of the disciples."

"You are," she corrected. "We will sit with the followers and attendants, behind the students. So you may have to survive conversation with strange disciples all on your own. If you don't want to make a fuss, be dull and don't say anything interesting. Otherwise," she said cheerfully, "be yourself."

Bahram's basilica was a monument to the man who made the church. In terms of its footprint, it was the largest structure in all of the city, with a dome that dominated skyline. From the inside it was even more magnificent, drawing the eye upward into a vision of clouds and saints and sunshine, to the oculus from which all the light shone.

"Don't say it out loud," Mila warned them, because they were all thinking the same thing. Bahram's Basilica was supposed to feature a Fragment of Sun, but the enchanted object above them was a disappointment. It was very bright, but it wasn't a Fragment. It didn't come close to the artifact Taylor had made and given to Girona's Basilica of Magnificent Light. This one was a fake.

"I'll catch up with you later," he told his crew, and went through the crowd to find himself a spot. Like everyone else on the east quarter past the center rows, Taylor wore a short stone knife hardly a dozen centimeters long (more symbolic than functional), a stole embroidered in green, and a simple wooden star. Unlike the rest of them he was only twelve years old. Instead of the silks that seemed common here, his outfit was fine wool with his bifur-lined cloak on the outside. In Enclave people mostly greeted each other with a hand over their heart and a slight bow of the head, a gesture he found easy to imitate.

"You look lost, little disciple," said a man in his forties sporting sharp teeth. He was wearing finery of silk and lace, with tiny gems sparkling from the embroidery in his stole. His attire was fit for a minor prince. "Who are you?"

"Disciple Phillip the Younger," Taylor said.

"Of what family?" said the toothy man, looming over him.

"Of no family you would know," responded Taylor. "I was anointed in the wilderness by Dean Garsharp."

"Oh, that one never had a proper respect for family ties."

"You're right about that," he agreed, "he's more interested in disciples who will dedicate themselves to the Work than he does about lineage. What trouble. It must irk you a great deal."

"It does," sneered the toothy disciple. "Oh, I've neglected to introduce myself. I'm Boras Namalous."

"Really," said Taylor with a small amount of excitement.

"Then you've heard of me."

"There's nothing in the *Luminous Histories*, so no." The barb drew a scowl from the silken disciple. "In fact, I don't recall seeing any Namalous at all since fifty years past, when your ancestor built a hundred kilometers of road in Mialta. There used to be a bunch of you back in the days of the first disciples."

"Ah yes, Saint Jerome Namalous and his many children. We are very proud of our long and distinguished history."

Taylor completely lost control of his tongue. "Not proud enough to follow in their footsteps."

Boras glared at Taylor hard enough to peel skin, and swooped away with a flip of his silken half-cape. Taylor realized then the space around him was vacant. He was socially so radioactive now, nobody wanted to share the same air as him.

Idiot, he admonished himself, *you've gone and been yourself again.*

"Phillip Young!" That voice sounded familiar. "Making all the right enemies, as usual!" Taylor spun around to find himself face-to-face with Dean Garsharp.

"Hello teacher. You need to read your mail. I sent you a message two days ago!"

"And I told you to just drop by at any time." Garsharp shook his hand, in Gallia fashion. "I let messenger boards age before having someone else read them. Less to do that way."

"Then I will stop by unannounced. But I feel like I have a whole day's worth of ideas to unload on you, plus I need your advice. I thought you'd want to schedule ahead."

"Sounds interesting. Skip the communion lunch and come to my place instead. Bring the cadre, too. My people will want to have a good long look at your people."

"Mine will have questions for yours. But first, what's going on with," Taylor pointed at the light in the oculus and lowered his voice. "Is the real one in a box somewhere?"

"As far as Enclave is concerned, that is the real one."

The service, when it finally began, was standard. The basilica's prelate gave an opening prayer, led them in a song, and recited a short sermon. The only surprise came at the end.

"We have among us today a young disciple, anointed in the wilderness. Although he is not new, he is new to us and so it falls to him to give the benediction. Disciple Phillip the Younger, will you please?"

Boras had probably arranged it, under the assumption that Taylor would stumble in the sudden spotlight. But Taylor was so accustomed to being called on for prayer he didn't even blink. He took the center of the room by the altar, and covered the crowd with his spirit. The sanctuary was far larger than usual, but that only made it a better fit for him. A number of heads snapped up the moment he did that.

Now I know who the most spirit sensitive practitioners are.

He said the prayer in his best presentation voice, letting the words rise and fall in supplication to the divine, and laid the prayer firmly on them all.

He didn't give them the party-drug version that would keep them dancing all night and sharing their innermost secrets until dawn. But they were going to feel it. And if anyone rejected the sense of communion ...

Several people in the sanctuary were looking ill enough to throw up or pass out, mostly among Leadership, and a large contingent of disciples wearing sparkly lace.

And now I know who the assholes are, he thought while memorizing their faces.

At the Garsharp house Taylor's entourage was introduced to Erdamon, Linsayer, Alwen, and Ebon. All were from Hyskos where Garsharp had first apprenticed, and the five of them had bounced around Tenobre for thirty five years before settling in Unity City. For a working disciple, teaching and being dean at the Art School was as close to retirement as one usually got.

"And this is Milara, a former student of mine." The woman who shook Taylor's hand had orange and red hair, sprouting horns that swooped dramatically backwards over her head. She was even better looked-after than Taylor was, and had probably dressed down to meet them at their own level.

Inez brought the last of their boxes of surprises and presents inside and shut the door. "Are those your men across the street, Milara?"

"That's a good trick," said Garsharp, surprised. "I blessed them with overlook myself." Inez didn't deign to explain, but she signaled her team that there were four armed people she could detect across the street, possibly friendly.

The dean respectfully didn't pry into her methods. "Come in to the parlor, everyone! Dinner will be a little while yet, so let's see what Taylor has learned about the arts while mendicating about."

Being called by his real name made Taylor cautious. Even his own people called him Phillip, even in private. "I'm not sure what you mean."

"Show me some new profound trick, Taylor. Don't worry, everyone here knows that the supposedly dead Taylor DeLanion is alive as Phillip the Younger. Milara is here because I want her to understand what you bring to the church. So, let's see something interesting."

"I'm willing to trust you, Dean Garsharp, but I don't know her," Taylor motioned to Milara. "And, I have an entire bag of crazy stuff to lay out today - any of which might make Leadership feel threatened and get me declared a heretic. No offense mam, but I'm here because I'm not sure how much of this I should even say out loud, and how much of it I should bury in a deep hole somewhere."

"I trust her with my life, lad. And whatever your new goals are, she's in a good position to help. But she has to return to her posting tomorrow, so it's either now or never."

Taylor only had a second to agonize over it before Inez made a suggestion. "Show her the bird, master."

Mila agreed with a bright smile. "The bird is my favorite." She produced a large amethyst stone and a small lump of coal from their gear and presented them to Taylor.

"You just like it because it's pretty," accused her cousin.

"There is nothing wrong with pretty," she insisted, pushing the objects in Taylor's direction. Inez set out a spirit lamp while Milo asked the house staff for a pair of clean wooden bowls and a mug of water.

Once everything was assembled Taylor said, "Let's begin." In the next moment, the lamp was lit.

"Did you just light the lamp without prayer?" Milara sounded impressed and, perhaps, slightly alarmed.

"No, you can never omit the prayer," he reassured her, "but you can say it silently. And, once you have crossed that hurdle, you can recite the entire prayer simultaneously as if it were a single mental Word."

"Instant prayer," said Garsharp wonderingly.

"A superb tactical advantage," said Linsayer.

"Fiendishly difficult," Taylor told them. "Silent prayer is pretty easy, once you believe it's possible. Learning prayers as Words is a lot harder."

"Keep going," said Milara, looking interested.

"Many prayers that we think we know well actually have more generalist underpinnings, and have much wider applications than most people know. For example, the prayer to purify water is at its core a prayer of separation." With that, Taylor held the amethyst and removed all of the iron, letting the metal dust fall into the smaller of the two bowls. What he had left was a perfect clear crystal of quartz. "You can separate anything from anything. Amethyst is quartz with impurities of iron. Remove the iron, and you have clear crystal.

"Contrary to what the school teaches, visualization is a fundamental skill. But I prefer the term conceptualization, because it extends into the realm too small to be seen, even by microscopes. If you can describe a shape, you can make a shape.

Taylor held the crystal over the large bowl then turned it into finely powdered sand. He added water and made sure the two were well mixed, then added a small measure of the iron and powdered charcoal, and stirred again. He then turned the bowl over and a smooth black substance oozed out onto the table, flattening itself into a thin disk.

"The structures I will create now are tiny spheres of sand and water, measured in billionths of a meter." He ran a finger along the disk, making stripes of different colors. "One hundred fifty nanometers, two hundred, two twenty five, two fifty, three hundred, three twenty five." Each line he drew was a different color from violet to red, and seemed to leap off the black surface.

Milara's eyes widened in recognition. "That's black opal!"

"If you'll indulge me for a few minutes, we can do something fun." While he talked, Taylor drew a brightly colored bird in flight, against a dark sky and rising to a yellow and gold moon. "After the ... Incident ... I had trouble regaining control of my spirit and wanted something challenging to do every morning, so this has been a daily practice for a few weeks now." Taylor couldn't actually draw very well, but he could do a credible job of the one picture he drew every day.

When he was finished, he passed the disk around so each person could admire the play of colors in the light of the spirit lamps. "The colors you see don't come from any substance in the stone. It comes from the way light interacts with the structure of opal. The light is refracted and interfered with by those tiny spheres, which are half of the wavelength of visible light. There are colors in this picture past red, which are visible only to people with heat vision. My eyes can see past violet, and there's some color in there for me, too.

The disk made its way back to Taylor. "And that is the next lesson. With enough knowledge of natural law you can very efficiently do amazing things with relatively little spirit. If we put enough effort into learning natural law, and combine that knowledge with the arts, we can do new and amazing things."

Taylor broke the opal into wet sand, to the cry of most who were in attendance. The carbon was removed and lumped into coal, the water was returned to its cup, and the remaining iron returned to the sand. Then Taylor liquified the sand and grew a new amethyst, slowly crystalizing while the audience watched. Soon the amethyst was whole again.

"Sand, iron, and water," said Alwen. "Now I've seen it all."

"You really have not," Taylor warned him. "I have a whole bag of stuff we haven't even touched yet."

Then they started opening boxes to reveal gifts and inventions: a proper microscope with two lenses and a stage; a telescope with a smoked lens for viewing the sun; the youngmeter; a board coated with a fluorescent material that shone bright green in the presence of spirit light; a few small spirit stones. The optical instruments came with a written dissertation on the properties of light, and schematics for making more. Taylor hadn't written the book himself: he had translated a famous treatise from memory. Making the paper and binding the materials into a book was time consuming, so he had only made one copy for himself and one for Garsharp.

"So that's it," said Taylor, "for the easy stuff. The rest of what I have for you is a lot harder to process."

Garsharp looked ready to retreat to his lab immediately, to play with the new inventions. His retired bulwark and Milara looked stunned. They elected to have dinner before tackling whatever came next.

Garsharp's house was what he called, "a little bit grand," and his dining room for twenty bore out that claim. With the servants around Taylor was Phillip again, and he regaled them with his last few months of adventures, with colorful notes added by his bulwark, for as long as Milara kept asking.

It was clear she had seen the summary in the histories, but was curious about the details.

Mila and Milo asked about what kinds of monsters Garsharp and his bulwark had faced, and if they had detailed tactical advice. They talked about the spear throwers and the properties of the new alloys Taylor's team was using for armaments. Milara skillfully dodged the few questions asked about herself, and Taylor's party was smart enough not to pursue the matter.

The food reminded Taylor of Lavradio. The vegetables were boiled, the meats were roasted, and everything was creatively sauced. Midway through dinner, Taylor's eyes met Inez's: she was watching their surroundings with most of her attention, and he gave her a nod of thanks for her dedication.

After dinner the followers all went to a separate room to plunder Garsharp's library of past monster encounters, while Taylor, Garsharp, and Milara returned to the parlor. Stiff drinks were poured for the two adults, and juice was found for the minor. Before they started, Taylor had Mila lay out a pair of meter-long cedar planks in the parlor, the kilabora's favor to Taylor: they were cut from the council chamber's tree stump and showed all the rings from the tree's sapling years to the alignment. Once Mila was out of the room, Taylor began to talk.

He started with the tree rings, and the eleven hundred and nine year cycle. He told them about the successive iterations of humanity using different strategies for survival, and the parts of kilabora lore that weren't secret. He told them where they were on the cycle, and how long he expected the current trend of increasing monster attacks to continue. Taylor wasn't the first person in the church to notice the problems: Leadership wouldn't be hiding data if someone hadn't noticed and made a fuss. Nor was he the first to make a connection between increased intensity of the sun and monster attacks: he was far from the only practitioner who could sense spirit. But Taylor was the first person to put a meaningful number on when the tide would turn in their favor, based on something other than wishful thinking. The cycle wouldn't peak for another three hundred fifty years, which was not good news.

Then he talked about the church. He knew 'Saint' Bahram had purged the disciples who refused to follow him to the Second Enclave. He knew Leadership was fudging the population summaries and aggregate data on monster incidents. He knew the first and second families weren't especially talented, and they were deliberately failing to teach outsiders. He knew Leadership was attempting to populate the healing and disciple positions almost entirely with their own family members, out of a dual desire for their own security and to advantage their own children.

And he knew the Unity had already lost the fight to preserve civilization. "Even if the monster attacks remain steady for the next twenty years, which they will not," he emphasized, "we've still lost. All the working disciples will be dead and there won't be anyone left to fight the cursed monsters. All you'll have left is some pointless privileged elite who would rather let the world burn than give up an ounce of their status or do any real work."

Taylor sat up straight. "Oh, and I thought of one more thing today. Every major city in Tenobre that I know of is built near an ancient underground ruin, except for Unity City. When things get really bad, where will the residents of Unity

City go? Bahram was so eager to break with the ancient civilization, but he should have been wondering if they were on to something."

Finally done, the disciple slouched into his chair and sipped juice while Milara and the dean put their heads together. The business of delivering cataclysmic news had put him in a funk. There was nothing about the situation that was fair to him. He shouldn't have to be here, and the church should have already planned for this. That two senior clerics were looking to an outlander kid to solve their problems for them was a ridiculous failure for a supposedly strong institution whose mission was to serve humanity.

"So," asked Milara, "what will you do now?"

"What will I do?" Taylor was suddenly feeling testy. "I'm here to find out what you will do. I can't exactly go home because someone wrecked the summoning room. Thanks for that, by the way. Since I'm stuck on this rock with the rest of you, I guess I'll have to do whatever I can. But if I go around turning everything upside down, Leadership will have me un-anointed and dead inside a year. They'll burn me in a pit like they did all those poor two-natured people back at the Alignment. So, what can I do? I'm not sure."

"That's a pile of gurantor crap." Taylor was shocked to hear Garsharp say something so profane. "You didn't come this far without a plan. You won't let Tenobre die any more than you would let nobles poison Girona. You have ideas, or you're not the boy I trained. So stop throwing a tantrum, and lay it out for us. What's your plan for saving Tenobre?"

Garsharp was someone he respected. He had done good work with the single-lens microscope, and he was the best healer Taylor knew. So, the rebuke stung.

"It depends on how much leeway we have to work in," Taylor said at last. "Plan A is the Turtle Plan: build an underground city for selected people. Everyone has to be literate, and most of them have to be practitioners. If I have to I can locate and train the practitioners myself. All I need the church for is their anointment. With the arts and a sufficient number of people we can save humanity though the next cycle. If I throw in enough technological know-how from my home world, the little city can thrive. The most dangerous moment is when everyone else in the world realizes they're about to be monster chow, and come knocking on the city's front door demanding to be let in. It'll be bloody, and I'll never sleep well again, but it's winnable."

"And the other plan?" asked Milara.

"Plan B is the Age of Discovery, and it's a little more involved. It doesn't threaten the church directly, but it threatens the first families. Of course they won't recognize the difference, so it's only a matter of time before Leadership comes for me and everyone else involved. That's the weakness." Taylor removed a paper scroll from one of the boxes he hadn't opened yet, but he hesitated to unroll it. At Garsharp's urging, he placed the scroll at one end of the planks and let it roll open, rolling past the end of the first plank and partially covering the second. On it, he had drawn a gantt chart. He gave them some time to look at it in silence.

"The goal of the Age of Discovery isn't to enact some master plan to save everyone. The goal is to raise the continent's technical and industrial capabilities so all the kingdoms can save themselves. Some might put protective walls or domes over their cities, others may go underground or, my personal favorite, build floating islands to avoid the monsters."

Milara looked at him like he was telling fairy tales. "I'm not joking, that's a real possibility. As bad as the sun storms are for us because of the monsters, it is also a massive source of energy that we can capture and put to use. Our ancestors may ultimately lament the end of the storms because it will force them to change their lifestyle. But that's a problem for them to deal with. Our job is to make sure those children get born."

Taylor pointed at the three main lines of effort, which had numerous smaller boxes attached to them. Vertical lines separated the entire "Age of Discovery" plan into phases. "Our first and most obvious need is more disciples. Instead of dozens in the field, we need hundreds within the next several years. Within twenty years we should be counting them in thousands. We need to train them on an entirely different scale than we have been. We teach them my method of spirit arts, and we teach Mobeen's method of fighting. Basically we train them like soldiers, with a strong emphasis on practical skills. They can be battle ready in under a year, but we want them to continue honing their skills for a lifetime. So they don't just leave school and never come back. They rotate back through the school to either teach or learn new techniques."

"We know from Matrix Lucia how to use a Fragment to awaken candidates," said Milara. "Filling a school won't be a problem. If we find them young enough we can ensure they read and write before sending them to school."

"That definitely makes the job easier. The second line is industry. Paper, printing, glass, and the new alloys are the first things we produce. We create a facility where we refine the techniques and train craftsmen. Then we license production in every kingdom and take a slight percentage to finance the school."

He spent a few minutes explaining movable type and mimeograph printing, which wasn't difficult because Tenobre already had block printing and silk screening. "I can't overstate the importance of paper and printing. If you make books cheap and can produce them by the hundreds or thousands, knowledge spreads quickly. Your transportation system is your most impressive achievement. Add printing to that, and new ideas will multiply as they spread over the continent.

"The third leg is basic research into natural law, especially its intersection with the spirit arts. I can prime this by translating some of my world's best books about natural law and publish them with printing, but there has to be a place and funding for people who want to push the boundaries of what's known and invent ways to exploit what we discover."

"Like your youngmeter." Garsharp put his finger on a box. "I see a task, here."

"Right. A lot of basic research and development went into that, and now that we have it we should make enough of them for every depot in the world to have one. Just like they record the weather every day, depot masters should be recording spirit readings every day. We can't know yet what that will tell us, but it's precisely the kind of activity that comes under basic research.

"To staff the research effort we need to put a special emphasis on recruiting anyone who has an intense interest in natural law and a knack for reasoning things out. We also want anyone with an exceptional facility for math.

"All of this gets located in one place: a basic research facility, an incubator for new industries, an arts school, and a school of math and letters. One place to teach what is known, expand the limits of knowledge, and turn that knowledge into tools."

"You're talking about building a kind of enclave," said Milara casually, "aren't you?"

"I would avoid that name," said Taylor dismissively, "or else people might think we're trying to compete with the church. In Emristar it was called it a nexus. If I thought this enterprise could survive in Unity City I'd build it right here, but Leadership would kill it in the cradle."

"You don't have much faith in us," said Milara. Taylor couldn't tell if by 'us' she meant Leadership or the church at large, so he chose his words carefully.

"I think there is no scenario in which the Second Enclave survives with its self-denial intact. It either deals with its deficiencies, or it dies. As of yesterday's adventure in the library it looks to me like denial is winning."

"What's this line," asked Garsharp, "ex-founder?"

"That's the point when I'm no longer necessary. When nations set up their own nexuses, poach our best people, and begin competing with each other on advanced research the whole culture becomes self-perpetuating. After that point, our biggest threat is warfare. I think as long as the Unity keeps the peace, civilization survives"

"You have tasks for 'floating island'," sighed Milara. "You're that serious about it?"

Taylor grinned, "why not? It would make a great summer home. And if the Unity fails to hold things together I'll have a place for my people. But, it's one of those notions where we can't even know yet how hard it is. I'm not getting my hopes up."

"He's right about not being able to do it in the city," Garsharp told Milara. "The vested interests would pull every string they could find to undermine it. We have to put it in a place where the first families will ignore it."

"And I can't go back to Lavradio," Taylor told them, "because some people there want to kill me."

ASSIGNMENTS

That night Taylor dreamed his teeth were crumbling. The grist got stuck between his lips and gums like sand. He couldn't close his mouth for fear the jagged remains would pierce his flesh. He awoke to Milo shaking him.

"Take a potion," he urged, pushing a half-vial of dreamless sleep into Taylor's hand. "We'll keep watch. You can't do anything if you don't sleep."

The next morning he woke in the strange house, and found his way to the garden with Inez close behind him. He found the garden cloaked in pristine snow, and placed himself cross-legged on the ground. He let his spirit unfurl fully, not caring how many people in a city full of practitioners might notice. He needed to stretch out. As he bent and shaped his spirit, compacting and expanding it in turn, his head began to clear.

He was having stress dreams. Of course he didn't need to do everything himself. Mostly, he needed to instigate things, train some arts users properly, and remove roadblocks. Like he had told Baron Fringe months before, he wasn't about to try and save Tenobre on his own.

When he made his opal painting that morning it was a little different. Actually, it was a little different every day, but on that day the bird seemed to be striving for the distant sun, unsure if he could reach it but unwilling to give in. Garsharp swooped in at the last minute and saved it from the usual fate.

"I'll make a present of it for Milara. You made a deep impression on her, lad. She's a good one to have in your corner." But he still wouldn't say what she did for the church.

They spent breakfast planning, adding and moving boxes around on his chart and assigning some of the responsibilities to the church. There were a few things they could do for him, especially in the realm of recruitment and deploying youngmeters to the depots. At Garsharp's request, Taylor made a Fragment of Sun before he left, with the promise of several more to come.

"You know, if you ever feel like messing with leadership," Taylor suggested while handing the orb of silver to Garsharp, "hang one of these in Bahram's Basilica, nice and low. See if they can talk at all without lying."

The plan was to spend at least a few weeks in Unity City. Garsharp and Milara organized the library research Taylor had been trying to complete, using students who were granted access to all of the relevant "unavailable" resources. That way the findings would be widely known and the youngsters who knew their math would understand exactly what was at stake.

Taylor focused on bulwark training, research, and making Fragments which were hand delivered by Inez to Dean Garsharp. Whenever he sent her out on a delivery Taylor enhanced her, just in case someone tried to intercept the cargo. Few people would think of interfering with such an intimidating warrior dashing through the Enclave fully armed, but it seemed like a reasonable precaution anyway.

The group used their brief respite in the afternoons to enjoy the city before returning to the Knight's Cup for dinner, followed by study group.

"Study group" was code for tutoring sessions Taylor ran in his suite for Khali and a group of similarly situated students who needed proper instruction. There were five in all: low born, smooth skinned, or otherwise ill-favored candidates whose main trouble with prayer was the lack of active instruction. Every one of them had been found by well-meaning disciples in far away cities and shipped to the Enclave with the promise of an education, only to have their arts talent neglected. The first families' goal was to convince most of them to take the less prestigious healer track or, better yet, drop out and go home. Fully half of such recruits went home un-anointed, while nearly all the remaining recruits became healers. That fed the belief that students outside the first and second families weren't worth teaching and couldn't become disciples.

Lector Herod visited one afternoon for tea tasting, bringing as his guest his younger sister Irina. Irina was Milos's age, with blue eyes and expressive feline ears. Together, Irina and Milo seemed to have a fun time brewing and serving the many teas Mila had bought, putting the tasters' portions into tiny shallow bowls. Herod and Irina were from a second family called Sestos who had turned out a long line of scholars and priests, but no practitioners.

Herod Sestos examined Phillip with a gimlet eye over a saucer of fine strong black tea. "This is excellent, but it should be blended with something if you want to serve it to anyone of note." He put the dish down. "You made a ruckus in the library, Phillip. We have students running amok in the closed stacks, tabulating things few people have ever read closely."

"Don't blame me for the ruckus, Herod. All I did was use the library." Taylor slurped from the dish and wished for bergamont. Maybe there was a similar citrus in Tenobre but he hadn't found it yet.

"You did more than that. You told someone very high up in the Unity, and they sent students to re-tabulate directly from the kingdoms' reports. The discrepancies are alarming, and the students know. It's unprecedented." Herod sipped from a blend Milo had crafted of several teas. "That's quite good, and very in keeping with the current style in the Enclave. Too delicate for my tastes personally, but you could serve it to nearly anyone without shame."

Milo accepted Herod's effusive praise with grace, and put the next set of selections in front of them.

"I shared my concerns with Dean Garsharp, but I don't know who he may have told after." Taylor carefully elided Milara's presence from the conversation. He didn't know who she was or if she had been there in any official capacity, so he pretended it had been him and Garsharp and no one else.

They slurped their way through a few more samples, taking water in between. Taylor had saved his personal favorite for last.

"Spiced havendish," said Herod, nostalgic for the red tea aged in barrels and flavored with a melange of spices. "I have missed this. It was very popular several years ago, but regrettably fell out of fashion. Yours is very intense."

"If you like it then we'll make a gift of some for you, and some of Milo's blend as well. That way you have something for guests, and something to keep for yourself."

"You have my thanks." With Herod's approval given, full-sized cups full of the havendish were served with a hearty march cake. It looked like too sparse a snack compared to most Enclave fare but it packed enough caffeine, calories, and vitamins to fuel hours of physical exertion. When toasted and topped with a swirl of whipped appalon butter it became a rare treat. A snob might turn it away for being too "rustic", but anyone who could admit what was actually good would eat it. Herod took seconds.

"How did you know," Herod asked between bites. "What tipped you off that there was something wrong with the yearly aggregates?"

"Mila, why don't you explain our reasoning for the lector?"

"Of course," she said, putting down her tea. "Master Phillip once observed that there were more ruins of villages than there were inhabited ones, and that many of the ruins looked recently abandoned. Once it was pointed out, the phenomenon was hard to ignore. We started keeping count of the villages we passed, populated and abandoned, and verified our information with locals. We discovered there were very few settlements of under a thousand people, and many settlements had been abandoned in living memory. Some people we talked to pegged the decline to the last ten years or so, while others insisted it went back much farther than that. We started getting truly suspicious when we tried to read the national reports that are supposed to be housed in the main temples of each nation: we were told they weren't present and we would have to come to the Enclave to read them.

"Our question at the Enclave library was twofold: was the pattern global, and how long had rural population been declining? When we saw some of the regional numbers for areas we had passed through, it was obvious the numbers were far higher than the populations actually living there. And then, Milo found the footnote."

"A change of methodology," added Milo, shaking his head. "Twenty years ago they decided to add numbers wherever they wanted to. But they did it badly: the end tallies for population were almost perfectly flat year over year. That by itself is suspicious."

Taylor summarized. "To us it was obvious. If they had fuzzed a few years it might have been hard to discover, but the errors have been accumulating for so long they're glaring. All anyone had to do was look and the lie fell apart. What I would like to know is how Leadership got away with it for so long."

"I suspect nobody was looking," said the librarian. "Those who do the Work don't concern themselves with governance. Those in governance mostly talk to each other and don't have to face realities of the Work. Everyone else lies low and hopes not to be assigned anything too difficult."

Taylor stared into his cup. Disciples like Lucia, Garsharp, Mobeen, and Leila deserved better. "It's all pretty disappointing," he said at last.

"If you're going to stay in the Enclave," Herod said with a trace of empathy, "you will have to get used to it."

"We're not staying," Taylor told him. "The Second Enclave will have to work out its problems without us."

Something about the comment seemed to strike Herod as odd, but before he could say anything there was a knock on the door. Mila answered and accepted a message board. "There's a Candidate Bolesloval Pearlcamp, a Guardian

Paraskevi Pearlcamp, and Warden Helen here to see us. They are here about a challenge to duel."

Taylor and his entourage stared at each other, silently asking who among them knew anything about a planned duel.

"Give them a hundred count, then let them come up," decided Taylor. Mila passed the word to whomever was on the other side of the door, and the re-arrangements began. Furniture was adjusted, dishes were cleared, and Milo gave his master a good once-over. Mila took the door position, Milo took over tea service, and Inez took the close guard position directly behind Taylor.

"We should probably go," announced Herod reasonably while the preparations were being made.

"I don't mind if you stay," Taylor told him, "but you should do what suits you. Whatever this is about, it could get uncomfortable."

Curious, Herod and Irina elected to stay but moved to the seats farthest away from their host.

There was a knock on the door and Mila admitted the new guests: the gate warden they had met previously, followed by a young man wearing an apprentice's star on a silk and lace doublet, followed by a woman who could have been his mother wearing the silver and aquamarine trimmed stole of Leadership. The room stood to greet the newcomers. Seats were taken and tea was poured: the elegant but delicate Milo blend. Boleslovas couldn't seem to take his eyes off the arkto rug.

"So," said Taylor casually, "what's this about a duel?"

The warden answered, "Boleslovas Pearlcamp has challenged Phillip the Younger to a duel, but has yet to receive an answer. He has come to make the necessary arrangements, with myself and his aunt Paraskevi Pearlcamp as witnesses."

"I don't remember receiving a challenge," said Taylor, looking to his bulwark. "Does anyone remember receiving a challenge?" They all shook their heads. "Someone needs to explain to me why I should kill this Boleslovas person. As far as I know, we've never met."

"That's a lie!" said the young man. "We met earlier today, in front the the library. You pretended to ignore me."

Inez leaned over and spoke softly to Taylor, "Red Face Guy".

"Oh! Red Face Guy. We were trying to decide where to have lunch, and you refused to walk around us. Your yelling was so distracting I put up a privacy barrier. You must have challenged me while the barrier was up. We didn't hear anything you said after, 'I'm first family do you know what I can do to you.'"

"I'm saying it again now!" he yelled, leaping to his feet and pointing rudely at Taylor. "You have insulted me for the last time! I challenge you to a duel!" His face turned beet red, which sparked Taylor's memory. This was definitely the same guy.

Taylor let the apprentice stand there, breathing hard and waiting for a response while he sipped his tea. Milo had done a good job with the blend. "This is very annoying," Taylor said at last. "Sit down while I talk to the warden."

The apprentice looked like he was about to start yelling again, but his aunt took hold of his arm and pulled him down into his chair. Looking closely at him, Red Face Guy didn't seem very fit or very coordinated. Whatever his specialty was, it wasn't combat.

"Warden Helen, if you would, please tell me about the protocol here for duels. I'm not very familiar with Enclave." Taylor ignored Boleslovas' smirk.

"If you accept his challenge you can name a condition under which the duel takes place. Then the challenger names a condition, then you name a condition, and so on until the time and place and manner of the duel are all decided. Then you meet and fight in front of at least two witnesses each, plus a healer in attendance. A popular location is in the school arena in front of the student body. Duels are fought until one side or the other is unable to continue."

"It seems like a waste of valuable personnel. Don't people die in these events?"

"Not often," said the warden, "but it happens. The most frequent result is forfeiture by spirit exhaustion."

"Not much of a duel." Taylor made the Lavradio hand gesture of derision. "If nobody is expected to die you should just call it something else. Can people really challenge anyone over any little thing?"

"They can."

"This just gets more and more stupid. What if I refuse?"

"The most likely outcome is the rebuffed challenger claims you were too afraid to face him."

"Is there any way I can refuse that prevents that, like on the grounds that it's dumb and I don't want to kill someone over petty insults? Or because he doesn't have standing to challenge me?"

"Normally," sighed the warden, "your status as a disciple would preclude any challenge from an apprentice. But, he's from a first family."

"Then I have a question for Aunt Paraskevi." Taylor's familiarity was deliberate. "Do you really want this duel to happen? It's strange that a guardian would come down here to the Knight's Cup over a nothing like this. He doesn't look like much of a fighter, whereas I've killed mercenaries and hunted dark monsters. We're all sitting next to one right now. My first condition would be that we fight one-on-one, no proxies. You have to know he'll loose, so why encourage him?"

"Boleslovas is my nephew, and he asked me to be his witness. I am only here in that capacity."

That could mean she was looking forward to seeing Red Face Guy humiliated, or she was plotting something and wasn't going give away her plans. Either way, her face wasn't saying much.

Taylor tried to think it through, figure out what the angle was and what might happen. He could fight the guy privately or publicly, to the death or just knock him out. Or he could try to intimidate Boleslovas into withdrawing the challenge. But Taylor kept coming back to the idea that only reason to do any of that was because he didn't want the candidate calling him names. It was a stupid reason to get drawn into fake dispute.

"I decline," he said at last. "The whole enterprise is just too idiotic to be involved with." He motioned for a refill, "more tea, anyone? Warden? We have several varieties if you want something different."

"I thought I smelled a spiced havendish on the way up," she said.

"Good choice. And I think we still have some march cake, too. It's a little rustic for Enclave, but we enjoy it. Guardian Paraskevi, can I tempt you?"

"We must be going," she said, standing and dragging Boleslovas up with her. Everyone else in the room had to stand, too.

"Coward! This isn't over," warned Red Face Guy, and flounced out of the room in his lace doublet. From somewhere in the room, there was a snort of arrested laughter. It could have been anyone.

The guardian pretended not to hear it and took her leave with dignity.

Sorry, Aunt Paraskevi, thought Taylor, *but you'll have to find someone else to terminate your embarrassing nephew.*

Their stay was cut short by a report from Girona. Most of the contents were known or inferred from Inez, but she had left the city before Guardian Maia had arrived so the news about Mobeen was new, and it was going to hit everyone hard. The disciple known as Sacred Blade had been in his prime and had hunted more monsters than anyone living. He had been huge, fast, smart, and had seemed un-killable. Taylor had always assumed they would meet again: he had been making a list of things he wanted to ask his combat tutor, and now the questions would go unasked.

Taylor was getting a preview of the news in the relative privacy of Garsharp's lab, on the second floor of Enclave's main infirmary. The building was a u-shaped marble affair with a central courtyard slippery with snow and laid out around a statue of Saint Eustratius, the first dedicated healer listed in the book *Disciples*. The dean had cleared out his office for the meeting by piling all the dirty dishes and unwanted message boards out in the hall so Taylor had somewhere to sit. They had shut and locked the door, and put up a privacy barrier inside that made the space stuffy but secure. Part of the reason for all the security was the way in which the message was delivered: it had been hand delivered directly to Her Holiness, bypassing the normal mail route. From there it had somehow found its way down to the dean.

The news about Mobeen was tough to take in, but reading about the school was just as surprising. Inez had relayed some of the information, but she hadn't done it justice. There were as many candidates in Girona as there were at the Art School, and they were all disciple class talents. Estevan was chairman of the glebe, with the full support of the royal family. He not only protected it from the predation of nobles, but had expanded it by absorbing the fortunes of the disgraced Colares family.

"It's perfect!" The death and fires and unrest were bad news, but Dean Garsharp was gleeful about it.

"It's not perfect!" growled Taylor, "do you know how hard we worked to get people back into decent housing? And they burned the archive, so the city will be unmanageable! The matrix is not recovering. We have no idea what Frenzio is doing or even what his goals are. Girona could be a war zone soon."

"I'm talking about your school. You have a city desperate to see your return, a royal family eager for alignment, and they owe you for trying to kill you."

Taylor interrupted his tirade. "There was no trying. They did it. I wouldn't be here if it weren't for Sandim's Return."

"So they really owe you," quipped the old man, "and they'll owe you again when you soothe the masses, raise some housing with the arts, and offer a full rapprochement with the church. Your industries will bring fortunes to Girona, and much of that will go to the school. The church will give you a free hand financially: they'll send auditors, but as long as you keep the books clean you can put everything into the school."

"I still need experienced bulwarks to teach combat enhancement and tactics."

"We'll get someone. Maybe two someones," agreed Garsharp.

"How? You're not on the assignments committee."

"Disciples know how to make things happen," said the cagey dean.

"Mobeen would have been my dream teacher," reflected Taylor with a pained expression, "but maybe this Edos apprentice of his would like a try. They were together for a year or two, right? Oh!" Taylor stood up so suddenly the dean started backward, nearly falling out of his chair. "Mobeen wrote everything down. He made reports of every engagement, I've seen some of them! Who gets his archive of reports?"

"He has no heirs, so they'll either go to the library or be destroyed if nobody wants them."

"I want them," insisted Taylor, "for the Mobeen Collection of Tactical Writings, or whatever catchy name we come up with for it."

"What are you going to do with it all? I've been to his house. There's practically a carriage full of them."

"I'm going to make students study them, old man! What else would I do with them? He was a terrifying opponent, and he could write a useful report. Give me his written corpus and an experienced bulwark or two who know his method, and I'll make sure Sacred Blade lives on for a thousand years!"

Garsharp was right. It was perfect, and not only for the reasons he had told Taylor. The Matriarch could bypass the old families who were keeping a stranglehold on the profession, and vastly expand her disciple corps. In Lavradio he would be out of sight and out of mind. By the time the lace disciples realized he was up to something they would be outnumbered and obsolete — irrelevant. If the experiment in Girona failed then the Matriarch's hands would be relatively clean: she had tried something new but had kept it from infecting Enclave.

Taylor realized he was being spun off into a separate concern from the Art School, like an innovative new business line that clashed with the parent company's culture. The parent company (the Unity) would continue to profit (gain more disciples for the Work) without the internecine fighting that comes with hiring a bunch of upstarts. To make it work, all Taylor had to do was muster every friend he had ever made in this world to help him.

"Keep this under your hat for now," warned the dean, "there's an all-school meeting tomorrow where we'll break the news, and tend to a few other items of business."

Garsharp put the report aside. "By the way, do you have any of that spirit-flourescent powder handy? I'd like a few grams for a project."

"I'll have Mila run some over to you."

"Good, good," said the dean, looking cagey again. "I also want you to do a few things to prepare for tomorrow..."

Like so much of the Enclave, Practitioner Hall was monumental, ornate, and tragically under-utilized. All of the staff and students of the Art School, priests and practitioners alike, filled less than a quarter of the vast space. Nobody seemed to notice.

Leadership was represented by two guardians, and three deans represented the practitioners. There were a great many students priests: about a hundred, plus fifteen lectors of scripture. Healers were a smaller group, numbering around thirty students (of both candidate and apprentice ranks) and four lectors. Finally, there were five disciple track candidates (Khali and her study group), five apprentice disciples, and two lectors.

Behind the rows of students sat a smattering of other interested parties. Some were mendicants who happened to be in the city, but most were healers and disciples dressed like Boras in silks and lace. Collectively they looked like they hadn't been outside in months. Maybe a few of them were doing something useful in Enclave, but Taylor felt sure he was looking at one of the central problems in the church. Too many clannish practitioners who didn't work and didn't want outsiders to join their esteemed ranks.

When the meeting convened and the news about Mobeen was read, there was the expected murmurs of shock. Dean

Galonzo announced the scheduled date for Morbeen's memorial service, and several other notices about buildings that would be closed for the remainder of winter.

Then Galonzo proceeded to active practitioner business. Healer business was first, with several promotions from apprentice to full healer. The new healers separated out from their fellow students, shook hands with the deans, and accepted their holy symbols that indicated their new rank. Healer symbols were more ornate than the disciple ones: a pair of hands, palm out, with a star in the center. People clapped, congratulations were made. Each of the five received assignments in the form of a scroll of parchment.

Disciple business came next. It would have been permissible at that point for the non-disciple personnel to leave, but they all stayed. Maybe it was because disciple business was interesting, or because there was free lunch after the meeting. For whatever reason, the entire school was present when Taylor was professionally sidelined.

Dean Galonzo announced the first order of disciple business was the church's disposition in Girona. The disciple currently stationed there was not much longer for this world and a replacement was urgently needed. With the city in unrest, Leadership decided to send Brother Phillip to fill the role at this delicate time.

Brother Boras Namalous, he of the sharp teeth and no works, was the first to offer his congratulations, saying the achievement was a worthy one and a great opportunity for one so young. It promised a stellar career. Taylor had a hard time hearing him over the sound of blood pumping through his ears. Boras was mocking him: everyone knew Lavradio was where the church ended your career.

Nearly all of the "lace disciples", as Taylor was starting to think of them, applauded in approval.

One of the Guardians spoke, a member of the assignment committee. "We can't force a disciple to take assignment. However, Brother Phillip, will you accept the post in Lavradio?"

Taylor stood to address the guardian. "Excuse me, but I'm not sure I understand. My record as a mendicant is short but, I thought, acceptable. I was hoping to be mendicant for a few more years and gain experience. Why send me to Lavradio?" He gestured to all the lace disciples on his row. "There are many other disciples, more illustrious than I. With the city in turmoil, shouldn't we be sending our best?"

"Brother Phillip," barked Dean Galonzo, "it is the wish of the deans you take this assignment. Will you accept, or not?"

Taylor opened and closed his mouth twice, as if to object. Everyone knew the deans were more important to disciples than Leadership was. After a short struggle with himself, clenching his hands and flaring his nostrils, Taylor put his hand over his heart and bowed his head. He accepted the assignment because it came from both Leadership and the deans of the Art School. The guardian from the Assignments Committee put his name on a roll of parchment and signed it then passed it to the dean for endorsement. The scroll was ultimately passed back towards Taylor through the audience.

Boras got hold of the scroll and hand-delivered it. "Congratulations," he said with a fake smile, "I'm sure you'll feel right at home."

Taking the assignment and acting reluctant about it was Taylor's plan, but having it rubbed in his face by the likes of

Boras was getting hard to take. Taylor snatched the scroll from his hands.

"Next," continued Dean Galonzo, "we have the matter of candidate Khali and four others. Will you please stand?" The only five disciple candidates in the school stood in a group, apprehensive. "You have defied your mentor's orders by taking instruction from another practitioner without his leave. Is that true?"

Khali held her head high, looked the dean in the eye and said loudly, "our so-called mentor wasn't teaching us anything! Brother Phillip taught us more in a week than we learned in six months with Lector Sulpiono."

"Lector Sulpiono, your thoughts?"

Sulpiono stood from among the ranks of teachers. "Thank you, Dean. Brother Phillip is well-meaning, but has permanently twisted the growth of these students by teaching them shortcuts before the basics of prayer are mastered."

"You aren't teaching us at all!" accused Kahli. The other students with her looked nervous, but didn't look down.

The guardian from the assignment committee fixed her with a powerful glare of his ebony eyes. "You question your mentor's decision? He graciously agreed to take you under his wing in spite of your lack of family history."

"I propose," said Sulpiono, "we be gracious and permit these five to remain as priests. It would be a shame to waste all the effort we have put into them so far, but they should be removed from the practitioner course immediately."

"That isn't fair," yelled one of the students. "You refuse to teach us anything, and then throw us out the moment anyone else does? You just shove aside anyone who's not from a first family and pretend nobody else can be a disciple!"

"Indeed, our families are precious," intoned Sulpiono, "for they hold the legacy of the first disciples. This is the way we have instructed new disciples at the School of Spiritual Arts for centuries. It is your own arrogance that led you to this point. If you are truly dedicated to Olyon, you may serve him as priests, but not as practitioners."

"I would rather go home in shame," Khali declared, "than spend one more day in your shady little school." The other four agreed with her. It was disciple training, or nothing at all.

"Then you are expelled." Sulpiono said the words with unseemly relish. "Pack your belongings and go. Now."

The five expelled candidates left their seats in a hurry, chased out the door by scattered applause. As they left, Sulpiono looked directly at Taylor and smiled, like the gurantor who had just plucked a massive melon off the ground and stuffed the whole thing into its mouth.

"Next order of business," read Dean Galonzo. There was a ripple of unease as a new figure entered from the side door, a woman in white robes trimmed in gold. Her face was covered with an embroidered veil, but her dramatic horns gave away her identity: Milara. Her costume was that of an aide to the Matriarch. She was trailed by two priests in black cossacks and red stoles, personal attendants of the Matriarch. Her veil was a symbol that she was here not as herself, but as the Voice of Her Holiness. She moved with stately grace to the empty chair in the center of the dais and sat, while her two attendants took up stations on either side of her. The entire room covered their hearts and bowed their heads.

"Continue," said the Voice.

"There are two open disciple stations," resumed Dean Galanzo, "that must be manned. The previous occupants were both killed by cursed monsters, which remain at large. The first opening is in the city of Jindalini in Mialta. There have been many monster attacks this year, and an experienced bulwark is recommended. Any volunteers?"

For several seconds it looked like there wouldn't be any takers, but then Disciple Souzane, a trim, muscular woman without any sign of lace on her, raised her hand. She was just a few seats down the row behind Taylor.

"Are you sure, Sister Souzane? You've just returned from your last posting."

"Temperate rain forest and people who like to dance naked? I better take it before someone else does." She laughed, then turned serious. "Besides, this place is getting too stuffy for us working disciples." She gave Taylor a wink and sat down.

"The position is yours." Like Taylor, she received a roll of parchment with her orders. She looked ready to walk out the door right away, but kept her seat.

"Next is Sand Castle, in southern Kravikas." There was some quiet scoffing from the lace disciples in Taylor's row. They were wondering what poor bastard was going to get stuck with such a bad post. "It is in the desert, but it guards the central land route across Tenobre. Are there any volunteers?"

Galonzo clearly wasn't expecting there to be any takers, since these postings were for three years and most people wouldn't want to be at a remote desert city for all that time. Half of the corps in the Enclave were septuagenarians who couldn't take the physical strain of the harsh environment.

That left the lace disciples who, by virtue of their family connections, could arrange to stay forever in Enclave without actual jobs.

"I am concerned," said the Voice. "The posting is strategically important. If Sand Castle falls to cursed monsters the gurantor trains cannot complete the desert crossing. Tenobre will be cut in half. The darkness continues to grow, year by year, feeding on the blood of the faithful. The Alignment will not hold if the Enclave allows such failures to continue.

"However, we are fortunate. We have among us the blood of the first disciples, carefully husbanded for centuries, until our hour of need. Long have we been reminded of their special value. We call upon that promise now. Brother Sulpiono, descendant of Saint Karolo, we call upon you to take up the post in Sand Castle."

"Your Holiness!" he stammered, rising from his seat, "what about my students?"

"They are all expelled! They could not rise to the heights of your bloodline and you have dismissed them. How fortunate we are to find you so unengaged. You will go to Sand Castle and inspire us all with the light of the first disciples that is so exquisitely preserved in your veins."

Sulpiono stood there, among the lace disciples, working his mouth like a fish out of water. It went on for an embarrassingly long time. The disciples near him all leaned away instinctively.

"Let the record show Sulpiono voices no objection. Prepare the order."

While the assignment guardians were putting Sulpiono'a name on the order, the Voice continued to speak.

"Creatures of darkness roam Tenobre, in greater numbers each year, feasting on the flesh of the devout. The deaths of Disciples Asmasu, Lyon, and Mobeen is the loss of a quarter of our monster-fighting ability. Every disciple will be called upon to defend the faithful. Every practitioner will be put to the Work. If we fail this test, then we fail the Treaty of Alignment. Without the treaty, Enclave becomes irrelevant. We must rise to meet the darkness, for that is our purpose."

Taylor didn't go to the free lunch. Instead he went to the training grounds to meet up with his followers and Khali's study group of expelled candidates. They were all waiting for him by the sling range, practicing. A fully enhanced bulwark could throw hardened bullets fast enough to destroy carriages and kill gurantors. They were set up on the short-distance range at the twenty meter mark.

"So what happened after we left?" Khali did the asking, but all of the candidates were eager to know.

"The Voice of Her Holiness showed up and shamed Lector Sulpiono into a desert posting. The place is literally called Sand Castle. He tried to decline of course, on the grounds he's a teacher whose students needed him."

"But he doesn't have any!" Khali and the others understood immediately. Taylor had told them ahead of time to push for expulsion and in return he would take them to Girona to train them for real. Now they knew why.

"Are we still going to Lavradio?"

"When do we leave?"

"Are you sure this is okay?"

The questions came so fast he couldn't answer them. "Hold on! You're going to pack right away and spend the night at the Knight's Cup. We leave by special post in the morning. But!" he had to interrupt their celebrations, "the school in Girona is not nearly as nice as here. You'll be living very close with students from minor nobility, merchants, tradesmen, and the slums. I can't promise you'll like it. I can promise we'll put a roof over your head, food in your belly, and we'll train you. When you come back here for your final tests you will be more than ready, and these clowns will be so desperate for more disciples they'll have to pass you even if they hate it."

"Assuming they're alive by then," said a new voice. "Her Holiness sounds ready to send them all to their deaths if they don't start being useful. Disciple Souzane. We meet in the Light."

"Phillip the Younger. Let's walk as brothers," Taylor responded.

Souzane introduced her three bulwark, and their friend James. James was wearing a lightweight vest in spite of the cold, partially revealing a torso covered in colorful interlocking tattoos. He was a former bulwark himself. Taylor made his introductions, including the expelled students. They looked ready to shrink into the ground.

"Any chance of Sulpiono showing up?"

Souzane laughed. "None. Dean Garsharp made the invitation at lunch, in front of everyone. Of course the idiot refused in the most insulting way. And then he tried to recruit a cadre by making a public announcement in the dining hall. No takers, obviously.

"So," she looked meaningfully at the long boxes stacked on the ground, "Garsharp said you had something new to fight dark monsters with. Are those it?"

"Yes. Some for practice, and some for fighting." He turned to the ex-students. "You lot can go pack. The Knight is expecting you. If you have any trouble, talk to Mila." Mila and the students took off, excited to leave Enclave.

"You're really taking them on as students?" asked Souzane.

"Definitely. We can't let that much talent go to waste. If the school hadn't wasted so much of their time they could be hunting cursed monsters already. Let's move back to the thirty meter line."

Inez demonstrated the atlatl, and Souzane's team (plus James) practiced enough to get the hang of it. They seemed to be having a good time, because they kept at it until every practice dart had shattered against the hillside. The thrower was a surprisingly easy tool to learn, especially for someone who knew how to throw a spear. All it really did was add length and a joint to one's arm. When they all had the basic idea Taylor moved them to the next range over and set them up on the fifty meter line.

"I've hardened the target wall. Could you have someone sling a rock at it, with full enhancements?"

Souzane said the necessary prayers over one of her followers, who slung a ten kilogram ball so fast it left a shockwave in its wake and screamed down range. It collided with the hillside with a loud clack and ricocheted directly back to them, at an only slightly reduced speed. It skipped over the ground, spraying dirt and leaving gouges. One of Souzane's bulwark uttered a curse and threw her to the ground, covering her with their body. Taylor put up a barrier (that he had been holding ready) to redirect the shot into the forest where it crashed and broke things before coming to a stop.

The woman's bulwark were not happy. "You could have warned us!"

"Inez, you're up," said Taylor, as he canceled the barrier.

Inez kicked open the long box containing the real throwing darts. Their heads weren't mere points, but broad-bladed and wicked looking, with a redder hue than most bronze. The tails had low-profile vanes, set at a slight angle to induce a stabilizing spin. Just behind the center of gravity was a slight bulge.

Inez loaded the specialist dart into the thrower and waited for Taylor to bless her with a full set of enhancements. When she launched the dart from the atlatl it moved at a deceptive speed. The extended length of the missile made it look slower than it really was, and unlike bullets hurled from a sling it barely whispered as it cut through the air. When the dart hit its target, it seemed to just disappear.

"It sank right up to the fletching." James was impressed.

Souzane's party forgot their anger at Taylor in their enthusiasm to get their hands dirty. It didn't take long to run through all one dozen darts. Then came the chore of retrieving the buried darts and recovering the broken practice ones. Souzane had to reshape part of the hillside just to pull out all the darts and their heads. The broad headed points were deformed from the trip into the hardened rock, still hot from the impact.

"Each set comes with this tool." Taylor showed them a finished slat of hardwood with holes and notches of different sizes cut into it. While they watched, he used it as a jig to straighten and refine a broken practice dart as he re-shaped it. "This way, every dart is the same, as long as you make them all from the same kind of wood. And I'm including a schematic for the tool, in case you ever need to remake the jig from scratch. Any decent finish carpenter can follow the diagram perfectly."

Taylor took one of the fighting darts, deformed by their impact with rock, and started repairing it. "These cutouts are for shaping the head, these are for positioning the vanes, and these are for making the thrower."

"So you've made a new weapon that gives deep penetration and massive damage. From a distance." Souzane was gratifyingly pleased.

"A modest distance, but yes."

"Its a lot better than trying to stick spears in them from up close," said James. "And it's field constructible. Mobeen would approve. Bows never last long."

"Can we use normal bronze with this?" asked one of Souzane's bulwark.

"You can. It won't take enhancements as well or give the same depth, but it'll work. And you can use a normal tip if you prefer: you'll need to play with the size to get the balance right. Since Sulpiono declined to show up today, you get to keep all twelve of these."

"How do we get more of this metal?" asked James. "It reminds me of moldonian bronze."

"I got the idea from moldonian, and improved it. It takes enhancements just as beautifully, can be work hardened to a higher degree, and has improved acid and corrosion resistance. The downside is I'm the only one who can make it right now. When I get to Lavradio I'll set up a refinery to make more. By summer we should be selling this stuff and a similar metal for armor, all over Tenobre. Disciples only, obviously. It's wasted on someone who won't put prayers on it."

James fingered the edge of one of the broadheads. "What do you call it?"

"I'm not sure," Taylor said thoughtfully, "but I was thinking of naming it after mobeen. He was skeptical about the stone knife tradition, and he was always looking for ways to improve his gear. I think he would have liked this."

Souzane stood tall, testing the balance of one of the darts. Taylor felt it was one of his better ideas: a sophisticated weapon system that was easy to build. And, importantly, it was documented.

"What can I do to repay you?"

"Kill dark monsters," Taylor told her solemnly. "For a while, that's going to be the Work."

On the day Phillip the Younger boarded the post train to Lavradio, a box arrived at the Enclave from the Lavradian ambassador. It was a small box: rectangular and just large enough to hold a few thin scrolls of parchment. The usual path of such parcels was to enter Unity City by carriage train, in a crate full of mail collected along the train's route, all addressed to destinations in the Enclave. The crates were picked up at the city depot by a pair of workers from the Enclave mail room, who loaded them onto a horse-drawn cart and hauled then through the Enclave gate, past the warden and into the building where mail was accepted, sorted, and delivered.

Like so many messages from Lavradio in recent months, the parcel did not arrive at its intended destination: the Leadership office that handled routine ambassadorial mail.

Normally such messages wouldn't be missed, or if they were then it was assumed they had been lost in transit.

This time, someone came looking for the message: Warden Helen entered the warehouse-like space a day after the message should have been delivered, with two additional wardens and a healer in tow. She ordered an immediate stop to all work and lined up the personnel. Clerk Damon, a priest of Olyon and head of the mail house, came down from his office that overlooked the sorting area and demanded to know what was going on. Helen put him in line with the others.

"You can't just come in here and stop work," complained the clerk, "the evening sort has just started!" Heaps of messages were in the midst of being sub-divided into smaller piles, which would be organized according to building and floor then shelved until the morning delivery.

"Here is the order from Her Holiness's office, authorizing a search. Is everyone accounted for?"

Clerk Damon read the order, blanched, then counted his people.

"We're missing one, Warden. Carrier Knut hasn't returned yet, but that's perfectly normal. She has the far residences and has a heavy load."

"Then we'll start. I want everyone to hold out their hands," said the warden, demonstrating. She held out her hands in front of her, waist high and palms up. The line of fifteen did as they were told, with some muttering.

The healer walked along the line of hands, moving slowly but hardly looking at them. He stopped in front of a tall man with hunter point ears whose hands began to glow a vivid green. Smears and handprints in green showed on his robes.

"Who is this?" asked Warden Helen.

"That's Deputy Clerk Serano." Clerk Damon swallowed hard. He didn't know what was happening, but he knew it was bad. Leadership kept assigning useless priests as his deputies, and he kept firing them because of their incompetence. He had thought Brother Serano a happy exception, someone reliable who could be promoted to Clerk when Damon retired, but now it seemed he was the worst deputy of all of them.

Serano turned and fled. Helen watched him with a bemused expression until he was halfway down the sorting area, breathing hard and pulling things down in his wake. With a snap and a pointed finger, she ordered the other wardens to give chase.

"Does Brother Serano have an office?" she asked, without bothering to watch as her deputies chased down and grappled his deputy.

Damon's response was automatic. "Please, follow me."

Serano's office was next to Damon's own, though smaller and full of shelves holding long rows of boards. The healer toured the space slowly, revealing spots and smears and splotches of green appearing and disappearing as he passed them. He soon focused on a section of shelves where all the boards glowed. He removed the boards to reveal a small alcove behind them, cut into the exterior wall. Inside alcove was a cast iron chest of curious design, not large but quite heavy, which he opened to reveal the missing scrolls. The scrolls glowed the brightest of anything in the room, reflecting the healer's spirit as visible light.

It was only a few moments' work to find the original box, broken down, in the deputy clerk's kindling pile next to the warming stove.

The iron chest, broken box, missing scrolls, and ex-deputy all went away with the wardens for examination. Damon didn't want to know where.

HOMECOMING

Ullidia

It started again, before they got to Lavradio. That feeling of being watched, being targeted, of some impending doom focused only on Taylor. Someone was about to summon him.

Of all the summons he had endured, none could be considered positive developments in his life. Reincarnations after death were sometimes good, like his rebirth in Emristar, but summonings were (so far) always bad. Taylor would suddenly find himself enslaved, or abandoned in the wilderness, or in some other awful situation. If he managed to survive long enough, which was less than half of the time, he could improve his situation. Just as soon as he hit his stride and felt he had a good future ahead, he would be yanked away from that life and have his consciousness installed somewhere new. Then the cycle would start again. These facts made early death a more likely route to a comfortable life than a long and successful climb through adversity.

When Taylor measured his current circumstances against his past ones, Tenobre was second best of a dozen worlds. It was a big step down from Emristar, and he wasn't enthusiastic about living in a bronze age world. But there were major upsides to his life in Tenobre. Being a disciple gave him significant status, he was free both in body and in conscience, and now that he had thrown off his self-imposed restraints the technology issues could be tackled. So he was in no mood to be pulled away to somewhere else.

A post train like theirs ran continuously, only stopping at depots long enough to change guarantors. At the first stop in Ullidia Taylor pulled aside his followers and explained the situation, while omitting the detail that Tenobre hadn't been the first world to summon him.

"Is Emristar trying to take you back?" Mila asked.

Taylor shook his head. "They don't have the arts for it. Just sending small objects across the world by magic is highly experimental and takes massive resources. I can't imagine them advancing far enough to pull me back to Emristar in less than a year.

"My guess is this is something else. Maybe now that I've been summoned once I'm easier to summon by anyone, and random summoning rooms will be trying to grab me all the time."

"What are you going to do?" Milo's voice was neutral, cautious. Mila looked worried about his answer, and Inez watched the pedestrians for trouble. Their gurantor was being led away for grooming and rest, and the new one would be hitched up soon.

"I'm going to try and stop it. I think I know how to stop the summoning with a barrier and a ton of stored spirit, but there's going to be some explosive blowback. If I order an emergency stop of the carriage you have to hang on. Don't follow me when I go charging out of the car, and don't let the students come near me until after it's done. Stay twenty meters away from me, minimum."

"Why twenty meters?" said Mila, clearly not liking the instruction.

"Because math. The number of youngs that the emerald rod will hold, suddenly converted to undifferentiated spirit energy, expanding in a sphere. What proportion will hit you at twenty meters?"

"One four-hundredth of the intensity as at point blank," said Mila after a moment, "by inverse square law."

"More. There's the ground to think about," said Inez. "It won't be a perfect sphere."

"A lot of dirt and stuff is going get thrown," said Milo. "We have to think about those guys," he motioned at the students stretching their legs, and two of the drivers backing a fresh gurantor into the harness. The third driver was probably running down the street to buy ale and food. "And the gurantor. You might get hurt, and we can't get you to a healer if the gurantor can't run."

"Then let's plan," said Taylor. "If it's at all like the last time, I'll have thirty seconds to react."

Days later when the summoning came, Taylor almost missed it because he was asleep. He woke up annoyed that someone was staring at him, but saw only Mila watching two of the moons out the window. Then he remembered.

I've lost ten seconds, he thought as he yelled for an emergency stop. He held tight to the handle by the right-side door as the order was relayed, the car shifted into sudden deceleration, and the students began yelling. They hadn't been briefed, so being thrown against the front of the car was a rude awakening.

While he waited, Taylor self-enhanced for protection and speed. Then he called up shaping and held it ready. When the car was going slow enough he jumped out and ran towards the rear of the carriage, which was now moving past him, and shaped a large section of road into a sloped wedge as tall as the train. The idea was that any shockwave or debris that hit the shield would be forced up and to the sides, protecting the cars and occupants from harm. Days ago he had reinforced the back of the rear-most carriage with a thin panel of mobeen as a backup.

He kept running, and kept counting. With eight seconds left he curled up in the fetal position with one hand on the emerald and put a barrier close around himself, the kind that prevented any spirit-enhanced object or effect from passing through. He only had two seconds before he felt the sense of doom peak, and he drained every last young of spirit from the red emerald and fed it into the barrier.

It was like having lightning strike next to you, a noise so violent it threw the mind into disarray. Then came a long period of time, it felt like several minutes, where everything was white noise and shaking. The sensations took up his whole head: he couldn't even think about what was happening to him. When it stopped, he wasn't in the road any more.

He must have passed out.

He was in the carriage, and it was moving.

Taylor started his body check. He found his toes, his arches, his calves and knees, and kept working his way up. His ears weren't working very well and his skin felt tender and hot, like he had a horrible sunburn and his entire head was going to shed multiple layers of skin like a snake. He decided not to move his face too much, because the skin might split open.

353

People sounded far away, or like he was listening to them through a pillow held over a keyhole.

"He's awake!" A face swam into view, some student whose name he didn't remember. "Huh, his eyes are green."

"He's out of spirit," said another muffled voice. Milo shouldered the student aside. "You need a healer, Master. We're an hour away from Fort Edge."

Taylor grunted as loud as he could, which wasn't enough. Somebody sitting next to his head applied a gel to his face and neck. It felt cold, then wet and soothing. Too soon, the gel began to dry and the pain started to return.

"Fringe," he managed to croak out at last. There. Now the Dowager Fringe couldn't complain he hadn't kept his promise.

"Edge is closer." Milo evidently cared about this part a great deal, and that warmed Taylor's heart, but the Monfortes were among the few nobles he had met anywhere whom he considered noble. He knew and trusted the family. They were friends. Also, he had promised to drop by if he was ever in the area, and here he was. Since he wasn't hiding his identity any more, he could keep his promise.

"Fringe," Taylor said again. This conversation was wearing him out.

He could hear Inez, far away on the other side of the car, calling out to the driver in tones that reached him weak and wavering. "Driver, take us all the way to Fringe."

"Edge is closer!" complained Milo, again. It wasn't the perfect time for Taylor's hearing to start clearing up. Or maybe he was just yelling that loud.

"Fringe is only a little farther. Edge puts him in the hands of strange nobles. He'll be fine for the few extra minutes, and he'll be a lot safer with the Monfortes."

Inez understood. When you were vulnerable then you wanted to be in friendly hands. The new king was in Alignment, and wasn't hunting disciples for cash. So, no divided loyalties for the Monfortes. It should be fine. Taylor tried to think about his social graph, to check if he should reconsider, but he fell asleep instead.

He started the body check-in procedure again, before he was fully conscious. Toes, arches, calves, knees, quads, and so on up the torso and down the arms and into the fingers. Neck and face seemed to be in working order. When he got his eyes open, all he could see was Amalia staring holes into him.

His voice was raspy, but he got it to work. "It's good to see you, Amalia."

"Is it? Because the last time you were in Fringe you left without even telling people who you were! Gonzo cried when you went missing! Did you know that? We could barely get him to eat for weeks. And you just breeze on through here like we were nobody to you."

"Maybe," he said slowly, "get everyone together for this. Long story. Are there pants?"

Amalia held up his pants in one hand. "Give me the short version, then you get pants."

"It was King Joaquim. Helping Taylor DeLanion could have been treason."

That was apparently good enough. Amelia left his pants on the bed and fetched Milo. For once, Taylor really needed the help and he was deeply grateful to his valet. Taylor barely had his top on when Gonzo bust into the room, breathless, Amelia chasing behind him. The boy was younger than Taylor, nine years old, with a mousy nose and whiskers -- the family trait of the Monfortes. Gonzo charged at Taylor and hugged him, forcing him to hug the boy back just to keep his balance.

"I'm fine, Gonzo. I'll explain everything." He signed to Amalia that this was fine, and she could leave Gonzo with him.

Milo pushed a handkerchief into Gonzo's hand. "Try not to get tears on the master's shirt, please."

Gonzo broke his grapple to wipe his eyes and pepper Taylor with questions. "Where have you been? Why is your hair like that? How many monsters did you kill? Is it true your eyes turn silver?"

The questions went on until Taylor laughed. "No stories until I can think straight. I'm starving. Food, then stories."

"Our master will need to rest soon, too," Milo told the boy sympathetically. "Try not to wear him out, okay? We'll be here overnight."

"Let's hurry," said Gonzo, "they're holding lunch for you." Gonzo was gone as fast as he had appeared.

Lunch was family-only, plus Taylor with only Milo to wait on him. However, the food was not immediately forthcoming: they were holding lunch hostage for information. The Monfortes had placed him at one end of the the table, directly opposite of the baron. Baron Rodrigo of Fringe, Dowager Marcia, Alicia, and Gonzo took most of the remaining chairs.

"Explain this issue of treason," said the baron, "Phillip or Taylor or whatever your name is. I especially want to know if I am committing treason by harboring you here."

"Duke Frenzio and Prelate DeGray tricked King Joaquim. They told him the Unity had put a bounty on my head of one ton of gold. The king decided to collect, and used his best people to kill me. There was no gold, of course, but all I knew at the time was the palace had tried to have me killed. I couldn't go to any citizens of Lavradio without them committing treason, so I took up my alternate disciple name, and didn't come back until Leadership sorted everything out."

"I'm shocked you got away with it," Alicia said sourly. She sounded remarkably like her grandmother, who was infamous for her acerbic manner.

"How would you describe Disciple Taylor to someone who had never seen him? You'd say he was smooth-skinned, outgoing, plays a strange instrument, and sings well. Disciple Phillip has silver eyes and brindle hair, is surly, and doesn't sing."

"It was wisely done," said the dowager.

"Grandmother, stop taking his side. We're angry about this, remember?"

"I have changed my mind, child. He thought revealing himself to us could place us in grave danger. I take it the matter has been resolved to everyone's satisfaction?" Dowager Marcia eyed Taylor with one of her skeptical, 'don't shovel any gurantor apples my way' glares.

"Officially, rogue elements of the palace and the church conspired to assassinate me, and I disappeared while Leadership investigated. Everyone involved has been dealt with, except Nurr who has been recessed. Few people know

Taylor is alive, so please don't go spreading it around until I've checked in at the basilica."

Taylor looked at Amalia. "I'm happy you're still mad at me, Amalia. Only a true friend would be so angry I didn't force her to risk treason."

"Let's table this for now." Baron Monforte rang a small bell by his place setting, which caused doors to open and servants to approach with drinks and food. Taylor wouldn't remember what the food was, only that he ate a lot of it.

Taylor made it almost to the end of the meal before his fatigue ambushed him. On his way to bed he thanked everyone. "I would stay a month if I could, but I'm on assignment now. I'll have to leave tomorrow even if I'm not recovered. But thank you for taking me in with no notice." With that he shuffled off to his assigned room and was asleep before Milo had his shoes off.

Having gone to sleep in the early afternoon, it was only natural that Taylor was up in the middle of the night. Gonzo was in his bed, and Amalia had re-occupied the visitor's chair wearing a robe over her night clothes. Gonzo was radiating a soft nimbus of spirit, which was a new and startling development. It took all of two seconds for Taylor to decide the boy's future.

"You look troubled, Lady Amalia. Two bits for your thoughts."

"We went to the coronation. They had it in the basilica, so we saw the Fragment." She stopped there, unwilling to go on.

"And now Gonzo's light is awake," he finished for her. "Did the matrix offer to teach him?"

Another sour look. She must have been practicing, because Taylor didn't remember her ever using that face when they were in the west palace together.

Taylor assembled his case. He wanted this kid, and convincing the family was key. "Gonzo is special, beyond his spirit ability. He's smart, Amalia." Taylor sat up cross-legged and made sure the younger boy was covered. "He's not just educated, but smart in a way few people are. A few minds like his could turn things around, let us face what's coming."

Amalia had already figured it out. Taylor could tell from her look. She was up in the dead of night not just because she was worried about her little brother, but because she was worried about the whole of Fringe. In her time among the auditors of Girona she had learned the importance of taking a wide view, mining the data, and asking questions other people would think were wild.

"You and Gonzo were at the basilica, so you visited the library in the crypt," he prompted her.

"And a hundred years ago cursed monsters were a myth, something in scripture you read about but they weren't real. Last year there were fifteen. Most of Fringe has been abandoned in the last twenty years. Not that it was ever crowded." Her smile was wry but affectionate. The Monfortes loved their highland domain, with its stark beauty and sudden storms that came crashing down from the mountains in the west and barreled over the hills in the east.

"How bad will it get?" she asked. That was the question, wasn't it? The thing people needed to know but that he couldn't answer. Net yet, anyway.

"I can tell you how long it will keep getting worse, but you won't like the answer."

"Didn't you teach us not to hide from ugly facts? Just tell me already."

"Three hundred and fifty years, give or take a few." She turned white. Taylor knew what she was thinking right then. She was trying to imagine how much worse the monster attacks could get, if they kept increasing for so long. Milara's and Garsharp's reactions hadn't been so strong, which made Taylor think they already had some idea of the scale of this problem, well before he blew into Enclave with his sack full of insanity. Maybe they hadn't known a concrete number, but they had suspected something along similar lines. Amalia was getting the news fresh.

"They'll wipe us out, just like the ancients."

"Some of the ancients survived," he reminded her, "or else you wouldn't be here. When you come to Girona for your palace rotation, I'll give you the long version."

"If we send him to you," she meant Gonzo, "can you guarantee his safety?"

"If he stays in the Fringe, can you? I can promise to prepare him. And I can promise he'll make a difference. Isn't that enough for a son of the Fringe?"

There was a quiet knock on the door, followed by Inez's head. "Julian wants to check in on you."

"Let him in."

Healer Julian looked amused at the tension between Taylor and Amalia, as he put down his bag and a dimly lit spirit lamp. He gave Taylor a quick once over. "Your skin has healed up very well. And your eyes are back to silver, which is normal for you. Bloom out for me."

Taylor let his spirit unfurl, without reaching for more or trying to shape it at all. He didn't have even a fifth of his normal strength, but that would be solved with rest.

"You're very stable, which is good." Julian was comparing his current state to the last time they met, but didn't go into details because Amalia was in the room. Instead, he handed over a bead of silver. "Shape this."

Taylor transformed the tiny bead into a meter-wide flower with a thousand petals made of delicate silver foil, so thin they fluttered as he handed the flower to Amalia. She grabbed it in a fist and angrily wadded it into a misshapen ball. Still not satisfied, she rolled it between her palms to shrink it even smaller.

"Pity." Julian still looked very amused for some reason, as he scooped up the foil ball and dropped it into a pocket. "Rest. No heavy spirit use, just for a few days until you're full again. Let your carriage full of students do all the heavy lifting for a while."

"Thanks Julian." Taylor flipped him a small brass triangle that was worth eight bits, which the healer caught. It was a token payment between practitioners, a way of saying "I respect what you've done for me, but we're too awesome to swap real money."

"Next time we're in the same town, let's get a drink. I'll buy."

"You drink now?" The healer looked concerned about the young disciple's habits.

"Vegetable juice, sure. You can have spirits in yours. I have it on good authority that it's a delicious drink."

"Keep your root juice, I'll take my spirits straight." He picked up his bag and lamp, and wished them a good night.

Taylor caught Gonzo watching, awake and grinning. "Enjoy the show?"

"Practitioners are so sway!"

"Is that what the kids are saying these days? Sway?"

"You sound like my dad," he said, still grinning. "'You kids and your misuse of language. What nonsense! In my day everything was sharp.'"

"Sharp, huh? If I show you something sway, can we all go back to sleep?"

He had Amalia put out the candle. In the darkened room Taylor lit a thousand tiny lights, arranged like stars in the sky above Emristar. "These are the stars of my home world. A sky you have never seen. Sway?"

"Sway," agreed Gonzo.

"If you want to sleep next to Gonzo it's okay with me," Taylor told Amalia. If he could convince the baron, this would be the last time she saw her little brother until summer. With both of her brothers living in the capital, she would be without any siblings for the first time in her life.

Taylor was asleep before the siblings finished getting comfortable. He was dimly aware of the change of guard from Inez to Mila, but he was otherwise dead to the world until after dawn.

Taylor awoke to an empty bed. Amalia had briefed the baron on what she had learned the night before, and Gonzo was packing in hopes of leaving right away. As soon as Taylor was dressed and had checked in with his students (they were all fine, and had spent the extra day practicing with the spear throwers) he spent the next two hours at "breakfast" briefing the baron. He started with the same material he had given to the Voice, omitting the deficiencies of Enclave. And he told them about the nexus.

"Until now, I've been holding back most of my knowledge," he told them, "because I didn't want to accidentally transform your whole culture. That has to change. Now I'm pushing math, natural law, and technology into the world as fast as I can. And that's what I need Gonzo for. He's capable of learning all the new stuff faster than most people, and he'll come up with ideas no one else would."

Taylor sighed. "Your son is smarter than I am. One day he's going to look at me and realize he's surpassed anything I could ever do. Then it'll be him and a few others like him, inventing the world the rest of us will live in. In fifty years you won't even recognize the world, it'll be so different. And we need to start right away, because right now we're losing."

"What else can we do?" asked the baron.

"We're going to need your mineral wealth, including some things you're used to throwing away. There's enough profit to make it worth your while, but there will be startup costs." Taylor passed him a list. "In a few days, send someone who can negotiate on your behalf. Or, come yourself."

The carriage had a new passenger in Gonzo, who looked so excited he could jump out of his skin. By gurantor post they were only two days out from Girona, so Taylor set Khali to teaching Gonzo the Prayer for Light. In a few hours Gonzo was able to enchant a stone with a soft, happy light. The other students were better at it, and they had more spirit, but they were obviously bitter.

"They're not mad at you, Gonzo," Taylor explained, "they're mad because their old teacher wasted so much of their time."

As the carriage finally ground its way through the slushy streets of Girona, Taylor looked upon a city changed by fire. West town was missing several buildings from its skyline, and a quarter of Plaza Hall was destroyed and not being rebuilt. He was glad to see the Basilica of Magnificent Light was untouched. They stopped the carriage at the basilica because that was the protocol: when you were on assignment you checked in with the prelate in a timely fashion, and no time was more timely than right now.

They didn't need to make much of an effort to make a showy entrance. They were all in uniform with their bifur cloaks, brigandine, and black-hilted weapons of mobeen. The four of them left the students in the carriage and climbed the stair to the foyer. Within minutes they were being greeted by the prelate and ambassador, Sister Kasryn. Taylor sat patiently while she reviewed his order from Leadership, then reviewed a scroll of secret orders from the Matriarch. Taylor was granted certain extra privileges and Kasryn was to cooperate with him fully. Certain reports were to be sent for hand-delivery to the Matriarch, bypassing Leadership.

"So Phillip the Younger is Taylor DeLanion." She didn't look very pleased about that. "Why didn't you come forward sooner? It would have made my job much easier."

"Why would I? First Brother Serano tries to kill me in open court, and then Prelate DeGray has me assassinated. The news I had at the time was Leadership put a bounty on my head. Under those circumstances..." He left the sentence hanging, inviting her to disagree.

"You believed Unity wanted you dead." She had more questions, but she was holding them for another time. "Her Holiness says you'll brief me. So," said Kasryn, "brief me."

"I would rather brief you when I brief the local nobles. It's pretty extreme, and it takes a while."

Kasryn shook her head emphatically. "As ambassador, and your ally here, I need to know what I'm dealing with. We need to learn to trust each other, so earn a little trust by briefing me."

"Here's the short version. Dark monsters will continue to increase in number, for another three hundred fifty years. We have no idea how bad it's going to get, but it will be much, much worse than it is today." Kasryn had the good sense to turn green. "I'm here to train as many disciples as we can, at an accelerated rate, so the monsters don't eat us all. At the same time I'll be flooding Tenobre with new inventions and knowledge, so the collective ingenuity of the human race can propel us to victory. To make all that happen we're going to build three institutions, all adjacent to each other: a school (which we have), a research facility, and an industrial center. The working name for it is Nexus. Girona's will be the first, but eventually I'd like to see a few more across Tenobre."

Kasyn chewed on that information, almost literally. Taylor could see her jaw clenching. She read the Matriarch's orders again, then put the scroll down.

"It will take a few days to get your audience with the king. Maybe a month, if he's not feeling cooperative."

"If he tries to stall, just remind him that his parents killed me after I worked so hard to save his capital. Oh, and I don't want the Dowager Queen or her ladies in attendance. I'm still pretty mad about them murdering me, and I can't guarantee I won't kill them on sight. If it takes more than a day to meet him, I'll give you the full hour-long presentation."

The party boarded the train again for the DeLanion School for Math, Scripture, and Music where they pulled to a stop in front of a what could charitably be called the beginnings of a campus. The buildings were plain gray brick, drawn from whatever vast stockpile kept the slums of bricktown from running out of material. Piled four stories tall and boasting several chimneys, the main building was classrooms on the first two floors and dorms on the top two floors. From the street Taylor could see two smaller buildings and a training yard large enough for a hundred students to practice martial arts. They were met by none other than Brother Mika, who had a teenage boy at his elbow.

"We meet in the Light, Brother Mika." Taylor fairly leapt out of the carriage.

Mika took in Taylor's brindle hair and silvered eyes. "Let's walk as brothers, Brother Phillip." A bow or a handshake was not enough for either of them, so they went for the hug.

"How is the matrix?"

"Not well. She doesn't have an abundance of time. You should see her right away."

"I brought you more students, good ones I think. The little one is new to the church, but the five older ones I rescued from the neglect of Enclave's Art School." The six new students had lined up along the first car of the train, while their baggage was being unloaded by the drivers.

"Ah! No first families among you? Good. Here at DeLanion's we care about what you can do, and we care about the tenets. Everyone is here to perform Olyon's Work. We do not tolerate bullying. Any objections?"

A round of "no, Brother" rose up from the clutch of new students.

"Good. Gavoto here will show you to your beds, get you fed, and otherwise get you settled."

Gavoto took charge of the newcomers while Mika, Taylor, and Mila made the short walk to the Chapel of Compassionate Light and its small but comfortable parsonage. Milo and Inez redirected the train to the Vagos-Avelar hotel where the cadre would be staying until some permanent housing was sorted out.

When Taylor took the visitor's chair next to Lucia, he was speechless. She was rail thin, skin so white it was transparent. Her light waxed and waned with her breathing as if it could go out on any exhalation. She was on her way out. It was painful to watch her, but Taylor couldn't bring himself to leave too soon. He sat there for several minutes, unable to say or do anything.

"Chondra!" The clouded eyes turned in Taylor's direction. "Why aren't you in class? Lee will be angry."

Taylor improvised, just so he could talk to her. "The lector didn't arrive, something about an enhancement gone wrong. The rumor," he tried to sound as if the news was delicious gossip, "is he's in the infirmary."

"That Lee is so incompetent. I'm surprised he had the nerve to try anything at all. He's such a coward."

"Well he tried something today, and now I have a free class period."

"Serves him right, lecherous nut-muncher. Oh! But Loukas is in his history class. Now I won't get to see Loukas today. Lector Lee is such an idiot."

Taylor leaned in to the friend-at-school persona. "Oh, you have a thing for that Loukas guy, huh?"

"He makes my womb throb," she said with a wicked laugh. "I've been taking my nightclothes to study group every night. If he doesn't invite me soon, I'm going to hit him with a maximized benediction."

This was so much more than Taylor needed to know.

"Chandra? You can't be Chandra!" Lucia was alarmed, and withdrew her hand. "She died."

"I know," said Taylor, switching roles. "Do you miss her?"

"Oh, so terribly." Her fear seemed to drain away. The kind stranger was asking about her dead friend. "Except high holy days. She was so useless for the big services. She would panic and run. Brave against monsters and kings, but a coward against crowds."

"I wish I could have met her." He had her hand again.

"How are you, Taylor?" It might not last long, but it was reassuring to have her in the here and now.

"Alive again. Don't ask me why."

"You don't remember? Passing over and back again? Nothing?" The urgency in her voice gave away her fears. She was about to make that journey herself, and she didn't want to go unprepared. It was normal to want to know.

Taylor shook his head. "All I know is our souls are eternal. We fall like meteors into our new lives, touching thousands when we enter their atmosphere. You will too, and they will be lucky to have you."

"It wasn't supposed to be this way." Her trembling, thinly skinned hand gripped his own with feeble strength. "We thought it would be over in a few years, but it keeps getting worse. But you're so bright. And you're such a good boy. You will keep an eye on things, won't you?"

"Yes, Lucia. I know what to do. I have a plan."

After she fell asleep Taylor hugged Mika again. He tried to tell the older man a lot in that embrace: his appreciation for Lucia; compassion for the man's impending loss; a general message of support. He left Mika alone in the matrix's room, but only made it half way through the house before breaking down in tears himself.

Only at that moment, days before her death, did he realize he had loved her.

Tha Vagos-Avelar was a match for nearly any other hotel in Tenobre. It was not lost on Taylor what it meant that Unity had put him up in that particular establishment. The wealthy and influential had their own enclaves and the Vagos-Avelar was one of them. Nor was it lost on the opulent hotel that they had been chosen to host the Missing Disciple, returned in victory and cloaked in trophies. Within an hour of taking his suite, boards were dispatched to every level of Grirona's society, serving notice he had returned. They went to the King (via the ambassador), healers, priests, inner city, merchants, guilds, unions, plaza hall, peacekeepers, slums, and shops. The boards came in two varieties. Some were requests to "get together at a near date", while others effectively said "let's meet when things have calmed down." By the end of the day everyone would know the Missing Disciple was no longer missing.

Plaza Hall was the first to respond, in the person of Second Prince Estevan Odemira, who fast-walked across the plaza, cutting across traffic while his guard urgently flagged down oncoming appalons and carriages. He barreled through the front doors and climbed the stairs two at a time, making the silver ties and ornaments in his mane (a trait of the Odemira family) sparkle and chime. The happy ornaments were at odds with the anger in his stride. The staff's pleas that he wait to be announced went ignored as he prepared to kick down door 301, but he was denied his act of destruction when the portal opened on its own.

Inez held the door to the foyer, and had the nerve to look at Estevan as if she barely recognized him.

"Second Prince Estevan Odemira has arrived," she called over her shoulder.

"He may enter," came another woman's voice.

"You may enter," offered Inez.

Estevan stared at her hard as he passed through the door. Inez had guarded him for as long as he could remember. Then two months ago she had retired suddenly and disappeared. He stalked across the foyer and found the open door to the salon where Taylor had displayed himself. He sat in a wingback chair, like he used to in the Pegasus Workshop, reading boards from a pile set before him on a low table. The bricktown cousins were behind him. At his elbow was a matching table holding a mug of something, probably fruit juice. It was so typically Taylor that Estevan at first didn't notice the change in hair and eyes.

What he did notice was the massive arkto rug baring its tusks in warning to all who entered, and the bifur lined cloak thrown over the back of the throne. His boyish friend of a few months ago had gone full disciple and had been off hunting. The trader and musician had become a conqueror of dark monsters, and now sat armed and armored among his trophies.

Then Estevan realized what Taylor had done.

"Oh, very nice pose, you three. The stacks of boards leading the eye, and the lighting. Did you think I wouldn't notice?"

"I thought you'd be appreciative, Vanni: I worked hard on this composition for entire minutes." Taylor pretended to read the board in profile while looking at Estevan from the corner of his eye.

"It's all right," said the prince. He almost added "but my mother does it better," then remembered his mother had tried to kill his friend and instead took the seat he was offered. "The minister is somewhere behind me."

"Accept a cup of jota from over your shoulder when he comes in, left arm over the divan. Yes, like that."

"What's with your hair? And your eyes?"

"The hair is part of my disguise. Don't scoff, it was very effective! The eyes are harder to explain."

When the minister was announced and shown through they struck their pose for several seconds, letting him get a good look. Marvao was not a man known for smiling, but the tableau was clearly pleasing to him.

"Are we playing the picture game?"

"There's a game?" asked Taylor, surprised. "I was just messing around."

"Obviously," said Estevan. "How many more are coming?"

"I wouldn't know," said the minister, "but I noticed a brace of union men across the square, headed this way."

Milo had the place nearest the window, and opened the shutters to look out. "I see them, and healers a ways behind them."

"They all had your idea, Estevan: charge in without an appointment and get an early look at our Missing Disciple. I believe the next scene is mine. Taylor, did you bring props?"

"Props?" The messing about had escaped his control and turned into something unexpected. But he had an idea. "Mila, get the bag of crazy." Mila went to the next room to fetch the inventions and other materials they kept on hand for his presentations.

When the union men arrived they were treated to a vision of the minister and the prince frozen in the act of drinking or accepting jota from the hotel staff. In front of them was the tree rings and the gantt chart, with a few spirit gems scattered about for color. Again, the lines subtly lead the eye to Taylor. They took in the scene for several seconds and applauded.

"That's a pretty picture," said Master Clemens, who had laid in the facade of the grander buildings in Girona. "Let me do the next one. What else do we have for props?"

And so it went, with each new group being treated to a surprise vignette, then improvising changes for whomever came next. The builders got architectural drawings of proposed school building, which they argued over with Estevan. The microscope went to Healer Praetor and two apprentice healers, who set it up on a table and gathered around it to take turns looking into the eyepiece. Guild leaders complemented the scene, and took up ingots of manganese, mobeen, and a cut crystal goblet to consider.

By this time Taylor had completely lost control of the proceedings, whose nuances he wasn't sure he understood. "You're doing fine," Praetor assured him. "Is that a stack of Garsharp's notes on the microscope I see over there? Move them here so we can read them."

Someone brought in hotel staff, or maybe they came on their own, to reflect light with silver trays and add a sideboard with the requisite miniature foods. When the depot master arrived she received a youngmeter, since they would be added to each station's weather tracking routine. The head of the commodities exchange received a thick sheaf of paper but traded it to the guild for ingots of metal instead, to which Taylor added ingots of silicon and silver.

Sister Lorena, who would be matrix of the chapel when Lucia died, arrived with Head Priest Javach from the basilica. It was Javach who warned them the royal carriage was on its way. This prompted the popular election of Master Clemens to compose the final scene. He shuffled the older and wiser near the tree rings (yet to be explained) and the gantt chart (which was easier to understand) and put the younger players around them with all the inventions in poses suggesting critical examination and discussion.

Clemens wasn't quite done when Alice Tabua was announced. She burst into the room without waiting for permission to enter, and so caught a few of them off-guard. Her face went from eagerness, to joy at the picture, to maternal anger.

"Months gone, young man. Missing! Not a word! And now I find you playing games!" Her embrace would have powdered Taylor's bones if he wasn't enhanced. By the time the royals arrived they had finished their composition, with new allowances made for Alice's gorgeous but imposing physique.

"Their Royal Majesties," announced Inez, "King Leonardo Odemira and Queen Farava Odemira." The normal protocol was to stand and bow before royalty, but they kept their positions.

Guards (none other than Nunio and Malisa) preceded them through the door and took up posts to either side before the the king entered. Leo paused at the door, looked aside at his queen and said, "our idea was not so original after all."

Larava appraised the scene, radiating an aura of critical approval. "It would have been a shame to miss all of this. But husband, doesn't that boy with the silver eyes seem familiar? We came to see Taylor DeLanion, but instead we find Phillip the Younger." Behind her appeared Ambassador Kasryn, craning her neck to get a view of the picture.

"Great monster hunter or not, some explanation is in order," he agreed.

Minister Marvao broke the tableau first as a signal for everyone else to do the same. The room bowed and remained so until granted the king's leave, with the exception of the priests and practitioners. They bowed just enough to show respect to a foreign monarch and rose on their own.

The Vagos-Avelar staff brought in a divan just big enough for their majesties and placed it opposite the minister, and when the royal couple sat down the entire room pivoted to make them the center of attention. The man was born and raised to be king, so of course he could commandeer a room. Taylor could only take notes and hope to learn something. With the king's leave, everyone who had seats resumed them.

"Brother Phillip the Younger," said King Leonardo, "explain."

Not for the last time, Taylor gave the sanitized-for-the-public explanation about his double anointment, and the attempt on his life by "rogue forces of the palace and the church".

"I won't apologize for keeping my friends ignorant," he told them all, but looking at Prince Estevan. "From what I knew at the time, helping me might be treason. Removing myself from the picture seemed like the smartest move. And, I wanted to hunt monsters." People nodded and chuckled.

"Since you have everyone here, why not give us a briefing." Marvao's eyes were twinkling, as if he was trying to catch Taylor off guard. "All of this," he motioned to everything in the room, "tells me you have something big on your mind."

Marvao addressed the king, "it might be best to get it over with your majesties. It's likely to be quite shocking."

"It's been a long time since we had a DeLanion briefing," said Estevan.

Taylor was caught by surprise, but it wasn't as if he weren't prepared. "If their majesties have the time, I do have a some important news to relate."

"Well, here we go," said the leader of the hospitality guild.

"Do we need helmets for this?" asked someone.

"I've missed these," said one of the junior healers.

"I've never been, but I've heard rumors," said the other.

King Leonardo grandly allowed it. "As you say, Minister. We are all assembled. We will hear the news."

Taylor was about to begin, but was interrupted the ambassador, who was also prelate. "But first, benediction."

Taylor blessed them with prayer, out loud and very gently. The staff made sure their drinks were filled. Then Taylor gave them what would later become known as The Talk. He told them about the long cycle of the sun, of civilizations' rise and fall, their current place in the cycle, and the attempts to find out more about it. He told them about training new disciples in unheard-of numbers, the new technology which would be brought to bear, and his long-term plan to spark an age of discovery and invention.

All of that, and how Girona would be the center of it all if their majesties gave their permission.

Taylor fielded questions for about an hour before the hotel staff let them know dinner was prepared. The king had wisely ordered a supper, to let the conversation continue.

"I didn't intend to put such a large hole in your majesty's schedule." Taylor was given the honor of walking next to the king, from the salon to a large dining hall on the first floor. The collection of nobles, church people, and commoners paraded down the grand stairway through the second-floor mezzanine. Queen Larava walked on the king's right side, and Taylor on his left. The ambassador, Marvao, and Estevan were directly behind them. The pace was stately, testing Taylor's patience. Palace guards lined the staircase at intervals, not only as protection but to lend ceremony to the event: the king was passing by in full view of hundreds of staff and guests of the Vagos-Avelar, all of them gathered to bow and to witness his august passage from one room to another.

"My family owes you a great deal, Taylor of Emristar. Not only for what you have done for us, but for all we have taken from you, things that can never be returned." Taylor thought this was a terrible place for that conversation: people were watching. He might get angry and yell at the king, because they had taken from him. They had taken everything twice over.

"And yet you have returned to Girona for the sake of my people, and the the people of Tenobre. I am at a loss for how to reward you. Titles and domains are forbidden to you, and if my brother is to be believed great wealth would only be given away. What can the King of Lavradio offer as thanks to the Outlander?"

Taylor took a few steps to think about it. He honestly didn't need anything he couldn't either make or earn for himself.

"Mostly what I want, your majesty, is for the nexus to succeed and the people of Tenobre to survive. Hardly anything else matters."

There was a small cough from behind them, and it sounded feminine. The ambassador was trying to tell him something, but Taylor didn't know what it was. A cough just wasn't that useful as a means of communication.

The young king graced him with a patient smile. "That simply won't do, Taylor. A king must not only acknowledge others, he must be seen acknowledging them." Leonardo said this while sweeping his eyes across the small crowd gathered at the railings of the mezzanine to watch the procession.

That was when Taylor got it. He was walking at the left hand of the king, armed and armored in his presence even though he owed the monarch no oath of loyalty. He was caught in some kind of performance whose full meaning wasn't clear to him, but the king wanted to show favor and make amends. And because these performances mattered,

Taylor really need to think of something to ask for. If he was smarter he would have planned for this ahead of time.

What, of all that he had lost, could they even come close to replacing? The king's uncle had yanked him from his home on whim, then stranded him, then killed him for money. The replaceable stuff, mainly all of Pegasus Workshop, had been rebuilt in Tegea. He didn't lack anything except...

"An instrument, your majesty. Janocas burned my guitar and I haven't replaced it, because it would be too identifiable. I could make one myself, but if a master were to be employed the outcome would be far better."

"You will have the best Lavradio has to offer. It will nearly play itself."

"I'll provide a design to get them started. And don't forget the case, your majesty. The old one was a gift from palace craftsmen and hand-tooled by Gabriel. The new one has to travel well under difficult conditions." He was doing Leo a favor at this point, asking for extras. "Considering the fate of the last one, a fire resistant material might be good idea, if such a thing exists in this world."

Leo favored him with a laugh. "I know how you feel. A great instrument needs a secure home. But these are still small matters."

"They're not small to me, your majesty. I miss my guitar terribly. Just the thought of being able to play again improves my morale. Oh, there is one other thing. I found an appalon in the forest near your hunting lodge. He seemed lost so I took him with me, but he might be one of yours. His tack said Hateful Ben."

"So that's what happened to him," said Nunio.

"I can have him exchanged for a good mount," offered Leonardo.

"I don't want to exchange him," said Taylor with alarm, "I want your permission to keep him."

"That monster?" said Queen Larava. "He was always head butting us and knocking us over. You can't want to keep that beast."

"I have found him to be a sensitive and loyal friend. I call him Magnificent Ben, and I don't want any other mount. Your majesties."

"Then he is yours," said the king.

"Thank you, your majesty."

Nunio sighed with relief.

Larava muttered, "thank goodness."

"You're all welcome." The young king smiled with genuine, if restrained, mirth.

As they turned at the bottom of the stairs Taylor stole a glance at Ambassador Kasryn. She gave him the barest of nods. Less 'well done' than 'it'll do', but it was enough.

What remained of winter slouched and sloshed its way towards spring with the death of Matrix Lucia. Losing her was not as hard as learning she was dying, but it was hard enough to stop everything else for a few days. Her followers clothed in her priestess robes, with her disciple stole and star her only adornments, and a thin stone knife her only weapon. Thus attired, she was wrapped in a simple winding sheet. Disciples didn't need much when they went out into the world, and they needed even less as they went out of it.

Her service was delivered by her follower and successor matrix, Sister Lorena, at the Chapel of Compassionate Light. It was attended by most of the residents of bricktown, all of the healers of the city, with Prince Estevan there to represent the royal family. Taylor and his followers were there too, as were many students from the academy. Quite a few priests from other temples in the city came to pay their respects, including Prelate Kasryn.

The procession carried her for over a kilometer outside the city and buried her in a hilltop cemetery. They lowered her into the ground, said the final words, and took turns shoveling the dirt in. Taylor could have done it all himself in a few seconds using the arts but he took his turn with the shovel instead, then handed it on to the next person.

After, Taylor took Ben into the coppiced woods trailed by his silent followers, and meandered among the stumps shorn of their trunks. New growth came out of the stumps as smaller shoots grouped in threes and fours, which would be cut down in several years when they reached the desired width. He hoped someone was planing an expansion to the coppice woods to handle the increase in population. Nexus would have a lot of implications like that for the city.

Taylor tried to formulate how much the woods would have to expand, but the numbers kept sliding away from him. Finally he had to admit that being out there wasn't helping: he was just as sad alone (or as alone as he could ever be any more) as he was while surrounded by other mourners, so he decided instead to race his three followers home.

They weaved their way through the wood, people and mounts breathing hard and splattering thick brown mud on themselves and each other. Wordless they charged over and around obstacles, passing by two kilometers of the skeletal woodland until they broke free of it and jumped a drainage ditch to land on the highway. Ben turned three quick circles to the left, and three to the right in victory. The four of them laughed and, after the mounts had recovered their breath, took a medium pace into the city. Somewhere in the excitement Taylor had realized he didn't want to miss Lucia's reception. How else would he hear all the unexpected stories about her?

He had made a choice when he used the prayer of Sandim's Return, the choice not to be taken from Tenobre. He made the same choice again when he refused to be summoned away. He was making a life here, and he was going to live it. If some other world wanted him, they would have to wait their turn.

THE LIBRARIAN

Lavradio

Vizana was thirty years old, unmarried, unsuccessful, and in exile. And she was stuck in a gurantor car with Mobeen's ridiculous ex-bulwark who refused to wear a proper shirt. He was a huge man, covered in a dense tapestry of tattoos, wearing a torso garment with no sleeves. His vest, if it could be called such, was so scant that it didn't close in the middle. At least twice a day he would vault out of the door of the moving car and swing himself up onto the roof, then spend a half hour slinging stones at whatever passing objects made for interesting targets. Then he would swing back in through the doorway as dramatically as he had gone.

On their first day traveling together James (that was the improperly clothed man's name) had the nerve to ask her what kind of books she liked to read. She was surprised to learn a man of his intense physicality could read, much less was able to talk about books. Since they were to be stuck together for a while she allowed the familiarity.

Her other companion was a merchant girl. The four-car train, its two gurantors, and most of its cargo were technically hers, and the Unity was merely renting space. Vizana and James had waited in Kashmar for four days for the girl to arrive, but it had been worth their time. Kashmar was an amusing city to be in, the Unity was footing the bill, and James was excellent company when she had the option of sending him to a separate room whenever she got tired of him. The merchant girl's train was slower than a regular carriage train due to the heavy cargo, but it was roomy and gave a smooth ride. Compared to traveling by coach car, it was luxurious.

The girl's name was Laura and she looked too young to be in charge of so many of her own goods, never mind Vizana's precious cargo.

Vizana was a librarian. At least, that is what she had always wanted to be. But fate had different ideas in store for her. There were only so many libraries big enough to warrant a full-time minder, and even fewer willing to pay a decent wage. Library arts wasn't even a proper field of study. For six months, a brief and glorious moment, she had served an internship at Enclave's Art School library. She hadn't even minded the nasty stares from all the first and second family descendants. But when the time came to fill her position permanently it went to a dull, talentless boy who had failed his priest exam repeatedly but had good family connections.

Vizana left the library in a hot rage, with nothing but a box of things from her desk, a tear-stained handkerchief, and a scribbled note telling her to talk to Disciple Mobeen about a job.

The note had been slipped to her by one of the reference librarians, and it saved her life. The disciple known as Sacred Blade had started young and hunted monsters into the prime of his life. Along the way, he had written all of it down.

Mobeen wasn't from a first or even a second family, but got adopted by the Fortuna family as a way to launder his lack of heritage and thus save the Art School some embarrassment. In truth, he was from a family of knights in Dace who got picked up as a bulwark, then turned disciple when it was discovered he had the talent for it.

Vizana entered the picture because Mobeen's housekeeper insisted he do something with all his records, or else throw it away. All the records of his monster hunts was sitting in heaps, stacked up in spare rooms like so much kindling. Vizara spent months cataloguing. Along the way she repaired reports that had faded or were written on non-standard scrap wood. And when it was all done, nobody had wanted it. The housekeeper wanted it out of the house, and the Art School literally didn't have any more room, given the number of pointless dissertations on first family trees they were required to keep in perpetuity.

And then Mobeen had died. Without an heir. Probate courts moved at glacial speed, but the day after they received news of his death people started coming by to look at the house. A few tried to submit bills for non-existent services rendered, but the housekeeper turned them away by brandishing a mace at them. Nonetheless, the future was clear: the house would be sold and the life's work of Sacred Blade would be tossed out like garbage. Or, more likely, burnt for kindling.

Vizana's only plan was to pile up the boards in tall stacks in a corner of a guest bedroom, as if they were unwanted. All the "valuable" works by first family authors were shelved in the office as if they were the real treasures. When the court-appointed assessor inventoried the house, Mobeen's writings weren't even listed as property. Since they weren't on the inventory, Vizara could simply take them, but she still had to have a place to put them.

In her search for a new home it was Dean Garsharp who finally threw her a lifeline. A former student wanted the whole collection, but he wanted it in Lavradio. At first she refused, but as the day of her eviction loomed she got desperate enough to let them go into the unknown. She went back to the dean, but he told her it was no longer enough to ship them away. Vizana would have to go with them to the place where church careers went do die: Lavradio. Confronted by the fact her only other option was to hope for a late marriage she agreed to take the long ride with Mobeen's collected writings to the east end of the continent.

Laura's train, with James and Vizana, two drivers, and all their combined cargo on board, entered through Girona's west gate, then stopped at the depot just long enough to detach one gurantor and the two back cars. A city driver joined them to pilot them through the city. That was a new and novel requirement in Lavradio, instituted to reduce deaths related to collisions between the massive gurantor trains and other users of the roads. There were several major construction projects under way in the city and too many trains were trying to pull too much heavy cargo along the roads all at once. Signal men had been set up at important intersections to keep the traffic from stagnating, and gurantors were banned from the narrower roads. To ensure every gurantor train obeyed the rules, either your driver had to pass a test and be licensed to pilot the beasts through the city, or you hired a driver at the depot to do it for you.

Laura's carriage took a turn onto a "heavy road", one reinforced for constant heavy traffic, that looped through the north end of the city. Their stop was in front of a tall rectangular building with two floors of stone and a wooden third story, with a shed roof. The narrow side of the building faced the road, which was odd, and a short distance away were a bunch of people, mostly children, standing around in a deep rectangular hole. Beyond them stood a small chapel and a dormitory. Just to the east of the chapel was bricktown: tiny gray brick houses lined up in neat rows, enough to make a whole town on its own.

None of it inspired confidence.

For some reason, Laura the merchant girl was checking her appearance in a hand mirror concealed in a wooden clamshell. Vizana wondered who there was to impress in this place. One of the adults outside raced off at improbable speed into the far side of the tall building and returned soon with an old priest and a young boy with silver eyes. By the time their driver had properly set the brakes on the cars and pulled down the stairs for his passengers, the odd pair were already waiting for them.

Laura went first aided down by the boy, who kissed her hand.

"It's been months. How are you, and did you bring my stuff?"

The girl laughed and handed him a pair of boards. "I'm doing very well. Here is your manifest, and I've missed you too."

The boy's face lit up as he scanned the list. "Mobeen is finally here. Excellent! James, I'm glad you could make it."

James paused halfway down the steps to inhale the city's air deeply, and let everyone get a good look at his tattoos. "I thought I'd check this place out. Garsharp won't shut up about it."

"We'll give you a full tour tomorrow." The disciple watched Vizana being handed down the steps by James. "You must be Vizana. How was your trip?"

"Long," she told the boy, put off by his presumption. Looking directly at him, she realized he was wearing disciple gear. Instead of the usual stone knife he bore a bronze blade of unusual color. "Can you show me where the collection will be stored."

"Of course. Right this way," but then he paused after the old man cleared his throat. After a meaningful look from the priest he realized what he had forgotten.

"Oh, right. I am Disciple Phillip the Younger, a lector here. This is Mika, our rector. He keeps the place running. There's Mistress Manu, our architect and also a lector here," he indicated a woman approaching from the muddy pit. "The rest here are students, mostly candidates. They're in a big hole because they're preparing the foundation for the other wing of this building."

"It looks like a giant shed," said James as they followed the boy inside. It was exactly what Vizana had been thinking.

"From this angle it does," agreed the disciple while leading them inside, "but this is what the finished building will look like." Taylor stopped in front of a large architectural drawing displayed near the entrance, well lit by a bright spirit lantern. The shed roof on the current building would be joined to a similar roof on the building next door by an arched skyway, forming ...

"An arch of triumph," James said, impressed, "with a statue of Mobeen in the center."

"This is just a small, temporary structure," explained Mistress Manu. "When we aren't so desperate for time we'll build the full-scale one. This should do for at least a few years."

Taylor explained the internal layout. "This half of the building is dedicated to the library, all three floors. Reading room on the ground, stacks on first, and a scriptorium in the garret. All at the librarian's discretion, of course."

Then he turned his uncanny silver eyes on Vizana. "How is Mobeen's archive organized?"

"The author and title are the same for all of the reports, which puts them together in the Unity classification system." Vizana felt easier, being asked about her own area of competence. "So they are ordered by date."

Taylor hummed to himself. "If I wanted to know about all the encounters with salamanders..."

"I would direct you to the catalog. I have cross-referenced location and monster type."

"What if I didn't want to use the catalog?" The boy was going to be difficult.

"I would assist you, because you are a disciple. But I would urge you to learn the catalog." Vizana put on her patron-friendly voice. "Understanding the catalog system truly does help in one's research."

"Would you have any misgivings about teaching new readers to use the catalog?"

"Not at all. The best time to learn to use a library is as soon as one is able. Excuse me, but can we get back to what we are here for? I'd like to see where you intend to store Mobeen's archive."

Taylor paused for a second as if he didn't understand her, mouth half-open. "I see," he said finally, "Dean Garsharp didn't tell you."

"All he said was, if I wanted to save Mobeen's collection then I had to deliver it in person."

It was Mika who cleared up the confusion. "We don't want you to store the collection, Vizana. We want you to shelve it so students can read it."

Taylor went a step further. "Mobeen was the most prolific monster hunter since the first disciples, and he kept excellent records. We are training more monster hunters today than Enclave has deployed in the last decade. Enclave might not want Mobeen's legacy, but we do. And, we're in need of a full-time librarian to look after it. And everything else that goes here."

The rector, sensing her confusion, elaborated. "There are multiple schools here: music, basic literacy, civil service, and spiritual arts. There is also a nearby industrial workshop and a research facility. All of them use this library. We expect it to grow rapidly, which is why we plan to build a bigger one a few years from now.

"We would like you to be our head librarian," he concluded. "Full time, housing included, and you'll find the stipend goes a lot farther here than it did in Unity City. You would also have a budget for paid student help."

Young people, most of them just boys and girls, marched in line. Each carried a heavy box on one shoulder, and they neatly stacked up the boxes under James' direction. He watched them with appraising eyes.

All of this. Her little collection of Mobeen's writings didn't take up even a tenth of the shelves on the ground floor. Vizana could see the downstairs shelves already held boards, sorted by topic using the unity system. There were quite a few bound volumes too, the precious books right out in the

389

open where any student could take one and read it at the tables lit by spirit lamps. The shelving directly around the reading area was nearly full already, but there were plenty of empty shelves on the ground floor plus an entire floor above them. They intended to fill all of it, then build a bigger library.

She wanted the job. She just didn't want it in dead-end Lavradio.

"What if you just took the job temporarily, to help us set up our library properly," suggested the boy. "You can see the state we're in. If you want to stay permanently and everybody is happy, then you can stay. If not, we'll have to make do with student volunteers until we find another real librarian. There's no first family laggards or brothers-in-law lurking around corners to take the position from you, so there's no pressure to make an immediate decision. Will you help out a new library for three months while you make up your mind?"

All at once the students who had been carrying boxes lined up and bowed at her. A single vulpine-eared girl spoke for them, "Please be our librarian, Lector Vizana."

"Well," she breathed, trying not to sound like she was leaping at the offer. Having the title of Lector thrown at her was a very pleasant shock. "If it means so much to you, I'll take the temporary position."

"Thank you very much," they said in unison, and they bowed again.

James nodded at the line of students. "How long has this lot been doing self-enhancements?"

"At least a month, some of them longer."

"Their control isn't bad. You could start them all on bulwarks right now."

"We could," said the rector with a glance at Taylor, "but our only qualified teacher is too busy. If only we had another person who could teach Mobeen's method."

"You're in luck!" James stood with arms akimbo. "Mobeen didn't invent his method alone, you know. He worked it out with his bulwark, of which I was one. And we kept our practice up to date, even after he started traveling alone. You're looking at Tenobre's leading expert on the Mobeen Method of Bulwark Tactics!"

Taylor and Mika exchanged a silent look before Mika spoke. "Oh! You're that James. We mistook you for some other tattooed giant."

"It was the vest," mused Taylor, "we were expecting less coverage."

"The same arrangement is offered to you, authentic James," smiled Rector Mika. "You become Lector James for three months, with housing and a stipend. If everyone is happy, then you can stay permanently."

"Done!" Vizana couldn't decide if his certainty was admirable for its honesty, or foolish for its transparency. Certainly nobody in Enclave encouraged that kind of attitude.

Keys were handed out, and the carriage was sent off to unload their possessions. James and Vizana each received a student to take them to their new homes, part of a line of conjoined townhomes. Hers (number five) was compact, simply furnished, and entirely her own. No siblings or parents or roommates. Her helper was Lourdes, a scholarship student who was also something called a class president. Evidently she had certain logistical duties, such as organizing students to plead with prospective staff members to join the fledgling campus. She was adept at helping Vizana unpack, and even started a list of things she needed.

"If you don't mind used items, there are some inexpensive places you can shop," Lourdes told her, "we can have someone show you around the city tomorrow." Then she went to answer a knock at the door: a message arrived by runner, which the girl read aloud. "Depart for tonight's evening services at the basilica in one hour, followed by a welcoming dinner at the Purple Beast. Will you be able to attend?

"You're lucky," added Lourdes, "the Beast is legendary for its music. It would be a shame to miss this, Lector Vizana."

"I don't know if I have anything good enough to wear," worried the new librarian.

Lourdes spoke to the messenger. "Find Mary, and Mila if she's available. And get Bibia too, if you happen to run into her." The messenger took off at impressive speed, probably enhanced with the arts.

"We'll sort it out, Lector Vizana. You have some nice dresses here, and Mary will know what's best for the occasion. The others can help with hair and makeup. I admire our Rector Mika and Lector Phillip very much, but I wish at least one of them was a woman. Matrix Lucia would have given you more notice."

Lourdes and her chosen helpers had Vizana turned out nicely in spite of the short notice, and she soon found herself inside an appalon-pulled carriage. On the way Rector Mika, as her new superior, advised her on how to greet nobility and royalty, should the need arise.

"Is that likely to happen?" she said with alarm.

"The school has close ties to the second prince and the city minister. They often take evening services in the basilica. So yes, you're likely to be introduced to them tonight."

Once inside the basilica Vizana went through the same sequence of awe, incredulity, and surprise as Guardian Maia had weeks before, but without the nausea at the end. The basilica's Fragment was so obviously genuine that it made Enclave's version a farce. People from the slums prayed near the nobility. Benediction was sung and mutually given, not handed down from priests. And the free mixing of people continued after the service. Vizana was introduced to the second prince, who apparently had something to do with the school's glebe. The merchant girl Laura was with two older women who might have been her family, negotiating with Taylor to have him stay overnight. The city minister was in conversation with union workers. Healer practitioners were laughing at something said by a glamorous woman in silks, whom Vizana suspected might be the madam of a bordello. Students from the school who were reputedly from the slums were discussing tax policy with legal experts from Plaza Hall.

It dawned on Vizana that, for all their talk about love across borders and Alignment, people in the Enclave didn't practice it very much. Maybe that's why all these people, church people who believed in the thing Enclave was always talking about, were here instead of some more favored post. The first family scions were uncomfortable around people who actually practiced what Enclave had been preaching, and so put them all in the same place. They didn't realize they were creating an alternate, more radical, enclave.

For the first time in her life Vizana felt a sense of possibility, beyond the almost unobtainable goal of being a paid librarian. Something big was happening in Lavradio, something that would sweep her along for the ride if she let it.

METAMORPHOSIS

Videocast, Channel Seven

Hello, I'm Osso Salamanca and this is Great Arts. Today we're visiting the Grand Mobeen Library to view a fresco by Pieto Nieva popularly called "Homecoming" but which he called "Metamorphosis". It depicts a very real moment in time, a spontaneous event that occurred when Taylor DeLanion, the famed disciple, returned to Girona.

Prior to this moment nearly everyone in Girona believed DeLanion to be dead, assassinated by Duke Frenzio as part of his scheme to secede from the kingdom. Even the palace believed this young, immensely talented disciple had been killed. In truth he was not dead, but had taken up his secret disciple name of Phillip the Younger and set out on a mendicant expedition. It would be one of his shorter forays, but it was uniquely productive and his discoveries would upend the world as they knew it.

When DeLanion arrives in Girona he installs himself in a suite at the opulent Vargos-Avelar and he sends out messages, written on stiff little boards, to all of his acquaintances in the city. And these messages are just to let people know that he has returned, that he can be reached at the hotel, and won't it be nice to get together some time soon for jota. Normally in those days, if you received such a board, you would write a return note welcoming them to the city and perhaps invite them over for a meal. But when DeLanion's boards are received there is this rush to be the first to see him, to verify with one's own eyes that he is alive, and all of these people set out immediately to the Vargos-Avelar. They kept arriving, one after the other, in a slow-moving invasion of his drawing room.

Here is Estevan Odemira, Second Prince and city planner for Girona sitting next to City Minister Marvao. They were the first to arrive because they were the closest to the hotel: Plaza Hall was just across the square. In front of them you can see the famous cut of wood from an ancient tree that illustrates the long solar cycle. On top of that is this large work diagram, mapping their future plans. Here you see healers, led by Healer Mataba, examining one of the first two-lens microscopes. There's Depot Master Ayuso, handling a prototype youngmeter. There are craftsmen and guild masters, standing shoulder to shoulder, admiring the glass and paper they would soon be manufacturing in large quantities. Master Clemmens the architect is here, Matrix Lorena from the Chapel, Head Priest Javach from the Basilica, and the beautiful woman behind DeLanion is Alice Tabua. She was like his adoptive mother in Girona.

What's unique about this painting is it's quite literal. As these impromptu guests arrived, those who were present would pose themselves for whomever entered the room. It was an improvised game played by children and their families called 'making pictures'. You would try to surprise anyone coming into the room with a scene that was beautiful, or funny, or shocking. The new arrivals are added to the picture, and as more people arrive the scene becomes more elaborate. Because that's the kind of game you play when you don't have videocast channels. People who were there made sketches and recorded the details, so Nieva had excellent contemporaneous notes to work from. As a result we know who these people are, that they really held these items, looked like this, wore these clothes, and stood like so. And there's all these wonderful little details. Here you can see a woman who worked for the hotel, dressed in her winter uniform, and she's holding up a silver tray to add dramatic lighting to the scene. And there you see Milo, one of DeLanion's followers, casting a suspicious eye at Alice because she has muscled him aside and insisted on standing in his spot just behind his master. On the sideboard is an array of delicate little sandwiches, next to a rather unsightly mass of meat with the thin slices coming off of it. That's cured arkto meat, made from the same animal whose skin is on the floor, and you can see another hotel worker daintily adding this greenery around it, trying to dress it up and failing. All of this is in quite good fun, and you sense how much they enjoy being in on this prank.

And it is a prank, a royal one at that, because this would be the scene that greeted King Leonardo and Queen Farava as they entered the room. They were the farthest away and, like everyone else, expected to catch the disciple alone. Instead, they walk in on all of this. As they were the last to arrive they got to see the final picture but didn't get to be part of it. We're told that the king took it very well.

My favorite detail in this painting might be the one face that wasn't there at the time. If you look closely in this reflection, you can see an old woman with horns watching the proceedings with this beautiful, beatific smile. That is Matrix Lucia, and when this event is happening she is on her death bed. She was a beloved figure in Girona, and

397

DeLanion's mentor: it was she who inducted him into the church, she taught him his first prayers, and she was the first rectress of the DeLanion school. DeLanion went to see his mentor the moment he arrived in Girona, and had only just come from her bedside when he sent out his messages, so he knew she wasn't well and she was certainly on his mind while this was taking place. When Nieva first presented his plans for the mural to DeLanion, the disciple insisted she be represented in some way. So we get this lovely reflection of her in the room, present in spirit but not in body.

In the middle of all of this sits DeLanion himself. He's seated in this wingback chair rather like a throne, still wearing the brindle hair that was his principle form of disguise, casually reading a book while all of this is going on around him. Printing hasn't been introduced yet, so this is one of his prototypes. You see the pattern of shiny rivets in this long tunic that reaches his knees? He's wearing armor, probably made from tirun scale. His sword is a new style of bronze, which he's enhanced by adding a hilt of dark monster bone. He's armed and armored as he receives his guests because that is how a working, monster hunting, serious disciple lives. He's quite beautifully dressed but in a minimalist, functional way because he considered it improper for a priest to over-adorn himself with things like lace or jewels. The star he wears is simple wood, and his stole is wool rather than silk.

But then, you have this incongruous cloak thrown over the back of his chair, lined with bifurdactica fur, and at his feet is this monstrous, lavish arkto rug. These are not luxury items: they're trophies. He had left the city on the run for his life and he's returned victorious, laden with trophies, and full of inventions and ideas that would change Girona and the world.

And that, I think, is the most astonishing aspect of this painting. It is literal to an exceptional degree for this kind of art, and yet it works so well at a symbolic level. The bottom center of the painting is occupied by the central problem these people faced: the so-called rings of doom that foretold an age of sun storms and dark monsters. Gathered immediately around it are the oldest and most powerful who would plan the future, raise the money, lead the armies, and wrestle the political obstacles. Behind those central figures are arrayed the people who would build that future, holding the very tools they would use to reshape the world. They came from different backgrounds, but they had in common a thirst for the new and a burning desire to make humanity strong enough to face the centuries to come. It's very exciting, this moment when everything begins to change.

That is why Nieva called his fresco Metamorphosis. The change had already begun, just by the virtue of these people being in the same room, working together. They would redefine what was normal, and then redefine it again. It was the end of the stagnant days of Alignment, and the dawn of something new: an Age of Discovery.

I hope you've enjoyed this look at Pieto Nieva's fresco, Metamorphosis. I'm Osso Salamanca, and this has been Great Arts.

AFTERWORD

We've come to the end of another book, of a series I hadn't planned to write. It's Q1 of 2023, and the technology job market continues to be lousy, even for experienced programmers. I spend some of my days job hunting and updating my skills, and the rest of my time writing. The fact that I've finished a second book and started a third says something about the way my job hunt has been going.

Again, I must credit my wonderful wife. Her advice has been instrumental, and her criticisms on point. This goes for both the novels, and all those cover letters I have to write.

Finally, let us not forget the chairman of Bongosian Press, Mister Bongosian. His doggie determination to keep the family entertained and exercised is a credit to his kind.

Taylor will return, in *Isekai Veteran: Heretic.*